STREET SCENE

There were cyclists and pedestrains on the street—all recorded. They were solid rather than ghostly, but it was an eerie kind of solidity; unstoppable, unswayable, they were like infinitely strong, infinitely disinterested robots.

When Paul reached the corner, the visual illusion of the city continued off into the distance; but when he tried to step forward, the concrete pavement under his feet started sliding backward, like a treadmill.

He was on the edge of his universe.

Books by Greg Egan
Quarantine
Permutation City

Published by HarperPrism

GREG EGAN

PERMUTATION CITY

HarperPrism
An Imprint of HarperPaperbacks

This is a work of fiction. The characters, incidents, and dialogues are products of the author's imagination and are not to be construed as real. Any resemblance to actual events or persons, living or dead, is entirely coincidental.

HarperPaperbacks   *A Division of* HarperCollins*Publishers*
10 East 53rd Street, New York, N.Y. 10022

A trade paperback edition of this book was published in 1994 by Millennium, an imprint of Orion Books Ltd.

Skyline photograph © Craig Aurness/Westlight
Computer chip photograph © Chuck O'Rear/Westlight

ISBN#   0-06-105481-X

Printed in the United States of America

HarperPrism is an imprint of HarperPaperbacks. HarperPaperbacks, HarperPrism, and colophon are trademarks of HarperCollins*Publishers*

ACKNOWLEDGMENTS

Parts of this novel are adapted from a story called "Dust," which was first published in *Isaac Asimov's Science Fiction Magazine,* July 1992.

Thanks to Deborah Beale, Charon Wood, Peter Robinson, David Pringle, Lee Montgomerie, Gardner Dozois and Sheila Williams.

Into a mute crypt, I
Can't pity our time
Turn amity poetic
Ciao, tiny trumpet!
Manic piety tutor
Tame purity tonic
Up, meiotic tyrant!
I taint my top cure
To it, my true panic
Put at my nice riot

To trace impunity
I tempt an outcry, I
Pin my taut erotic
Art to epic mutiny
Can't you permit it
To cite my apt ruin?
My true icon: tap it
Copy time, turn it; a
Rite to cut my pain
Atomic putty? *Rien!*

————————

*Found in the memory of a discarded notepad in
the Common Room of the Psychiatric Ward,
Blacktown Hospital, June 6, 2045.*

PROLOGUE

(Rip, tie, cut toy man)

JUNE 2045

Paul Durham opened his eyes, blinking at the room's unexpected brightness, then lazily reached out to place one hand in a patch of sunlight at the edge of the bed. Dust motes drifted across the shaft of light which slanted down from a gap between the curtains, each speck appearing for all the world to be conjured into, and out of, existence—evoking a childhood memory of the last time he'd found this illusion so compelling, so hypnotic: *He stood in the kitchen doorway, afternoon light slicing the room; dust, flour and steam swirling in the plane of bright air.* For one sleep-addled moment, still trying to wake, to collect himself, to order his life, it seemed to make as much sense to place these two fragments side by side—watching sunlit dust motes, forty years apart—as it did to follow the ordinary flow of time from one instant to the next. Then he woke a little more, and the confusion passed.

Paul felt utterly refreshed—and utterly disinclined to give up his present state of comfort. He couldn't think why he'd slept so late, but he didn't much care. He spread his fingers on the sun-warmed sheet, and thought about drifting back to sleep.

He closed his eyes and let his mind grow blank—and then caught himself, suddenly uneasy, without knowing why. *He'd done something foolish, something insane, something he was going to regret, badly* . . . but the details remained elusive, and he began to suspect that it was nothing more than the lingering mood of a dream. He tried to recall exactly what he'd dreamed, without much hope; unless he was catapulted awake by a nightmare, his dreams were usually evanescent. And yet—

He leaped out of bed and crouched down on the carpet, fists to his eyes, face against his knees, lips moving soundlessly. The shock of realization was a palpable thing: a red lesion behind his eyes, pulsing with blood . . . like the aftermath of a hammer blow to the thumb—and tinged with the very same mixture of surprise, anger, humiliation and idiot bewilderment. Another childhood memory: *He held a nail to the wood, yes—but only to camouflage his true intentions. He'd seen his father injure himself this way—but he knew that he needed first-hand experience to understand the mystery of pain. And he was sure that it would be worth it, right up to the moment when he swung the hammer down—*

He rocked back and forth, on the verge of laughter, trying to keep his mind blank, waiting for the panic to subside. And eventually, it did—to be replaced by one simple, perfectly coherent thought: *I don't want to be here.*

What he'd done to himself was insane—and it had to be undone, as swiftly and painlessly as possible. *How could he have ever imagined reaching any other conclusion?*

Then he began to remember the details of his preparations. He'd anticipated feeling this way. He'd planned for it. However bad he felt, it was all part of the expected progression of responses. Panic. Regret. Analysis. Acceptance.

Two out of four; so far, so good.

Paul uncovered his eyes, and looked around the room. Away from a few dazzling patches of direct sunshine, everything glowed softly in the diffuse light: the matte white brick walls, the imitation (imitation) mahogany furniture; even the posters—Bosch, Dali, Ernst, and Giger—looked harmless, domesticated. Wherever he turned his gaze (if nowhere else), the simulation was utterly convincing; the spotlight of his attention made it so. Hypothetical light rays were being traced backward from individual rod and cone cells on his simulated retinas, and projected out into the virtual environment to determine exactly what needed to be computed: a lot of detail near the center of his vision, much less toward the periphery.

Objects out of sight didn't 'vanish' entirely, if they influenced the ambient light, but Paul knew that the calculations would rarely be pursued beyond the crudest first-order approximations: Bosch's *Garden of Earthly Delights* reduced to an average reflectance value, a single gray rectangle—because once his back was turned, any more detail would have been wasted. Everything in the room was as finely resolved, at any given moment, as it needed to be to fool him—no more, no less.

He had been aware of the technique for decades. It was something else to experience it. He resisted the urge to wheel around suddenly, in a futile attempt to catch the process out—but for a moment it was almost unbearable, just *knowing* what was happening at the edge of his vision. The fact that his view of the room remained flawless only made it worse, an irrefutable paranoid fixation: *No matter how fast you turn your head, you'll never even catch a glimpse of what's going on all around you . . .*

He closed his eyes again for a few seconds. When he opened them, the feeling was already less oppressive. No doubt it would pass; it seemed too bizarre a state of mind to be sustained for long. Certainly, none of the other Copies had reported anything similar . . . but then, none of them had volunteered much useful data at all. They'd just ranted abuse, whined about their plight, and then terminated themselves—all within fifteen (subjective) minutes of gaining consciousness.

And this one? How was he different from Copy number four? Three years older. *More stubborn? More determined? More desperate for success?* He'd believed so. If he hadn't felt more committed than ever—if he hadn't been convinced that he was, finally, prepared to see the whole thing through—he would never have gone ahead with the scan.

But now that he was "no longer" the flesh-and-blood Paul Durham—"no longer" the one who'd sit outside and watch the whole experiment from a safe distance—all of that determination seemed to have evaporated.

Suddenly he wondered: *What makes me so sure that I'm not still flesh and blood?* He laughed weakly, hardly daring to take the possibility seriously. His most recent memories seemed to be of lying on a trolley in the Landau Clinic, while technicians prepared him for the scan—on the face of it, a bad sign—but he'd been overwrought, and he'd spent so long psyching himself up for "this," that perhaps he'd forgotten coming home, still hazy from the anesthetic, crashing into bed, dreaming . . .

He muttered the password, "Abulafia"—and his last faint hope vanished, as a black-on-white square about a meter wide, covered in icons, appeared in midair in front of him.

He gave the interface window an angry thump; it resisted him as if it was solid, and firmly anchored. *As if he was solid, too.* He didn't really need any more convincing, but he gripped the top edge and lifted himself off the floor. He instantly regretted this; the realistic cluster of effects of exertion—down to the plausible twinge in his right elbow—pinned him to this "body," anchored him to this "place," in exactly the way he knew he should be doing everything he could to avoid.

He lowered himself to the floor with a grunt. *He was the Copy.* Whatever his inherited memories told him, he was "no longer" human; he would never inhabit his real body "again." Never inhabit *the real world* again . . . unless his cheapskate original scraped up the money for a telepresence robot—in which case he could spend his time blundering around in a daze, trying to make sense of the lightning-fast blur of human activity. *His model-of-a-brain ran seventeen times slower than the real thing.* Yeah, sure, if he hung around, the technology would catch up, eventually—and seventeen times faster for him than for his original. And in the meantime? He'd rot in this prison, jumping through hoops, carrying out Durham's precious research—while the man lived in his apartment, spent his money, slept with Elizabeth . . .

Paul leant against the cool surface of the interface, dizzy and confused. *Whose precious research?* He'd wanted this so badly—and he'd done this to himself with his eyes wide open. Nobody had forced him, nobody had deceived him. He'd known exactly what the drawbacks would be—but he'd hoped that he would have the strength of will (this time, at last) to transcend them: to devote himself, monk-like, to the purpose for which he'd been brought into being, content in the knowledge that his other self was as unconstrained as ever.

Looking back, that hope seemed ludicrous. Yes, he'd made the decision freely—for the fifth time—but it was mercilessly clear, now, that he'd never really faced up to the consequences. All the time he'd spent, supposedly "preparing himself" to be a Copy, his greatest source of resolve had been to focus on the outlook for the man who'd remain flesh and blood. He'd told himself that he was rehearsing "making do with vicarious freedom"—and no doubt he had been genuinely struggling to do just that . . . but he'd also been taking secret comfort in the knowledge that *he* would "remain" on the outside—that his future, then, still included a version with absolutely nothing to fear.

And as long as he'd clung to that happy truth, he'd never really swallowed the fate of the Copy at all.

People reacted badly to waking up as Copies. Paul knew the statistics. Ninety-eight percent of Copies made were of the very old, and the terminally ill. People for whom it was the last resort—most of whom had spent millions beforehand, exhausting all the traditional medical options; some of whom had even died between the taking of the scan and the time the Copy itself was run. Despite this, fifteen percent decided on awakening—usually in a matter of hours—that they couldn't face living this way.

And of those who were young and healthy, those who were merely curious, those who knew they had a perfectly viable, living, breathing body outside?

The bale-out rate so far had been one hundred percent.

Paul stood in the middle of the room, swearing softly for several minutes, acutely aware of the passage of time. He didn't feel ready—but the longer the other Copies had waited, the more traumatic they seemed to have found the decision. He stared at the floating interface; its dreamlike, hallucinatory quality helped, slightly. He rarely remembered his dreams, and he wouldn't remember this one—but there was no tragedy in that.

He suddenly realized that he was still stark naked. Habit—if no conceivable propriety—nagged at him to put on some clothes, but he resisted the urge. One or two perfectly innocent, perfectly ordinary actions like that, and he'd find he was taking himself seriously, thinking of himself as real, making it even harder . . .

He paced the bedroom, grasped the cool metal of the doorknob a couple of times, but managed to keep himself from turning it. There was no point even starting to explore this world.

He couldn't resist peeking out the window, though. The view of north Sydney was flawless; every building, every cyclist, every tree, was utterly convincing—but that was no great feat; it was a recording, not a simulation. Essentially photographic—give or take some computerized touching up and filling in—and totally predetermined. To cut costs even further, only a tiny part of it was "physically" accessible to him; he could see the harbor in the distance, but he knew that if he tried to go for a stroll down to the water's edge . . .

Enough. Just get it over with.

Paul turned back to the interface and touched a menu icon labelled UTILITIES; it spawned another window in front of the first. The function he was seeking was buried several menus deep—but he knew exactly where to look for it. He'd watched this, from the outside, too many times to have forgotten.

He finally reached the EMERGENCIES menu—which included a cheerful icon of a cartoon figure suspended from a parachute. *Baling out* was what everyone called it—but he didn't find that too cloyingly euphemistic; after all, he could hardly commit "suicide" when he wasn't legally human. The fact that a bale-out option was compulsory had nothing to do with anything so troublesome as the "rights" of the Copy; the requirement arose solely from the ratification of certain, purely technical, international software standards.

Paul prodded the icon; it came to life, and recited a warning spiel. He scarcely paid attention. Then it said, "Are you absolutely sure that you wish to shut down this Copy of Paul Durham?"

Nothing to it. Program A asks Program B to confirm its request for orderly termination. Packets of data are exchanged.

"Yes, I'm sure."

A metal box, painted red, appeared at his feet. He opened it, took out the parachute, strapped it on.

Then he closed his eyes and said, "Listen to me. *Just listen!* How many times do you need to be told? I'll skip the personal angst; you've heard it all before—and ignored it all before. It doesn't matter how I feel. But . . . when are you going to stop wasting your time, your money, your energy—*when are you going to stop wasting your life*—on something which you just don't have the strength to carry through?"

Paul hesitated, trying to put himself in the place of his original, hearing those words—and almost wept with frustration. He still didn't know what he could say that would make a difference. He'd shrugged off the testimony of all the earlier Copies himself; he'd never been able to accept their claims to know his own mind better than he did. Just because they'd lost their nerve and chosen to bale out, who were they to proclaim that he'd *never* give rise to a Copy who'd choose otherwise? All he had to do was strengthen his resolve, and try again . . .

He shook his head. "It's been ten years, and nothing's changed. *What's wrong with you?* Do you honestly still believe that you're brave enough—or crazy enough—to be your own guinea pig? *Do you?*"

He paused again, but only for a moment; he didn't expect a reply.

He'd argued long and hard with the first Copy, but after that, he'd never had the stomach for it.

"Well, I've got news for you: *You're not.*"

With his eyes still closed, he gripped the release lever.

I'm nothing: a dream, a soon-to-be-forgotten dream.

His fingernails needed cutting; they dug painfully into the skin of his palm.

Had he never, in a dream, feared the extinction of waking? Maybe he had—but a dream was not a life. If the only way he could "reclaim" his body, "reclaim" his world, was to wake and forget—

He pulled the lever.

After a few seconds, he emitted a constricted sob—a sound more of confusion than any kind of emotion—and opened his eyes.

The lever had come away in his hand.

He stared dumbly at this metaphor for . . . what? A bug in the termination software? Some kind of hardware glitch?

Feeling—at last—truly dreamlike, he unstrapped the parachute, and unfastened the neatly packaged bundle.

Inside, there was no illusion of silk, or Kevlar, or whatever else there might plausibly have been. Just a sheet of paper. A note.

> *Dear Paul,*
> *The night after the scan was completed, I looked back over the whole preparatory stage of the project, and did a great deal of soul-searching. And I came to the conclusion that—right up to the very last moment— my attitude had been poisoned with ambivalence.*
> *With hindsight, I realized just how foolish my qualms were—but that was too late for you. I couldn't afford to ditch you, and have myself scanned yet again. So, what could I do?*
> *This: I put your awakening on hold for a while, and tracked down someone who could make a few alterations to the virtual-environment utilities. I know that wasn't strictly legal . . . but you know how important it is to me that you—that we—succeed this time.*
> *I trust you'll understand, and I'm confident that you'll accept the situation with dignity and equanimity.*
> *Best wishes,*
> *Paul*

He sank to his knees, still holding the note, staring at it with disbelief. *I can't have done this. I can't have been so callous.* No?

He could never have done it to anyone else. He was sure of that. He wasn't a monster, a torturer, a sadist.

And he would never have gone ahead himself without the bale-out option as a last resort. Between his ludicrous fantasies of stoicism, and the sanity-preserving cop-out of relating only to the flesh-and-blood version, he must have had moments of clarity when the bottom line had been: *If it's that bad, I can always put an end to it.*

But as for making a Copy, and then—once its future was no longer *his* future, no longer anything for *him* to fear—taking away its power to escape . . . and rationalizing this *hijacking* as nothing more than an over-literal act of self-control . . .

It rang so true that he hung his head in shame.

Then he dropped the note, raised his head, and bellowed with all the strength in his non-existent lungs: "DURHAM! YOU *PRICK!*"

Paul thought about smashing furniture. Instead, he took a long, hot shower. In part, to calm himself; in part, as an act of petty vengeance: twenty virtual minutes of gratuitous hydrodynamic calculations would annoy the cheapskate no end. He scrutinized the droplets and rivulets of water on his skin, searching for some small but visible anomaly at the boundary between his body—computed down to subcellular resolution—and the rest of the simulation, which was modelled much more crudely. If there were any discrepancies, though, they were too subtle to detect.

He dressed, and ate a late breakfast, shrugging off the surrender to normality. *What was he meant to do? Go on a hunger strike? Walk around naked, smeared in excrement?* He was ravenous, having fasted before the scan, and the kitchen was stocked with a—literally—inexhaustible supply of provisions. The muesli tasted exactly like muesli, the toast exactly like toast, but he knew there was a certain amount of cheating going on with both taste and aroma. The detailed effects of chewing, and the actions of saliva, were being faked from a patchwork of empirical rules, not generated from first principles; there *were no* individual molecules being dissolved from the food and torn apart by enzymes—just a rough set of evolving nutrient concentration values, associated with each microscopic "parcel" of saliva. Eventually, these would lead to plausible increases in the concentrations of amino acids, various carbohydrates, and other substances all the way down to humble sodium and chloride ions, in similar 'parcels' of gastric juices . . . which in turn would act as input data to the models of his intestinal villus cells. From there, into the bloodstream.

Urine and feces production were optional—some Copies wished to retain every possible aspect of corporeal life—but Paul had chosen to do without. (So much for smearing himself in excrement.) His bodily wastes would be magicked out of existence long before reaching bladder or bowel. Ignored out of existence; passively annihilated. All that it took to destroy something, here, was to fail to keep track of it.

Coffee made him feel alert, but also slightly detached—as always. Neurons were modeled in the greatest detail, and whatever receptors to caffeine and its metabolites had been present on each individual neuron in his original's brain at the time of the scan, his own model-of-a-brain incorporated every one of them—in a simplified, but functionally equivalent, form.

And the physical reality behind it all? A cubic meter of silent, motionless optical crystal, configured as a cluster of over a billion individual processors, one of a few hundred identical units in a basement vault . . . somewhere on the planet. Paul didn't even know what city he was in; the scan had been made in Sydney, but the model's implementation would have been contracted out by the local node to the lowest bidder at the time.

He took a sharp vegetable knife from the kitchen drawer, and made a shallow cut across his left forearm. He flicked a few drops of blood onto the sink—and wondered exactly which software was now responsible for the stuff. Would the blood cells 'die off' slowly—or had they already been surrendered to the extrasomatic general-physics model, far too unsophisticated to represent them, let alone keep them "alive"?

If he tried to slit his wrists, when exactly would Durham intervene? He gazed at his distorted reflection in the blade. Most likely, his original would let him die, and then run the whole model again from scratch, simply leaving out the knife. He'd rerun all the earlier Copies hundreds of times, tampering with various aspects of their surroundings, trying in vain to find some cheap trick, some distraction which would keep them from wanting to bale out. It was a measure of sheer stubbornness that it had taken him so long to admit defeat and rewrite the rules.

Paul put down the knife. He didn't want to perform that experiment. Not yet.

Outside his own apartment, everything was slightly less than convincing; the architecture of the building was reproduced faithfully enough, down to the ugly plastic potted plants, but every corridor was deserted, and every door to every other apartment was sealed shut—concealing, literally, nothing. He kicked one door, as hard as he could; the wood seemed to give slightly, but when he examined the surface, the paint wasn't even marked. The model would admit to no damage here, and the laws of physics could screw themselves.

There were pedestrians and cyclists on the street—all purely recorded. They were solid rather than ghostly, but it was an eerie kind of solidity; unstoppable, unswayable, they were like infinitely strong, infinitely disinterested robots. Paul hitched a ride on one frail old woman's back for a while; she carried him down the street, heedlessly. Her clothes, her skin, even her hair, all felt the same: hard as steel. Not cold, though. Neutral.

The street wasn't meant to serve as anything but three-dimensional wallpaper; when Copies interacted with each other, they often used cheap, recorded environments full of purely decorative crowds. Plazas, parks, open-air cafés; all very reassuring, no doubt, when you were fighting off a sense of isolation and claustrophobia. Copies could only receive realistic external visitors if they had friends of relatives willing to slow down their mental processes by a factor of seventeen. Most dutiful next-of-kin preferred to exchange video recordings. Who wanted to spend an afternoon with great-grandfather, when it burnt up half a week of your life? Paul had tried calling Elizabeth on the terminal in his study—which should have granted him access to the outside world, via the computer's communications links—but, not surprisingly, Durham had sabotaged that as well.

When he reached the corner of the block, the visual illusion of the city continued, far into the distance, but when he tried to step forward onto the road, the concrete pavement under his feet started acting like a treadmill, sliding backward at precisely the rate needed to keep him motionless, whatever pace he adopted. He backed off and tried leaping over the affected region, but his horizontal velocity dissipated—without the slightest pretense of any "physical" justification—and he landed squarely in the middle of the treadmill.

The people of the recording, of course, crossed the border with ease. One man walked straight at him; Paul stood his ground—and found himself pushed into a zone of increasing viscosity, the air around him becoming painfully unyielding, before he slipped free to one side.

The sense that discovering a way to breach this barrier would somehow "liberate" him was compelling—but he knew it was absurd. Even if he did find a flaw in the program which enabled him to break through, he knew he'd gain nothing but decreasingly realistic surroundings. The recording could only contain complete information for points of view within a certain, finite zone; all there was to "escape to" was a region where his view of the city would be full of distortions and omissions, and would eventually fade to black.

He stepped back from the corner, half dispirited, half amused. What had he hoped to find? A door at the edge of the model, marked EXIT, through which he could walk out into reality? Stairs leading metaphorically down to some boiler-room representation of the underpinnings of this world, where he could throw a few switches and blow it all apart? He had no right to be dissatisfied with his surroundings; they were precisely what he'd ordered.

What he'd ordered was also a perfect spring day. Paul closed his eyes and turned his face to the sun. In spite of everything, it was hard not to take solace from the warmth flooding onto his skin. He stretched the muscles in his arms, his shoulders, his back—and it felt like he was reaching out from the "self" in his virtual skull to all his mathematical flesh, imprinting the nebulous data with meaning; binding it all together, staking some kind of claim. He felt the stirrings of an erection. *Existence was beginning to seduce him.* He let himself surrender for a moment to a visceral sense of identity which drowned out all his pale mental images of optical processors, all his abstract reflections on the software's approximations and short-cuts. This body didn't want to evaporate. This body didn't want to bale out. It didn't much care that there was another—"more real"—version of itself elsewhere. It wanted to retain its wholeness. It wanted to endure.

And if this was a travesty of life, there was always the chance of improvement. Maybe he could persuade Durham to restore his communications facilities; that would be a start. And when he grew bored with libraries, news systems, databases, and—if any of them would deign to meet him—the ghosts of the senile rich? He could always have himself suspended until processor speeds caught up with reality—when people would be able to visit without slowdown, and telepresence robots might actually be worth inhabiting.

He opened his eyes, and shivered in the heat. He no longer knew what he wanted—the chance to bale out, to declare this bad dream *over* . . . or the possibility of virtual immortality—but he had to accept that there was only one way he could make the choice his own.

He said quietly, "I won't be your guinea pig. A collaborator, yes. An equal partner. If you want my cooperation, then you're going to have to treat me like a colleague, not a . . . *piece of apparatus.* Understood?"

A window opened up in front of him. He was shaken by the

sight, not of his predictably smug twin, but of the room behind him. It was only his study—and he'd wandered through the virtual equivalent, unimpressed, just minutes before—but this was still his first glimpse of the real world, in real time. He moved closer to the window, in the hope of seeing if there was anyone else in the room—*Elizabeth?*—but the image was two-dimensional, the perspective remained unchanged as he approached.

The flesh-and-blood Durham emitted a brief, high-pitched squeak, then waited with visible impatience while a second, smaller window gave Paul a slowed-down replay, four octaves lower:

"Of course that's understood! We're collaborators. That's exactly right. Equals. I wouldn't have it any other way. We both want the same things out of this, don't we? We both need answers to the same questions."

Paul was already having second thoughts. "Perhaps."

But Durham wasn't interested in his qualms.

Squeak. "You know we do! We've waited ten years for this . . . and now it's finally going to happen. And we can begin whenever you're ready."

PART ONE

The
Garden-of-Eden
Configuration

1

(Remit not paucity)

Maria Deluca had ridden past the stinking hole in Pyrmont Bridge Road for six days running, certain each time, as she'd approached, that she'd be greeted by the reassuring sight of a work team putting things right. She knew that there was no money for road works or drainage repairs this year, but a burst sewage main was a serious health risk; she couldn't believe it would be neglected for long.

On the seventh day, the stench was so bad from half a kilometer away that she turned into a side street, determined to find a detour.

This end of Pyrmont was a depressing sight; not every warehouse was empty, not every factory abandoned, but they all displayed the same neglected look, the same peeling paint and crumbling brickwork. Half a dozen blocks west, she turned again—to be confronted by a vista of lavish gardens, marble statues, fountains and olive groves, stretching into the distance beneath a cloudless azure sky.

Maria accelerated without thinking—for a few seconds, almost believing that she'd chanced upon a park of some kind, an impossibly well-kept secret in this decaying corner of the city. Then, as the illusion collapsed—punctured by sheer implausibility as much as any visible flaw—she pedaled on wilfully, as if hoping to blur the imperfections and contradictions out of existence. She braked just in time, mounting the narrow footpath at the end of the cul-de-sac, the front wheel of her cycle coming to a halt centimeters from the warehouse wall.

Close up, the mural was unimpressive, the brushstrokes

clearly visible, the perspective obviously false. Maria backed away—and she didn't have to retreat far to see why she'd been fooled. At a distance of twenty meters or so, the painted sky suddenly seemed to merge with the real thing; with a conscious effort, she could make the border reappear, but it was hard work keeping the slight difference in hue from being smoothed out of existence before her eyes—as if some subsystem deep in her visual cortex had shrugged off the unlikely notion of a sky-blue wall and was actively collaborating in the deception. Further back, the grass and statues began to lose their two-dimensional, painted look—and at the corner where she'd turned into the cul-de-sac, every element of the composition fell into place, the mural's central avenue now apparently converging toward the very same vanishing point as the interrupted road.

Having found the perfect viewing position, she stood there awhile, propping up her cycle. Sweat on the back of her neck cooled in the faint breeze, then the morning sun began to bite. The vision was entrancing—and it was heartening to think that the local artists had gone to so much trouble to relieve the monotony of the neighborhood. At the same time, Maria couldn't help feeling cheated. She didn't mind having been taken in, briefly; what she resented was not being able to be fooled again. She could stand there admiring the artistry of the illusion for as long as she liked, but nothing could bring back the surge of elation she'd felt when she'd been deceived.

She turned away.

Home, Maria unpacked the day's food, then lifted her cycle and hooked it into its frame on the living-room ceiling. The terrace house, one hundred and forty years old, was shaped like a cereal box; two stories high, but scarcely wide enough for a staircase. It had originally been part of a row of eight; four on one side had been gutted and remodeled into offices for a firm of architects; the other three had been demolished at the turn of the century to make way for a road that had never been built. The lone survivor was now untouchable under some bizarre piece of heritage legislation, and Maria had bought it for a quarter of the price of the cheapest modern flats. She liked the odd proportions—and with more space, she was certain, she would have felt less in control. She had as clear a mental image of the layout and contents of the house as she had of her own body, and she couldn't recall ever misplacing even the smallest object. She couldn't have shared the place with anyone, but having it to herself seemed to strike the right balance between her territorial and organizational needs. Besides, she believed that houses were meant to be thought of as vehicles—physically fixed, but logically mobile—and compared to a one-person space capsule or submarine, the size was more than generous.

Upstairs, in the bedroom that doubled as an office, Maria switched on her terminal and glanced at a summary of the twenty-one items of mail which had arrived since she'd last checked. All were classified as "Junk"; there was nothing from anyone she knew—and nothing remotely like an offer of paid work. **Camel's Eye,** her screening software, had identified six pleas for donations from charities (all worthy causes, but Maria hardened her heart); five invitations to enter lotteries and competitions; seven retail catalogues (all of which boasted that they'd been tailored to her personality and "current lifestyle requirements"—but **Camel's Eye** had assessed their contents and found nothing of interest); and three interactives.

The "dumb" audio-visual mail was all in standard transparent data formats, but interactives were executable programs, machine code with heavily encrypted data, intentionally designed to be easier for a human to talk to than for screening software to examine and summarize. **Camel's Eye** had run all three interactives (on a doubly quarantined virtual machine—a simulation of a computer running a simulation of a computer) and tried to fool them into thinking that they were making their pitch to the real Maria Deluca. Two sales programs—superannuation and health insurance—had fallen for it, but the third had somehow deduced its true environment and clammed up before disclosing anything. In theory, it was possible for **Camel's Eye** to analyze the program and figure out exactly what it would have said if it *had* been fooled; in practice, that could take weeks. The choice came down to trashing it blind, or talking to it in person.

Maria ran the interactive. A man's face appeared on the terminal; "he" met her gaze and smiled warmly, and she suddenly realized that "he" bore a slight resemblance to Aden. Close enough to elicit a flicker of recognition which the mask of herself she'd set up for **Camel's Eye** would not have exhibited? Maria felt a mixture of annoyance and grudging admiration. She'd never shared an address with Aden—but no doubt the data analysis agencies correlated credit card use in restaurants, or whatever, to pick up relationships which didn't involve cohabitation. Mapping useful connections between consumers had been going on for decades—but employing the data in this way, as a reality test, was a new twist.

The junk mail, now rightly convinced that it was talking to a human being, began the spiel it had refused to waste on her digital proxy. "Maria, I know your time is valuable, but I hope you can spare a few seconds to hear me out." It paused for a moment, to make her feel that her silence was some kind of assent. "I also know that you're a highly intelligent, discerning woman, with no interest whatsoever in the muddled, irrational superstitions of the past, the fairy tales that comforted humanity in its infancy." Maria guessed what was coming next; the interactive saw it on her face—she hadn't bothered to hide behind any kind of filter—and it rushed to get a hook in. "No truly intelligent person, though, ever dismisses an idea without taking the trouble to evaluate it—skceptically, but fairly—and here at the Church of the God Who Makes No Difference—"

Maria pointed two fingers at the interactive, and it died. She wondered if it was her mother who'd set the Church onto her, but that was unlikely. They must have targeted their new member's family automatically; if consulted, Francesca would have told them that they'd be wasting their time.

Maria invoked **Camel's Eye** and told it, "Update my mask so it reacts as I did in that exchange."

A brief silence followed. Maria imagined the synaptic weighting parameters being juggled in the mask's neural net, as the training algorithm hunted for values which would guarantee the required response. She thought: *If I keep on doing this, the mask is going to end up as much like me as a fully fledged Copy. And what's the point of saving yourself from the tedium of talking to junk mail if . . . you're not?* It was a deeply unpleasant notion . . . but masks were orders of magnitude less sophisticated than Copies; they had about as many neurons as the average goldfish—organized in a far less human fashion. Worrying about their "experience" would be as ludicrous as feeling guilty about terminating junk mail.

Camel's Eye said, "Done."

It was only 8:15. The whole day loomed ahead, promising nothing but bills. With no contract work coming in for the past two months, Maria had written half a dozen pieces of consumer software—mostly home-security upgrades, supposedly in high demand. So far, she'd sold none of them; a few thousand people had read the catalogue entries, but nobody had been persuaded to download. The prospect of embarking on another such project wasn't exactly electrifying—but she had no real alternative. And once the recession was over and people started buying again, it would have been time well spent.

First, though, she needed to cheer herself up. If she worked in the Autoverse, just for half an hour or so—until nine o'clock at the latest—then she'd be able to face the rest of the day . . .

Then again, she could always try to *face the rest of the day* without bribing herself, just once. The Autoverse was a waste of money, and a waste of time—a hobby she could justify when things were going well, but an indulgence she could ill afford right now.

Maria put an end to her indecision in the usual way. She logged on to her Joint Supercomputer Network account—paying a fifty-dollar fee for the privilege, which she now had to make worthwhile. She slipped on her force gloves and prodded an icon, a wireframe of a cube, on the terminal's flatscreen—

and the three-dimensional workspace in front of the screen came to life, borders outlined by a faint holographic grid. For a second, it felt like she'd plunged her hand into some kind of invisible vortex: magnetic fields gripped and twisted her glove, as start-up surges tugged at the coils in each joint at random—until the electronics settled into equilibrium, and a message flashed up in the middle of the workspace: YOU MAY NOW PUT ON YOUR GLOVES.

She jabbed another icon, a starburst labeled FIAT. The only visible effect was the appearance of a small menu strip hovering low in the foreground—but to the cluster of programs she'd invoked, the cube of thin air in front of her terminal now corresponded to a small, empty universe.

Maria summoned up a single molecule of *nutrose*, represented as a ball-and-stick model, and, with a flick of a gloved forefinger, imparted a slow spin. The vertices of the crimped hexagonal ring zig-zagged above and below the molecule's average plane; one vertex was a divalent *blue* atom, linked only to its neighbors in the ring; the other five were all tetravalent *greens*, with two bonds left over for other attachments. Each *green* was joined to a small, monovalent *red*—on the top side if the vertex was raised, on the bottom if it was lowered—and four of them also sprouted short horizontal spikes, built from a *blue* and a *red*, pointing away from the ring. The fifth *green* held out a small cluster of atoms instead: a *green* with two *reds*, and its own *blue-red* spike.

The viewing software rendered the molecule plausibly solid, taking into account the effects of ambient light; Maria watched it spin above the desktop, admiring the not-quite-symmetrical form. A real-world chemist, she mused, would take one look at this and say: *Glucose. Green is carbon, blue is oxygen, red is hydrogen . . . no?* No. They'd stare awhile; put on the gloves and give the impostor a thorough grope; whip a protractor out of the toolbox and measure a few angles; invoke tables of bond formation energies and vibrational modes; maybe even demand to see nuclear magnetic resonance spectra (not available—or, to put it less coyly, *not applicable*). Finally, with the realization of blasphemy dawning, they'd tear their hands

from the infernal machinery, and bolt from the room screaming, "There is no Periodic Table but Mendeleev's! There is no
Periodic Table but Mendeleev's!"

The Autoverse was a "toy" universe, a computer model
which obeyed its own simplified "laws of physics"—laws far
easier to deal with mathematically than the equations of real-
world quantum mechanics. Atoms could exist in this stylized
universe, but they were subtly different from their real-world
counterparts; the Autoverse was no more a faithful simulation
of the real world than the game of chess was a faithful simulation of medieval warfare. It was far more insidious than chess,
though, in the eyes of many real-world chemists. The false
chemistry it supported was too rich, too complex, too seductive by far.

Maria reached into the workspace again, halted the
molecule's spin, deftly plucked both the lone *red* and the
blue-red spike from one of the *greens,* then reattached them,
swapped, so that the spike now pointed upward. The gloves'
force and tactile feedback, the molecule's laser-painted image,
and the faint *clicks* that might have been plastic on plastic as
she pushed the atoms into place, combined to create a convincing impression of manipulating a tangible object built out
of solid spheres and rods.

This virtual ball-and-stick model was easy to work with—
but its placid behavior in her hands had nothing to do with
the physics of the Autoverse, temporarily held in abeyance.
Only when she released her grip was the molecule allowed
to express its true dynamics, oscillating wildly as the
stresses induced by the alteration were redistributed from
atom to atom, until a new equilibrium geometry was found.

Maria watched the delayed response with a familiar sense
of frustration; she could never quite resign herself to accepting the handling rules, however convenient they were. She'd
thought about trying to devise a more authentic mode of interaction, offering the chance to feel what it was "really like" to
grasp an Autoverse molecule, to break and re-form its
bonds—instead of everything turning to simulated plastic at
the touch of a glove. The catch was, if a molecule obeyed only

Autoverse physics—the internal logic of the self-contained computer model—then how could she, outside the model, interact with it at all? By constructing little surrogate hands in the Autoverse, to act as remote manipulators? Construct them out of *what?* There were no molecules small enough to build anything finely structured, at that scale; the smallest rigid polymers which could act as "fingers" would be half as thick as the entire *nutrose* ring. In any case, although the target molecule would be free to interact with these surrogate hands according to pure Autoverse physics, there'd be nothing authentic about the way *the hands themselves* magically followed the movements of her gloves. Maria could see no joy in simply shifting the point where the rules were broken—and the rules had to be broken, somewhere. Manipulating the contents of the Autoverse meant violating its laws. That was obvious . . . but it was still frustrating.

She saved the modified sugar, optimistically dubbing it *mutose.* Then, changing the length scale by a factor of a million, she started up twenty-one tiny cultures of *Autobacterium lamberti,* in solutions ranging from pure *nutrose,* to a fifty-fifty mixture, to one hundred percent *mutose.*

She gazed at the array of Petri dishes floating in the workspace, their contents portrayed in colors which coded for the health of the bacteria. "False colors" . . . but that phrase was tautological. Any view of the Autoverse was necessarily stylized: a color-coded map, displaying selected attributes of the region in question. Some views were more abstract, more heavily processed than others—in the sense that a map of the Earth, color-coded to show the health of its people, would be arguably more abstract than one displaying altitude or rainfall—but the real-world ideal of an unadulterated, naked-eye view was simply untranslatable.

A few of the cultures were already looking decidedly sick, fading from electric blue to dull brown. Maria summoned up a three-dimensional graph, showing population versus time for the full range of nutrient mixtures. The cultures with only a trace of the new stuff were, predictably, growing at almost the pace of the control; with increasing *mutose* substitution the ascent gradually slowed, until, around the eighty-five percent line, the population was static. Beyond that were ever steeper trajectories into extinction. In small doses, *mutose* was simply irrelevant, but at high enough concentrations it was insidious: similar enough to *nutrose*—*A. lamberti*'s usual food—to be taken part-way through the metabolic process, competing for the same enzymes, tying up valuable biochemical resources . .

but eventually reaching a step where that one stray *blue-red* spike formed an insurmountable barrier to the reaction geometry, leaving the bacterium with nothing but a useless byproduct and a net energy loss. A culture with ninety percent *mutose* was a world where ninety per cent of the food supply had no nutritional value whatsoever—but had to be ingested indiscriminately along with the worthwhile ten percent. Consuming ten times as much for the same return wasn't a viable solution; to survive in the long term, *A. lamberti* would have to chance upon some means of rejecting *mutose* before wasting energy on it—or, better still, find a way to turn it back into *nutrose,* transforming it from a virtual poison into a source of food.

Maria displayed a histogram of mutations occurring in the bacteria's three *nutrose epimerase* genes; the enzymes these genes coded for were the closest things *A. lamberti* had to a tool to render *mutose* digestible—although none, in their original form, would do the job. No mutants had yet persisted for more than a couple of generations; all the changes so far had evidently done more harm than good. Partial sequences of the mutant genes scrolled by in a small window; Maria gazed at the blur of codons, and mentally urged the process on—if not straight toward the target (since she had no idea what that was), then at least . . . *outward,* blindly, into the space of all possible mistakes.

It was a nice thought. The only trouble was, certain portions of the genes were especially prone to particular copying errors, so most of the mutants were "exploring" the same dead ends again and again.

Arranging for *A. lamberti* to mutate was easy; like a real-world bacterium, it made frequent errors every time it duplicated its analogue of DNA. Persuading it to mutate "usefully" was something else. Max Lambert himself—inventor of the Autoverse, creator of *A. lamberti,* hero to a generation of cellular-automaton and artificial-life freaks—had spent much of the last fifteen years of his life trying to discover why the subtle differences between real-world and Autoverse biochemistry made natural selection so common in one system, and so elusive in the other. Exposed to the kind of stressful opportunities which *E. coli* would have exploited within a few dozen generations, strain after strain of *A. lamberti* had simply died out.

Only a few die-hard enthusiasts still continued Lambert's work. Maria knew of just seventy-two people who'd have the slightest idea what it meant if she ever succeeded. The artificial life scene, now, was dominated by the study of Copies—patchwork creatures, mosaics of ten thousand different *ad hoc* rules . . . the antithesis of everything the Autoverse stood for.

Real-world biochemistry was far too complex to simulate in every last detail for a creature the size of a gnat, let alone a human being. Computers *could* model all the processes of life—but not on every scale, from atom to organism, all at the same time. So the field had split three ways. In one camp, traditional molecular biochemists continued to extend their painstaking calculations, solving Schrödinger's equation more or less exactly for ever larger systems, working their way up to entire replicating strands of DNA, whole mitochondrial sub-assemblies, significant patches of the giant carbohydrate chain-link fence of a cell wall . . . but spending ever more on computing power for ever diminishing returns.

At the other end of the scale were Copies: elaborate refinements of whole-body medical simulations, originally designed to help train surgeons with virtual operations, and to take the place of animals in drug tests. A Copy was like a high-resolution CAT scan come to life, linked to a medical encyclopedia to spell out how its every tissue and organ should behave . . . walking around inside a state-of-the-art architectural simulation. A Copy possessed no individual atoms or molecules; every organ in its virtual body came in the guise of specialized sub-programs which knew (in encyclopedic, but not atomic, detail) how a real liver or brain or thyroid gland functioned . . . but which couldn't have solved Schrödinger's equation for so much as a single protein molecule. All physiology, no physics.

Lambert and his followers had staked out the middle ground. They'd invented a new physics, simple enough to allow several thousand bacteria to fit into a modest computer simulation, with a consistent, unbroken hierarchy of details existing right down to the subatomic scale. Everything was driven from the bottom up, by the lowest level of physical laws, just as it was in the real world.

The price of this simplicity was that an Autoverse bacterium didn't necessarily behave like its real-world counterparts. *A. lamberti* had a habit of confounding traditional expectations in bizarre and unpredictable ways—and for most serious microbiologists, that was enough to render it worthless.

For Autoverse junkies, though, that was the whole point.

Maria brushed aside the diagrams concealing her view of the Petri dishes, then zoomed in on one thriving culture, until a single bacterium filled the workspace. Color-coded by "health," it was a featureless blue blob; but even when she switched to a standard chemical map there was no real structure visible, apart from the cell wall—no nucleus, no organelles, no flagella; *A. lamberti* wasn't much more than a sac of protoplasm. She played with the representation, making the fine strands of the unraveled chromosomes appear; highlighting regions where protein synthesis was taking place; rendering visible the concentration gradients of *nutrose* and its immediate metabolites. Computationally expensive views; she cursed herself (as always) for wasting money, but failed (as always) to shut down everything but the essential analysis software (and the Autoverse itself), failed to sit gazing into thin air, waiting patiently for a result.

Instead, she zoomed in closer, switched to atomic colors (but left the pervasive *aqua* molecules invisible), temporarily halted time to freeze the blur of thermal motion, then zoomed in still further until the vague specks scattered throughout the workspace sharpened into the intricate tangles of long-chain lipids, polysaccharides, peptidoglycans. Names stolen unmodified from their real-world analogues—but screw it, who wanted to spend their life devising a whole new biochemical nomenclature? Maria was sufficiently impressed that Lambert had come up with distinguishable colors for all thirty-two Autoverse atoms, and unambiguous names to match.

She tracked through the sea of elaborate molecules—all of them synthesized by *A. lamberti* from nothing but *nutrose, aqua, pneuma,* and a few trace elements. Unable to spot any *mutose* molecules, she invoked **Maxwell's Demon** and asked it to find one. The perceptible delay before the program responded always drove home to her the sheer quantity of information she was playing with—and the way in which it was organized. A traditional biochemical simulation would have been keeping track of every molecule, and could have told her the exact location of the nearest altered sugar almost instantaneously. For a traditional simulation, this catalogue of molecules would have been the "ultimate truth"—nothing would have "existed," except by virtue of an entry in the Big List. In contrast, the "ultimate truth" of the Autoverse was a vast array of cubic cells of subatomic dimensions—and the primary software dealt only with these cells, oblivious to any larger structures. Atoms in the Autoverse were like hurricanes in an atmospheric model (only far more stable); they arose from the simple rules governing the smallest elements of the system. There was no need to explicitly calculate their behavior; the laws governing individual cells drove everything that happened at higher levels. Of course, a swarm of demons could have been used to compile and maintain a kind of census of atoms and molecules—at great computational expense, rather defeating the point. And the Autoverse itself would have churned on, regardless.

Maria locked her viewpoint to the *mutose* molecule, then restarted time, and everything but that one hexagonal ring smeared into translucence. The molecule itself was only slightly blurred; the current representational conventions made the average positions of the atoms clearly visible, with the deviations due to bond vibration merely suggested by faint ghostly streaks.

She zoomed in until the molecule filled the workspace. She didn't know what she was hoping to see: a successful mutant *epimerase* enzyme suddenly latch onto the ring and shift the aberrant *blue-red* spike back into the horizontal position? Questions of probability aside, it would have been over before she even knew it had begun. That part was easily fixed: she instructed **Maxwell's Demon** to keep a rolling buffer of a few million clock ticks of the molecule's history, and to replay it at a suitable rate if any structural change occurred.

Embedded in a "living" organism, the *mutose* ring looked exactly the same as the prototype she'd handled minutes before: red, green and blue billiard balls, linked by thin white rods. It seemed like an insult for even a bacterium to be composed of such comic-book molecules. The viewing software was constantly inspecting this tiny region of the Autoverse, identifying the patterns that constituted atoms, checking for overlaps between them to decide which was bonded to which, and then displaying a nice, neat, stylized picture of its conclusions. Like the handling rules which took this representation at face value, it was a useful fiction, but . . .

Maria slowed down the Autoverse clock by a factor of ten billion, then popped up the viewing menu and hit the button marked RAW. The tidy assembly of spheres and rods melted into a jagged crown of writhing polychromatic liquid metal, waves of color boiling away from the vertices to collide, merge, flow back again, wisps licking out into space.

She slowed down time a further hundredfold, almost freezing the turmoil, and then zoomed in to the same degree. The individual cubic cells which made up the Autoverse were visible now, changing state about once a second. Each cell's "state"—a whole number between zero and two hundred and fifty-five—was recomputed every clock cycle, according to a simple set of rules applied to its own previous state, and the states of its closest neighbors in the three-dimensional grid. The cellular automaton which was the Autoverse did nothing whatsoever but apply these rules uniformly to every cell; these were its fundamental "laws of physics." Here, there were no daunting quantum-mechanical equations to struggle with—just a handful of trivial arithmetic operations, performed on integers. And yet the impossibly crude laws of the Autoverse still managed to give rise to "atoms" and "molecules" with a "chemistry" rich enough to sustain "life."

Maria followed the fate of a cluster of golden cells spreading through the lattice—the cells themselves didn't move, by definition, but the pattern advanced—infiltrating and conquering a region of metallic blue, only to be invaded and consumed in turn by a wave of magenta.

If the Autoverse had a "true" appearance, this was it. The palette which assigned a color to each state was still "false"—still completely arbitrary—but at least this view revealed the elaborate three-dimensional chess game which underpinned everything else.

Everything except the hardware, the computer itself.

Maria reverted to the standard clock rate, and a macroscopic view of her twenty-one Petri dishes—just as a message popped up in the foreground:

> *JSN regrets to advise you that your resources have been diverted to a higher bidder. A snapshot of your task has been preserved in mass storage, and will be available to you when you next log on. Thank you for using our services.*

Maria sat and swore angrily for half a minute—then stopped abruptly, and buried her face in her hands. *She shouldn't have been logged on in the first place.* It was insane, squandering her savings playing around with mutant *A. lamberti*—but she kept on doing it. The Autoverse was so seductive, so hypnotic . . . so addictive.

Whoever had elbowed her off the network had done her a favor—and she'd even have her fifty-dollar log-on fee refunded, since she'd been thrown right out, not merely slowed down to a snail's pace.

Curious to discover the identity of her unintentional benefactor, she logged on directly to the QIPS Exchange—the marketplace where processing power was bought and sold. The connection to JSN had passed through the Exchange, transparently; her terminal was programmed to bid at the market rate automatically, up to a certain ceiling. Right now, though, some outfit calling itself Operation Butterfly was buying QIPS—quadrillions of instructions per second—at *six hundred times* that ceiling, and had managed to acquire one hundred percent of the planet's traded computing power.

Maria was stunned; she'd never seen anything like it. The pie chart of successful bidders—normally a flickering kaleidoscope of thousands of needle-thin slices—was a solid, static disk of blue. Aircraft would not be dropping out of the sky, world commerce would not have ground to a halt . . . but tens of thousands of academic and industrial researchers relied on the Exchange every day for tasks it wasn't worth owning the power to perform in-house. Not to mention a few thousand Copies. For one user to muscle in and outbid everyone else was unprecedented. Who needed that much computing power? Big business, big science, the military? All had their own private hardware—usually in excess of their requirements. If they traded at all, it was to sell their surplus capacity.

Operation Butterfly? The name sounded vaguely familiar. Maria logged on to a news system and searched for reports which mentioned the phrase. The most recent was three months ago:

> **Kuala Lumpar—Monday, August 8th, 2050:** *A meeting of environmental ministers from the Association of South-East Asian Nations (ASEAN) today agreed to proceed with the latest stage of Operation Butterfly, a controversial plan to attempt to limit the damage and loss of life caused by Greenhouse Typhoons in the region.*
>
> *The long-term aim of the project is to utilize the so-called Butterfly Effect to divert typhoons away from*

vulnerable populated areas—or perhaps prevent them from forming in the first place.

Maria said, "Define 'Butterfly Effect.'" A second window opened up in front of the news report:

Butterfly Effect: This term was coined by meteorologist Edward Lorenz in the late 1970s, to dramatize the futility of trying to make long-term weather forecasts. Lorenz pointed out that meteorological systems were so sensitive to their initial conditions that a butterfly flapping its wings in Brazil could be enough to determine whether or not there was a tornado in Texas a month later. No computer model could ever include such minute details—so any attempt to forecast the weather more than a few days in advance was doomed to failure.

However, in the 1990s the term began to lose its original, pessimistic connotations. A number of researchers discovered that, although the effects of small, random influences made a chaotic system unpredictable, under certain conditions the same sensitivity could be deliberately exploited to steer the system in a chosen direction. The same kind of processes which magnified the flapping of butterflies' wings into tornadoes could also magnify the effects of systematic intervention, allowing a degree of control out of all proportion to the energy expended.

The Butterfly Effect now commonly refers to the principle of controlling a chaotic system with minimum force, through a detailed knowledge of its dynamics. This technique has been applied in a number of fields, including chemical engineering, stock-market manipulation, fly-by-wire aeronautics, and the proposed ASEAN weather-control system, Operation Butterfly.

There was more, but Maria took the cue and switched back to the article.

Meteorologists envisage dotting the waters of the tropical western Pacific and the South China Sea with a grid of hundreds of thousands of "weather-control" rigs— solar-powered devices designed to alter the local temperature on demand by pumping water between different depths. Theoretical models suggest that a sufficient number of rigs, under elaborate computer control, could be used to influence large-scale weather patterns, "nudging" them toward the least harmful of a number of finely balanced possible outcomes.

Eight different rig prototypes have been tested in the open ocean, but before engineers select one design for mass production, an extensive feasibility study will be conducted. Over a three-year period, any potentially threatening typhoon will be analyzed by a computer model of the highest possible resolution, and the effects of various numbers and types of the as yet nonexistent rigs will be included in the model. If these simulations demonstrate that intervention could have yielded significant savings in life and property, ASEAN's ministerial council will have to decide whether or not to spend the estimated sixty billion dollars required to make the system a reality.

Other nations are observing the experiment with interest.

Maria leaned back from the screen, impressed. *A computer model of the highest possible resolution.* And they'd meant it, literally. They'd bought up all the number-crunching power on offer—paying a small fortune, but only a fraction of what it would have cost to buy the same hardware outright.

Nudging typhoons! Not yet, not in reality . . . but who could begrudge Operation Butterfly their brief monopoly, for such a grand experiment? Maria felt a vicarious thrill at the sheer scale of the endeavor—and then a mixture of guilt and resentment at being a mere bystander. She had no qualifications in atmospheric or oceanic physics, no PhD in chaos theory—but in a project of that size, there must have been a few hundred jobs offered to mere programmers. When the tenders had gone out over the network, she'd probably been busy on some shitty contract to improve the tactile qualities of beach sand for visitors to the Virtual Gold Coast—either that, or tinkering with the genome of *A. lamberti,* trying to become the first person in the world to bludgeon a simulated bacterium into exhibiting natural selection.

It wasn't clear how long Operation Butterfly would spend monitoring each typhoon—but she could forget about returning to the Autoverse for the day.

Reluctantly, she logged off the news system—fighting the temptation to sit and wait for the first reports of the typhoon in question, or the response of other supercomputer users to the great processing buy-out—and began reviewing her plans for a new intruder surveillance package.

2

(Remit not paucity)

"What I'm asking for is two million ecus. What I'm offering you is immortality."

Thomas Riemann's office was compact but uncluttered, smartly furnished without being ostentatious. The single large window offered a sweeping view of Frankfurt—looking north across the river, as if from Sachsenhausen, toward the three jet-black towers of the Siemens/Deutsche Bank Center—which Thomas believed was as honest as any conceivable alternative. Half the offices in Frankfurt itself looked out over recorded tropical rainforests, stunning desert gorges, Antarctic ice shelves—or wholly synthetic landscapes: rural-idyllic, futuristic, interplanetary, or simply surreal. With the freedom to choose whatever he liked, he'd selected this familiar sight from his corporeal days; sentimental, perhaps, but at least it wasn't ludicrously inappropriate.

Thomas turned away from the window, and regarded his visitor with good-natured skepticism. He replied in English; the office software could have translated for him—and would have chosen the very same words and syntax, having been cloned from his own language centers—but Thomas still preferred to use the version "residing inside" his own "skull."

"Two million? What's the scheme? Let me guess. Under your skillful management, my capital will grow at the highest possible rate consistent with the need for total security. The price of computation is sure to fall again, sooner or later; the fact that it's risen for the last fifteen years only makes that more likely than ever. So: it may take a decade or two—or three, or four—but eventually, the income from my modest investment will be enough to keep me running on the latest hardware, indefinitely . . . while also providing you with a small commission, of course." Thomas laughed, without malice. "You don't seem to have researched your prospective client very thoroughly. You people usually have immaculate intelligence—but I'm afraid you've really missed the target with me. I'm in no danger of being shut down. The hardware we're using, right now, isn't leased from anyone; it's wholly owned by a foundation I set up before my death. My estate is being managed to my complete satisfaction. I have no problems—financial, legal, *peace of mind*—for you to solve. And the last thing in the world I need is a cheap and nasty perpetuity fund. Your offer is useless to me."

Paul Durham chose to display no sign of disappointment. He said, "I'm not talking about a perpetuity fund. I'm not selling any kind of financial service. Will you give me a chance to explain?"

Thomas nodded affably. "Go ahead. I'm listening." Durham had flatly refused to state his business in advance, but Thomas had decided to see him anyway—anticipating a perverse satisfaction in confirming that the man's mysterious coyness hid nothing out of the ordinary. Thomas almost always agreed to meet visitors from outside—even though experience had shown that most were simply begging for money, one way or another. He believed that anyone willing to slow down their brain by a factor of seventeen, solely for the privilege of talking to him face to face, deserved a hearing—and he wasn't immune to the intrinsic flattery of the process, the unequal sacrifice of time.

There was more to it, though, than flattery.

When other Copies called on him in his office, or sat beside him at a boardroom table, everyone was "present" in exactly the same sense. However bizarre the algorithmic underpinnings of the encounter, it was a meeting of equals. No boundaries were crossed.

A visitor, though, who could lift and empty a coffee cup, who could sign a document and shake your hand—but who was, indisputably, lying motionless on a couch in another (higher?) metaphysical plane—came charged with too many implicit reminders of the nature of things to be faced with the same equanimity. Thomas valued that. He didn't want to grow complacent—or worse. Visitors helped him to retain a clear sense of what he'd become.

Durham said, "Of course I'm aware of your situation—you have one of the most secure arrangements I've seen. I've read the incorporation documents of the Soliton Foundation, and they're close to watertight. Under present legislation."

Thomas laughed heartily. "But you think you can do better? Soliton pays its most senior lawyers almost a million a year; you should have got yourself some forged qualifications and asked me to employ you. *Under present legislation!* When the laws change, believe me, they'll change for the better. I expect you know that Soliton spends a small fortune lobbying for improvement—and it's not alone. The trend is in one direction: there are more Copies every year, and most of them have *de facto* control over virtually all of the wealth they owned when they were alive. I'm afraid your timing's atrocious if you're planning on using scare tactics; I received a report last week predicting full human rights—in Europe, at least—by the early sixties. Ten years isn't long for me to wait. I've grown used to the current slowdown factor; even if processor speeds improve, I could easily choose to keep living at the rate I'm living now, for another six or seven subjective months, rather than pushing all the things I'm looking forward to—like European citizenship—further into the future."

Durham's puppet inclined its head in a gesture of polite assent; Thomas had a sudden vision of a second puppet—one Durham truly felt himself to be inhabiting—hunched over a control panel, hitting a button on an etiquette sub-menu. *Was that paranoid?* But any sensible mendicant visitor would do just that, conducting the meeting at a distance rather than exposing their true body language to scrutiny.

The visible puppet said, "Why spend a fortune upgrading, for the sake of effectively slowing down progress? And I agree with you about the outlook for reform—in the short term. Of course people begrudge Copies their longevity, but the PR has been handled remarkably well. A few carefully chosen terminally ill children are scanned and resurrected every year: better than a trip to Disney World. There's discreet sponsorship of a sitcom about working-class Copies, which makes the whole idea less threatening. The legal status of Copies is being framed as a human rights issue, especially in Europe: Copies are disabled people, no more, no less—really just a kind of radical amputee—and anyone who talks about *decadent rich immortals getting their hands on all the wealth* is shouted down as a neo-Nazi.

"So you might well achieve citizenship in a decade. And if you're lucky, the situation could be stable for another twenty or thirty years after that. But . . . what's twenty or thirty years to you? Do you honestly think that the status quo will be tolerated for ever?'"

Thomas said, "Of course not—but I'll tell you what would be "tolerated": scanning facilities, and computing power, so cheap that everyone on the planet could be resurrected. Everyone who wanted it. And when I say *cheap,* I mean at a cost comparable to a dose of vaccine at the turn of the century. Imagine that. Death could be eradicated—like smallpox or malaria. And I'm not talking about some solipsistic nightmare; by then, telepresence robots will let Copies interact with the physical world as fully as if they were human. Civilization wouldn't have deserted reality—just transcended biology."

"That's a long, long way in the future."

"Certainly. But don't accuse me of thinking in the short term."

"And in the meantime? The privileged class of Copies will grow larger, more powerful—and more threatening to the vast majority of people, who still won't be able to join them. The costs will come down, but not drastically—just enough to meet some of the explosion in demand from the executive class, once they throw off their qualms, *en masse.* Even in secular Europe, there's a deeply ingrained prejudice that says dying is the responsible, the *moral* thing to do. There's a Death Ethic—and the first substantial segment of the population abandoning it will trigger a huge backlash. A small enough elite of giga-rich Copies is accepted as a freak show; tycoons can get away with anything, they're not expected to act like ordinary people. But just wait until the numbers go up by a factor of ten."

Thomas had heard it all before. "We may be unpopular for a while. I can live with that. But you know, even now we're vilified far less than people who strive for *organic* hyper-longevity—transplants, cellular rejuvenation, whatever—because at least *we're* no longer pushing up the cost of health care, competing for the use of overburdened medical facilities. Nor are we consuming natural resources at anything like the rate we did when we were alive. If the technology improves sufficiently, the environmental impact of the wealthiest Copy could end up being less than that of the most ascetic living human. Who'll have the high moral ground then? We'll be the most ecologically sound people on the planet."

Durham smiled. The puppet. "Sure—and it could lead to some nice ironies if it ever came true. But even low environmental impact might not seem so saintly, when the same computing power could be used to save tens of thousands of lives through weather control."

"Operation Butterfly has inconvenienced some of my fellow Copies very slightly. And myself not at all."

"Operation Butterfly is only the beginning. Crisis management, for a tiny part of the planet. Imagine how much computing power it would take to render sub-Saharan Africa free from drought."

"Why should I imagine that, when the most modest schemes are still unproven? And even if weather control turns out to be viable, more supercomputers can always be built. It doesn't have to be a matter of Copies versus flood victims."

"There's a limited supply of computing power right now, isn't there? Of course it will grow—but the demand, from Copies, and for weather control, is almost certain to grow faster. Long before we get to your deathless utopia, we'll hit a bottleneck—and I believe that will bring on a time when Copies are declared *illegal*. Worldwide. If they've been granted human rights, those rights will be taken away. Trusts and foundations will have their assets confiscated. Supercomputers will be heavily policed. Scanners—and scan files—will be destroyed. It may be forty years before any of this happens—or it may be sooner. Either way, you need to be prepared."

Thomas said mildly, "If you're fishing for a job as a futurology consultant, I'm afraid I already employ several—highly qualified—people who do nothing but investigate these trends. Right now, everything they tell me gives me reason to be optimistic—and even if they're wrong, Soliton is ready for a very wide range of contingencies."

"If your whole foundation is eviscerated, do you honestly believe it will be able to ensure that a snapshot of you is hidden away safely—and then resurrected after a hundred years or more of social upheaval? A vault full of ROM chips at the bottom of a mine shaft could end up taking a one-way trip into geological time."

Thomas laughed. "And a meteor could hit the planet tomorrow, wiping out this computer, all of my backups, *your* organic body . . . anything and everything. Yes, there could be a revolution which pulls the plug on my world. It's unlikely, but it's not impossible. Or there could be a plague, or an ecological disaster, which kills billions of organic humans but leaves all the Copies untouched. There are no certainties for anyone."

"But Copies have so much more to lose."

Thomas was emphatic; this was part of his personal litany. "I've never mistaken what I have—a very good chance of a prolonged existence—for a *guarantee of immortality.*"

Durham said flatly, "Quite right. You have no such thing. Which is why I'm here offering it to you."

Thomas regarded him uneasily. Although he'd had all the ravages of surgery edited out of his final scan file, he'd kept a scar on his right forearm, a small memento of a youthful misadventure. He stroked it, not quite absentmindedly; conscious of the habit, conscious of the memories that the scar encoded—but practiced at refusing to allow those memories to hold his gaze.

Finally, he said, "Offering it how? What can you possibly

do—for two million ecus—that Soliton can't do a thousand times better?"

"I can run a second version of you, entirely out of harm's way. I can give you a kind of insurance—against an anti-Copy backlash . . . or a meteor strike . . . or whatever else might go wrong."

Thomas was momentarily speechless. The subject wasn't entirely taboo, but he couldn't recall anyone raising it quite so bluntly before. He recovered swiftly. "I have no wish to run a *second version,* thank you. And . . . what do you mean, "out of harm's way"? Where's your invulnerable computer going to be? In orbit? Up where it would only take a pebble-sized meteor to destroy it, instead of a boulder?"

"No, not in orbit. And if you don't want a second version, that's fine. You could simply move."

"Move *where?* Underground? To the bottom of the ocean? You don't even know where this office is being implemented, do you? What makes you think you can offer a superior site— for such a ridiculous price—when you don't have the faintest idea how secure I am already?" Thomas was growing disappointed, and uncharacteristically irritable. "Stop making these inflated claims, and get to the point. What are you selling?"

Durham shook his head apologetically. "I can't tell you that. Not yet. If I tried to explain it, out of the blue, it would make no sense. You have to do something first. Something very simple."

"Yes? And what's that?"

"You have to conduct a small experiment."

Thomas scowled. "What kind of *experiment?* Why?"

And Durham—the software puppet, the lifeless shell animated by a being from another plane—looked him in the eye and said, "You have to let me show you exactly what you are."

3

(Rip, tie, cut toy man)

JUNE 2045

Paul—or the flesh-and-blood man whose memories he'd inherited—had traced the history of Copies back to the turn of the century, when researchers had begun to fine-tune the generic computer models used for surgical training and pharmacology, transforming them into customized versions able to predict the needs and problems of individual patients. Drug therapies were tried out in advance on models which incorporated specific genetic and biochemical traits, allowing doses to be optimized and any idiosyncratic side-effects anticipated and avoided. Elaborate operations were rehearsed and perfected in Virtual Reality, on software bodies with anatomical details—down to the finest capillaries—based on the flesh-and-blood patient's tomographic scans.

These early models included a crude approximation of the brain, perfectly adequate for heart surgery or immunotherapy—and even useful to a degree when dealing with gross cerebral injuries and tumours—but worthless for exploring more subtle neurological problems.

Imaging technology steadily improved, though—and by 2020, it had reached the point where individual neurons could be mapped, and the properties of individual synapses measured, non-invasively. With a combination of scanners, every psychologically relevant detail of the brain could be read from the living organ—and duplicated on a sufficiently powerful computer.

At first, only isolated neural pathways were modeled: portions of the visual cortex of interest to designers of machine vision, or sections of the limbic system whose role had been in dispute. These fragmentary neural models yielded valuable results, but a functionally complete representation of the whole organ—embedded in a whole body—would have allowed the most delicate feats of neurosurgery and psychopharmacology to be tested in advance. For several years, though, no such model was built—in part, because of a scarcely articulated unease at the prospect of what it would mean. There were no formal barriers standing in the way—government regulatory bodies and institutional ethics committees were concerned only with human and animal welfare, and no laboratory had yet been fire-bombed by activists for its inhumane treatment of physiological software—but still, someone had to be the first to break all the unspoken taboos.

Someone had to make a high-resolution, whole-brain Copy—and let it wake, and talk.

In 2024, John Vines, a Boston neurosurgeon, ran a fully conscious Copy of himself in a crude Virtual Reality. Taking slightly less than three hours of real time (pulse racing, hyperventilating, stress hormones elevated), the first Copy's first words were: "This is like being buried alive. I've changed my mind. Get me out of here."

His original obligingly shut him down—but then later repeated the demonstration several times, without variation, reasoning that it was impossible to cause additional distress by running exactly the same simulation more than once.

When Vines went public, the prospects for advancing neurological research didn't rate a mention; within twenty-four hours—despite the Copy's discouraging testimony—the headlines were all immortality, mass migration into Virtual Reality, and the imminent desertion of the physical world.

Paul was twenty-four years old at the time, with no idea what to make of his life. His father had died the year before—leaving him a modest business empire, centered on a thriving retail chain, which he had no interest in managing. He'd spent seven years traveling and studying—science, history and philosophy—doing well enough at everything he tried, but unable to discover anything that kindled real intellectual passion. With no struggle for financial security ahead, he'd been sinking quietly into a state of bemused complacency.

The news of John Vines's Copy blasted away his indifference. It was as if every dubious promise technology had ever made to transform human life was about to be fulfilled, with a vengeance. Longevity would only be the start of it; Copies could *evolve* in ways almost impossible for organic beings: modifying their minds, redefining their goals, endlessly transmuting themselves. The possibilities were intoxicating—even as the costs and drawbacks of the earliest versions sank in, even as the inevitable backlash began. Paul was a child of the millennium; he was ready to embrace it all.

But the more time he spent contemplating what Vines had done, the more bizarre the implications seemed to be.

The public debate the experiment had triggered was heated, but depressingly superficial. Decades-old arguments raged again over just how much computer programs could ever have in common with human beings (psychologically, morally, metaphysically, information-theoretically . . .) and even whether or not Copies could be "truly" intelligent, "truly" conscious. As more workers repeated Vines's result, their Copies soon passed the Turing test: no panel of experts quizzing a group of Copies and humans—by delayed video, to mask the time-rate difference—could tell which were which. But some philosophers and psychologists continued to insist that this demonstrated nothing more than "simulated consciousness,' and that Copies were merely programs capable of faking a detailed inner life which didn't actually exist at all.

Supporters of the Strong AI Hypothesis insisted that consciousness was a property of certain algorithms—a result of information being processed in certain ways, regardless of what machine, or organ, was used to perform the task. A computer model which manipulated data about itself and its "surroundings" in essentially the same way as an organic brain would have to possess essentially the same mental states. "Simulated consciousness" was as oxymoronic as "simulated addition."

Opponents replied that when you modeled a hurricane, nobody got wet. When you modeled a fusion power plant, no energy was produced. When you modeled digestion and metabolism, no nutrients were consumed—no *real digestion* took place. So, when you modeled the human brain, why should you expect *real thought* to occur? A computer running a Copy might be able to generate plausible descriptions of human behavior in hypothetical scenarios—and even appear to carry on a conversation, by correctly predicting what a human *would have done* in the same situation—but that hardly made the machine itself conscious.

Paul had rapidly decided that this whole debate was a distraction. For any human, absolute proof of a Copy's sentience was impossible. For any Copy, the truth was self-evident: *cogito ergo sum.* End of discussion.

But for any human willing to grant Copies the same reasonable presumption of consciousness that they granted their fellow humans—and any Copy willing to reciprocate—the real point was this:

There were questions about the nature of this shared condition which the existence of Copies illuminated more starkly than anything which had come before them. Questions which needed to be explored, before the human race could confidently begin to bequeath its culture, its memories, its purpose and identity, to its successors.

Questions which only a Copy could answer.

Paul sat in his study, in his favorite armchair (unconvinced that the texture of the surface had been accurately reproduced), taking what comfort he could from the undeniable absurdity of being afraid to experiment on himself further. He'd already "survived" the "transition" from flesh-and-blood human to computerized physiological model—the most radical stage of the project, by far. In comparison, tinkering with a few of the model's parameters should have seemed trivial.

Durham appeared on the terminal—which was otherwise still dysfunctional. Paul was already beginning to think of him as a bossy little *djinn* trapped inside the screen—rather than a vast, omnipotent deity striding the halls of Reality, pulling all the strings. The pitch of his voice was enough to deflate any aura of power and grandeur.

Squeak. "Experiment one, trial zero. Baseline data. Time resolution one millisecond—system standard. Just count to ten, at one-second intervals, as near as you can judge it. Okay?"

"I think I can manage that." He'd planned all this himself, he didn't need step-by-step instructions. Durham's image vanished; during the experiments, there could be no cues from real time.

Paul counted to ten. The *djinn* returned. Staring at the face on the screen, Paul realized that he had no inclination to think of it as "his own." Perhaps that was a legacy of distancing himself from the earlier Copies. Or perhaps his mental image of himself had never been much like his true appearance—and now, in defence of sanity, was moving even further away.

Squeak. "Okay. Experiment one, trial number one. Time resolution five milliseconds. Are you ready?"

"Yes."

The *djinn* vanished. Paul counted: "One. Two. Three. Four. Five. Six. Seven. Eight. Nine. Ten."

Squeak. "Anything to report?'

"No. I mean, I can't help feeling slightly apprehensive, just knowing that you're screwing around with my . . . infrastructure. But apart from that, nothing."

Durham's eyes no longer glazed over while he was waiting for the speeded-up reply; either he'd gained a degree of self-discipline, or—more likely—he'd interposed some smart editing software to conceal his boredom.

Squeak. "Don't worry about apprehension. We're running a control, remember?"

Paul would have preferred not to have been reminded. He'd known that Durham must have cloned him, and would be feeding exactly the same sensorium to both Copies—while only making changes in the model's time resolution for one of them. It was an essential part of the experiment—but he didn't want to dwell on it. A third self, shadowing his thoughts, was too much to acknowledge on top of everything else.

Squeak. "Trial number two. Time resolution ten milliseconds."

Paul counted. The easiest thing in the world, he thought, when you're made of flesh, when you're made of matter, when the quarks and the electrons just do what comes naturally. Human beings were embodied, ultimately, in fields of fundamental particles—incapable, surely, of being anything other than themselves. Copies were embodied in computer memories as vast sets of *numbers*. Numbers which certainly *could be* interpreted as describing a human body sitting in a room . . . but it was hard to see that meaning as intrinsic, as *necessary*, when tens of thousands of arbitrary choices had been made about the way in which the model had been coded. *Is this my blood sugar here . . . or my testosterone level? Is this the firing rate of a motor neuron as I raise my right hand . . . or a signal coming in from my retina as I watch myself doing it?* Anybody given access to the raw data, but unaware of the conventions, could spend a lifetime sifting through the numbers without deciphering what any of it meant.

And yet no Copy buried in the data itself—ignorant of the details or not—could have the slightest trouble making sense of it all in an instant.

Squeak. "Trial number three. Time resolution twenty milliseconds."

"One. Two. Three."

For time to pass for a Copy, the numbers which defined it had to change from moment to moment. Recomputed over and over again, a Copy was a sequence of snapshots, frames of a movie—or frames of computer animation.

But . . . when, exactly, did these snapshots give rise to conscious thought? While they were being computed? Or in the brief interludes when they sat in the computer's memory, unchanging, doing nothing but representing one static instant of the Copy's life? When both stages were taking place a thousand times per subjective second, it hardly seemed to matter, but very soon—

Squeak. "Trial number four. Time resolution fifty milliseconds."

What am I? The data? The process that generates it? The relationships between the numbers?

All of the above?

"One hundred milliseconds."

"One. Two. Three."

Paul listened to his voice as he counted—as if half expecting to begin to notice the encroachment of silence, to start perceiving the gaps in himself.

"Two hundred milliseconds."

A fifth of a second. "One. Two." Was he strobing in and out of existence now, at five subjective hertz? The crudest of celluloid movies had never flickered at this rate. "Three. Four." He waved his hand in front of his face; the motion looked perfectly smooth, perfectly normal. And of course it did; he wasn't watching from the outside. "Five. Six. Seven." A sudden, intense wave of nausea passed through him but he fought it down, and continued. "Eight. Nine. Ten."

The *djinn* reappeared and emitted a brief, solicitous squeak. "What's wrong? Do you want to stop for a while?"

"No, I'm fine." Paul glanced around the innocent, sun-dappled room, and laughed. *How would Durham handle it if the control and the subject had just given two different replies?* He tried to recall his plans for such a contingency, but couldn't remember them—and didn't much care. It wasn't his problem any more.

Squeak. "Trial number seven. Time resolution five hundred milliseconds."

Paul counted—and the truth was, he felt no different. A little uneasy, yes—but factoring out any squeamishness, everything about his experience seemed to remain the same. And that made sense, at least in the long run—because nothing was being omitted, in the long run. His model-of-a-brain was only being fully described at half-second (model time) intervals—but each description still included the results of everything that "would have happened" in between. Every half-second, his brain was ending up in exactly the state it would have been in if nothing had been left out.

"One thousand milliseconds."

But . . . what was going on, in between? The equations controlling the model were far too complex to solve in a single step. In the process of calculating the solutions, vast arrays of partial results were being generated and discarded along the way. In a sense, these partial results *implied*—even if they didn't directly represent—events taking place within the gaps between successive complete descriptions. And when the whole model was arbitrary, who was to say that these implied events, buried a little more deeply in the torrent of data, were any "less real" than those which were directly described?

"Two thousand milliseconds."

"One. *Two.* Three. *Four.*"

If he seemed to speak (and hear himself speak) every number, it was because the effects of having said "three" (and having heard himself say it) were implicit in the details of calculating how his brain evolved from the time when he'd just said "two" to the time when he'd just said "four."

"Five thousand milliseconds."

"One. Two. Three. Four. *Five.*"

Besides, hearing words that he'd never "really" spoken wasn't much stranger than a Copy hearing anything at all. Even the standard millisecond clock rate of this world was far too coarse to resolve the full range of audible tones. Sound wasn't represented in the model by fluctuations in air pressure values—which couldn't change fast enough—but in terms of audio power spectra: profiles of intensity versus frequency. Twenty kilohertz was just a number here, a label; nothing could actually *oscillate* at that rate. Real ears analyzed pressure waves into components of various pitch; Paul knew that his brain was being fed the preexisting power spectrum values directly, plucked out of the nonexistent air by a crude patch in the model.

"Ten thousand milliseconds."

"One. Two. Three."

Ten seconds free-falling from frame to frame.

Fighting down vertigo, still counting steadily, Paul prodded the shallow cut he'd made in his forearm with the kitchen knife. It stung, convincingly. *So where was this experience coming from?* Once the ten seconds were up, his fully described brain would *remember* all of this . . . but that didn't account for what was happening *now.* Pain was more than the memory of pain. He struggled to imagine the tangle of billions of intermediate calculations, somehow "making sense" of themselves, bridging the gap.

And he wondered: *What would happen if someone shut down the computer, just pulled the plug—right now?*

He didn't know what that meant, though. In any terms but his own, he didn't know when "right now" *was.*

"Eight. Nine. *Ten.*"

Squeak. "Paul—I'm seeing a slight blood pressure drop. Are you okay? How are you feeling?"

Giddy—but he said, "The same as always." And if that wasn't quite true, no doubt the control had told the same lie. Assuming . . .

"Tell me—which was I? Control, or subject?"

Squeak. Durham replied, "I can't answer that—I'm still speaking to both of you. I'll tell you one thing, though: the two of you are still identical. There were some very small, transitory discrepancies, but they've died away completely now—and whenever the two of you were in comparable representations, all firing patterns of more than a couple of neurons were the same."

Paul grunted dismissively; he had no intention of letting Durham know how unsettling the experiment had been. "What did you expect? Solve the same set of equations two different ways, and of course you get the same results—give or take some minor differences in round-off errors along the way. You *must.* It's a mathematical certainty."

Squeak. "Oh, I agree." The *djinn* wrote with one finger on the screen:

$$(1 + 2) + 3 = 1 + (2 + 3)$$

Paul said, "So why bother with this stage at all? *I know*—I wanted to be rigorous, I wanted to establish solid foundations. But the truth is, it's a waste of our resources. Why not skip the bleeding obvious, and get on with the kind of experiment where the answer isn't a foregone conclusion?'

Squeak. Durham frowned reprovingly. "I didn't realize you'd grown so cynical so quickly. AI isn't a branch of pure mathematics; it's an empirical science. Assumptions have to be tested. Confirming the so-called "obvious" isn't such a dishonourable thing, is it? And if it's all so straightforward, why should you be afraid?"

"I'm not afraid: I just want to get it over with. But . . . go ahead. Prove whatever you think you have to prove, and then we can move on."

Squeak. "That's the plan. But I think we could both use a break now. I'll enable your communications—for incoming data only." He turned away, reached off-screen, and hit a few keys on a second terminal.

Then he turned back to the camera, smiling—and Paul knew exactly what he was going to say.

Squeak. "By the way, I just deleted one of you. I couldn't afford to keep you both running, when all you're going to do is laze around."

Paul smiled back at him, although something inside him was screaming. "Which one did you terminate?"

Squeak. "What difference does it make? I told you, they were identical. And you're still here, aren't you? Whoever you are. *Whichever you were.*"

Three weeks had passed outside since the day of the scan, but it didn't take Paul long to catch up with the state of the world; most of the fine details had been rendered irrelevant by subsequent events, and much of the ebb and flow had simply canceled itself out. Israel and Palestine had come close to war again, over alleged water treaty violations on both sides—but a joint peace rally had brought more than a million people onto the glassy plain that used to be Jerusalem, and the two governments had been forced to back down. Former US President Martin Sandover was still fighting extradition to Palau, to face charges arising from his role in the bloody *coup d'état* of thirty-five; the Supreme Court had finally reversed a long-standing ruling which had granted him immunity from all foreign laws, and for a day or two things had looked promising—but then his legal team had discovered a whole new set of delaying tactics. In Canberra, another leadership challenge had come and gone, with the Prime Minister remaining undeposed. In a week-old report, one journalist described this, straight-faced, as "high drama." Paul thought: *I guess you had to be there.* Inflation had fallen by half a percentage point; unemployment had risen by the same amount.

Paul scanned the old news reports rapidly, skimming over articles and fast-forwarding scenes which he felt sure he would have studied scrupulously, had they been fresh. He felt a curious sense of resentment, at having "missed" so much—it was all there in front of him, *now,* but that wasn't the same at all.

And yet, he wondered, shouldn't he be relieved that he hadn't wasted his time on so much ephemeral detail? The very fact that he was now less than enthralled only proved how little of it had really mattered, in the long run.

Then again, what did? People didn't inhabit geological time. People inhabited hours and days; they had to care about things on that time scale.

People.

Paul plugged into real-time TV, and watched an episode of *The Unclear Family* flash by in less than two minutes, the soundtrack an incomprehensible squeal. A game show. A war movie. The evening news. It was as if he was in deep space, rushing back toward the Earth through a sea of Doppler-shifted broadcasts. The image was strangely comforting; his situation wasn't so bizarre, after all, if flesh-and-blood humans could find themselves in much the same relationship with the world as he did. Nobody would claim that the Doppler shift could rob someone of their humanity.

Dusk fell over the recorded city. He ate a microwaved soya protein stew—wondering if there was any good reason, moral or otherwise, to continue to be a vegetarian.

He listened to music until long after midnight. Tsang Chao, Michael Nyman, Philip Glass. It made no difference that each note "really" lasted seventeen times as long as it should have, or that the audio ROM sitting in the player "really" possessed no microstructure, or that the "sound" itself was being fed into his model-of-a-brain by a computerized sleight-of-hand that bore no resemblance to the ordinary process of hearing. The climax of Glass's *Mishima* still seized him like a grappling hook through the heart.

And if the computations behind *all this* had been performed over millennia, by people flicking abacus beads, would he have felt exactly the same?

It was outrageous to admit it—but the answer had to be *yes.*

He lay in bed, wondering: *Do I still want to wake from this dream?*

The question remained academic, though; he still had no choice.

4

(Remit not paucity)

Maria had arranged to meet Aden at the Nadir, an Oxford Street nightclub where he sometimes played and often went to write. He could usually get them both in for free, and the door—an intimidating, airlock-like contraption of ribbed black anodized steel—let her pass unchallenged after a brief security scan. Maria had once had a nightmare in which she'd been trapped in that chamber, a knife inexplicably strapped to her right boot—and, worse, her credit rating canceled. The thing had digested her like an insect in a Venus flytrap, while Aden stood on stage, singing one of his cut-up love songs.

Inside, the place was crowded for a Thursday night, and poorly lit as always; she finally spotted Aden sitting at a table near a side wall, listening to one of the bands and jotting down music, his face catching the glow of his notepad. So far as Maria could tell, he never seemed to be unduly influenced by anything he listened to while composing, but he claimed to be unable to work in silence, and preferred live performances for inspiration—or catalysis, or whatever it was.

She touched him on the shoulder. He looked up, took off his headset, and stood to kiss her. He tasted of orange juice.

He gestured with the headset. "You should listen. Crooked Buddhist Lawyers on Crack. They're quite good."

Maria glanced at the stage, although there was no way of telling who he meant. A dozen performers—four bands in all—stood enclosed in individual soundproof plastic cylinders. Most of the patrons were tuned in, wearing headsets to pick up one band's sound, and liquid crystal shades, flickering in synch with one group of cylinders, to render the other bands invisible. A few people were chatting quietly—and of the room's five possible soundtracks, Maria decided that this tranquil near-silence best suited her mood. Besides, she never much liked using nerve current inducers; although physically unable to damage the eardrums (sparing the management any risk of litigation), they always seemed to leave her ears—or her auditory pathways—ringing, regardless of the volume setting she chose.

"Maybe later."

She sat beside Aden, and felt him tense slightly when their shoulders brushed, then force himself to relax. Or maybe not. Often when she thought she was reading his body language, she was making signals out of noise. She said, "I got some junk mail today that looked just like you."

"How flattering. I think. What was it selling?"

"The Church of the God Who Makes No Difference."

He laughed. "Every time I hear that, I think: they've got to change the name. A God which makes no difference doesn't rate the definite article or the pronoun 'who.'"

"I'll rerun the program, and the two of you can fight it out."

"No thanks." He took a sip of his drink. "Any non-junk mail? Any contracts?"

"No."

"So . . . another day of terminal boredom?"

"Mostly." Maria hesitated. Aden usually only pressed her for news when he had something to announce himself—and she was curious to find out what it was. But he volunteered nothing, so she went on to describe her encounter with Operation Butterfly.

Aden said, "I remember hearing something about that. But I thought it was decades away."

"The real thing probably is, but the simulations have definitely started. In a big way."

He looked pained. "*Weather control?* Who do they think they're kidding?"

Maria suppressed her irritation. "The theory must look promising, or they wouldn't have taken it this far. Nobody spends a few million dollars an hour on supercomputer time without a good chance of a payoff."

Aden snickered. "Oh yes they do. And it's usually called *Operation* something-or-other. Remember Operation Radiant Way?"

"Yes, I remember."

"They were going to seed the upper atmosphere with nanomachines which could monitor the temperature—and supposedly do something about it."

"Manufacture particles which reflected certain wavelengths of solar radiation—and then disassemble them, as required."

"In other words, cover the planet with a giant thermostatic blanket."

"What's so terrible about that?"

"You mean, apart from the sheer technocratic hubris? And apart from the fact that releasing any kind of replicator into the environment is—still, thankfully—illegal? *It wouldn't have worked.* There were complications nobody had predicted—unstable mixing of air layers, wasn't it?—which would have counteracted most of the effect."

Maria said, "Exactly. But how would anyone have known that, if they hadn't run a proper simulation?"

"Common sense. This whole idea of throwing technology at problems *created by* technology . . . "

Maria felt her patience desert her. "What would you rather do? Be humble in the presence of nature, and hope you'll be rewarded for it? You think *Mother Gaia* is going to forgive us, and put everything right—just as soon as we throw away our wicked computers and promise to stop trying to fix things ourselves?" *Should have made that "Nanny Gaia."*

Aden scowled. "No—but the only way to "fix things" is to have *less* impact on the planet, not more. Instead of thinking up these grandiose schemes to bludgeon everything into shape, we have to back off, leave it alone, give it a chance to heal."

Maria was bemused. "It's too late for that. If that had started a hundred years ago . . . fine. Everything might have turned out differently. But it's not enough any more; too much damage has already been done. Tip-toeing through the debris, hoping all the systems we've fucked up will magically restore themselves—and tip-toeing twice as carefully every time the population doubles—just won't work. The whole planetary ecosystem is as much of an artifact, now, as . . . a city's microclimate. Believe me, I wish that wasn't the case, but it is—and now that we've created an artificial world, intentionally or not, we'd better learn to control it. Because if we stand back and leave it all to chance, it's just going to collapse around us in some random fashion that isn't likely to be any better than our worst well-intentioned mistakes."

Aden was horrified. "An *artificial world?* You honestly believe that?"

"Yes."

"Only because you spend so much time in Virtual Reality you don't know the difference anymore."

Maria was indignant. "I hardly ever—" Then she stopped herself, realizing that he meant the Autoverse. She'd long ago given up trying to drum the distinction into his head.

Aden said, "I'm sorry. That was a cheap shot." He made a gesture of retraction, a wave of the hand more impatient than apologetic. "Look, forget all this depressing ecoshit. I've got some good news, for a change. We're going to Seoul."

Maria laughed. "Are we? Why?"

"I've been offered a job. University Music Department."

She looked at him sharply. "Thanks for telling me you'd applied."

He shrugged it off lightly. "I didn't want to get your hopes up. Or mine. I only heard this afternoon; I can still hardly believe it. Composer-in-residence, for a year; a couple of hours a week teaching, the rest of the time I can do what I like: writing, performing, producing, whatever. And they throw in free accommodation. For two."

"Just . . . hold it. *A few hours' teaching?* Then why do you have to go there in person?"

"They want me, physically. It's a prestige thing. Every Mickey Mouse university can plug into the networks and bring in a dozen lecturers from around the world—"

"That's not Mickey Mouse, it's efficient."

"Cheap and efficient. This place doesn't want to be cheap. They want a piece of exotic cultural decoration. Stop laughing.

Australia is flavor of the month in Seoul; it only happens once every twenty years, so we'd better take advantage of it. And they want a composer-in-residence. In residence."

Maria sat back and digested it.

Aden said, "I don't know about you, but I have a lot of trouble imagining us ever being able to afford to spend a year in Korea, any other way."

"And you've said yes?"

"I said maybe. I said probably."

"Accommodation for two. What am I supposed to do while you're being exotic and decorative?"

"Whatever you like. Anything you do here, you could do just as easily there. You're the one who keeps telling me how you're plugged into the world, you're a node in a logical data space, your physical location is entirely irrelevant . . . "

"Yes, and the whole point of that is *not having to move*. I like it where I am."

"That shoebox."

"A campus apartment in Seoul won't be much bigger."

"We'll go out! It's an exciting city—there's a whole *cultural renaissance* going on there, it's not just the music scene. And who knows? You might find some exciting project to work on. Not everything gets broadcast over the nets."

That was true enough. Korea had full membership of ASEAN, as opposed to Australia's probationary status; if she'd been living in Seoul at the right time, if she'd had the right contacts, she might have ended up part of Operation Butterfly. And even if that was wishful thinking—*the right contacts* probably took a decade to make—she could hardly do worse than she'd been doing in Sydney.

Maria fell silent. It was good news, a rare opportunity for both of them, but she still couldn't understand why he was unloading it on her out of the blue. He should have told her everything when he'd applied, however poorly he'd rated his chances.

She glanced at the stage, at the twelve sweating musicians playing their hearts out, then looked away. There was something disconcertingly voyeuristic about watching them without tuning in: not just the sight of them emoting in silence, but also the realization that none of the bands could see each other, despite the fact that she could see them all.

Aden said, "There's no rush to make up your mind. The academic year starts on January ninth. Two months away."

"Won't they need to know, long before then?"

"They'll need to know by Monday if I've accepted the job—but I don't think the accommodation will be a big deal. I mean, if I end up alone in an apartment for two, it'll hardly be the end of the world." He looked at her innocently, as if daring her to give the time and place he'd ever promised to turn down a chance like this, just because she didn't want to come along for the ride.

Maria said, "No, of course not. How stupid of me."

Home, Maria couldn't resist logging on to the QIPS Exchange, just to find out what was going on. Operation Butterfly had vanished from the market. **Omniaveritas,** her knowledge miner, had picked up no news reports of a typhoon in the region; perhaps the predicted one had failed to eventuate—or perhaps it was yet to appear, but the simulations had already given their verdict. It was strange to think that it could all be over before the storm was a reality . . . but then, by the time anything newsworthy happened, the actual meteorological data would—hopefully—bear no relationship at all to what would have happened if the weather control rigs had been in use. The only real-world data needed for the simulations was the common starting point, a snapshot of the planet's weather the moment before intervention would have begun.

The QIPS rate was still about fifty percent higher than normal, as ordinary users jostled to get their delayed work done. Maria hesitated; she felt like she needed cheering up, but running the Autoverse now would be stupid; it would make far more sense to wait until morning.

She logged on to the JSN, slipped on her gloves, activated the workspace. An icon of a man tripping on a banana skin, frozen in mid-fall, represented the snapshot of her interrupted task. She prodded it, and the Petri dishes reappeared in front of her instantly, the *A. lamberti* feeding, dividing and dying, as if the past fifteen hours had never happened.

She could have asked Aden to his face: *Do you want to go to Seoul alone? Do you want a year away from me? If that's it, why don't you just say so?* But he would have denied it, whether or not it was the truth. And she wouldn't have believed him, whether or not he was lying. Why ask the question, if the answer told you nothing?

And it hardly seemed to matter, now: Seoul or Sydney, welcome or not. She could reach *this* place from anywhere—geographically or emotionally. She stared into the workspace, ran a gloved finger around the rim of one of the Petri dishes, and declaimed mockingly, "My name is Maria, and I am an Autoverse addict."

As she watched, the culture in the dish she'd touched faded from muddy blue to pure brown, and then began to turn transparent, as the viewing software ceased classifying dead *A. lamberti* as anything more than chance arrangements of organic molecules.

As the brown mass dissolved, though, Maria noticed something she'd missed.

A tiny speck of electric blue.

She zoomed in on it, refusing to leap to conclusions. The speck was a small cluster of surviving bacteria, growing slowly—but that didn't prove anything. Some strains always lasted longer than others; in the most pedantic sense, there was always a degree of "natural selection" taking place—but the honor of being the last of the dinosaurs wasn't the kind of evolutionary triumph she was looking for.

She summoned up a histogram showing the prevalence of different forms of the *epimerase* enzymes, the tools she'd been pinning her hopes on to turn *mutose* back into *nutrose* . . . but there was nothing out of the ordinary, just the usual scatter of short-lived, unsuccessful mutations. No hint of how this strain was different from all of its extinct cousins.

So why was it doing so well?

Maria "tagged" a portion of the *mutose* molecules in the culture medium, assigning multiple clones of **Maxwell's Demon** to track their movements and render them visible . . . the Autoverse equivalent of the real-world biochemist's technique of radioactive labeling—along with something like nuclear magnetic resonance, since the demons would signal any chemical changes, as well as indicating position. She zoomed in on one surviving *A. lamberti,* rendered neutral gray now, and watched a swarm of phosphorescent green pinpricks pass through the cell wall and jostle around the protoplasm in the sway of Brownian motion.

One by one, a fraction of the tags changed from green to red, marking passage through the first stage of the metabolic pathway: the attachment of an energy-rich cluster of atoms—more or less the Autoverse equivalent of a phosphate group. But there was nothing new in that; for the first three stages of the process, the enzymes which worked with *nutrose* would squander energy on the impostor as if it were the real thing.

Strictly speaking, these red specks weren't *mutose* any more, but Maria had instructed the demons to turn an unmistakable violet, not only in the presence of *nutrose* itself, but also if the molecules under scrutiny were rehabilitated at a later stage—salvaged in mid-digestion. With the *epimerase* enzymes unchanged, she doubted that this was happening . . . but the bacteria *were* thriving, somehow.

The red-tagged molecules wandered the cell at random, part-digested mixed with raw indiscriminately. Neat process diagrams of metabolism—the real-world Embden-Meyerhof pathway, or the Autoverse's Lambert pathway—always gave the impression of some orderly molecular conveyor belt, but the truth was, life in either system was powered by nothing at the deepest level but a sequence of chance collisions.

A few red tags turned orange. Stage two: an enzyme tightening the molecule's hexagonal ring into a pentagon, transforming the spare vertex into a protruding cluster, more exposed and reactive than before.

Still nothing new. And still no hint of violet.

Nothing further seemed to happen for so long that Maria glanced at her watch and said "Globe," to see if some major population center had just come on-line for the day—but the authentic Earth-from-space view showed dawn well into the Pacific. California would have been busy since before she'd arrived home.

A few orange tags turned yellow. Stage three of the Lambert pathway, like stage one, consisted of bonding an energy-rich group of atoms to the sugar. With *nutrose,* there was a payoff for this, eventually, with twice as many of the molecules which supplied the energy ending up "recharged" as had been "drained." Stage four, though—the cleaving of the ring into two smaller fragments—was the point where *mutose* gummed up the works irretrievably . . .

Except that one yellow speck had just split into two, before her eyes . . . and both new tags were colored violet.

Maria, startled, lost track of the evidence. Then she caught sight of the same thing happening again. And then a third time.

It took her a minute to think it through, and understand what this meant. The bacterium *wasn't* reversing the change she'd made to the sugar, converting *mutose* back into *nutrose*—or doing the same to some part-digested metabolite. Instead, it must have modified the enzyme which broke the ring, coming up with a version which worked directly on the metabolite of *mutose.*

Maria froze the action, zoomed in, and watched a molecular-scale replay. The enzyme in question was constructed of thousands of atoms; it was impossible to spot the difference at a glance—but there was no doubt about what it was doing. The two-atom *blue-red* spike she'd repositioned on the sugar was never shifted back into its "proper" place; instead, the enzyme now accommodated the altered geometry perfectly.

She summoned up old and new versions of the enzyme, highlighted the regions where the tertiary structure was different, and probed them with her fingertips—confirming, palpably, that the cavity in the giant molecule where the reaction took place had changed shape.

And once the ring was cleaved? The fragments were the same, whether the original sugar had been *nutrose* or *mutose.* The rest of the Lambert pathway went on as if nothing had changed.

Maria was elated, and a little dazed. People had been trying to achieve a spontaneous adaptation like this for *sixteen years.* She didn't even know why she'd finally succeeded; for five years she'd been tinkering with the bacterium's error correction mechanisms, trying to force *A. lamberti* to mutate, not more rapidly, but *more randomly.* Every time, she'd ended up with a strain which—like Lambert's original, like those of other workers—suffered the same handful of predictable, useless mutations again and again . . . almost as if something deep in the clockwork of the Autoverse itself ruled out the exuberant diversity which came so effortlessly to real-world biology. Calvin and others had suggested that, because Autoverse physics omitted the deep indeterminacy of real-world quantum mechanics—because it lacked this vital inflow of "true unpredictability"—the same richness of phenomena could never be expected, at any level.

But that had always been absurd—*and now she'd proved it was absurd.*

For a moment she thought of phoning Aden, or Francesca—but Aden wouldn't understand enough to do more than nod politely, and her mother didn't deserve to be woken at this hour.

She got up and paced the tiny bedroom for a while, too excited to remain still. She'd upload a letter to *Autoverse Review* (total subscription, seventy-three), with the genome of the strain she'd started out with appended as a footnote, so everyone else could try the experiment . . .

She sat down and began composing the letter—popping up a word processor in the foreground of the workspace—then decided that was premature; there was still a lot more to be done to form the basis of even a brief report.

She cloned a small colony of the *mutose*-eating strain, and watched it grow steadily in a culture of pure *mutose.* No surprise, but it was still worth doing.

Then she did the same, with pure *nutrose,* and the colony, of course, died out at once. The original ring-cleaving enzyme had been lost; the original roles of *nutrose* and *mutose* as food and poison had been swapped.

Maria pondered this. *A. lamberti* had adapted—but not in the way she'd expected. Why hadn't it found a means of consuming both sugars, instead of exchanging one kind of exclusive reliance for another? It would have been a far better strategy. *It was what a real-world bacterium would have done.*

She brooded over the question for a while—then started laughing. *Sixteen years,* people had been hunting for a single, convincing example of natural selection in the Autoverse—and here she was worrying that it wasn't the best of all possible adaptations. Evolution was a random walk across a minefield, not a preordained trajectory, onward and upward toward "perfection." *A. lamberti* had stumbled on a successful way to turn poison into food. It was tough luck if the corollary was: *vice versa.*

Maria ran a dozen more experiments. She lost all track of time; when dawn came, the software brightened the images in front of her, keeping the daylight from washing them out. It was only when her concentration faltered, and she looked around the room, that she realized how late it was.

She started again on the letter. After three drafts of the first paragraph—all eliciting the same response from **Camel's Eye:** *You'll hate this when you reread it later. Trust me.*—she finally admitted to herself that she was wasted. She shut down everything and crawled into bed.

She lay there awhile in a stupor, burying her face in the pillow, waiting for the ghost images of Petri dishes and enzymes to fade. Five years ago, she could have worked all night, and suffered nothing worse than a fit of yawning in the middle of the afternoon. Now, she felt like she'd been hit by a train—and she knew she'd be a wreck for days. *Thirty-one is old, old, old.*

Her head throbbed, her whole body ached. She didn't care. All the time and money she'd squandered on the Autoverse was worth it, now. Every moment she'd spent there had been vindicated.

Yeah? She rolled onto her back and opened her eyes. *What, exactly, had changed?* It was still nothing but a self-indulgent hobby, an elaborate computer game. She'd be famous with seventy-two other anal-retentive Autoverse freaks. *How many bills would that pay? How many typhoons would it neutralize?*

She wrapped her head in the pillow, feeling crippled, stupid, hopeless—and defiantly happy—until her limbs went numb, her mouth went dry, and the room seemed to rock her to sleep.

5

(Remit not paucity)

Peer anchored the soles of both feet and the palm of one hand firmly against the glass, and rested for a while. He tipped his head back to take in, one more time, the silver wall of the skyscraper stretching to infinity above him. Cotton-wool clouds drifted by, higher than any part of the building—even though the building went on forever.

He freed his right foot, reanchored it higher up the wall, then turned and looked down at the neat grid of the city below, surrounded by suburbs as orderly as ploughed fields. The foreshortened countryside beyond formed a green-brown rim to the hemispherical bowl of the Earth; a blue-hazed horizon bisected the view precisely. The features of the landscape, like the clouds, were "infinitely large," and "infinitely distant"; a finite city, however grand, would have shrunk to invisibility, like the base of the skyscraper. The distance was more than a trick of perspective, though; Peer knew he could keep on approaching the ground for as long as he liked, without ever reaching it. Hours, day, centuries.

He couldn't remember beginning the descent, although he understood clearly—cloud-knowledge, cloud-memories—the sense in which there was a beginning, and the sense in which there was none. His memories of the skyscraper, like his view of it, seemed to converge toward a vanishing point; looking back from the present moment, all he could recall was the act of descending, punctuated by rest. And although his mind had wandered, he'd never lost consciousness; his past seemed to stretch back seamlessly, forever—yet he could hold it all in his finite gaze, thanks to some law of mental perspective, some calculus of memory limiting the sum of ever diminishing contributions to his state of mind from ever more distant moments in the past. But he had his cloud-memories, too; memories from before the descent. He couldn't join them to the present, but they existed nonetheless, a backdrop informing everything else. He knew exactly who he'd been, and what he'd done, in that time before the time he now inhabited.

Peer had been exhausted when he'd stopped, but after a minute's rest he felt, literally, as energetic and enthusiastic as ever. Back in cloud-time, preparing himself, he'd edited out any need or desire for food, drink, sleep, sex, companionship, or even a change of scenery, and he'd preprogrammed his exoself—the sophisticated, but nonconscious, supervisory software which could reach into the model of his brain and body and fine-tune any part of it as required—to ensure that these conditions remained true. He resumed the descent gladly, a happy Sisyphus. Making his way down the smooth mirrored face of the skyscraper was, still, the purest joy he could imagine: the warmth of the sun reflecting back on him, the sharp cool gusts of wind, the faint creak of steel and concrete. Adrenaline and tranquility. The cycle of exertion and perfect recovery. Perpetual motion. Touching infinity.

The building, the Earth, the sky, and his body vanished. Stripped down to vision and hearing, Peer found himself observing his Bunker: a cluster of display screens floating in a black void. Kate was on one screen; two-dimensional, black-and-white, nothing but her lips moving.

She said, "You set your threshold pretty damn high. You'd be hearing about this a decade later if I hadn't called you in."

Peer grunted—disconcerted for a moment by the lack of tactile feedback from the conventional organs of speech—and glanced, by way of eye-movement-intention, at the screen beside her, a graph of the recent history of Bunker time versus real time.

Observing the Bunker—"being in it" would have been an overstatement—was the most computing-efficient state a Copy could adopt, short of losing consciousness. Peer's body was no longer being simulated at all; the essential parts of his model-of-a-brain had been mapped into an abstract neural network, a collection of idealized digital gates with no pretensions to physiological verisimilitude. He didn't enter this state very often, but Bunker time was still a useful standard as a basis for comparisons. At best—on the rare occasions when demand slackened, and he shared a processor cluster with only two or three other users—his Bunker-time slowdown factor dropped to about thirty. At worst? Up until a few minutes ago, the worst had been happening: a section of the graph was perfectly flat. For more than ten hours of real time, he hadn't been computed at all.

Kate said, "Operation Butterfly. Weather control simulations. The fuckers bought up everything."

She sounded shaken and angry. Peer said calmly, "No great loss. Solipsist Nation means making your own world, on your own terms. Whatever the risks. Real time doesn't matter. Let them give us one computation per year. What would it change? *Nothing.*" He glanced at another display, and realized that he'd only been in the skyscraper model for seven subjective minutes. The false memories had meshed perfectly; he would never have believed it had been so short a time. Pre-computing the memories had taken time, of course—but far less than it would have taken to accumulate the same effect by conventional experience.

Kate said, "You're wrong. You don't—"

"Let them run *one moment* of model time for *one Copy* on every processor cluster, the day it's commissioned—and then dedicate it entirely to other users. Each Copy would thread its way from machine to machine, with a slowdown of a few billion . . . and it wouldn't matter. The manufacturers could run us all for free—turn it into a kind of ritual, a blessing of the hardware by the spirits of the dead. Then we could abolish all the trust funds, and stop worrying about money altogether. The cheaper we are, the less vulnerable we are."

"That's only half the truth. The more we're marginalized, the more we're at risk."

Peer tried to sigh; the sound that emerged was plausible enough, but the lack of sensation was annoying.

"Is there any reason to stay in emergency mode? Is there some snap decision I'm going to have to make? Are there missiles heading for—" He checked a display. "—Dallas?" *Dallas?* The US dollar must have fallen sharply against the yen.

Kate said nothing, so Peer glanced at icons for a body and a room, and willed them to be active. His disembodied consciousness, and the floating screens of the Bunker, fleshed out into a young man, barefoot in blue jeans and a T-shirt, sitting in a windowless control room—what might have been the operations center for a medium-sized office building.

The body's physiological state continued directly from its last moments on the wall of the skyscraper—and it felt good: loose-limbed, invigorated. Peer recorded a snapshot, so he could get the feeling back again at will. He looked at Kate imploringly; she relented and joined him, vanishing from the screen and appearing on a chair beside him.

She said, "I *am* Solipsist Nation. What happens outside doesn't matter to me . . . but we still need certain guarantees, certain minimum standards."

Peer laughed. "So what are you going to do? Become a lobbyist now? Spend all your time petitioning Brussels and Geneva? "Human rights" are for people who want to play at being human. I know who I am. I am *not* human." He plunged his fist into his chest, effortlessly penetrating shirt, skin and ribs, and tore his heart out. He felt the parting of his flesh, and the aftermath—but although aspects of the pain were "realistic," preprogrammed barriers kept it isolated within his brain, a perception without any emotional, or even metabolic, consequences. And his heart kept beating in his hand as if nothing had happened; the blood passed straight between the ragged ends of each broken artery, ignoring the "intervening distance."

Kate said, "Blink and ten hours are gone. That's no disaster—but where is it heading? State-of-emergency decrees, nationalizing all the computing power in Tokyo for weather control?"

"Tokyo?"

"Some models show Greenhouse Typhoons reaching the Japanese islands in the next thirty years."

"Fuck Tokyo. We're in Dallas."

"Not any more." She pointed to the status display; exchange-rate fluctuations, and the hunt for the cheapest QIPS, had flung them back across the Pacific. "Not that it matters. There are plans for the Gulf of Mexico, too."

Peer put his heart on the floor and shrugged, then groped around in his chest cavity in search of other organs. He finally settled on a handful of lung. Torn free, the pink tissue continued to expand and contract in time with his breathing; functionally, it was still inside his rib cage. "Start looking for *security,* and you end up controlled by the demands of the old world. Are you Solipsist Nation, or not?"

Kate eyed his bloodless wound, and said quietly, "Solipsist Nation doesn't mean dying of stupidity. You take your body apart, and you think it proves you're invulnerable? You plant a few forced-perspective memories, and you think you've already lived forever? I don't want some cheap illusion of immortality. I want the real thing."

Peer frowned, and started paying attention to her latest choice of body. It was still recognizably "Kate"—albeit the most severe variation on the theme he'd seen. Short-haired, sharp-boned, with piercing gray eyes; leaner than ever, plainly dressed in loose-fitting white. She looked ascetic, functional, determined.

She said—mock-casually, as if changing the subject—"Interesting news: there's a man—a visitor—approaching the richest Copies, selling prime real estate for second versions at a ludicrous rate."

"How much?"

"Two million ecus."

"What—per month?"

"No. Forever."

Peer snorted. "It's a con."

"And outside, he's been contracting programmers, designers, architects. Commissioning—and paying for—work that will need at least a few dozen processor clusters to run on."

"Good move. That might actually persuade a few of the doddering old farts that he can deliver what he's promising. Not many, though. Who's going to pay without getting the hardware on-line and running performance tests? How's he going to fake that? He can show them simulations of glossy machines, but if the things aren't real, they won't crunch. End of scam."

"Sanderson has paid. Repetto has paid. The last word I had was he'd talked to Riemann."

"I don't believe any of this. They all have their own hardware—why would they bother?"

"They all have a high profile. People *know* that they have their own hardware. If things get ugly, it can be confiscated. Whereas this man, Paul Durham, is nobody. He's a broker for someone else, obviously—but whoever it is, they're acting like they have access to more computing power than Fujitsu, at about a thousandth of the cost. And none of it is on the open market. Nobody officially knows it exists."

"Or unofficially. Because it doesn't. *Two million ecus!*"

"Sanderson has paid. Repetto has paid."

"According to your sources."

"Durham's getting money from somewhere. I spoke to Malcolm Carter myself. Durham's commissioned a city from him, thousands of square kilometers—and none of it passive. Architectural detail everywhere down to visual acuity, or better. Pseudo-autonomous crowds—hundreds of thousands of people. Zoos and wildlife parks with the latest behavioral algorithms. A waterfall the size of nothing on Earth."

Peer pulled out a coil of intestine and playfully wrapped it around his neck. "You could have a city like that, all to yourself, if you really wanted it—if you were willing to live with the slowdown. Why are you so interested in this con man Durham? Even if he's genuine, you can't afford his price. Face it: you're stuck here in the slums with me—*and it doesn't matter.*" Peer indulged in a brief flashback to the last time they'd made love. He merged it with the current scene, so he saw both Kates, and the new lean gray-eyed one seemed to look on as he lay on the floor gasping beneath his tangible memory of her earlier body—although in truth she saw him still sitting in the chair, smiling faintly.

All memory is theft, Daniel Lebesgue had written. Peer felt a sudden pang of post-coital guilt. But what was he guilty of? Perfect recollection, nothing more.

Kate said, "I can't afford Durham's price—but I can afford Carter's."

Peer was caught off guard for a second, but then he grinned at her admiringly. "You're serious, aren't you?"

She nodded soberly. "Yes. I've been thinking about it for some time, but after being flatlined for ten hours—"

"Are you sure *Carter* is serious? How do you know he really has something to sell?"

She hesitated. "I hired him myself, when I was outside. I used to spend a lot of time in VR, as a visitor, and he made some of my favorite places: the winter beach; that cottage I took you to. And others. He was one of the people I talked it over with, before I made up my mind to come in for good."

Peer regarded her uneasily—she rarely talked about the past, which suited him fine—and mercifully, she returned to the point. "With slowdown, filters, masks, it's hard to judge anyone . . . but I don't think he's changed that much. I still trust him."

Peer nodded slowly, absentmindedly sliding his intestine back and forth across his shoulders. "But how much does Durham trust him? How thoroughly will he check the city for stowaways?"

"Carter's sure he can hide me. He has software that can break up my model and bury it deep in the city's algorithms— as a few billion trivial redundancies and inefficiencies."

"*Inefficiencies* can get optimized out. If Durham—"

Kate cut him off impatiently. "Carter's not stupid. He knows how optimizers work—and he knows how to keep them from touching his stuff."

"Okay. But . . . once you're in there, what sort of communications will you have?"

"Not much. Only limited powers to eavesdrop on what the legitimate inhabitants choose to access—and if the whole point of this place is secrecy, that may not be much. I get the impression from Carter that they're planning to drag in everything they need, then pull up the drawbridge."

Peer let that sink in, but chose not to ask the obvious question, or to show that he'd even thought of it. "So what do you get to take with you?"

"All the software and all the environments I've been using here—which doesn't amount to all that much data, compared to me. And once I'm in, I'll have read-only access to all of the city's public facilities: all the information, all the entertainment, all the shared environments. I'll be able to walk down the main street—invisible and intangible—staring at the trillionaires. But my presence won't *affect* anything—except to slow it all down by a negligible amount—so even the most rigorous verification should pass the total package as contamination-free."

"What rate will you run at?"

Kate snorted. "I should refuse to answer that. You're the champion of *one computation per year.*"

"I'm just curious."

"It depends how many QIPS are allocated to the city." She hesitated. "Carter has no real evidence for this—but he thinks there's a good chance that Durham's employers have got their hands on some kind of new high-powered hardware—"

Peer groaned. "Please, this whole deal is already suspect enough—don't start invoking the mythical *breakthrough.* What makes people think that anyone could keep that a secret? Or that anyone would even want to?"

"They might not want to, in the long run. But the best way to exploit the technology might be to sell the first of the new generation of processors to the richest Copies—before they hit the open market and the QIPS rate crashes."

Peer laughed. "Then why stow away at all? If that happens, there'll be nothing to fear from weather control."

"Because there might not have been any breakthrough. The only thing that's certain is that some of the wealthiest—and best-informed—Copies have decided that it's worth going into this . . . sanctuary. And I've got the chance to go with them."

Peer was silent for a while. Finally, he asked, "So are you moving—or cloning yourself?"

"Cloning."

He could have concealed his relief, easily—but he didn't. He said, "I'm glad. I would have missed you."

"And I'd have missed you. I want you to come with me."

"You want—?"

Kate leaned toward him. "Carter has said he'll include you—and your baggage—for another fifty percent. *Clone yourself and come with me.* I don't want to lose you—either of me."

Peer felt a rush of excitement—and fear. He took a snapshot of the emotion, then said, "I don't know. I've never—"

"A second version, running on the most secure hardware on the planet. That's *not* surrendering to outside—it's just finally gaining some true independence."

"*Independence?* What if these Copies get bored with Carter's city and decide to trash it—trade it in for something new?"

Kate was unfazed. "That's not impossible. But there are no guarantees on the public networks, either. This way, at least you have a greater chance that one version will survive."

Peer tried to imagine it. "Stowaways. No communications. Just us, and whatever software we bring."

"You're Solipsist Nation, aren't you?"

"You know I am. But . . . I've never run a second version before. I don't know how I'll feel about that, after the split."

How *who* will feel about it?

Kate bent over and picked up his heart. "Having a second version won't bother you." She fixed her new gray eyes on him. "We're running at a slowdown of sixty-seven. Carter will be delivering his city to Durham, six real-time months from now. But who knows when Operation Butterfly will flatline us again? So you don't have long to decide."

Peer continued to show Kate his body sitting in the chair, thinking it over, while in truth he rose to his feet and walked across the room, escaping her formidable gaze.

Who am I? Is this what I want?

He couldn't concentrate. He manually invoked a menu on one of the control screens, an array of a dozen identical images: a nineteenth-century anatomical drawing of the brain, with the surface divided into regions labeled with various emotions and skills. Each icon represented a package of mental parameters: snapshots of previous states of mind, or purely synthetic combinations.

Peer hit the icon named CLARITY.

In twelve short real-time years as a Copy, he'd tried to explore every possibility, map out every consequence of what he'd become. He'd transformed his surroundings, his body, his personality, his perceptions—but he'd always owned the experience himself. The tricks he'd played on his memory had added, never erased—and whatever changes he'd been through, there was always only one person, in the end, taking responsibility, picking up the pieces. One witness, unifying it all.

The truth was, the thought of finally surrendering that unity made him dizzy with fear. It was the last vestige of his delusion of humanity. The last big lie.

And as Daniel Lebesgue, founder of Solipsist Nation, had written: "My goal is to take everything which might be revered as quintessentially human . . . and grind it into dust."

He returned to his seated body, and said, "I'll do it."

Kate smiled, raised his beating heart to her lips, and gave it a long, lingering kiss.

6

(Rip, tie, cut toy man)

JUNE 2045

Paul woke without any confusion. He dressed and ate, trying to feel optimistic. He'd demonstrated his willingness to cooperate; now it was time to ask for something in return. He walked into the study, switched on the terminal, and called his own number. The *djinn* answered at once.

Paul said, "I'd like to talk to Elizabeth."

Squeak. "That's not possible."

"Not possible? Why don't you just ask her?"

Squeak. "I can't do that. She doesn't even know you exist."

Paul stared at him coldly. "Don't lie to me, it's a waste of time. As soon as I had a Copy who survived, I was going to explain everything—"

Squeak. The *djinn* said drily, "Or so we thought."

Paul's certainty wavered. "You're telling me that your great ambition is finally being fulfilled—and you haven't even mentioned it to the one woman . . . ?"

Squeak. Durham's face turned to stone. "I really don't wish to discuss it. Can we get on with the experiment, please?"

Paul opened his mouth to protest—and then found he had nothing to say. All his anger and jealousy suddenly dissipated into . . . embarrassment. It was as if he'd just come to his senses from a daydream, an elaborate fantasy of a relationship with someone else's lover. *Paul and Elizabeth. Elizabeth and Paul.* What happened between them was none of his business. Whatever his memories suggested, that life wasn't his to live anymore.

He said, "Sure, let's get on with the experiment. Time is just rushing by. You must have turned forty-five . . . what, a day ago? Many happy returns."

Squeak. "Thanks—but you're wrong. I took some shortcuts while you were asleep: I shut down part of the model—and cheated on most of the rest. It's only the fourth of June; you got six hours' sleep in ten hours' real time. Not a bad job, I thought."

Paul was outraged. "You had no right to do that!"

Squeak. Durham sighed. "Be practical. Ask yourself what you'd have done in my place."

"It's not a *joke!*"

Squeak. "So you slept without a whole body. I cleaned a few toxins out of your blood at a non-physiological rate." The *djinn* seemed genuinely puzzled. "Compared to the experiments, that's nothing. Why should it bother you? You've woken up in exactly the same condition as you'd be in if you'd slept in the normal way."

Paul caught himself. He didn't want to explain how vulnerable it made him feel to have someone reach through the cracks in the universe and relieve him of unnecessary organs while he slept. And the less the bastard knew about his Copy's insecurities, the better—he'd only exploit them.

He said, "It *bothers me* because the experiments are worthless if you're going to intervene at random. Precise, controlled changes—that's the whole point. You have to promise me you won't do it again."

Squeak. "You're the one who was complaining about waste. Someone has to think about conserving our dwindling resources."

"Do you want me to keep on cooperating? Or do you want to start everything again from scratch?"

Squeak. The *djinn* said mildly, "All right, you don't have to threaten me. You have my word: no more *ad hoc* intervention."

"Thank you."

Conserving our dwindling resources? Paul had been trying hard not to think about money. What would the *djinn* do when he could no longer afford to keep him running—if Paul chose not to bale out once the experiments were over? Store a snapshot of the model, of course, until he could raise the cash flow to start it up again. In the long term, set up a trust fund; it would only have to earn enough to run him part-time, at first: keep him in touch with the world, stave off excessive culture shock . . . until the technology became cheap enough to let him live continuously.

Of course, all these reassuring plans had been made by a man with two futures. *Would he really want to keep an old Copy running, when he could save his money for a deathbed scan, and "his own" immortality?*

Squeak. "Can we get to work, now?"

"That's what I'm here for."

This time, the model would be described at the standard time resolution of one millisecond, throughout—but the order in which the states were computed would be varied.

Squeak. "Experiment two, trial number one. Reverse order."

Paul counted. "One. Two. Three." *Reverse order.* After an initial leap into the future, he was now traveling backward through real time. It would have been a nice touch if he'd been able to view an external event on the terminal—some entropic cliché like a vase being smashed—knowing that it was *himself,* and not the scene, that was being "rewound" . . . but he knew that it couldn't be done (quite apart from the fact that it would have ruined the experiment, betraying the difference between subject and control). In real time, the first thing to be computed would be his model-time-final brain state, complete with memories of everything that "had happened" in the "preceding" ten seconds. Those memories couldn't include having seen a real broken vase assemble itself from fragments, if the vase hadn't even been smashed yet. The trick could have been done with a simulation, or a video recording of the real thing—but that wouldn't have been the same.

"Eight. Nine. Ten." Another imperceptible leap into the future, and the *djinn* reappeared.

Squeak. "Trial number two. Odd numbered states, then even."

In external terms: he would count to ten, skipping every second model-time moment . . . then forget having done so, and count again, going back and filling in the gaps.

And from his own point of view? As he counted, once only, the external world—even if he couldn't see it—was flickering back and forth between two separate regions of time, which had been chopped up into seventeen-millisecond portions, and interleaved.

So . . . who was right? Paul thought it over, half seriously. Maybe both descriptions were equally valid; after all, relativity had abolished absolute time. Everybody was entitled to their own frame of reference; crossing deep space at close to lightspeed, or skimming the event horizon of a black hole. Why shouldn't a Copy's experience of time be as sacrosanct as that of any astronaut?

The analogy was flawed, though. Relativistic transformations were smooth—possibly extreme, but always continuous. One observer's space-time could be stretched and deformed in the eyes of another—but it couldn't be sliced like a loaf of bread and then shuffled like a deck of cards.

"Every tenth state, in ten sets."

Paul counted—and for argument's sake, tried to defend his own perspective, tried to imagine the outside world actually cycling through fragments of time drawn from ten distinct periods. The trouble was . . . this allegedly shuddering universe contained the computer which ran the whole model, the infrastructure upon which everything else depended. If its orderly chronology had been torn to shreds, what was keeping *him* together, enabling him to ponder the question?

"Every twentieth state, in twenty sets."

Nineteen episodes of amnesia, nineteen new beginnings. (Unless, of course, he was the control.)

"Every hundredth state, in one hundred sets."

He'd lost any real feeling for what was happening. He just counted.

"Pseudo-random ordering of states."

"One. Two. Three."

Now he was . . . dust. To an outside observer, these ten seconds had been ground up into ten thousand uncorrelated moments and scattered throughout real time—and in model time, the outside world had suffered an equivalent fate. Yet the pattern of his awareness remained perfectly intact: somehow he found himself, "assembled himself" from these scrambled fragments. He'd been taken apart like a jigsaw puzzle—but his dissection and shuffling were transparent to him. Somehow—on their own terms—the pieces remained connected.

"Eight. Nine. Ten."

Squeak. "You're sweating."

"Both of me?"

Squeak. The *djinn* laughed. "What do you think?"

Paul said, "Do me one small favor. The experiment is over. Shut down one of me—control or subject, I don't care."

Squeak. "Done."

"Now there's no need to conceal anything, is there? So run the pseudo-random effect on me again—and stay on-line. This time, *you* count to ten."

Squeak. Durham shook his head. "Can't do it, Paul. Think about it: you can't be computed non-sequentially when past perceptions aren't known."

Of course; the broken vase problem all over again.

Paul said, "Record yourself, then, and use that."

The *djinn* seemed to find the request amusing, but he agreed; he even slowed down the recording so it lasted ten model-time seconds. Paul watched the blurred lips and jaws intently, listened carefully to the drone of white noise.

Squeak. "Happy now?"

"You did scramble *me,* and not the recording?"

Squeak. "Of course. Your wish is my command."

"Yeah? Then do it again."

Durham grimaced, but obliged.

Paul said, "Now, scramble *the recording.*"

It looked just the same. Of course.

"Again."

Squeak. "What's the point of all this?"

"Just do it."

Paul watched, the hairs on the back of his neck rising, convinced that he was on the verge of . . . *what?* Finally confronting the "obvious" fact that the wildest permutations in the relationship between model time and real time would be undetectable to an isolated Copy? He'd accepted the near certainty of that, tacitly, for almost twenty years . . . but the firsthand experience of having his mind literally scrambled—*to absolutely no effect*—was still provocative in a way that the abstract understanding had never been.

He said, "When do we move on to the next stage?"

Squeak. "Why so keen all of a sudden?"

"Nothing's changed. I just want to get it over and done with."

Squeak. "Lining up all the other machines is taking some delicate negotiations. The network allocation software isn't designed to accommodate whims about geography. It's a bit like going to a bank and asking to deposit some money . . . at a certain location in a particular computer's memory. Basically, people think I'm crazy."

Paul felt a momentary pang of empathy, recalling his own anticipation of these difficulties. Empathy verging on identification. He smothered it. The two of them were irreversibly different people now, with different problems and different goals—and the stupidest thing he could do would be to forget that.

Squeak. "I could suspend you while I finalize the arrangements, save you the boredom—if that's what you want."

"You're too kind. But I'd rather stay conscious. I've got a lot to think about."

7

(Remit not paucity)

"Twelve to eighteen months? Are they sure?"

Francesca Deluca said drily, "What can I say? They modeled it."

Maria did her best to sound calm. "That's plenty of time. We'll get you scanned. We'll get the money together. I can sell the house, and borrow some from Aden—"

Francesca smiled but shook her head. "No, darling." Her hair had grayed a little since Maria had last really looked at her, last consciously gauged her appearance, but she showed no obvious signs of ill health. "What's the point? Even if I wanted that—and I don't—what's the use of a scan that will never be run?"

"It *will* be run. Computing power will get cheaper. Everybody's counting on that. Thousands of people have scan files waiting—"

"How many frozen corpses have ever been revived?"

"That's not the same thing at all."

"How many?"

"Physically, none. But some have been scanned—"

"And proved non-viable. All the interesting ones—the celebrities, the dictators—are brain-damaged, and nobody cares about the rest."

"A scan file is nothing like a frozen corpse. You'd never *become* non-viable."

"No, but I'd never become worth bringing back to life, either."

Maria stared at her angrily. "*I'll* bring you back to life. Or don't you believe I'll ever have the money?"

Francesca said, "Maybe you will. But I'm not going to be scanned, so forget about it."

Maria hunched forward on the couch, not knowing how to sit, not knowing where to put her hands. Sunlight streamed into the room, obscenely bright, revealing every speck of lint on the carpet; she had to make an effort not to get up and close the blinds. *Why hadn't Francesca told her on the phone? All of this would have been a thousand times easier by phone.*

She said, "All right, you're not going to be scanned. Someone in the world must be making nanomachines for liver cancer. Even just experimental ones."

"Not for this cell type. It's not one of the common onco-genes, and nobody's sure of the cell surface markers."

"So? They can find them, can't they? They can look at the cells, identify the markers, and modify an existing nanoma-chine. All the information they need is there in your body."

Maria pictured the mutant proteins which enabled metastasis poking through the cell walls, highlighted in ominous yellow.

Francesca said, "With enough time and money and exper-tise, I'm sure that would be possible . . . but as it happens, nobody plans to do it in the next eighteen months."

Maria started shuddering. It came in waves. She didn't make a sound; she just sat and waited for it to pass.

Finally, she said, "There must be drugs."

Francesca nodded. "I'm on medication to slow the growth of the primary tumor, and limit further metastasis. There's no point in a transplant; I already have too many secondary tumors—actual liver failure is the least of my worries. There are general cytotoxic drugs I could take, and there's always radiation therapy—but I don't think the benefits are worth the side effects."

"Would you like me to stay with you?"

"No."

"It'd be no trouble. You know I can work from anywhere."

"There's no need for it. I'm not going to be an invalid."

Maria closed her eyes. She couldn't imagine feeling this way for another hour, let alone another year. When her father had died of a heart attack, three years before, she'd promised herself that she'd raise the money to have Francesca scanned by her sixtieth birthday. She was nowhere near on target. *I screwed up. I wasted time. And now it's almost too late.*

Thinking aloud, she said, "Maybe I'll get some work in Seoul."

"I thought you'd decided not to go."

Maria looked up at her, uncomprehending. *"Why don't you want to be scanned?* What are you afraid of? I'd protect you, I'd do whatever you asked. If you didn't want to be run until slowdown is abolished, I'd wait. If you wanted to wake up in a physical body—*an organic body*—I'd wait."

Francesca smiled. "I know you would, darling. That's not the point."

"Then what *is* the point?"

"I don't want to argue about it."

Maria was desperate. "I won't argue. But can't you tell me? Please?"

Francesca relented. "Listen, I was thirty-three when the first Copy was made. You were five years old, you grew up with the idea—but to me, it's still . . . too strange. It's something rich eccentrics do—the way they used to freeze their corpses. To me, spending hundreds of thousands of dollars for the chance to be imitated by a computer after my death is just . . . farcical. I'm *not* an eccentric millionaire, I don't want to spend my money—or yours—building some kind of . . . talking monument to my ego. I still have a sense of proportion." She looked at Maria imploringly. "Doesn't that count for anything any more?"

"You wouldn't be *imitated.* You'd be you."

"Yes and no."

"What's that supposed to mean? You always told me you believed—"

"I *do* believe that Copies are intelligent. I just wouldn't say that they are—or they aren't—"the same person as" the person they were based on. There's no right or wrong answer to that; it's a question of semantics, not a question of truth.

"The thing is, I have my own sense—right now—of *who I*

am . . . what my boundaries are . . . and it doesn't include a Copy of me, run at some time in the indefinite future. Can you understand that? Being scanned wouldn't make *me* feel any better about dying. Whatever a Copy of me might think, if one was ever run."

Maria said, angrily, "That's just being perverse. That's as stupid as . . . saying when you're twenty years old, "I can't picture myself at fifty, a woman that old wouldn't really be *me.*" And then killing yourself because there's nothing to lose but that older woman, and *she's* not inside your 'boundaries.'"

"I thought you said you weren't going to argue."

Maria looked away. "You never used to talk like this. You're the one who always told me that Copies had to be treated exactly like human beings. If you hadn't been brainwashed by that 'religion'—"

"The Church of the God Who Makes No Difference has no position on Copies, one way or the other."

"It has no *position* on anything."

"That's right. So it can hardly be their fault that I don't want to be scanned, can it?"

Maria felt physically sick. She'd held off saying anything on the subject for almost a year; she'd been astonished and appalled, but she'd struggled to respect her mother's choice—and now she could see that *that* had been insane, irresponsible beyond belief. *You don't stand by and let someone you love—someone who gave you your own understanding of the world—have their brain turned to pulp.*

She said, "It's their fault, because they've undermined your judgment. They've fed you so much bullshit that you can't think straight about anything, anymore."

Francesca just looked at her reprovingly. Maria felt a pang of guilt—*How can you make things harder for her, now? How can you start attacking her, when she's just told you that she's dying?*—but she wasn't going to fold now, take the easy way out, be "supportive."

She said, "'God makes no difference . . . because God is the reason why everything is exactly what it is?' That's supposed to make us all feel at peace with the cosmos, is it?"

Francesca shook her head. "At peace? No. It's just a matter of clearing away, once and for all, old ideas like divine intervention—and the need for some kind of proof, or even faith, in order to believe."

Maria said, "What *do* you need, then? *I* don't believe, so what am I missing?"

"Belief?"

"And a love of tautology."

"Don't knock tautology. Better to base a religion on tautology than fantasy."

"But it's worse than tautology. It's . . . redefining words arbitrarily, it's like something out of Lewis Carroll. Or George Orwell. "God is the reason for everything . . . whatever that reason is." So what any sane person would simply call *the laws of physics,* you've decided to rename G-O-D . . . solely because the word carries all kinds of historical resonances—all kinds of misleading connotations. You claim to have nothing to do with the old religions—so why keep using their terminology?"

Francesca said, "We don't deny the history of the word. We make a break from the past in a lot of ways—but we also acknowledge our origins. *God* is a concept people have been using for millennia. The fact that we've refined the idea beyond primitive superstitions and wish-fulfilment doesn't mean we're not part of the same tradition."

"But you haven't *refined* the idea, you've made it meaningless! And rightly so—but you don't seem to realize it. You've stripped away all the obvious stupidities—all the anthropomorphism, the miracles, the answered prayers—but you don't seem to have noticed that once you've done that, there's absolutely nothing left that needs to be called *religion.* Physics is *not* theology. Ethics is *not* theology. Why pretend that they are?"

Francesca said, "But don't you see? We talk about God for the simple reason that *we still want to.* There's a deeply ingrained human compulsion to keep using that word, that concept—to keep honing it, rather than discarding it—despite the fact that it no longer means what it did five thousand years ago."

"And you know perfectly well where that compulsion comes from! It has nothing to do with any real divine being; it's just a product of culture and neurobiology—a few accidents of evolution and history."

"Of course it is. What human trait isn't?"

"So why give in to it?"

Francesca laughed. "Why give in to anything? The religious impulse isn't some kind of . . . alien mind virus. It's not—in its purest form, stripped of all content—the product of brainwashing. It's a part of who I am."

Maria put her face in her hands. "Is it? When you talk like this, it doesn't sound like you."

Francesca said, "Don't you ever want to give thanks to God when things are going well for you? Don't you ever want to ask God for strength when you need it?"

"No."

"Well, I do. Even though I know God makes no difference. And if God is the reason for everything, then God includes the urge to use the word God. So whenever I gain some strength, or comfort, or meaning, from that urge, then God *is* the source of that strength, that comfort, that meaning.

"And if God—while making no difference—helps me to accept what's going to happen to me, why should that make you sad?"

On the train home, Maria sat next to a boy of about seven, who twitched all the way to the silent rhythms of a nerve-induced PMV—participatory music video. Nerve induction had been developed to treat epilepsy, but now its most common use seemed to bring about the symptoms it was meant to alleviate. Glancing at him sideways, she could see his eyeballs fluttering behind his mirror shades.

As the shock of the news diminished, slightly, Maria began to see things more clearly. It was really all about money, not religion. *She wants to be a martyr, to save me from spending a cent. All the rest is rationalization. She must have picked up a load of archaic bullshit from her own parents about the virtues of not being a "burden"—not imposing too much on the next generation, not "ruining the best years of their lives."*

She'd left her cycle in a locker at Central Station. She rode home slowly through the leisurely Sunday evening traffic, still feeling drained and shaky, but a little more confident, now that she'd had a chance to think it through. Twelve to eighteen months? She'd raise the money in less than a year. Somehow. She'd show Francesca that she could shoulder the burden— and once that was done, her mother could stop inventing excuses.

Home, she started some vegetables boiling, then went upstairs and checked for mail. There were six items under "Junk," four under "Autoverse"—and nothing under "Boring But Lucrative." Since her letter in *Autoverse Review,* almost every subscriber had been in touch, with congratulations, requests for more data, offers of collaboration, and a few borderline crank calls full of misunderstandings and complaints. Her success with *A. lamberti* had even made the big time—a slightly less specialized journal, *Cellular Automaton World.* It was all strangely anticlimactic— and in a way, she was glad of that; it put things in perspective.

She trashed all the junk mail with a sweep of her hand across the touch screen, then sat for a moment gazing at the icons for the Autoverse messages, contemplating doing the same to them. *I have to get my act together. Concentrate on earning money, and stop wasting time on this shit.*

She ran the first message. A teenage girl in Kansas City complained that she couldn't duplicate Maria's results, and proceeded to describe her own tortuous version of the experiment. Maria stopped and deleted the file after viewing twenty seconds; she'd already replied at length to half a dozen like it, and any sense of obligation she'd felt to the "Autoverse community" had vanished in the process.

As she started the second message running, she smelled something burning downstairs, and suddenly remembered that the stove had been brain-dead since Friday—everything had to be watched, and she couldn't even switch off the hotplates remotely. She turned up the volume on the terminal, and headed for the kitchen.

The spinach was a blackened mess. She threw the saucepan across the narrow room; it rebounded, almost to her feet. She picked it up again and started smashing it against the wall beside the stove, until the tiles began to crack and fall to the floor. Damaging the house was more satisfying than she'd ever imagined; it felt like rending her clothes, like tearing out her hair, like self-mutilation. She pounded the wall relentlessly, until she was breathless, giddy, running with sweat, her face flushed with a strange heat she hadn't felt since childhood tantrums. *Her mother touched her cheek with the back of her hand, brushing away tears of anger. The cool skin, the wedding ring. "Sssh. Look at the state you're in. You're burning up!"*

After a while, she calmed down, and noticed that the message was still playing upstairs; the sender must have programmed it to repeat indefinitely until she acknowledged it. She sat on the floor and listened.

"My name is Paul Durham. I read your article in *Autoverse Review*. I was very impressed by what you've done with *A. lamberti*—and if you think you might be interested in being funded to take it further, call me back on this number and we can talk about it."

Maria had to listen three more times before she was certain she'd understood the message. *Being funded to take it further.* The phrasing seemed deliberately coy and ambiguous, but in the end it could only really mean one thing.

Some idiot was offering her a job.

When Durham asked to meet her in person, Maria was too surprised to do anything but agree. Durham said he lived in north Sydney, and suggested that they meet the next morning in the city, at the Market Street Café. Maria, unable to think of a plausible excuse on the spot, just nodded—thankful that she'd made the call through a software filter which would erase any trace of anxiety from her face and tone of voice. Most programming contracts did not involve interviews, even by phone—the tendering process was usually fully automated, based entirely on the quotes submitted and the tenderer's audited performance record. Maria hadn't faced an interview in the flesh since she'd applied for part-time cleaning jobs as a student.

It was only after she'd broken the connection that she realized she still had no idea what Durham wanted from her. A real Autoverse fanatic might, just conceivably, part with money for the privilege of collaborating with her—perhaps footing the bills for computer time, for the sake of sharing the kudos of any further results. It was hard to think of any other explanation.

Maria lay awake half the night, looking back on the brief conversation, wondering if she was missing something blindingly obvious—wondering if it could be some kind of hoax. Just before two, she got up and did a hasty literature search of *Autoverse Review* and a handful of other cellular automaton journals. There were no articles by anyone named Durham.

Around three o'clock, she gave up pondering the question and managed to force herself to sleep. She dreamed that she was still awake, distraught at the news of her mother's illness—and then, realizing that she was only dreaming, cursed herself angrily because this proof of her love was nothing but an illusion.

8

(Remit not paucity)

Thomas took the elevator from his office to his home. In life, the journey had been a ten-minute ride on the S-Bahn, but after almost four subjective months he was gradually becoming accustomed to the shortcut. Today, he began the ascent without giving it a second thought—admiring the oak panelling, lulled by the faint hum of the motor—but halfway up, for no good reason, he suffered a moment of vertigo, as if the elegant coffin had gone into free fall.

When first resurrected, he'd worried constantly over which aspects of his past he should imitate for the sake of sanity, and which he should discard as a matter of honesty. A window with a view of the city seemed harmless enough—but to walk, and ride, through an artificial crowd scene struck him as grotesque, and the few times he'd tried it, he'd found it acutely distressing. It was too much like life—and too much like his dream of one day being among people again. He had no doubt that he would have become desensitized to the illusion with time, but he didn't want that. When he finally inhabited a telepresence robot as lifelike as his lost body—when he finally rode a real train again, and walked down a real street—he didn't want the joy of the experience dulled by years of perfect imitation.

He had no wish to delude himself—but apart from declining to mimic his corporeal life to the point of parody, it was hard to define exactly what that meant. He baulked at the prospect of the nearest door always opening magically onto his chosen destination, and he had no desire to snap his fingers and teleport. Acknowledging—and exploiting—the unlimited plasticity of Virtual Reality might have been the most "honest" thing to do . . . but Thomas needed a world with a permanent structure, not a dream city which reconfigured itself to his every whim.

Eventually, he'd found a compromise. He'd constructed an auxiliary geography—or architecture—for his private version of Frankfurt; an alternative topology for the city, in which all the buildings he moved between were treated as being stacked one on top of the other, allowing a single elevator shaft to link them all. His house "in the suburbs" began sixteen stories "above" his city office; in between were board rooms, restaurants, galleries and museums. Having decided upon the arrangement, he now regarded it as immutable—and if the view from each place, once he arrived, blatantly contradicted the relationship, he could live with that degree of paradox.

Thomas stepped out of the elevator into the ground floor entrance hall of his home. The two-story building, set in a modest ten hectares of garden, was his alone—as the real-world original had been from the time of his divorce until his terminal illness, when a medical team had moved in. At first, he'd had cleaning robots gliding redundantly through the corridors, and gardening robots at work in the flower beds— viewing them as part of the architecture, as much as the drain pipes, the air-conditioning grilles, and countless other "unnecessary" fixtures. He'd banished the robots after the first week. The drain pipes remained.

His dizziness had passed, but he strode into the library and poured himself a drink from two cut-glass decanters, a bracing mixture of Confidence and Optimism. With a word, he could have summoned up a full mood-control panel—an apparition which always reminded him of a recording studio's mixing desk—and adjusted the parameters of his state of mind until he reached a point where he no longer wished to change the settings . . . but he'd become disenchanted with that nakedly technological metaphor. Mood-altering "drugs," here, could function with a precision, and a lack of side effects, which no real chemical could ever have achieved—pharmacological accuracy was possible, but hardly mandatory—and it felt more natural to gulp down a mouthful of "spirits" for fortification than it did to make adjustments via a hovering bank of sliding potentiometers.

Even if the end result was exactly the same.

Thomas sank into a chair as the drink started to take effect—as a matter of choice, it worked gradually, a pleasant warmth diffusing out from his stomach before his brain itself was gently manipulated—and began trying to make sense of his encounter with Paul Durham.

You have to let me show you exactly what you are.

There was a terminal beside the chair. He hit a button, and one of his personal assistants, Hans Löhr, appeared on the screen.

Thomas said casually, "Find out what you can about my visitor, will you?"

Löhr replied at once, "Yes, sir."

Thomas had six assistants, on duty in shifts around the clock. All flesh-and-blood humans—but so thoroughly wired that they were able to switch their mental processes back and forth between normal speed and slowdown at will. Thomas kept them at a distance, communicating with them only by terminal; the distinction between a visitor "in the flesh" and a "mere image" on a screen didn't bear much scrutiny, but in practice it could still be rigorously enforced. He sometimes thought of his staff as working in Munich or Berlin . . . "far enough away" to "explain" the fact that he never met them in person, and yet "near enough" to make a kind of metaphorical sense of their ability to act as go-betweens with the outside world. He'd never bothered to find out where they really were, in case the facts contradicted this convenient mental image.

He sighed, and took another swig of C & O. It was a balancing act, a tightrope walk. A Copy could go insane, either way. Caring too much about the truth could lead to a pathological obsession with *the infrastructure*—the algorithms and optical processors, the machinery of "deception" which lay beneath every surface. Caring too little, you could find yourself gradually surrendering to a complacent fantasy in which life had gone on as normal, and everything which contradicted the illusion of ordinary physical existence was avoided, or explained away.

Was that Durham's real intention? To drive him mad?

Thomas had ordered the usual cursory screening before letting Durham in, revealing only that the man worked as a salesman for Gryphon Financial Products—a moderately successful Anglo-Australian company—and that he possessed no criminal record. Elaborate precautions were hardly warranted; visitors could do no harm. Thomas's VR consultants had assured him that nothing short of tampering with the hardware *in situ* could ever damage or corrupt the system; no mere signal coming down the fiber from the outside world could penetrate the protected layers of the software. Visitors who wreaked havoc, introducing viruses by the fiendishly clever binary-modulated snapping of their fingers, were the stuff of fiction. (Literally; Thomas had seen it happen once on *The Unclear Family*.)

Durham had said: "I'm not going to lie to you. I've spent time in a mental institution. Ten years. I suffered delusions. Bizarre, elaborate delusions. And I realize, now, that I was seriously ill. I can look back and understand that.

"But at the very same time, I can look back and remember what it was that I believed was happening when I was insane. And without for one moment ceasing to acknowledge my condition, I still find those memories *so convincing . . .*"

Thomas's skin crawled. He raised his glass . . . and then put it down. He knew that if he kept on drinking, nothing the man had said would unsettle him in the least—but he hadn't drunk enough, yet, to be absolutely sure that that was what he wanted.

"If you're not prepared to perform the experiment yourself, at least think about the implications. *Imagine* that you've modified the way in which you're computed—and imagine what the consequences would be. A *gedanken* experiment—is that too much to ask for? In a sense, that's all I ever performed myself."

The terminal chimed. Thomas took the call. Löhr said, "I have a preliminary report on Paul Durham. Would you like me to read it?"

Thomas shook his head. "I'll view the file."

He skimmed it, at level one detail. *Paul Kingsley Durham.* Born in Sydney on June 6, 2000. Parents: Elizabeth Anne Maddox and John Arthur Durham . . . joint owners of a delicatessen in the Sydney suburb of Concord, from 1996 to 2032 . . . retired to Mackay, Queensland . . . now both deceased by natural causes.

Educated at a government high school. 2017: Higher School Certificate aggregate score in third percentile; best subjects physics and mathematics. 2018: completed one year of a science degree at Sydney University, passed all examinations but discontinued studies. 2019 to 2023: traveled in Thailand, Burma, India, Nepal. 2024: on return to Australia, diagnosed with an organic delusional syndrome, probably congenital . . . condition partly controlled by medication. Numerous casual laboring jobs until May, 2029. Condition deteriorating . . . disability pension granted January, 2031. Committed to Psychiatric Ward of Blacktown Hospital on September 4, 2035.

Corrective nanosurgery to the hippocampus and prefrontal cerebral cortex performed on November 11, 2045 . . . declared a complete success.

Thomas switched to level two, to fill in the ten-year gap, but found little more than a long list of the drugs, neural grafts, and gene-therapy vectors which had been injected into Durham's skull during that period, to no apparent benefit. There were frequent notes that the treatments had been tested first on a set of partial brain models, but hadn't worked in practice. Thomas wondered if Durham had been told about this—and wondered what the man imagined *happened* when a drug was evaluated on fifteen separate models of different regions of the brain, which, taken together, encompassed the entire organ . . .

2046 to 2048: studying finance and administration at Macquarie University. 2049: graduated with first class honors, and immediately hired by Gryphon as a trainee salesman. As of January 17, 2050, working in the Artificial Intelligence Division.

Which meant selling protection, in various guises, to Copies who were afraid that their assets were going to be pulled out from under them. Durham's job description would certainly cover spending long hours as a visitor—if not quite stretching to matters like disclosing details of his personal psychiatric history, or suggesting metaphysical *gedanken* experiments to his clients. Or indeed, wasting time on Copies obviously far too secure to need Gryphon's services.

Thomas leaned back from the terminal. It was almost too simple: Durham had fooled his doctors into believing that they'd cured him—and then, with typical paranoid ingenuity and tenacity, he'd set about getting himself into a position where he could meet Copies, share the Great Truth that had been revealed to him . . . and try to extract a little money in the process.

If Thomas contacted Gryphon and told them what their mad salesman was up to, Durham would certainly lose his job, probably end up in an institution again—and hopefully benefit from a second attempt at nanosurgery. Durham probably wasn't harming anybody . . . but ensuring that he received treatment was, surely, the kindest thing to do.

A confident, optimistic person would make the call at once. Thomas eyed his drink, but decided to hold off a little longer before drowning the alternatives.

Durham had said: "I understand that everything I believe I've experienced was "due to" my illness—and I know there's no easy way to persuade you that I'm not still insane. But even if that were true . . . why should it make the question I've raised any less important to you?

"Most flesh-and-blood humans live and die without knowing or caring *what they are*—scoffing at the very idea that it should matter. But you're not flesh and blood, and you can't afford the luxury of ignorance."

Thomas rose and walked over to the mirror above the fireplace. Superficially, his appearance was still based largely on his final scan; he had the same unruly thick white hair, the same loose, mottled, translucent eighty-five-year-old skin. He had the bearing of a young man, though; the model constructed from the scan file had been thoroughly rejuvenated, internally, sweeping away sixty years' worth of deterioration in every joint, every muscle, every vein and artery. He wondered if it was only a matter of time before vanity got the better of him and he did the same with his appearance. Many of his business associates were un-aging gradually—but a few had leaped back twenty, thirty, fifty years, or changed their appearances completely. *Which was most honest?* Looking like an eighty-five-year-old flesh-and-blood human (which he was not), or looking the way he'd prefer to look . . . prefer to *be* . . . given the choice. And he did have the choice.

He closed his eyes, put his fingertips to his cheek, explored the damaged skin. If he believed these ruins defined him, they defined him . . . and if he learned to accept a new young body, the same would be true of it. And yet, he couldn't shake the notion that external rejuvenation would entail nothing more than constructing a youthful "mask" . . . while his "true face" continued to exist—and age—somewhere. Pure Dorian Gray—a stupid moralistic fable stuffed with "eternal" verities long obsolete.

And it was good just to *feel* healthy and vigorous, to be free of the arthritis, the aches and cramps and chills, the shortness of breath he could still remember vividly. Anything more seemed too easy, too arbitrary. Any Copy could become a Hollywood Adonis in an instant. And any Copy could outrace a bullet, lift a building, move a planet from its course.

Thomas opened his eyes, reached out and touched the surface of the mirror, aware that he was avoiding making a decision. But one thing still bothered him.

Why had Durham chosen *him?* The man might be deluded—but he was also intelligent and rational on some level. Of all the Copies whose insecurities he might have tried to exploit, why choose one with a watertight setup, secure hardware, a well-managed trust fund? Why choose a target who appeared to have absolutely nothing to fear?

Thomas felt the vertigo returning. *It had been sixty-five years.* Not one newspaper story or police report had mentioned his name; no database search, however elaborate, could link him to Anna. Nobody alive could know what he'd done—least of all a fifty-year-old ex-psychiatric patient from the other side of the world.

Even the man who'd committed the crime was dead. Thomas had seen him cremated.

Did he seriously think that Durham's offer of sanctuary was some elaborately coded euphemism for not dredging up the past? *Blackmail?*

No. That was ludicrous.

So why not make a few calls, and have the poor man seen to? Why not pay for him to be treated by the best Swiss neurosurgeon (who'd verify the procedure in advance, on the most sophisticated set of partial brain models . . .)

Or did he believe there was a chance that Durham was telling the truth? That he could run a second Copy, in a place nobody could reach in a billion years?

The terminal chimed. Thomas said, "Yes?"

Heidrich had taken over from Löhr; sometimes the shifts seemed to change so fast that it made Thomas giddy. "You have a meeting of the Geistbank board in five minutes, sir."

"Thank you, I'll be right down."

Thomas checked his appearance in the mirror. He said, "Comb me." His hair was made passably tidy, his complexion less pale, his eyes clear; certain facial muscles were relaxed, and others tightened. His suit required no attention; as in life, it could not be wrinkled.

He almost laughed, but his newly combed expression discouraged it. *Expediency, honesty, complacency, insanity.* It was a tightrope walk. He was ninety years old by one measure, eighty-five-and-a-half by another—and he still didn't know how to live.

On his way out, he picked up his Confidence & Optimism and poured it on the carpet.

9

(Rip, tie, cut toy man)

JUNE 2045

Paul took the stairs down, and circled the block a few times, hoping for nothing more than to forget himself for a while. He was tired of having to think about *what he was,* every waking moment. The streets around the building were familiar enough, not to let him delude himself, but at least to allow him to take himself for granted.

It was hard to separate fact from rumor, but he'd heard that even the giga-rich tended to live in relatively mundane surroundings, favoring realism over power fantasies. A few models-of-psychotics had reportedly set themselves up as dictators in opulent palaces, waited on hand and foot, but most Copies aimed for an illusion of continuity. If you desperately wanted to convince yourself that you *were* the same person as your memories suggested, the worst thing to do would be to swan around a virtual antiquity (with mod cons), pretending to be Cleopatra or Ramses II.

Paul didn't believe that he "was" his original. He knew he was nothing but a cloud of ambiguous data. The miracle was that he was capable of believing that he existed at all.

What gave him that sense of identity?

Continuity. Consistency. Thought following thought in a coherent pattern.

But where did that coherence come from?

In a human, or a Copy being run in the usual way, the physics of brain or computer meant that the state of mind at any one moment directly influenced the state of mind that followed. Continuity was a simple matter of cause and effect; what you thought at time A affected what you thought at time B affected what you thought at time C . . .

But when his subjective time was scrambled, the flow of cause and effect within the computer bore no relationship whatsoever to the flow of his experience—so how could it be an essential part of it? When the program spelled out his life DBCEA, but it still *felt* exactly like ABCDE . . . then surely the pattern was all, and cause and effect were irrelevant. The whole experience might just as well have arisen by chance.

Suppose an intentionally haywire computer sat for a thousand years or more, twitching from state to state in the sway of nothing but electrical noise. Might it embody consciousness?

In real time, the answer was: probably not—the probability of any kind of coherence arising at random being so small. Real time, though, was only one possible reference frame; what about all the others? If the states the machine passed through could be rearranged in time arbitrarily, then who could say what kind of elaborate order might emerge from the chaos?

Paul caught himself. Was that fatuous? As absurd as insisting that every room full of monkeys really *did* type the complete works of Shakespeare—they just happened to put the letters in a slightly different order? As ludicrous as claiming that every large-enough quantity of rock contained Michelangelo's *David,* and every warehouse full of paint and canvas contained the complete works of Rembrandt and Picasso—not in any mere latent form, awaiting some skillful forger to physically rearrange them, but *solely by virtue of the potential redefinition of the coordinates of space-time?*

For a statue or a painting, yes, it was a joke. Where was the observer who perceived the paint to be in contact with the canvas, who *saw* the stone figure suitably delineated by air?

If the pattern in question was *not* an isolated object, though, but *a self-contained world,* complete with at least one observer to join up the dots *from within* . . .

There was no doubt that it was possible. *He'd done it.* In the final trial of the second experiment, he'd assembled himself and his surroundings—effortlessly—from the dust of randomly scattered moments, from apparent white noise in real time. True, what the computer had done had been contrived, guaranteed to contain his thoughts and perceptions coded into its seemingly aimless calculations. But given a large enough collection of truly random numbers, there was no reason to believe that it wouldn't include, purely by accident, hidden patterns as complex and coherent as the ones which underlay *him*.

And wouldn't those patterns, however scrambled they might be in real time, be conscious of themselves, just as he'd been conscious, and piece their own subjective world together, just as he had done?

Paul returned to the apartment, fighting off a sense of giddiness and unreality. So much for forgetting himself; he felt more charged than ever with the truth of his strange nature.

Did he still want to bale out? No. *No!* How could he declare that he'd happily wake and forget himself—wake and "reclaim" his life—when he was beginning to glimpse the answers to questions which his original had never even dared to ask?

10

(Remit not paucity)

Maria arrived at the café fifteen minutes early—to find Durham already there, seated at a table close to the entrance. She was surprised, but relieved; with the long wait she'd been expecting suddenly canceled, she had no time to grow nervous. Durham spotted her as she walked in; they shook hands, exchanged pleasantries, ordered coffee from the table's touchscreen menus. Seeing Durham in the flesh did nothing to contradict the impression he'd made by phone: middle-aged, quiet, conservatively dressed; not exactly the archetypical Autoverse junkie.

Maria said, "I always thought I was the only *Autoverse Review* subscriber living in Sydney. I've been in touch with Ian Summers in Hobart a couple of times, but I never realized there was anyone so close."

Durham was apologetic. "There's no reason why you would have heard of me. I'm afraid I've always confined myself to reading the articles; I've never contributed anything or participated in the conferences. I don't actually work in the Autoverse, myself. I don't have the time. Or the skills, to be honest."

Maria absorbed that, trying not to appear too startled. It was like hearing someone admit that they studied chess but never played the game.

"But I've followed progress in the field very closely, and I can certainly appreciate what you've done with *A. lamberti.* Perhaps even more so than some of your fellow practitioners. I think I see it in a rather broader context."

"You mean . . . cellular automata in general?"

"Cellular automata, artificial life."

"They're your main interests?"

"Yes."

But not as a participant? Maria tried to imagine this man as a patron of the artificial life scene, magnanimously sponsoring promising young practitioners; Lorenzo the Magnificent to the Botticellis and Michelangelos of cellular automaton theory.

It wouldn't wash. Even if the idea wasn't intrinsically ludicrous, he just didn't look that rich.

The coffee arrived. Durham started paying for both of them, but when Maria protested, he let her pay for herself without an argument—which made her feel far more at ease. As the robot trolley slid away, she got straight to the point. "You say you're interested in funding research that builds on my results with *A. lamberti.* Is there any particular direction—?"

"Yes. I have something very specific in mind." Durham hesitated. "I still don't know the best way to put this. But I want you to help me . . . prove a point. I want you to construct a seed for a biosphere."

Maria said nothing. She wasn't even sure that she'd heard him correctly. *A seed for a biosphere* was terraforming jargon—for all the plant and animal species required to render a sterile, but theoretically habitable planet ecologically stable. She'd never come across the phrase in any other context.

Durham continued. "I want you to design a pre-biotic environment—a planetary surface, if you'd like to think of it that way—and one simple organism which you believe would be capable, in time, of evolving into a multitude of species and filling all the potential ecological niches."

"An environment? So . . . you want a Virtual Reality landscape?" Maria tried not to look disappointed. Had she seriously expected to be paid to work in *the Autoverse?* "With microscopic primordial life? Some kind of . . . Precambrian theme park, where the users can shrink to the size of algae and inspect their earliest ancestors?" For all her distaste for patchwork VR, Maria found herself almost warming to the idea. If Durham was offering her the chance to supervise the whole project—and the funds to do the job properly—it would be a thousand times more interesting than any of the tedious VR contracts she'd had in the past. And a lot more lucrative.

But Durham said, "No, please—forget about Virtual Reality. I want you to design an organism, and an environment—*in the Autoverse*—which would have the properties I've described. And forget about Precambrian algae. I don't expect you to recreate ancestral life on Earth, translated into Autoverse chemistry—if such a thing would even be possible. I just want you to construct a system with . . . the same potential."

Maria was now thoroughly confused. "When you mentioned a planetary surface, I thought you meant a full-scale virtual landscape—a few dozen square kilometers. But if you're talking about the Autoverse . . . you mean a fissure in a rock on a seabed, something like that? Something vaguely analogous to a microenvironment on the early Earth? Something a bit more 'natural' than a culture dish full of two different sugars?"

Durham said, "I'm sorry, I'm not making myself very clear. Of course you'll want to try out the seed organism in a number of microenvironments; that's the only way you'll be able to predict with any confidence that it would actually survive, mutate, adapt . . . flourish. But once that's established, I'll want you to describe the complete picture. Specify an entire planetary environment which the Autoverse could support— and in which the seed would be likely to evolve into higher lifeforms."

Maria hesitated. She was beginning to wonder if Durham had any idea of the scale on which things were done in the Autoverse. "What exactly do you mean by a 'planetary environment'?"

"Whatever you think is reasonable. Say—thirty million square kilometers?" He laughed. "Don't have a heart attack; I don't expect you to model the whole thing, atom by atom. I do realize that all the computers on Earth couldn't handle much more than a tide pool. I just want you to describe the essential features. You could do that in a couple of terabytes—probably less. It wouldn't take much to sum up the topography; it doesn't matter what the specific shape of every mountain and valley and beach is—all you need is a statistical description, a few relevant fractal dimensions. The meteorology and the geochemistry—for want of a better word—will be a little more complex. But I think you know what I'm getting at. You could summarize everything that matters about a pre-biotic planet with a relatively small amount of data. I don't expect you to hand over a giant Autoverse grid which contains every atom in every grain of sand."

Maria said, "No, of course not." This was getting stranger by the minute. "But . . . why specify a whole 'planet'—in any form?"

"The size of the environment, and the variation in climate and terrain, are important factors. Details like that will affect the number of different species which arise in isolation and later migrate and interact. They certainly made a difference to the Earth's evolutionary history. So they may or may not be crucial, but they're hardly irrelevant."

Maria said carefully, "That's true—but nobody will ever be able to run a system that big in the Autoverse, so what's the point of describing it? On Earth, the system *is* that big, we're stuck with it. The only way to explain the entire fossil record, and the current distribution of species, is to look at things on a planetary scale. Migration *has happened,* it has to be taken into account. But . . . in the Autoverse, it hasn't happened, and it never will. Effects like that will always be completely hypothetical."

Durham said, "Hypothetical? Absolutely. But that doesn't mean the results can't be considered, can't be imagined, can't be argued about. Think of this whole project as . . . an aid to a thought experiment. A sketch of a proof."

"A proof of what?"

"That Autoverse life could—in theory—be as rich and complex as life on Earth."

Maria shook her head. "I can't *prove* that. Modeling a few thousand generations of bacterial evolution in a few microenvironment. . . . "

Durham waved a hand reassuringly. "Don't worry; I don't have unrealistic expectations. I said 'a sketch of a proof,' but maybe even that's putting it too strongly. I just want . . . suggestive evidence. I want the best blueprint, the best recipe you can come up with for a world, embedded in the Autoverse, which *might* eventually develop complex life. A set of results on the short-term evolutionary genetics of the seed organism, plus an outline of an environment in which that organism could, plausibly, evolve into higher forms. All right, it's impossible to *run* a planet-sized world. But that's no reason not to contemplate what such a world would be like—to answer as many questions as can be answered, and to make the whole scenario as concrete as possible. I want you to create a package so thorough, so detailed, that if someone handed it to you out of the blue, it would be enough—not to prove anything—but to *persuade you* that true biological diversity *could* arise in the Autoverse."

Maria laughed. "I'm already persuaded of that, myself. I just doubt that there could ever be a watertight proof."

"Then imagine persuading someone a little more skeptical."

"Who exactly did you have in mind? Calvin and his mob?"

"If you like."

Maria suddenly wondered if Durham was someone she should have known, after all—someone who'd published in other areas of the artificial life scene. Why else would he be concerned with that debate? She should have done a much wider literature search.

She said, "So what it comes down to is . . . you want to present the strongest possible case that deterministic systems like the Autoverse can generate a biology as complex as real-world biology—that all the subtleties of real-world physics and quantum indeterminacy aren't essential. And to deal with the objection that a complex biology might only arise in a complex environment, you want a description of a suitable 'planet' that *could* exist in the Autoverse—if not for the minor inconvenience that the hardware that could run it will almost certainly never be built."

"That's right."

Maria hesitated; she didn't want to argue this bizarre project out of existence, but she could hardly take it on if she wasn't clear about its goals. "But when it's all said and done, how much will this really add to the results with *A. lamberti?*"

"In one sense, not a lot," Durham conceded. "As you said, there can never be a proof. Natural selection is natural selection, and you've shown that it can happen in the Autoverse; maybe that should be enough. But don't you think a—carefully designed—thought experiment with *an entire planet* is a bit more . . . evocative . . . than any number of real experiments with Petri dishes? Don't underestimate the need to appeal to people's imaginations. Maybe you can see all the consequences of your work, already. Other people might need to have them spelled out explicitly."

Maria couldn't argue with any of that—but who handed out research grants on the basis of what was *evocative?* "So . . . which university—?"

Durham cut her off. "I'm not an academic. This is just an interest of mine. A hobby, like it is with you. I'm an insurance salesman, in real life."

"But how could you get funding without—?"

"I'm paying for this myself." He laughed. "Don't worry, I can afford it; if you take me up on this, you're not going to be shortchanged, I can promise you that. And I know it's unusual for an amateur to . . . subcontract. But like I said, I don't work in the Autoverse. It would take me five years to learn to do, myself, what I'm asking of you. You'll be free to publish all of this under your own name, of course—all I ask is a footnote acknowledging financial support."

Maria didn't know what to say. *Lorenzo the insurance salesman?* A private citizen—not even an Autoverse junkie—was offering to pay her to carry out the most abstract piece of programming imaginable: not simulating a nonexistent world, but "preparing" a simulation that would never be performed. She could hardly be disdainful of anyone for throwing their hard-earned money away on "pointless" Autoverse research—but everything that had driven her to do that, herself, revolved around firsthand experience. However much intellectual pleasure it had given her, the real obsession, the real addiction, was a matter of putting on the gloves and reaching into that artificial space.

Durham handed her a ROM chip. "There are some detailed notes here—including a few ideas of mine, but don't feel obliged to follow any of them. What I want is whatever you think is most likely to work, not what's closest to my preconceptions. And there's a contract, of course. Have your legal expert system look it over; if you're not happy with anything, I'm pretty flexible."

"Thank you."

Durham stood. "I'm sorry to cut this short, but I'm afraid I have another appointment. Please—read the notes, think it all through. Call me when you've made a decision."

After he'd left, Maria sat at the table, staring at the black epoxy rectangle in her palm, trying to make sense of what had happened.

Babbage had designed the Analytical Engine with no real prospect of seeing it constructed in his lifetime. Space travel enthusiasts had been designing interstellar craft, down to every last nut and bolt, since the 1960s. Terraforming advocates were constantly churning out comprehensive feasibility studies for schemes unlikely to be attempted for a hundred years or more. *Why?* As aids to thought experiments. As sketches of proofs.

And if Durham, who'd never even worked in the Autoverse, had an infinitely grander vision of its long-term possibilities than she had, then maybe she'd always been too close to it, too wrapped up in the tedious contingencies, to see what he'd seen . . .

Except that this wasn't about *long-term possibilities.* The computer that could run an Autoverse world would be far bigger than the planet it was modeling. If such a device was ever to be constructed, however far into the future, there'd have to be far better reasons for building it than this. It wasn't a question of a visionary born a generation or two before his time; *Autoverse ecology* was an entirely theoretical notion, and it always would be. The project was a thought experiment in the purest sense.

It was also too good to be true. The Autoverse addict's dream contract. But short of some senseless, capricious hoax, why should Durham lie to her?

Maria pocketed the chip and left the café, not knowing whether to feel skeptical and pessimistic, or elated—and guilty. Guilty, because Durham—if he was genuine, if he honestly planned to pay her real money for this glorious, senseless exercise—had to be a little insane. If she took this job, she'd be taking advantage of him, exploiting his strange madness.

Maria let Aden into the house reluctantly; they usually met at his place, or on neutral ground, but he'd been visiting a friend nearby, and she could think of no excuse to turn him away. She caught a glimpse of the red cloudless sunset behind him, and the open doorway let in the hot concrete smell of dusk, the whirr of evening traffic. After seven hours cloistered in her room, reading Durham's notes for his Autoverse Garden of Eden, the street outside seemed strange, almost shocking—charged with the two-billion-year gulf between Earth's equivalent moment of primordial fecundity and all the bizarre consequences.

She walked ahead of Aden down the entrance hall and switched on the light in the living room, while he propped his cycle against the stairs. Alone, the house suited her perfectly, but it took only one more person to make it seem cramped.

He caught up with her and said, "I heard about your mother."

"How? Who told you?"

"Joe knows one of your cousins in Newcastle. Angela? Is that her name?"

He was leaning sideways against the doorframe, arms folded. Maria said, "Why don't you come right in if you're coming in?"

He said, "I'm sorry. Is there anything I can do?"

She shook her head. She'd been planning to ask him how much he could lend her to help with the scan, but she couldn't raise the subject, not yet. He'd ask, innocently, if Francesca was certain that she wanted to be scanned—and the whole thing would degenerate into an argument about her right to choose a natural death. As if there was any real choice, without the money for a scan.

Maria said, "I saw her yesterday. She's handling it pretty well. But I don't want to talk about it right now."

Aden nodded, then detached himself from the doorway and walked up to her. They kissed for a while, which was comforting in a way, but Aden soon had an erection, and Maria was in no mood for sex. Even at the best of times, it took a willing suspension of disbelief, a conscious decision to bury her awareness of the biological clockwork driving her emotions—and right now, her head was still buzzing with Durham's suggestion for building a kind of latent diploidism into *A. lamberti,* a propensity to "mistakenly" make extra copies of chromosomes, which might eventually pave the way to sexual reproduction and all of its evolutionary advantages.

Aden pulled free and went and sat in one of the armchairs.

Maria said, "I think I've finally got some work. If I didn't dream the whole thing."

"That's great! Who for?"

She described her meeting with Durham. The commission, the seed.

Aden said, "So you don't even know what he gets out of this—except not-quite-proving some obscure intellectual point about evolution?" He laughed, incredulous. "How will you know if you've not-quite-proved it well enough? And what if Durham disagrees?"

"The contract is all in my favor. He pays the money into a trust fund before I even start. All I have to do is make a genuine effort to complete the project within six months—and if there's any dispute, he's legally bound to accept an independent adjudicator's decision on what constitutes a 'genuine effort.' The expert system I hired gave the contract a triple-A rating."

Aden still looked skeptical. "You should get a second opinion; half the time those things don't even agree with each other—let alone predict what would happen in court. Anyway, if it all goes smoothly, what do you end up with?"

"Thirty thousand dollars. Not bad, for six months' work. Plus computing time up to another thirty thousand—billed directly to him."

"Yeah? How can he afford all this?"

"He's an insurance salesman. If he's good, he could be making, I don't know . . . two hundred grand a year?"

"Which is one hundred and twenty, after tax. And he's paying out *sixty* on this shit?"

"Yes. You have a problem with that? It doesn't exactly leave him poverty-stricken. And he could be earning twice as much, for all I know. Not to mention savings, investments . . . tax dodges. His personal finances are none of my business; once the money's in the trust fund, he can go bankrupt for all I care. I still get paid if I finish the job. That's good enough for me."

Aden shook his head. "I just can't see why he thinks it's worth it. There are God-knows-how-many-thousand Copies in existence, *right now*—running half the biggest corporations in the world, in case you hadn't noticed—and this man wants to spend sixty thousand dollars proving that artificial life can go beyond *bacteria?*"

Maria groaned. "We've been through this before. The Autoverse is *not* Virtual Reality. Copies are *not* the human equivalent of *A. lamberti*. They're a cheat, they're a mess. They do what they're meant to do, very efficiently. But there's no . . . underlying logic to them. Every part of their body obeys a different set of *ad hoc* rules. Okay, it would be insane to try to model an entire human body on a molecular level—but if you're interested in the way fundamental physics affects biology, Copies are irrelevant, because they *have no* fundamental physics. The behavior of a Copy's neurons doesn't arise from any deeper laws, it's just a matter of some "rules for neurons" which are based directly on what's known about neurons in the human body. But in the human body, that behavior is a consequence of the laws of physics, acting on billions of molecules. With Copies, we've cheated, for the sake of efficiency. There are no molecules, and no laws of physics; we've just put in the net results—the biology—by hand."

"And that offends your aesthetic sensibilities?"

"That's not the point. Copies have their place—and when

the time comes, I'd rather be a software mongrel than dead. All I'm saying is, they're useless for telling you what kind of physics can support what kind of life."

"A burning question of our time."

Maria felt herself flush with anger, but she said evenly, "Maybe not. I just happen to find it interesting. And apparently Paul Durham does too. And maybe it's too abstract a question to qualify as *science* . . . maybe working in the Autoverse is nothing but pure mathematics. Or philosophy. Or art. But you don't seem to have any qualms about spending a year in Seoul, practicing your own useless artform at the Korean taxpayers' expense."

"It's a private university."

"Korean students' expense, then."

"I never said there was anything wrong with you taking the job—I just don't want to see you get screwed if this man turns out to be lying."

"What could he possibly have to gain by lying?"

"I don't know—but I still don't see what he has to gain if he's telling the truth." He shrugged. "But if you're happy, I'm happy. Maybe it'll all be okay. And I know, the way things are going, you can't afford to be picky."

Picky? Maria started laughing. Discussing this on Aden's terms was ridiculous. Durham wasn't stringing her along, wasting her time; he was absolutely serious—his notes proved that. Three hundred pages—months of work. He'd taken the plan as far as he could, short of learning the intricacies of the Autoverse himself.

And maybe she still didn't understand his motives—but maybe there was nothing to be "understood." When she'd been immersed in his notes, there'd been no mystery at all. On its own terms, Durham's plan was . . . natural, obvious. An end in itself, requiring no dreary explanation rooted in the world of academic glory and monetary gain.

Aden said, "What's so funny?"

"Never mind."

He shifted in the chair, and looked at her oddly. "Well, at least you won't have to spend all your time in Seoul looking for work, now. That would have been a bore."

"I'm not going to Seoul."

"You're joking."

She shook her head.

"What's the problem? You can do this job anywhere, can't you?"

"Probably. Yes. I just—"

Maria felt a twinge of uncertainty. He seemed genuinely hurt. He'd made it clear that he'd go without her, if he had to—but that was understandable. Composer-in-residence was *his* perfect job—and she had nothing to weigh against that, nothing to lose by accompanying him. He might have put his position more diplomatically, instead of making her feel like optional baggage—but that was neither proof that he was trying to drive her away, nor an unforgivable crime in itself. He was tactless sometimes. She could live with that.

"What's wrong with you? You'd love it in Seoul. You know you would."

She said, "I'd love it too much. There'd be too many distractions. This project is going to be hard work, the hardest thing I've ever done, and if I can't give it all my attention, it's going to be impossible." It had started as an *ad lib* excuse, but it was true. She had six months, if not to build a world, at least to sketch one; if she didn't eat, sleep and breathe it, it would never come together, it would never come to life.

Aden snorted. "That's ludicrous! You don't even have to write a program that *runs*. You said yourself, as long as you make a reasonable effort, whatever you hand over will be good enough. What's Durham going to say? 'Sorry, but I don't think this slime mould would ever invent the wheel'?"

"Getting it right matters to me."

Aden said nothing. Then, "If you want to stay behind because of your mother, why can't you just say so?"

Maria was startled. "Because it's not true."

He stared at her angrily. "You know, I was going to offer to stay here with you. But you didn't want to talk about it."

Maria untangled that. "That's what you came here to tell me? That if I planned to stay in Sydney because of Francesca, you'd turn down the job in Seoul?"

"Yes." He said it as if it should have been obvious to her all along. "She's dying. Do you think I'd walk off and leave you to cope with that alone? What kind of shit do you think I am?"

She's not dying; she's going to be scanned.

But she didn't say that. "Francesca doesn't care if I go or stay. I offered to move in with her, but she doesn't want to be looked after by anyone. Let alone by me."

"Then come to Seoul."

"Why, exactly? So you won't feel bad about leaving me? That's what it all comes down to, isn't it? Your peace of mind."

Aden thought about that for a while. Then he said, "All right. Fuck you. Stay."

He got to his feet and walked out of the room. Maria listened to him fumbling with his cycle, then opening the front door, slamming it closed.

She tidied up in the kitchen, checked the locks, switched off the lights. Then she went upstairs and lay on her bed, leaving the room in darkness, trying to picture the likely course of events over the next few weeks. Aden would phone before he left, trying to patch things up, but she could see how easy it would be, now, to break things off permanently. And now that it had reached that stage, it seemed like the obvious thing to do. She wasn't upset, or relieved—just calm. It always made her feel that way: burning bridges, driving people away. Simplifying her life.

She'd left the terminal switched on after reading Durham's ROM; the screen was blank, and supposedly pure black, but as her eyes adapted to the dark she could see it glowing a faint gray. Every now and then there was a brief flash at a random point on the screen—a pixel activated by background radiation, struck by a cosmic ray. She watched the flashes, like a slow rain falling on a window to another world, until she fell asleep.

11

(Remit not paucity)

Malcolm Carter presented as a tall, solid, vigorous-looking man in late middle age—and in fact he was fifty-eight, so his visitor's body might easily have been styled directly on his real one. Peer remembered seeing photographs of Carter in the early thirties, when he rose to prominence as one of the first architect-programmers to concentrate on the needs of Copies, rather than catering to the human visitors who used virtual environments merely for work or entertainment. Visitors had ended up hiring him too, though—visitors like Kate who were on their way in. And Kate had moved in a similar orbit then, a young computer artist snatched out of obscurity in Oregon and adopted by the San Francisco glitterati at about the same time as Carter's own ascent from a small Arizona software house. Peer wasn't sure he would have recognized the man from those old magazine shots—but then, nobody continued to look the way they'd looked in the thirties, if they could possibly help it.

Carter shook hands with Peer, and nodded at Kate; Peer wondered, curious but not really jealous, if they were greeting each other a little more warmly in a private detour from the version of the meeting he was seeing. They were standing in a spacious reception area, the walls and high ceiling decorated with a motif of tiered concentric circles moulded into the cream-colored plaster, the floor tiled in black-and-white diamonds. This was Carter's publicly listed VR address; anyone at all could call the number and "come here." The room spawned separate versions for separate callers, though; Peer and Kate had taken steps to arrive together, but there had been no risk of them accidentally bumping into one of Carter's—or Durham's—wealthy clients.

Carter said, "I hope you don't mind if we keep this brief and to the point. I don't like to use inducers for more than twenty-four hours at a stretch."

Peer said, "It's good of you to make the time to see us at all." He cursed himself silently; he was contemplating paying this man a substantial portion of his entire wealth—and trusting him with the fate of an autonomous version of his own consciousness. He had a right to an audience. *Still, at a slowdown of sixty . . .*

Carter—if it really was Carter, and not just a convincing mask—pointed out a door at the end of the room. "There's a rough sketch of the city through there, if you want to take the tour later on; just call out for a guide if you need one. But I expect the city itself's not your main concern. What you really want to know is, can I fit you safely into the cracks?"

Peer glanced at Kate. She remained silent. She was already convinced; this was all for his benefit.

Carter held out a hand toward the middle of the room. "See that fountain?" A ten-meter-wide marble wedding cake, topped with a winged cherub wrestling a serpent, duly appeared. Water cascaded down from a gushing wound in the cherub's neck. Carter said, "It's being computed by redundancies in the sketch of the city. I can extract the results, because I know exactly where to look for them—but nobody else would have a hope in hell of picking them out."

Peer walked up to the fountain. Even as he approached, he noticed that the spray was intangible; when he dipped his hand in the water around the base he felt nothing, and the motion he made with his fingers left the foaming surface unchanged. They were spying on the calculations, not interacting with them; the fountain was a closed system.

Carter said, "In your case, of course, nobody will need to know the results. Except you—and you'll know them because you'll *be* them."

Peer replied, almost without thinking, "Not me. My clone."

"Whatever." Carter clapped his hands, and a multicolored,

three-dimensional lattice appeared, floating in the air above the fountain. "This is a schematic of part of the software running the sketch of the city. Each cube represents a process. Packets of data—those blips of colored light—flow between them.

"There's nothing so crude as a subset of processes dedicated to the fountain. Every individual process—and every individual packet of data—is involved with some aspect of the city. But there are some slightly inefficient calculations going on here and there, and some 'redundant' pieces of information being exchanged." Pin-pricks in a smattering of the cubes, and some of the data, glowed bright blue. "One of the simplest tricks is to use a vector when only a direction is needed—when the magnitude of the vector is irrelevant. Perfectly reasonable operations on the vector, entirely justified in their own context, incidentally perform arithmetic on the magnitude. But that's just one technique; there are dozens of others." He clapped his hands again, and everything but the blue highlights vanished. The diagram re-formed, the scattered processes coming together into a compact grid. "The point is, the fountain gets computed along with the city, without any of the software explicitly stealing time for a parasitic task. Every line of every program makes sense in terms of computing the city."

Peer said, "And if Durham runs your code through an optimizer which rescales all the unnecessary vectors, trims away all the inefficiencies . . . ?"

Carter shook his head. "I don't believe he'd meddle with the code at all, but even if he does, optimizers can only track things so far. In the full version of the city, the results of your calculations will propagate so widely that it would take months for any program to deduce that the data's not actually needed somewhere—that it ultimately makes no difference to the legitimate inhabitants." He grinned. "Optimizing anything to do with Copies is a subtle business. You must have heard about the billionaire recluse who wanted to run as fast as possible—even though he never made contact with the outside world—so he fed his own code into an optimizer. After analyzing it for a year, the optimizer reported THIS PROGRAM WILL

PRODUCE NO OUTPUT, and spat out the optimized version—which did precisely nothing."

Peer laughed, although he'd heard the joke before.

Carter said, "The fact is, the city is so complex, there's so much going on, that even if it had all been left to chance, I wouldn't be surprised if there were some quite sophisticated secondary computations taking place, purely by accident. I haven't gone looking for them, though—it would burn up far too much processor time. And the same applies to anyone searching for you. It's just not a practical proposition. Why would anyone spend millions of dollars scanning for something which can do no harm?"

Peer gazed up at the blue schematic skeptically. Carter came across as if he knew what he was talking about, but a few plausible-looking graphics proved nothing.

Carter seemed to read his mind. "If you have any doubts, take a look at the software I used." A large, fat book appeared, floating in front of Peer. "This modifies program A to surreptitiously carry out program B, given A is sufficiently more algorithmically complex than B. What that means, exactly, is in the technical appendix. Try it out, show it to your favorite expert system . . . verify it any way you like."

Peer took hold of the book, squeezed it down to credit-card size, and slipped it into the back pocket of his jeans. He said, "There's no reason why you shouldn't be able to do everything you claim: piggyback us onto the city, hide us from searches, protect us from optimization. But . . . why? What do you get out of this? What you're asking for is nothing, compared to what Durham must be paying you. So why take the risk? Or do you screw all your clients as a matter of principle?"

Carter chose to seem amused, not offended. "The practice of skimming off a percentage of a construction project has a long, honorable tradition. All the more honorable if the client's needs aren't seriously compromised. In this case, there's also some elegant programming involved—worth doing for its own sake. As for the money, I'm charging you enough to cover my costs." He exchanged a look with Kate—for Peer's benefit, or he wouldn't have seen it. "But in the end, I'm only making the offer as a favor. So if you think I'm going to cheat you, you're welcome to decline."

Peer changed tack. "What if Durham is cheating *his* clients? You're only screwing them out of a few QIPS—but what if Durham doesn't plan to run the city at all, just vanish with the money? Have you ever seen his hardware? Have you used it?"

"No. But he never claimed—to me—that he had his own hardware. The version of the story I got is that the city's going to run on the public networks. That's bullshit, of course; the Copies funding him wouldn't wear that for a second—it's just a polite way of telling me that the hardware is none of my business. And as for vanishing with the money, from what I can deduce about his cash flow, he'll be lucky to break even on the project. Which suggests to me that someone else entirely is handling the true financial arrangements; Durham is just a front man, and the real owner of the hardware will pay him for his troubles, once the whole thing is wrapped up."

"The owner of *what?* This hypothetical 'breakthrough machine' that nobody's laid eyes on?"

"If he's persuaded Sanderson and Repetto to pay him, then you can be sure he's shown them something that he hasn't shown me."

Peer was about to protest, but Carter's expression said: *take it or leave it, believe what you like. I've done this much for my ex-lover, but the truth is, I don't care if you're convinced or not.*

Carter excused himself. When he turned and walked away across the room, footsteps echoing in the cavernous space, Peer couldn't believe he would have hung around for the fifteen real-time minutes it took to reach the exit. Not a busy man like that. In fact, he'd probably conducted two or three other meetings with Copies while he'd been talking to them, dropping in and out of the conversation, leaving a mask to animate his features in his absence.

Kate said, "What's the worst that can happen? If Durham is a con man, if the city's a hoax, what have we lost? All money can buy us is QIPS—and you're the one who's so sure that it doesn't matter how slowly we run."

Peer scowled, still staring at the exit Carter had used, surprised to find himself reluctant to drag his gaze away. The door meant nothing to him. He said, "Half the charm of this lies in stealing a free ride. Or bribing Carter to steal it for us. There's not much . . . dignity in stowing away on a ship going nowhere."

"You could choose not to care."

"I don't want to do that. I don't pretend to be human, but I still have a . . . core personality. And I don't want equanimity. Equanimity is death."

"On the skyscraper—"

"On the skyscraper I rid myself of distractions. And it's confined to that one context. When I emerge, I still have goals. I still have desires." He turned to her, reached out and brushed her cheek with his fingers. "You could *choose not to care* about security. Or QIPS rates, weather control, the politics of computing—you could choose to view all the threatening noises of the outside world as so much flatulence. Then you wouldn't need, or want, to do this at all."

Kate left the body he was touching where it was, but took a step backward in another just like it. Peer let his hand drop to his side.

She said, "Once I'm part of this billionaires' city, I'll happily forget about the outside world. Once I have all that money and influence devoted to my survival."

"Do you mean, that will be enough to satisfy you—or do you intend making a conscious decision to *be* satisfied?"

She smiled enigmatically—and Peer made a conscious decision to be moved by the sight. She said, "I don't know yet. You'll have to wait and see."

Peer said nothing. He realized that, in spite of his doubts, he'd almost certainly follow her—and not just for the shock of creating a second version, not just for the sake of undermining his last anthropomorphic delusions. The truth was, he wanted to be with her. All of her. If he backed out and she went ahead, the knowledge that he'd passed up his one opportunity to have a version of himself accompany her would drive him mad. He wasn't sure if this was greed or affection, jealousy or loyalty—

but he knew he had to be a part of whatever she experienced in there.

It was an unsettling revelation. Peer took a snapshot of his state of mind.

Kate gestured toward the door which led to the sketch of the city.

Peer said, "Why bother with that? There'll be plenty of time to explore the real thing."

She looked at him oddly. "Don't you want to satisfy your curiosity? Now—and forever, for the one who'll stay behind?"

He thought about it, then shook his head. "One clone will see the finished city. One won't. Both will share a past when they'd never even heard of the place. The clone outside, who never sees the city, will try to guess what it's like. The clone inside will run other environments, and sometimes he won't think about the city at all. When he does, sometimes he'll mis-remember it. And sometimes he'll dream about wildly dis-torted versions of what he's seen.

"I define all those moments as part of me. So . . . what is there to be curious about?"

Kate said, "I love it when you go all doctrinaire on me." She stepped forward and kissed him—then as he reached out to hold her, she slipped away into yet another body, leaving him embracing nothing but dead weight. "Now shut up and let's go take a look."

Peer doubted that he'd ever know exactly why he'd died. No amount of agonized introspection, tortuous video-postcard interrogation of ex-friends, or even expert system analysis of his final scan file, had brought him any nearer to the truth. The gap was too wide to be bridged; the last four years of his corpo-real life had been lost to him—and the events of the period seemed more like an ill-fated excursion into a parallel world than any mere episode of amnesia.

The coroner had returned an open finding. Rock-climbing accidents were rare, the best technology was almost foolproof—

but David Hawthorne had scornfully eschewed all the mollycoddling refinements (including the black box implants which could have recorded the actions leading up to his death, if not the motives behind them). No pitons full of microchips, which could have performed ultrasound tomography of the cliff face and computed their own load-bearing capacity; no harness packed with intelligent crash balloons, which could have cushioned his sixty-meter fall onto jagged rocks; no robot climbing partner, which could have carried him twenty kilometers over rugged terrain with a broken spine and delivered him into intensive care as if he'd floated there on a cloud of morphine.

Peer could empathize, to a degree. What was the point of being scanned, only to remain enslaved by an obsolete respect for the body's fragility? Having triumphed over mortality, how could he have gone on living as if nothing had changed? Every biological instinct, every commonsense idea about the nature of *survival* had been rendered absurd—and he hadn't been able to resist the urge to dramatize the transformation.

That didn't prove that he'd wanted to die.

But whether his death had been pure misfortune, unequivocal suicide, or the result of some insanely dangerous stunt not (consciously) intended to be fatal, the four-years-out-of-date David Hawthorne had awakened in the virtual slums to realize that, personally, he'd given the prospect about as much serious consideration as that of awakening in Purgatory. Whatever he'd come to believe in those missing years, whatever he'd imagined in his last few seconds of life on that limestone overhang, up until his final scan he'd always pictured his virtual resurrection as taking place in the distant future, when either he'd be seriously wealthy, or the cost of computing would have fallen so far that money would scarcely matter.

He'd been forty-six years old, in perfect health; a senior executive with Incite PLC—Europe's twenty-fifth largest marketing firm—second-in-charge of the interactive targeted mail division. With care, he could have died at the age of a hundred and fifty, to become an instant member of the elite—perhaps, by then, in a cybernetic body barely distinguishable from the real thing.

But having paid for the right not to fear death, at some level he must have confused the kind of abstract, literary, morally-charged, beloved-of-fate immortality possessed by mythical heroes and virtuous believers in the afterlife, with the highly specific free-market version he'd actually signed up for. And whatever the convoluted psychological explanation for his death, in financial terms the result was very simple. He'd died too soon.

In a real-time week—a few subjective hours—he had gone from a model of flesh and blood in the lavish virtual apartment he'd bought at the time of his first scan, to a disembodied consciousness observing his Bunker. Even that hadn't been enough to let him cling to his role in the outside world. Full life insurance was not available to people who'd been scanned—let alone those who also indulged in dangerous recreations—and the coroner's verdict had even ruled out payment from the only over-priced watered-down substitute policy he'd been able to obtain. At a slowdown of thirty, the lowest Bunker-to-real-time factor the income from his investments could provide, communication was difficult, and productive work was impossible. Even if he'd started burning up his capital to buy the exclusive use of a processor cluster, the time-rate difference would still have rendered him unemployable. Copies whose trust funds controlled massive shareholdings, deceased company directors who sat on the unofficial boards which met twice a year and made three or four leisurely decisions, could live with the time-dilated economics of slowdown. Hawthorne had died before achieving the necessary financial critical mass—let alone the kind of director-emeritus status where he could be paid for nothing but his name on the company letterhead.

As the reality of his situation sank in, he'd spiraled into the blackest depression. Any number of expensive, disabling diseases might have dragged him from upper-middle-class comfort into comparitive poverty and isolation—but dying "poor" had an extra sting. In corporeal life, he'd happily gone along with the consensus: money as the deepest level of reality, ownership records as the definition of truth . . . while escaping most weekends to the manicured garden of the English countryside, camping beneath the clouds, clearing his head of the City's byzantine fictions—reminding himself how artificial, how arbitrary, it all was. He'd never quite deluded himself that he could have lived off the land: "vanishing" into a forest mapped twice a day by EarthSat on a centimeter scale; surviving on the flesh of protected species, tearing the radio-tracking collars off foxes and badgers with his bare teeth; stoically enduring any rare diseases and parasitic infestations to which his childhood vaccinations and polyclonal T-cell boosts hadn't granted him immunity. The truth was, he almost certainly would have starved, or gone insane—but that wasn't the point. What mattered was the fact that his genes were scarcely different from those of his hunter-gatherer ancestors of ten thousand years before; that air was still breathable, and free; that sunshine still flooded the planet, still drove the food chain, still maintained a climate in which he could survive. It wasn't physically impossible, it wasn't biologically absurd, to imagine *life without money.*

Watching the screens of his Bunker, he'd looked back on that trite but comforting understanding with a dizzying sense of loss—because it was no longer in his power to distance himself, however briefly, from the mass hallucination of commerce-as-reality, no longer possible to wrench some half-self-mocking sense of dignity and independence out of his hypothetical ability to live naked in the woods. Money had ceased to be a convenient fiction to be viewed with appropriate irony—because the computerized financial transactions which flowed from his investments to the network's QIPS providers now underpinned everything he thought, everything he perceived, everything he was.

Friendless, bodiless, the entire world he'd once inhabited transformed into nothing but a blur of scenery glimpsed through the window of a high-speed train, David Hawthorne had prepared to bale out.

It was Kate who had interrupted him. She'd been delegated to make a "welcoming call" by a slum-dwellers' committee, which she'd only joined in the hope that they'd sponsor one of her projects. This was before she'd made the conscious decision not to desire an audience for any of her art, rendering its quota of computing time relative to any other process irrelevant.

Hawthorne's only contact since his death had been brief recorded messages from ex-friends, ex-lovers, ex-relations and ex-colleagues, all more or less bidding him farewell, as if he'd embarked on a one-way voyage to a place beyond the reach of modern communications. There'd also been an offer of counseling from his scanning clinic's Resurrection Trauma expert system—first ten subjective minutes absolutely free. When Kate had appeared on his communications screen, synched to his time rate and talking back, he'd poured out his soul to her.

She'd persuaded him to postpone baling out until he'd considered the alternatives. She hadn't had to argue hard; the mere fact of her presence had already improved his outlook immeasurably. Thousands of Copies, she'd said, survived with slowdown factors of thirty, sixty, or worse—playing no part in human society, earning no money but the passive income from their trust funds, living at their own speed, defining their worth on their own terms. He had nothing to lose by trying it himself.

And if he couldn't accept that kind of separatist existence? He always had the choice of suspending himself, in the hope that the economics of ontology would eventually shift in his favor—albeit at the risk of waking to find that he'd matched speeds with a world far stranger, far harder to relate to, than the present in fast motion.

For someone whose fondest hope had been to wake in a robot body and carry on living as if nothing had changed, the slums were a shock. Kate had shown him around the Slow Clubs—the meeting places for Copies willing to synch to the rate of the slowest person present. Not a billionaire in sight. At the Cabaret Andalou, the musicians presented as living saxophones and guitars, songs were visible, tangible, psychotropic radiation blasting from the mouths of the singers— and on a good night, a strong enough sense of camaraderie, telepathy, synergy, could by the mutual consent of the crowd take over, melting away (for a moment) all personal barriers, mental and mock-physical, reconstructing audience and performers into a single organism: one hundred eyes, two hundred limbs, one giant neural net resonating with the memories, perceptions and emotions of all the people it had been.

Kate had shown him some of the environments she'd bought—and some she'd built herself—where she lived and worked in solitude. An overgrown, oversized, small-town back garden in early summer, an enhanced and modified childhood memory, where she carved solid sculptures out of nothing but the ten-to-the-ten-thousandth possibilities of color, texture and form. A bleak gray stretch of shoreline under eternally threatening clouds, the sky dark oil on canvas, a painting come to life, where she went to calm herself when she chose not to make the conscious decision to be calm.

She'd helped him redesign his apartment, transforming it from a photorealist concrete box into a system of perceptions which could be as stable, or responsive, as he wished. Once, before sleep, he'd wrapped the structure around himself like a sleeping bag, shrinking and softening it until the kitchen cradled his head and the other rooms draped his body. He'd changed the topology so that every window looked in through another window, every wall abutted another wall; the whole thing closed in on itself in every direction, finite but borderless, universe-as-womb.

And Kate had introduced him to Daniel Lebesgue's interactive philosophical plays: *The Beholder, The Sane Man* (his adaptation of Pirandello's *Enrico IV*), and, of course, *Solipsist Nation.* Hawthorne had taken the role of John Beckett, a reluctant Copy obsessed with keeping track of the outside world—who ends up literally becoming an entire society and culture himself. The play's software hadn't enacted that fate upon Hawthorne—intended for visitors and Copies alike, it worked on the level of perceptions and metaphors, not neural reconstruction. Lebesgue's ideas were mesmerizing, but imprecise, and even he had never tried to carry them through—so far as anyone knew. He'd vanished from sight in 2036; becoming a recluse, baling out, or suspending himself, nobody could say. His disciples wrote manifestos, and prescriptions for virtual utopias; in the wider vernacular, though, to be "Solipsist Nation" simply meant to have ceased deferring to the outside world.

Three subjective weeks—almost four real-time years—after his resurrection, Hawthorne had stepped off the merry-go-round long enough to catch up with the news from outside. There'd been nothing especially dramatic or unexpected in the summaries—no shocking political upheavals, no stunning technological breakthroughs, no more nor less civil war or famine than in the past. The BBC's headlines of the day: Five hundred people had died in storms in southeast England. The European Federation had cut its intake of environmental refugees by forty percent. Korean investors had gone ahead with a threatened embargo on US government bonds, as part of a trade war over biotechnology tariffs, and utilities had begun disconnecting power, water and communications services from federal buildings. Up-to-the-minute details notwithstanding, it had all seemed as familiar as some brand-name breakfast food: the same texture, the same taste, as he remembered from four, from eight, years before. With his eyes locked on the terminal in front of him, the oddly soothing generic images drawing him in, the three hallucinatory weeks of dancing saxophones and habitable paintings had receded into insignificance, as if they'd been nothing but a vivid dream. Or at least something on another channel, with no risk of being mistaken for news.

Kate had said, "You know, you can sit here forever, watch this forever, if that's what you want. There are Copies—we call them Witnesses—who refine themselves into . . . systems . . . which do nothing but monitor the news, as thoroughly as their slowdown allows. No bodies, no fatigue, no distractions. Pure observers, watching history unfold."

"That's not what I want."

He hadn't taken his eyes off the screen, though. Inexplicably, he'd started to cry, softly, grieving for something that he couldn't name. Not the world defined by the news systems; he'd never inhabited that place. Not the people who'd sent him their recorded farewells; they'd been useful at the time, but they meant nothing to him anymore.

"But?"

"But outside is still what's real to me—even if I can't be a part of it. *Flesh and blood. Solid ground. Real sunlight.* It's still the only world that matters, in the end. I can't pretend I don't know that. Everything in here is just beautiful, inconsequential fiction." *Including you. Including me.*

Kate had said, "You can change that."

"Change what? Virtual Reality is Virtual Reality. I can't transform it into something else."

"You can change your perspective. Change your attitudes. Stop viewing your experiences here as *less than real.*"

"That's easier said than done."

"But it isn't."

She'd summoned up a control panel, shown him the software he could use: a program which would analyze his model-of-a-brain, identify his qualms and misgivings about turning his back on the world—and remove them.

"A do-it-yourself lobotomy."

"Hardly. There's no 'physical' excision. The program carries out trial-and-error adjustment of synaptic weights, until it finds the minimum possible alteration which achieves the desired goal. A few billion short-lived stripped-down versions of your brain will be tested and discarded along the way, but don't let that bother you."

"You've run this on yourself?"

She'd laughed. "Yes. Out of curiosity. But it found nothing to change in me. I'd already made up my mind. Even on the outside, I knew this was what I wanted."

"So . . . I press a button and there's someone new sitting here? One instant synthetic satisfied customer? I annihilate myself, just like that?"

"You're the one who jumped off a cliff."

"No. I'm the one who didn't."

"You won't 'annihilate yourself.' You'll only change as much as you have to. And you'll still call yourself David Hawthorne. What more can you ask for? What more have you ever done?"

They'd talked it through for hours, debating the fine philosophical and moral points; the difference between "naturally" accepting his situation, and imposing acceptance upon himself. In the end, though, when he'd made the decision, it had seemed like just another part of the dream, just another inconsequential fiction. In that sense, the old David Hawthorne had been true to his beliefs—even as he rewired them out of existence.

Kate had been wrong about one thing. Despite the perfect continuity of his memories, he'd felt compelled to mark the transition by choosing a new name, plucking the whimsical monosyllable out of thin air.

The "minimum possible alteration"? Perhaps if he had ended up less radically Solipsist Nation, far more of his personality would have to have been distorted for him to have been convinced at all. A few bold necessary cuts had squared the circle, instead of a thousand finicky mutilations.

That first change, though, had cleared the way for many more, a long series of self-directed mutations. Peer (by choice) had no patience with nostalgia or sentimentality; if any part of his personality offended him, he struck it out. Some traits had (most likely) vanished forever: a horde of petty jealousies, vanities, misgivings and pointless obsessions; a tendency to irrational depression and guilt. Others came and went. Peer had acquired, removed and restored a variety of talents, mood predispositions and drives; cravings for knowledge, art and physical experience. In a few subjective days, he could change from an ascetic bodiless student of Sumerian archaeology, to a hedonistic gastronome delighting in nothing more than the preparation and consumption of lavishly simulated feasts, to a disciplined practitioner of Shotokan karate.

A core remained; certain values, certain emotional responses, certain aesthetic sensibilities had survived these transitions unscathed.

As had the will to survive itself.

Peer had once asked himself: Was that kernel of invariants—and the more-or-less unbroken thread of memory— enough? Had David Hawthorne, by another name, achieved the immortality he'd paid for? Or had he died somewhere along the way?

There was no answer. The most that could be said, at any moment, was that someone existed who knew—or believed—that they'd once been David Hawthorne.

And so Peer had made the conscious decision to let that be enough.

12

(Rip, tie, cut toy man)

JUNE 2045

Paul switched on the terminal and made contact with his old
organic self. The *djinn* looked tired and frayed; all the begging and bribery required to set up the latest stage of the
experiment must have taken its toll. Paul felt more alive than
he'd ever felt, in any incarnation; his stomach was knotted
with something like fear, but the electric tingling of his skin
felt more like the anticipation of triumph. His body was about
to be mutilated, carved up beyond recognition—and yet he
knew he would survive, suffer no harm, feel no pain.

Squeak. "Experiment three, trial zero. Baseline data. All
computations performed by processor cluster number four six
two, Hitachi Supercomputer Facility, Tokyo."

"One. Two. Three." It was nice to be told where he was, at
last; Paul had never visited Japan before. "Four. Five. Six."
And on his own terms, he still hadn't. The view out the window
was Sydney, not Tokyo; why defer to the external geography,
when it made no difference at all? "Seven. Eight. Nine. Ten."

Squeak. "Trial number one. Model partitioned into five
hundred sections, run on five hundred processor clusters, dis-
tributed globally."

Paul counted. *Five hundred clusters.* Five only for the
crudely modeled external world; all the rest were allocated
to his body—and most to the brain. He lifted his hand to
his eyes—and the information flow that granted him motor
control and sight traversed tens of thousands of kilometers
of optical cable. There was no (perceptible) delay; each
part of him simply hibernated when necessary, waiting for
the requisite feedback from around the world.

It was, of course, pure lunacy, computationally and economically; Paul guessed that he was costing at least a hundred times as much as usual—not quite five hundred, since each cluster's capacity was only being partly used—and his slowdown factor had probably risen from seventeen to as much as fifty. Once, it had been hoped that devoting hundreds of computers to each Copy might improve the slowdown problem, not worsen it—but the bottlenecks in shifting data between processor clusters kept even the richest Copies from reducing the factor below seventeen. It didn't matter how many supercomputers you owned, because splitting yourself between them wasted more time on communications than was saved by the additional computing power.

Squeak. "Trial number two. One thousand sections, one thousand clusters."

Brain the size of a planet—and here I am, counting to ten. Paul recalled the perennial—naive and paranoid—fear that all the networked computers of the world might one day spontaneously give birth to a global hypermind; but he was, almost certainly, the first planet-sized intelligence on Earth. He didn't feel much like a digital Gaia, though. He felt exactly like an ordinary human being sitting in a room a few meters wide.

Squeak. "Trial number three. Model partitioned into fifty sections and twenty time sets, implemented on one thousand clusters."

"One. Two. Three." Paul struggled to imagine the outside world on his own terms, but it was almost impossible. Not only was he scattered across the globe, but widely separated machines were simultaneously computing different moments of his subjective time frame. Was the distance from Tokyo to New York now the length of his *corpus callosum?* Had the world shrunk to the size of his skull—and vanished from time altogether, except for the fifty computers which contributed at any one time to what he called "the present"?

Maybe not—although in the eyes of some hypothetical space traveler the whole planet was virtually frozen in time, and flat as a pancake. Relativity declared that this point of view was perfectly valid—but Paul's was not. Relativity permitted continuous deformation, but no cutting and pasting. *Why not?* Because it had to allow for *cause and effect.* Influences had to be localized, traveling from point to point at a finite velocity; chop up space-time and rearrange it, and the causal structure would fall apart.

What if you were an observer, though, who had no causal structure? A self-aware pattern appearing by chance in the random twitches of a noise machine, your time coordinate dancing back and forth through causally respectable "real time"? Why should you be declared a second-class being, with no right to see the universe your way? Ultimately, what difference was there between so-called cause and effect, and any other internally consistent pattern?

Squeak. "Trial number four. Model partitioned into fifty sections and twenty time sets; sections and states randomly allocated to one thousand clusters."

"One. Two. Three."

Paul stopped counting, stretched his arms wide, stood up slowly. He wheeled around once, to examine the room, checking that it was still intact, still complete. Then he whispered, "This is dust. *All dust.* This room, this moment, is scattered across the planet, scattered across five hundred seconds or more—*but it still holds itself together.* Don't you see what that means?"

The *djinn* reappeared, but Paul didn't give him a chance to speak. The words flowed out of him, unstoppable. *He understood.*

"Imagine . . . a universe entirely without structure, without shape, without connections. A cloud of microscopic events, like fragments of space-time . . . except that there *is no* space or time. What characterizes one point in space, for one instant? Just the values of the fundamental particle fields, just a handful of numbers. Now, take away all notions of position, arrangement, order, and what's left? A cloud of random numbers.

"That's it. That's all there is. The cosmos has no shape at all—no such thing as time or distance, no physical laws, no cause and effect.

"But . . . if the pattern that is *me* could pick itself out from all the other events taking place on this planet . . . why shouldn't the pattern we think of as 'the universe' assemble *itself,* find *itself,* in exactly the same way? If I can piece together my own coherent space and time from data scattered so widely that it might as well be part of some giant cloud of random numbers . . . *then what makes you think that you're not doing the very same thing?"*

The *djinn*'s expression hovered between alarm and irritation.

Squeak. "Paul . . . what's the point of all this? 'Space-time is a construct; the universe is really nothing but a sea of disconnected events . . . ' Assertions like that are meaningless. You can believe it if you want to . . . but what difference would it make?"

"What difference? We perceive—we *inhabit*—one arrangement of the set of events. *But why should that arrangement be unique?* There's no reason to believe that the pattern we've found is the only coherent way of ordering the dust. There must be billions of other universes coexisting with us, made of the very same stuff—just differently arranged. If *I* can perceive events thousands of kilometers and hundreds of seconds apart to be side by side and simultaneous, there could be worlds, and creatures, built up from what we'd think of as points in space-time scattered all over the galaxy, all over the universe. We're one possible solution to a giant cosmic anagram . . . but it would be ludicrous to believe that we're *the only one.*"

Squeak. Durham snorted. "A cosmic anagram? So where are all the leftover letters? If any of this were true—and the primordial alphabet soup really is random—don't you think it's highly unlikely that we could structure the whole thing?"

Paul thought about it. "We *haven't* structured the whole thing. The universe *is* random, at the quantum level. Macroscopically, the pattern seems to be perfect; microscopically, it decays into uncertainty. We've swept the residue of randomness down to the lowest level."

Squeak. The *djinn* strived visibly for patience. "Paul . . . none of this could ever be tested. How would anyone ever observe a planet whose constituent parts were scattered across the universe, let alone communicate with its hypothetical inhabitants? What you're saying might have a certain—purely mathematical—validity: grind the universe into fine enough dust, and maybe it could be rearranged in other ways that make as much sense as the original. If those rearranged worlds are inaccessible, though, it's all angels on the heads of pins."

"How can you say that? I've *been* rearranged! I've *visited* another world!"

Squeak. "If you did, it was an artificial world; created, not discovered."

"Found, created . . . there's no real difference."

Squeak. "What are you claiming? Some influence from this *other world* flowed into the computers, changed the way the model ran?"

"Of course not! Your pattern hasn't been violated; the computers did exactly what was expected of them. That doesn't invalidate my perspective. Stop thinking of explanations, causes and effects; there are only *patterns*. The scattered events that formed my experience had an internal consistency every bit as real as the consistency in the actions of the computers. And perhaps the computers didn't provide all of it."

Squeak. "What do you mean?"

"The gaps, in experiment one. What filled them in? What was I *made of,* when the processors weren't describing me? Well . . . it's a big universe. Plenty of dust to *be me,* in between descriptions. Plenty of events—nothing to do with your computers, maybe nothing to do with your planet or your epoch—out of which to construct ten seconds of experience."

Squeak. The *djinn* looked seriously worried now. "You're a Copy in a virtual environment under computer control. Nothing more, nothing less. These experiments prove that your internal sense of space and time is invariant. That's exactly what we always expected—remember? Come down to Earth. Your states are *computed,* your memories *have to be* what they would have been without manipulation. You haven't visited any other worlds, you haven't built yourself out of fragments of distant galaxies."

Paul laughed. "Your stupidity is . . . surreal. What did you *create me for,* if you're not even going to listen to what I have to say? I've had a glimpse of the truth behind . . . everything: space, time, the laws of physics. You can't shrug that off by saying that what happened to me was *inevitable*."

Squeak. "Control and subject are still identical."

"Of course they are! That's the whole point! Like . . . gravity and acceleration in General Relativity—it all depends on what you *can't tell apart*. This is a new Principle of Equivalence, a new symmetry between observers. Relativity threw out absolute space and time—but it didn't go far enough. We have to throw out absolute cause and effect!"

Squeak. The *djinn* muttered, dismayed, "Elizabeth said this would happen. She said it was only a matter of time before you'd lose touch."

Paul stared at him, jolted back to the mundane. "*Elizabeth?* You said you hadn't even told her."

Squeak. "Well, I have now. I didn't tell you, because I didn't think you'd want to hear her reaction."

"Which was?"

Squeak. "I was up all night arguing with her. She wanted me to shut you down. She said I was . . . seriously disturbed, to even think about doing this."

Paul was stung. "What would she know? Ignore her."

Squeak. Durham frowned apologetically—an expression Paul recognized at once, and his guts turned to ice. "Maybe I should pause you, while I think things over. Elizabeth raised some . . . valid ethical questions. I think I should talk it through with her again."

"Fuck that! I'm not here for you to put on ice every time you have a change of heart. And if Elizabeth wants to have a say in my life, she can damn well talk it through with *me*."

Paul could see exactly what would happen. If he was paused, Durham wouldn't restart *him*—he'd go back to the original scan file and start again from scratch, handling his prisoner differently, hoping to end up with a more cooperative subject. Maybe he wouldn't even perform the first set of experiments at all.

The ones which had given him this insight.

The ones which had made him who he was.

Squeak. "I need time to think. It would only be temporary. I promise."

"*No!* You have no right!"

Durham hesitated. Paul felt numb, disbelieving. Some part of him refused to acknowledge any danger—refused to accept that it could be this easy to die. Being paused wouldn't kill him, wouldn't harm him, wouldn't have the slightest effect. What would kill him would be not being restarted. He'd be passively annihilated, ignored out of existence. The fate that befell his own shit.

Durham reached offscreen.

13

(Remit not paucity)

Maria said, "Recalculate everything up to epoch five, then show me sunrise on Lambert. Latitude zero, longitude zero, altitude one."

She waited, staring into the blank workspace, fighting the temptation to change her instructions and have the software display every stage of the simulation, which would have slowed things down considerably. After several minutes, a fissured dark plain appeared, raked with silver light. The unnamed sun—dazzling and swollen, and, so low in the sky, too white by far—turned a chain of extinct volcanoes on the horizon into black silhouettes like a row of pointed teeth. In the foreground, the surface looked glassy, inhospitable.

Maria raised her viewpoint to a thousand meters, then sent it skimming east. The terrain repeated itself, the eerily symmetric cones of dead volcanoes the only relief from the fractured igneous plains. This specific, detailed scenery was nothing more than a series of computerized "artist's impressions," manufactured on demand from purely statistical data about the planet's topography; the simulation itself hadn't dealt with anything so finicky as individual volcanoes. Touring the planet was a wasteful means of finding out anything—but it was hard to resist playing explorer, treating this world as if its secrets had to be deduced painstakingly from its appearance . . . even when the truth was the exact opposite. Reluctantly, Maria froze the image and went straight to the underlying numerical data. The atmosphere was much too thin, again. And this time, there was almost no *aqua* at all.

She backtracked through the simulation's history to see when the *aqua* had been lost, but this version of Lambert had never possessed significant oceans—or ice caps, or atmospheric vapor. She'd made a slight change in the composition of the primordial gas-and-dust cloud, increasing the proportion of *blue* and *yellow* atoms, in the hope that this would ultimately lead to a denser atmosphere for Lambert. Instead, she'd caused more than half of the debris in the Kuiper belt to condense into a whole new stable outer planet. As a consequence, far fewer ice-rich comets from the belt had ended up striking Lambert, robbing it of its largest source of *aqua* by far—and much of its atmosphere. Gas released by volcanic eruptions provided a poor substitute; the pressure was far too low, and the chemistry was all wrong.

Maria was beginning to wish she'd kept her mouth shut. It had taken her almost an hour on the phone to persuade Durham that it was worth trying to give Lambert a proper astronomical context, and a geological history that stretched back to the birth of its sun.

"If we present this world as a *fait accompli,* and say: "Look, it can exist in the Autoverse" . . . the obvious response to that will be: "Yes, it can *exist*—if you put it there by hand—but that doesn't mean it's ever likely to have *formed.*" If we can demonstrate a range of starting conditions that lead to planetary systems with suitable worlds, that will be one less element of uncertainty to be used against us."

Durham had eventually agreed, so she'd taken an off-the-shelf planetary-system modeling program—irreverently titled **The Laplacian Casino**—and adapted it to Autoverse chemistry and physics; not the deep physics of the Autoverse cellular automaton, but the macroscopic consequences of those rules. Mostly, that came down to specifying the properties of various Autoverse molecules: bond energies, melting and boiling points versus pressure, and so on. *Aqua* was not just water by another name, *yellow* atoms were not identical to nitrogen—and although some chemical reactions could be translated as if there was a one-to-one correspondence, in the giant fractionating still of a protostellar nebula subtle differences in relative densities and volatilities could have profound effects on the final composition of each of the planets.

There were also some fundamental differences. Since the Autoverse had no nuclear forces, the sun would be heated solely by gravitational energy—the velocity its molecules acquired as the diffuse primordial gas cloud fell in on itself. In the real universe, stars unable to ignite fusion reactions ended up as cold, short-lived brown dwarfs—but under Autoverse physics, gravitational heating could power a large enough star for billions of years. (Units of space and time were not strictly translatable—but everybody but the purists did it. If a *red* atom's width was taken to be that of hydrogen, and one grid-spacing per clock-tick was taken as the speed of light, a more or less sensible correspondence emerged.) Similarly, although Planet Lambert would lack internal heating from radioisotope decay, its own gravitational heat of formation would be great enough to drive tectonic activity for almost as long as the sun shone.

Without nuclear fusion to synthesize the elements, their origin remained a mystery, and a convenient gas cloud with traces of all thirty-two—and the right mass and rotational velocity—had to be taken for granted. Maria would have liked to have explored the cloud's possible origins, but she knew the project would never be finished if she kept lobbying Durham to expand the terms of reference. The point was to explore the potential diversity of Autoverse life, not to invent an entire cosmology.

Gravity in the Autoverse came as close as real-world gravity to the classical, Newtonian inverse-square law for the range of conditions that mattered, so all the usual real-world orbital dynamics applied. At extreme densities, the cellular automaton's discrete nature would cause it to deviate wildly from Newton—and Einstein, and Chu—but Maria had no intention of peppering her universe with black holes, or other exotica.

In fact, gravity had been seen as an irrelevant side effect of Lambert's original choice of automaton rules—since running an Autoverse large enough for it to make the slightest difference was blatantly impossible—and several people had tried to remove the redundancy, while leaving everything else intact. Nobody had succeeded, though; their "rationalized" versions had always failed to generate anything remotely like the rich chemistry of the original. A Peruvian mathematician, Ricardo Salazar, had eventually proved that they shouldn't have bothered: the Autoverse rules were poised on the border between two radically different levels of algorithmic complexity, and any tinkering in the hope of improved efficiency was necessarily self-defeating. The presence or absence of gravity, in itself, had no bearing on Autoverse chemistry—but the roots of both phenomena in the simple automaton rules seemed to be inextricably entwined.

Maria was aiming for a star with four planets. Three small worlds, one giant. The seed-world, Lambert, second from the sun—with a decent-sized moon if possible. Whether or not tidal pools had been a driving force in real-world evolution, life's bridge from sea to land (and even though the sun itself would cause small tides, regardless), it couldn't hurt to make Lambert as generally Earth-like as possible, since Earth was still the only example to turn to for inspiration. With so much about terrestrial evolution still in dispute, the safest policy was to cover every factor which might have been significant. The gravitational effects of the other planets would ensure a reasonably complex set of Milankovitch cycles: minor orbital changes and axis wobbles, providing long-term climate variations, ice ages and interglacials. A belt of comets and other debris would complete the picture; not merely supplying an atmosphere, early on, but also offering the chance of occasional mass-extinctions for billions of years to come.

The trick was to ensure that all of these supposedly evolution-enhancing features coincided with a version of Lambert which could support the seed organism in the first place. Maria had half a dozen possible modifications to *A. lamberti* in mind, to render it self-sufficient, but she was waiting to see what kind of environments were available before making a final decision.

That still left unanswered the question of whether the seed organism—or life of any kind—could have *arisen* on Lambert, rather than being placed there by human hands. Max Lambert's original reason for designing the Autoverse had been the hope of observing self-replicating molecular systems—primitive life—arising from simple chemical mixtures. The Autoverse was meant to provide a compromise between real-world chemistry—difficult and expensive to manipulate and monitor in test-tube experiments, and hideously slow to compute in faithful simulations—and the tantalizing abstractions of the earliest "artificial life": computer viruses, genetic algorithms, self-replicating machines embedded in simple cellular automaton worlds; all trivially easy to compute, but unable to throw much light on the genesis of real-world molecular biology.

Lambert had spent a decade trying to find conditions which would lead to the spontaneous appearance of Autoverse life, without success. He'd constructed *A. lamberti*—a twelve-year project—to reassure himself that his goal wasn't absurd; to demonstrate that a living organism could at least *function* in the Autoverse, however it had come to be there. *A. lamberti* had permanently side-tracked him; he'd never returned to his original research.

Maria had daydreamed about embarking on her own attempt at abiogenesis, but she'd never done anything about it. That kind of work was open-ended; in comparison, any problems with mutation in *A. lamberti* seemed utterly tractable and well-defined. And although, in a sense, it went to the heart of what Durham was trying to prove, she was glad he'd chosen to compromise; if he'd insisted on starting his "thought experiment" with a totally sterile world, the uncertainties in the transition from inanimate matter to the simplest Autoverse life would have overwhelmed every other aspect of the project.

She scrapped the desert Planet Lambert and returned to the primordial gas cloud. She popped up a gadget full of slider controls and adjusted the cloud's composition, taking back half the increases she'd made in the proportions of *blue* and *yellow*. Planetology by trial and error. The starting conditions for real-world systems with Earth-like planets had been mapped out long ago, but nobody had ever done the equivalent for the Autoverse. Nobody had ever had a reason.

Maria felt a flicker of unease. Each time she stopped to remind herself that these worlds would never exist—not even in the sense that a culture of *A. lamberti* "existed"—the whole project seemed to shift perspective, to retreat into the distance like a mirage. The work itself was exhilarating, she couldn't have asked for anything more, but each time she forced herself to put it all into context—not in the Autoverse, but in the real world—she found herself light-headed, disoriented. Durham's reasons for the project were so much flimsier than the watertight internal logic of the thing itself; stepping back from the work was like stepping off a rock-solid planet and seeing it turn into nothing but a lightly tethered balloon.

She stood and walked over to the window, and parted the curtains. The street below was deserted; the concrete glowed in the hyperreal glare of the midday sun.

Durham was paying her good money—money that would help get Francesca scanned. That was reason enough to press on. And if the project was ultimately useless, at least it did no harm; it was better than working on some hedonistic VR resort or some interactive war game for psychotic children. She let the curtain fall back into place and returned to her desk.

The cloud floated in the middle of the workspace, roughly spherical, rendered visible in spite of the fact that its universe was empty of stars. That was a shame; it meant the future citizens of Lambert were destined to be alone. They'd have no prospect of ever encountering alien life—unless they built their own computers, and modeled other planetary systems, other biospheres.

Maria said, "Recalculate. Then show me sunrise again."

She waited.

And this time—*false colors, by definition*—the disk of the sun was bright cherry red, beneath a thick bank of clouds streaked orange and violet, spread across the sky—and the whole scene was repeated, stretched out before her, shimmering, inverted. Mirrored in the face of the waters.

By a quarter to eight, Maria was thinking about logging off and grabbing some food. She was still on a high, but she could feel how close she was coming to the point where she'd be useless for the next thirty-six hours if she pushed herself any further.

She'd found a range of starting conditions for the cloud which consistently gave rise to hospitable versions of Lambert, along with all the astronomical criteria she'd been aiming for—except for the large satellite, which would have been a nice touch but wasn't critical. Tomorrow, she could begin the task of providing *A. lamberti* with the means of surviving alone on this world, manufacturing its own *nutrose* from thin air, with the help of sunlight. Other workers had already designed a variety of energy-trapping pigment molecules; the "literal translation" of chlorophyll lacked the right photochemical properties, but a number of useful analogues had been found, and it was a matter of determining which could be integrated into the bacteria's biochemistry with the fewest complications. Bringing photosynthesis to the Autoverse would be the hardest part of the project, but Maria felt confident; she'd studied Lambert's notes, and she'd familiarized herself with the full range of techniques he'd developed for adapting biochemical processes to the quirks of Autoverse chemistry. And even if the pigment she chose, for the sake of expediency, wasn't the most efficient molecule for the task, as long as the seed organism could survive and reproduce it would have the potential to stumble on a better solution itself, eventually.

The potential, if not the opportunity.

She was about to shut down **The Laplacian Casino** when a message appeared in the foreground of the workspace:

Juno: Statistical analysis of response times and error rates suggests that your link to the JSN is being monitored. Would you like to switch to a more heavily encrypted protocol?

Maria shook her head, amused. It had to be a bug in the software, not a bug on the line. **Juno** was a public-domain program (free, but all donations welcome) which she'd downloaded purely as a gesture of solidarity with the US privacy lobby. Federal laws there still made bug-detection software, and any half-decent encryption algorithms, illegal for personal use—lest the FBI be inconvenienced—so Maria had sent **Juno**'s authors a donation to help them fight the good fight. Actually installing the program had been a joke; the idea of anyone going to the trouble of listening in to her conversations with her mother, her tedious VR contract work, or her self-indulgent excursions into the Autoverse, was ludicrous.

Still, the joke had to be carried through. She popped up a word processor on the JSN—the terminal's local one wouldn't have shown up to an eavesdropper tapping the fiber—and typed:

Whoever you are, be warned: I'm about to display the Langford Mind-Erasing Fractal Basilisk, so

The doorbell rang. Maria checked the peephole camera's view. There was a woman on the front step, nobody she knew. Early forties, conservatively dressed. The not-so-subtle giveaway was clearly visible behind her: one compact two-seater Mitsubishi "Avalon" electric car. The New South Wales Police Department were probably the only people in the world who'd bought that model, before the Bankstown factory closed down in forty-six. Maria had often wondered why they didn't give in and fit blue flashing lights to all their supposedly unmarked cars; acknowledging the situation would have been more dignified than carrying on as if nobody knew.

Dredging her memory for recent misdemeanors—but finding none—she hurried downstairs.

"Maria Deluca?"

"Yes."

"I'm Detective-Sergeant Hayden. Computer Fraud Squad. I'd like to ask you a few questions, if that's convenient."

Maria rescanned for guilty secrets; still no trace—but she would have preferred a visitor from Homicide or Armed Robbery, someone who'd clearly come to the wrong house. She said, "Yes, of course. Come in." Then, as she backed away from the door, "Ah—I nearly forgot, I suppose I should verify . . . ?"

Hayden, with a thin smile of blatantly insincere approval, let Maria plug her notepad into the socket of her Police Department badge. The notepad beeped cheerfully; the badge knew the private code which matched the current public key being broadcast by the Department.

Seated in the living room, Hayden got straight to the point. She displayed a picture on her notepad.

"Do you know this man?"

Maria cleared her throat. "Yes. His name's Paul Durham. I'm . . . working for him. He's given me some contract programming." She felt no surprise; just the jolt of being brought down to earth. *Of course the Fraud Squad were interested in Durham. Of course the whole fantasy of the last three months was about to unravel before her eyes.* Aden had warned her. She'd known it herself. It was a dream contract, too good to be true.

An instant later, though, she backed away from that reaction, furious with herself. Durham had paid the money into the trust fund, hadn't he? He'd met the costs of her new JSN account. He hadn't cheated her. *Too good to be true* was idiot fatalism. Two consenting adults had kept all their promises to each other; the fact that no outsider would understand the transaction didn't make it a crime. And after all he'd done for her, at the very least she owed him the benefit of the doubt.

Hayden said, "What kind of 'contract programming'?"

Maria did her best to explain without taking all night. Hayden was—not surprisingly—reasonably computer literate, and even knew what a cellular automaton was, but either she hadn't heard of the Autoverse, or she wanted to hear it all again from Maria.

"So you believe this man's paying you thirty thousand dollars . . . to help him state his position on a purely theoretical question about artificial life?"

Maria tried not to sound defensive. "I've spent tens of thousands of dollars on the Autoverse, myself. It's like a lot of other hobbies; it's a world unto itself. People can get obsessive, extravagant. It's no stranger than . . . building model airplanes. Or reenacting battles from the American Civil War."

Hayden didn't argue the point, but she seemed unmoved by

the comparisons. "Did you know that Paul Durham sold insurance to Copies?"

"I knew he was an insurance salesman. He told me that himself. Just because he's not a professional programmer doesn't mean he can't—"

"Did you know he was also trying to sell his clients shares in some kind of sanctuary? A place to go—or to send a clone—in case the political climate turned against them?"

Maria blinked. "No. What do you mean—a sanctuary? A privately owned supercomputer? He's been trying to raise money, form a consortium . . . ?"

Hayden said flatly, "He's certainly raising money—but I doubt he'll ever raise enough to purchase the kind of hardware he'd need for the kind of service he's offering."

"So, what are you accusing him of doing? Embarking on a business venture which you don't happen to believe will be successful?" Hayden said nothing. "Have you spoken to him about this? There might be a simple explanation for whatever you've been told. Some senile Copy might have taken his sales pitch for a perpetuity fund the wrong way." *Senile Copy?* Well . . . some postdementia scan file might have proved resistant to the cognitive repair algorithms.

Hayden said, "Of course we've spoken to him. He's refused to cooperate, he won't discuss the matter. That's why we're hoping you'll be able to assist us."

Maria's defiant optimism wavered. *If Durham had nothing to hide, why would he refuse to defend himself?*

She said, "I don't see how I can help you. If you think he's been misleading his clients, go talk to his clients. It's their testimony you need, not mine."

There was an awkward pause, then Hayden said, "The testimony of a Copy has no standing; legally, they're just another kind of computer software."

Maria opened her mouth, then realized that any excuse she offered would only make her sound more foolish. She salvaged some pride with the silent observation that the legal position of Copies was so farcical that any sane person could have trouble keeping it in mind.

Hayden continued. "Durham could be charged with defrauding the executors of the estates, by means of supplying misleading data to the software they use to advise them. There are precedents for that; it's like publishing false prospectus information that causes automated share-buying programs to buy your stock. But there's still the question of evidence. We can interview Copies as an informal source of information, to guide an investigation, but nothing they say will stand up in court."

Maria recalled an episode of *The Unclear Family* where a similar problem had arisen. Babette and Larry Unclear had witnessed bank accounts being pilfered, when the relevant data trail had—inexplicably—taken solid form as an accusing tableau of ice-sculptures in their cyber-suburban backyard. She couldn't recall exactly how the plot had turned out; ten-year-old Leroy had probably done something marginally illegal, but morally unimpeachable, to trick the thieves into giving themselves away to the authorities . . .

She said, "I don't know what you expect me to tell you. Durham hasn't defrauded *me*. And I don't know anything about this scheme."

"But you're working on it with him."

"I certainly am not!"

Hayden said drily, "You're designing a planet for him. What do you think that's for?"

Maria stared at her blankly for a second, then almost laughed. "I'm sorry, I can't have explained things very well. I'm designing a planet that "could" exist in the Autoverse, in the broadest sense of the word. It's a *mathematical possibility*. But it's too large to be run on a real computer. It's not some VR—"

Hayden cut her off. "I understand that perfectly. That doesn't mean Durham's clients would have grasped the distinction. Technical details about the Autoverse aren't exactly general knowledge."

True. Maria hesitated. But—

"It still makes no sense. For a start, these people would have advisers, researchers, who'd tell them that anyone promising them an Autoverse planet was full of shit. And why would Durham *offer them* an Autoverse planet—covered in primordial slime—when he could offer them a standard set of VR environments which would be a thousand times more attractive and a thousand times more plausible?"

"I believe he's offering them both. He's hired an architect in the US to work on the VR part."

"But why *both?* Why not just VR? You couldn't fit a single Copy into the Autoverse—and if you did, it would die on the spot. It would take fifty or sixty years of research to translate human biochemistry into Autoverse terms."

"They wouldn't know that."

"They could find out in ten seconds flat. Forget about advisers; it would take one call to a knowledge miner, total cost five dollars. So why tell a lie that could be so easily uncovered? What's the advantage—from a Copy's point of view—of an Autoverse planet over patchwork VR?"

Hayden was unfazed. "You're the Autoverse expert. So you tell me."

"I don't know." Maria stood up. She was beginning to feel claustrophobic; she hated having strangers in the house. "Can I get you something to drink? Tea? Coffee?"

"No. But you go ahead—"

Maria shook her head and sat down again; she had a feeling that if she went into the kitchen, she wouldn't want to return.

She couldn't see why Durham would refuse to talk to the police, unless he was involved in something dubious enough to have him thrown out of his job, at the very least. *Fuck him.* He might not have intended to cheat her, but he'd screwed her nonetheless. She wouldn't get a cent for the work she'd completed; other creditors would have no call on the trust fund if Durham merely went bankrupt—but if the money was the proceeds of crime . . .

Lorenzo the Magnificent. Yeah.

The worst of it was, for all she knew, Hayden believed she was a willing accomplice. And if Durham intended to remain silent, she'd have to clear her own name.

How?

First, she had to find out about the scam, and untangle her role in it.

She said, "What exactly is he promising these Copies?"

"A refuge. A place where they'll be safe from any kind of backlash—because they won't be connected to the outside world. No telecommunications; nothing to trace. He feeds them a long spiel about the coming dark age, when the unwashed masses will no longer put up with being lorded over by rich immortals—and evil socialist governments will confiscate all the supercomputers for weather control."

Hayden seemed to find the prospect laughable. Maria suspended judgement; what mattered was how Durham's clients felt, and she could imagine Operation Butterfly making a lot of Copies feel threatened. "So they send their clones in, and slam the door, in case the originals don't make it through the purges. But then what? How long is this "dark age" supposed to last?"

Hayden shrugged. "Who knows? Hundreds of years? Presumably Durham himself—or some trustworthy successor, several generations later—will decide when it's safe to come out. The two Copies whose executors filed complaints didn't wait to hear the whole scenario; they threw him out before he could get down to details like that."

"He must have approached other Copies."

"Of course. No one else has come forward, but we have a tentative list of names. All with estates incorporated overseas, unfortunately; I haven't been able to interview any of them, yet—we're still working on the jurisdictional red tape. But a few have made it clear already, through their lawyers, that they won't be willing to discuss the matter—which presumably means that they've swallowed Durham's line, and now they don't want to hear a word against him."

Maria struggled to imagine it: *No communications. Cut off from reality, indefinitely.* A few "Solipsist Nation" Copies might relish the prospect—but most of them had too little money to be the targets of an elaborate scam. And even if Durham's richest, most paranoid clients seriously believed that the world was on the verge of turning against them . . .

what if things went so badly wrong, outside, that links were *never* restored? The humans guarding the sanctuary could die out—or just walk away. How could any but the most radically separatist of Copies face the risk of being stranded inside a hidden computer, buried in the middle of a desert somewhere, with no means of discovering for themselves when civilization was worth rejoining—and no means of initiating contact in any case?

Radioisotope power sources could run for thousands of years; multiply redundant hardware of the highest standard could last almost as long, in theory. All these Copies would have, to remember reality by, would be the information they'd brought in with them at the start. If it turned into a one-way trip, they'd be like interstellar colonists, carrying a snapshot of Earth culture off into the void.

Except that *interstellar colonists* would merely face a growing radio time lag, not absolute silence. And whatever they were leaving behind, at least they'd have something to look forward to: a new world to explore.

A new world—and the possibility of new life.

So what better cure could there be for claustrophobia than the promise of dragging an entire planet into the refuge, seeded with the potential for developing its own exotic life?

Maria didn't know whether to be outraged or impressed. If she was right, she had to admire Durham's sheer audacity. When he had asked for a package of results which would persuade "the skeptics" about the prospects for an Autoverse biosphere, he hadn't been thinking of academics in the artificial life scene. He'd wanted to convince *his clients* that, even in total isolation, they'd have everything reality could ever offer the human race—including a kind of "space exploration," complete with the chance of alien contact. And these would be genuine *aliens;* not the stylish designer creatures from VR games, constructs of nothing but the human psyche; not the slick, unconvincing biomorphs of the high-level phenotype-selection models, the Darwinian equivalent of Platonic ideals. Life which had come the whole tortuous way, molecule by molecule, just like the real thing. Or,

almost the whole way; with a biogenesis still poorly understood, Durham had had enough sense to start with "hand-
made" microbes—otherwise his clients might never have
believed that the planet would bear life at all.

Maria explained the idea, tentatively. "He'd have to have
convinced these Copies that running the Autoverse is much
faster than modeling real biochemistry—which it is—without
being too specific about the actual figures. And I still think
it's a crazy risk to take; anyone could easily find out the
truth."

Hayden thought it over. "Would it matter if they did? If the
point of this world is mainly psychological—a place to "escape
to" if the worst happens, and reality becomes permanently inaccessible—then it wouldn't matter how slowly it ran. Once
they'd given up hope of reestablishing contact, slowdown
would become irrelevant."

"Yes, but there's *slow*—and there's physically impossible.
Sure, they could take in a crude sketch of the planet—which is
what Durham's asked me to provide—but they wouldn't have
a fraction of the memory needed to bring it to life. And even if
they found a way around that, it could take a billion years of
Autoverse time before the seed organism turned into anything
more exciting than blue-green algae. Multiply that by a slowdown of a trillion . . . I think you get the picture."

"Flat batteries?"

"Flat universe."

Hayden said, "Still . . . if they don't want to think too seriously about the prospect of ending up permanently trapped,
they might not want to look too closely at any of this. Thanks
to you, Durham will have a thick pile of impressive technical
details that he can wave in their faces, convincing enough to
take the edge off their fear of cabin fever. Maybe that's all
they want. The only part that matters, if everything goes
smoothly, is the conventional VR—good enough to keep them
amused for a couple of real-time centuries—and *that* checks
out perfectly."

Maria thought this sounded too glib by far, but she let it pass.
"What about the hardware? How does that check out?"

"It doesn't. There'll never be any hardware. Durham will vanish long before he has to produce it."

"Vanish with what? Money handed over with no questions asked—no safeguards, no guarantees?"

Hayden smiled knowingly. "Money handed over, mostly, for legitimate purposes. He's commissioned a VR city. He's commissioned an Autoverse planet. He's entitled to take a percentage of the fees—there's no crime in that, so long as it's disclosed. For the first few months, everything he does will be scrupulously honest. Then at some point, he'll ask his backers to pay for a consultants' report—say, a study of suitably robust hardware configurations. Tenders will be called for. Some of them will be genuine—but the most attractive ones will be forged. Later, Durham will claim to have received the report, the "consultants" will be paid . . . and he'll never be seen again."

Maria said, "You're guessing. You have no idea what his plans are."

"We don't know the specifics—but it will be something along those lines."

Maria slumped back in her chair. "So, what now? What do I do? Call Durham and tell him the whole thing's off?"

"Absolutely not! Keep working as if nothing had happened—but try to make contact with him more often. Find excuses to talk to him. See if you can gain his trust. See if you can get him to talk about his work. His clients. The refuge."

Maria was indignant. "I don't remember volunteering to be your informant."

Hayden said coolly, "It's up to you, but if you're not willing to cooperate, that makes our job very difficult . . . "

"There's a difference between *cooperation* and playing unpaid spy!"

Hayden almost smiled. "If you're worried about money, you'll have a far better chance of being paid if you help us to convict Durham."

"Why? What am I meant to do—try suing him after he's already gone bankrupt repaying the people he's cheated?"

"You won't have to sue him. The court is almost certain to

award you compensation as one of the victims—especially if you've helped bring the case to trial. There's a fund, revenue from fines. It doesn't *matter* whether Durham can pay you himself."

Maria digested that. The truth was, it still stank. What she wanted to do was cut her losses and walk away from the whole mess. Pretend it had never happened.

And then what? Go crawling back to Aden for money? There were still no jobs around; she couldn't afford to write off three months' work. A few thousand dollars wouldn't get Francesca scanned—but the lack of it could force her to sell the house sooner than she wanted to.

She said, "What if I make him suspicious? If I suddenly start asking all these questions . . . "

"Just keep it natural. Anyone in your position would be curious; it's a strange job he's given you—he must expect questions. And I know you went along with what he told you at the start, but that doesn't mean you can't have given it more thought and decided that there are a few things that still puzzle you."

Maria said, "All right, I'll do it." *Had she ever had a choice?* "But don't expect him to tell me the truth. He's already lied to me; he's not going to change his story now."

"Maybé not. But you might be surprised. He might be desperate to have someone to take into his confidence—someone to boast to. Or he might just drop a few oblique hints. Anything's possible, as long as you keep talking to him."

When Hayden had left, Maria sat in the living room, too agitated to do anything but run through the whole exchange again in her head. An hour before, she'd been exhausted, but triumphant; now she just felt weary and stupid. *Keep working as if nothing had happened!* The thought of tackling photosynthesis in *A. lamberti*—for the sake, now, of ingratiating herself with *the Fraud Squad*—was so bizarre it made her giddy.

It was a pity Durham hadn't been honest with her, and invited her in on the scam. It she'd known all along that she was meant to be helping to screw rich Copies out of their petty cash, at least the work would have had the real-world foundation she'd always felt was missing.

She finally went upstairs, without having eaten. Her connection to the JSN had been logged off automatically, but the message from **Juno,** locally generated, still hovered in the workspace. As she gestured to the terminal to switch itself off, she wondered if she should have asked Hayden: *Is it you who's been tapping my phone line?*

14

(Remit not paucity)

Seated in his library, Thomas viewed the final report in his knowledge miner's selection from the last real-time week of news. A journalist in a fur-lined coat appeared to address the camera, standing in light snow in front of the US Supreme Court building—although she was more likely to have been seated in a warm studio, watching a software puppet mime to her words.

"Today's five-to-one majority decision means that the controversial Californian statute will remain in force. Authorities taking possession of computer storage media to check for simulations of the brain, body or personality of a suspected felon, dead or alive, are *not* violating the Fourth Amendment rights of either the next of kin or the owners of the computer hardware. Chief Justice Andrea Steiner stressed that the ruling does not affect the status of Copies themselves, one way or another. The software, she said, can be confiscated and examined—but it will not stand trial."

The terminal blinked back to a menu. Thomas stretched his arms above his head, acutely conscious for a moment of the disparity between his frail appearance and the easy strength he felt in his limbs. *He had become his young self again, after all. Become him in the flesh—whether or not he chose to face him in the mirror.* But the thought led nowhere.

Thomas had been following the saga of the Californian legislation from the start. He hoped Sanderson and her colleagues knew what they were doing; if their efforts backfired, it could have unpleasant ramifications for Copies everywhere. Thomas's own public opinion model had shrugged its stochastic shoulders and declared that the effects of the law could go either way, depending on the steps taken to follow through—and several other factors, most of which would be difficult to anticipate, or manipulate.

Clearly, the aim was to shock apathetic US voters into supporting human rights for Copies—lest the alternative be *de facto* kidnap, mind pillage, and possibly even execution, all without trial. The computer-literate would understand just how useless the law would be in practice—but they'd already been largely won over. *The Unclear Family* rated highest with the demographics least likely to grasp the technical realities—a storehouse of good will that had yet to be fully exploited. Thomas could see the possibilities. Resurrected blue-collar worker Larry Unclear could turn out to have been under suspicion of murder at the time of his death. Flashback: Misunderstanding in bar leads to heated, highly visible, argument between Larry and guest-star X. Comic escalation to full-scale brawl. Taking advantage of the confusion, guest-star Y smashes a bottle over the skull of guest-star X—while Larry, with his usual endearing ineffectuality, has ended up comatose under a table. The new law could see him dragged from his home and family in the dead of night for a Kafkaesque virtual interrogation, in which his guilty dreams of being responsible are taken to be memories of *actually committing the crime . . .* while guest-star Y, still a living human, receives a civilized trial, lies through his teeth, and is acquitted. Son Leroy could save the day somehow, at the last minute, as usual.

Thomas closed his eyes and buried his face in his hands. Most of the room ceased being computed; he pictured himself adrift in Durham's sea of random numbers, carrying the chair and a fragment of floor with him, the only objects granted solidity by his touch.

He said, "I'm not in any danger." The room flickered halfway back into existence, subtly modified the sound of his words, then dissolved into static again.

Who did he believe would accuse him? There was no one left to care about Anna's death. He'd outlived them all.

But as long as the knowledge of what he'd done continued

to exist, inside him, he could never be certain that it wouldn't be revealed.

For months after the crime, he'd dreamed that Anna had come to his apartment. He'd wake, sweating and shouting, staring into the darkness of his room, waiting for her to show herself. Waiting for her to tear the skin of normality from the world around him, to reveal the proof of his damnation: blood, fire, insanity.

Then he'd started rising from his bed when the nightmare woke him, walking naked into the shadows, daring her to be there. Willing it. He'd enter every room in the apartment, most of them so dark that he had to feel his way with an outstretched hand, waiting for her fingers suddenly to mesh with his.

Night after night, she failed to appear. And gradually, her absence became a horror in itself; vertiginous, icy. The shadows were empty, the darkness was indifferent. Nothing lay beneath the surface of the world. He could have slaughtered a hundred thousand people, and the night would still have failed to conjure up a single apparition to confront him.

He wondered if this understanding would drive him mad.

It didn't.

After that, his dreams had changed; there were no more walking corpses. Instead, he dreamed of marching into Hamburg police station and making a full confession.

Thomas stroked the scar on the inside of his right forearm, where he'd scraped himself on the brickwork outside the window of Anna's room, making his clumsy escape. No one, not even Ilse, had ever asked him to account for it; he'd invented a plausible explanation, but the lie had remained untold.

He knew he could have his memories of the crime erased. Edited out of his original scan file, his current brain model, his emergency snapshots. No other evidence remained. It was ludicrous to imagine that anyone would ever have the slightest reason—let alone the legal right, let alone the power—to seize and examine the data which comprised him . . . but if it eased his paranoid fears, *why not?* Why not neutralize his unease at the technical possibility of his mind being read like a book— or a ROM chip—by turning the metaphor, or near-literal truth, to his own advantage? Why not rewrite the last incriminating version of his past? Other Copies exploited *what they'd become* with inane sybaritic excesses. Why not indulge himself in some peace of mind?

Why not? Because it would rob him of his identity. For sixty-five years, the tug on his thoughts of that one night in Hamburg had been as constant as gravity; everything he'd done since had been shaped by its influence. To tear out the entire tangled strand of his psyche—render half of his remaining memories incomprehensible—would be to leave himself a baffled stranger in his own life.

Of course, any sense of loss, or disorientation, could be dealt with, too, subtracted out . . . but where would the process of amputation end? Who would remain to enjoy the untroubled conscience he'd manufactured? Who'd sleep the sleep of the just in his bed?

Memory editing wasn't the only option. Algorithms existed which could transport him smoothly and swiftly into a state of enlightened acceptance: rehabilitated, healed, at peace with himself and his entire uncensored past. He wouldn't need to forget anything; his absurd fear of incrimination by mind-reading would surely vanish, along with his other neuroses-of-guilt.

But he wasn't prepared to swallow that fate, either—however blessed he might have felt once the transformation was complete. He wasn't sure that there was any meaningful distinction between *redemption* and the *delusion of redemption* . . . but some part of his personality—though he cursed it as masochistic and sentimental—baulked at the prospect of instant grace.

Anna's killer was dead! He'd burnt the man's corpse! What more could he do, to put the crime behind him?

On his "deathbed," as his illness had progressed—as he'd flirted giddily every morning with the prospect of ordering his final scan—he'd felt certain that witnessing the fate of his body would be dramatic enough to purge him of his stale, mechanical, relentless guilt. Anna was dead; nothing could change that. A lifetime of remorse hadn't brought her back. Thomas had never believed that he'd "earned" the right to be

free of her—but he'd come to realize that he had nothing left
to offer the little tin metronome in his skull but an extravagant
ritual of atonement: the death of the murderer himself.

But the murderer had never really died. The corpse con-
signed to the furnace had been nothing but shed skin. Two
days before being scanned, Thomas had lost his nerve and
countermanded his earlier instructions: that his flesh-and-
blood self be allowed to regain consciousness after the scan.

So the dying human had never woken, never known that he
was facing death. And there had been no separate, mortal
Thomas Riemann to carry the burden of guilt into the flames.

Thomas had met Anna in Hamburg in the summer of 1983, in
a railway station café. He was in town to run errands for his
father. She was on her way to West Berlin, for a concert. Nick
Cave and the Bad Seeds.

The café was crowded, they shared a table. Anna's appearance wasn't striking—dark-haired, green-eyed, her face round
and flat. Thomas would never have looked twice at her if
they'd passed in the street—but she soon made an impression.

She looked him over appraisingly, then said, "I'd kill for a
shirt like that. You have expensive tastes. What do you do to
support them?"

Thomas lied carefully. "I was a student. Engineering. Up
until a few months ago. It was hopeless, though; I was failing
everything."

"So what do you do now?"

He looked doleful. "My father owns a merchant bank. I
went into engineering to try to get away from the family business, but—"

She wasn't sympathetic at all. "But you screwed up, and
now he's stuck with you?"

"And vice versa."

"Is he very rich?"

"Yes."

"And you hate him?"

"Of course."

She smiled sweetly. "Why don't I kidnap him for you? You give me all the inside information, and we'll split the ransom money, fifty-fifty."

"You kidnap bankers for a living, do you?"

"Not exclusively."

"I think you work in a record store."

"You're wrong."

"Or a second-hand clothes shop."

"You're getting colder."

"Who are you meeting in Berlin?"

"Just some friends."

When her train was announced, he asked her for her number. She wrote it on the sleeve of his shirt.

For the next few months whenever he was traveling north, he phoned her. Three times, she made excuses. He almost gave up, but he kept recalling the mocking expression on her face, and he knew he wanted to see her again.

Early in November, she finally said, "Drop round, if you like. I'm not doing anything."

He'd planned to take her to a nightclub, but she had a child with her, a baby just a few months old. "He's not mine. I'm looking after him for a friend." They watched TV, then had sex on the sofa. Climbing off him, Anna said, "You're really quite sweet." She kissed him on the cheek, then vanished into the bedroom, locking him out. Thomas fell asleep watching an old John Wayne movie. Two teenage girls with smeared mascara pounded on the door around two in the morning and Anna sold them a plastic sachet of white powder.

Thomas, still on the couch, asked her if the powder was heroin, or cocaine.

"Heroin."

"Do you use that shit?"

"No." She regarded him with mild amusement; she didn't care if he believed her or not.

He woke again at half past five. Anna had gone. The baby was still in his crib, screaming. Thomas changed him and fed him; Anna had shown him where everything was. He wanted a shower, but there was no hot water. He shaved, and left in time for his meeting, telling himself Anna would be back soon. All morning, and all through lunch, he could smell the sour odor of the child's skin on his hands, and he wondered if the smiling property developers could smell it too.

He phoned from the hotel, paying for the night he hadn't spent there, knowing that his father would scrutinize his expenses. Anna was home; he'd woken her. Someone nearby grunted with displeasure. Thomas didn't mention the child.

The next time, he came on a Saturday afternoon, with no need to be anywhere else in a hurry. They met at the Alsterpavillon, drank their coffee looking down on the buffoons in rowboats on the Binnenalster, then went shopping on Jungfernstieg. Thomas paid for the clothes Anna chose, authenthic gothic designer trash that looked far worse than the cheapest imitation; it seemed she didn't really want to dress like him, after all. They walked arm-in-arm from shop to shop, and in the entrance to the most expensive boutique, they stopped and kissed for several minutes, blocking the way of customers trying to get past, then went in and spent a lot of money.

Later, in a nightclub with a bad live band who dressed like the Beatles and did Sex Pistols covers, they ran into Martin, a tall wiry blond youth who Anna introduced as a friend. Martin was all vicious back-slapping amiability, trying so hard to be intimidating that he was almost comical. They all staggered back to Anna's flat together, and sat on the floor listening to records. When Anna went to the toilet, Martin drew a knife and told Thomas he intended to kill him. He was very drunk. Thomas stood up, kicked him once in the face, breaking his nose, then took away the knife and dragged him moaning out into the hall. Thomas turned him on his side so he wouldn't choke on the blood, then locked the door.

Anna came out of the bathroom. Thomas told her what had happened. She went out and checked on Martin, and put a pillow under his head.

While Anna was undressing him, Thomas said, "On TV once, I saw an English soldier who'd just come back from Northern Ireland. And he said, 'It was hell there, but at least it

was real. At least I've lived now.'" Thomas laughed sadly.
"The poor fool had it all upside down. Slaughtering people is
real—and living an ordinary life is some kind of dream, some
kind of delusion? Poor fucked-up kid."

He searched Anna for needle marks, but he couldn't find a
single one.

Back in his office in Frankfurt, alone in his apartment, at the
dinner table in his parents' home, Thomas thought about Anna,
in images and scents. The memories never distracted him; he
could carry on a conversation, or keep reading a mortgage
schedule, while she played in his head like wallpaper music.

His father cornered him at Easter. "You should think about
getting married. It makes no difference to me, but there are
social advantages you're going to need sooner or later. And
think how happy it would make your mother."

Thomas said, "I'm twenty-four years old."

"I was engaged when I was twenty-four."

"Maybe I'm gay. Or perhaps I have an incurable venereal
disease."

"I don't see why either should be an obstacle."

Thomas saw Anna every second weekend. He bought her
whatever she asked for. Sometimes she had the child with her.
The boy was called Erik.

Thomas asked her, "Who's the mother? Have I met her?"

She said, "You don't want to."

He worried about her sometimes—afraid she'd get herself
arrested, or beaten up by junkies or rivals—but she seemed to
be able to take care of herself. He could have hired private
detectives to uncover the mysteries of her life, and bodyguards
to watch over her, but he knew he had no right. He could have
bought her an apartment, set her up with investments—but she
never suggested anything of the kind, and he suspected she'd be
deeply insulted if he made the offer. His gifts were lavish, but
he knew she could have lived without them. They were using
each other. She was, he told himself, as independent as he was.

He wouldn't have said he loved her. He didn't ache when
they were apart; he just felt pleasantly numb, and looked forward to the next time he'd see her. He was jealous, but not

obsessive, and she kept her other lovers out of the way; he rarely had to acknowledge their existence. He never saw Martin again.

Anna traveled with him to New York. They fell asleep in the middle of a Broadway show, saw the Pixies play at the Mudd Club, climbed the stairs to the top of Manhattan Chase.

Thomas turned twenty-five. His father promoted him. His mother said, "Look at all your gray hairs."

In the spring, Erik disappeared. Anna said casually, "His mother's gone, she's moved away."

Thomas was hurt; he'd liked having the boy around. He said, "You know, I used to think he might be yours."

She was baffled. "Why? I told you he wasn't. Why would I have lied?"

Thomas had trouble sleeping. He kept trying to picture the future. When his father died, would he still be seeing Anna, once a fortnight in Hamburg, while she dealt heroin and fucked pimps and junkies? The thought made him sick. Not because he didn't want everything to stay the same, but because he knew that it couldn't.

The Saturday in June was, almost, the second anniversary of the day they'd met. They went to a flea market in the afternoon, and he bought her cheap jewelery. She said, "Anything nicer would be asking for trouble."

They ate junk food, went dancing. They ended up back at Anna's flat at half past two. They danced around the tiny living room, propping each other up, more tired than drunk.

Thomas said, "God, you're beautiful." *Marry me.*

Anna said, "I'm going to ask you for something I've never asked for before. I've been trying to work up the courage all day."

"You can ask for anything." *Marry me.*

"I have a friend, with a lot of cash. Almost two hundred thousand marks. He needs someone who can—"

Thomas stepped back from her, then struck her hard across the face. He was horrified. He'd never hit her before; the thought had never even occurred to him. She started punching him in the chest and face; he stood there and let her do it for a while, then grabbed both her hands by the wrists.

She caught her breath. "Let go of me."

"I'm sorry."

"Then let go of me."

He didn't. He said, "I'm not a money-laundering facility for your *friends*."

She looked at him pityingly. "Oh, what have I done? Offended your high moral principles? All I did was ask. You might have made yourself useful. Never mind. I should have known it was too much to expect."

He pushed his face close to hers. "Where are you going to be, in ten years' time? In prison? At the bottom of the Elbe?"

"Fuck off."

"Where? Tell me?"

She said, "I can think of worse fates. I could end up playing happy families with a middle-aged banker."

Thomas threw her toward the wall. Her feet slipped from under her before she hit it; her head struck the bricks as she was going down.

He crouched beside her, disbelieving. There was a wide gash in the back of her head. She was breathing. He patted her cheeks, then tried to open her eyes; they'd rolled up into her skull. She'd ended up almost sitting on the floor, legs sprawled in front of her, head lolling against the wall. Blood pooled around her.

He said, "Think fast. Think fast."

He knelt over her, one knee to either side, took her face in his hands, then closed his eyes. He brought her head forward, then slammed it back against the wall. Five times. Then he held his fingers near her nostrils, without opening his eyes. He felt no exhalation.

He backed away from her, turned away and opened his eyes, then walked around the flat, wiping things he might have touched with his handkerchief. Avoiding looking at her. He was crying and shaking, but he couldn't think why.

There was blood on his hands, his shirt, his trousers, his shoes. He found a garbage bag, put all his clothes in it, then washed the blood from his skin. There was a black spot in the center of his vision, but he worked around it. He put the garbage bag in his suitcase, and put on fresh clothes: blue jeans and a black T-shirt. He went through the flat, packing away everything that belonged to him. He almost took Anna's address book, but when he checked he saw that he wasn't in it. He looked for diaries, but found none.

Dozens of people had seen them together, month after month. Anna's neighbors, Anna's friends. Dozens of people had seen them leave the nightclub. He wasn't sure how many of her friends knew what he did, where he was from. He'd never told any of them more than his first name, he'd always lied about the rest—but Anna might have told them everything she knew.

Having been seen with her alive was bad enough; he couldn't risk being seen walking out the front door the night she was killed.

The flat was two flights up. The bathroom window opened onto an alley. Thomas threw the suitcase down; it landed with a soft thud. He thought of jumping—almost believing that he could land unhurt, or almost believing that he wouldn't care—but there was a gray clarity underneath those delusions, and an engine in his skull a billion years old which only wanted to survive.

He climbed up into the window frame, into the gap left by the sliding half-pane, one foot either side of the track. There was no ledge, as such, just the double brickwork of the wall itself. He had to crouch to fit, but he found he could keep his balance by pushing his left hand up against the top of the frame, jamming himself in place.

He turned sideways, then reached across the outside wall, and into the frame of the bathroom window of the neighboring flat. He could hear traffic, and music somewhere, but no lights showed from within the flat, and the alley below was deserted. The two windows were scarcely a meter apart, but the second one was closed, halving its width. With one hand on each edge, he shifted his right foot to the neighbor's window. Then, gripping the intervening wall tightly between his forearms, he moved his left foot across. Finally, securing himself by pressing up with his right hand, he let go of the first frame completely.

He shuffled across the one-brick's-width ledge, fighting an impulse to mutter Ave Marias. *Pray for us sinners?* He realized that he'd stopped weeping. A drain pipe ran close to the far side of the window. He imagined tearing his palms open on jagged rusty metal, but the pipe was smooth; it took all his strength to hold himself in place, gripping it with hands and knees. When he touched the ground with his feet, his legs gave way. But not for long.

He hid in a public toilet for three hours, staring up at one corner of the room. The lights, the tiles, could have belonged to a prison or an asylum. He found himself disconnected, from the world, the past; his time breaking up into moments, shocks of awareness, shimmering droplets of mercury, beads of sweat.

This isn't me. This is something else that believes it's me. And it's wrong, wrong, wrong.

Nobody disturbed him. At six o'clock he walked out into the morning light, and caught a train home.

15

(Remit not paucity)

Durham's north Sydney flat was small, and very sparsely furnished; not at all what Maria had expected. The combined living room and kitchen was all she'd seen, but it was clear from the outside that there wasn't space for much more. Durham was on the sixteenth floor, but the building was hemmed in on all sides by ugly late-twenties office towers, blue and pink ersatz-marble monstrosities; no expensive harbor views here. For someone who was ripping off gullible millionaires—or even someone who merely sold them insurance—Durham didn't seem to have much to show for it. Maria thought it unlikely that the place had been set up entirely for her benefit, to fit the story he'd told her: to demonstrate the frugal lifestyle which supposedly enabled him to pay her out of his own pocket. He'd invited her out of the blue; she would never have had a reason to insist on seeing where he lived.

She put her notepad down on the scratched dining table, and turned it so that Durham could read the graphs. "These are the latest results for the two most promising species. *A. lithophila* has the higher mutation rate, per generation, but it reproduces much more slowly, and it's more vulnerable to climate change. *A. hydrophila* is more prolific, with a stabler genome. It's not intrinsically hardier; it's just better protected by the ocean."

Durham said, "What's your gut feeling?"

"What's yours?"

"*A. litho* evolves into a few promising species—which all get wiped out by one major crisis. *A. hydro* slowly builds up a huge stock of survival-neutral mutations, some of which turn out to be useful on land. The first few hundred thousand species which blow out of the sea don't make it—but it doesn't matter, there are always more. Or am I just being swayed too much by terrestrial preconceptions?"

"The people you're trying to convince will almost certainly think the same way."

Durham laughed. "It wouldn't hurt to be *right*, as well as persuasive. If they're not mutually exclusive ambitions."

Maria didn't reply. She stared down at the notepad; she couldn't look Durham in the eye. Talking to him by phone, with software filters, had been bearable. And the work itself had been an end in itself; immersed in the elaborate game of Autoverse biochemistry, she'd found it all too easy to carry on, as if it made no difference what it was *for.* But she'd done next to nothing to make Durham more likely to take her into his confidence. That was why she'd agreed to this meeting— and why she had to take advantage of it.

The trouble was, now that she was here, she was so ill at ease that she could barely discuss the most neutral technicalities without her voice faltering. If he started spouting lies about his hopes of debating the skeptics of the artificial life mafia in some future issue of *Cellular Automaton World,* she'd probably start screaming. Or, more likely, throw up on the bare linoleum floor.

He said, "By the way, I signed the release on your fee this morning—I've authorized the trust fund to pay you in full. The work's been going so well, it seemed only fair."

Maria glanced up at him, startled. He looked perfectly sincere, but she couldn't help wondering—not for the first time—if he knew that she'd been approached by Hayden, knew exactly what she'd been told. She felt her cheeks flush. She'd spent too many years using phones and filters; she couldn't keep anything from showing on her face.

She said, "Thank you. But aren't you afraid I might take the first plane to the Bahamas? There's still a lot of work to be done."

"I think I can trust you."

There wasn't a trace of irony in his voice—but there really didn't need to be.

He said, "Speaking of trust . . . I think your phone may be bugged. I'm sorry; I should have told you that sooner."

Maria stared at him. "How did you know?"

"Know? You mean, it is? You've had definite signs?"

"I'm not sure. But how . . . ?"

"Mine is. Bugged. So it makes sense that yours would be, too."

Maria was bewildered. What was he going to do—announce that the Fraud Squad were watching him? If he came right out and said it, she didn't think she could dissemble any longer. She'd have to confess that she already knew—and then she'd have to tell him everything Hayden had said.

Taking the pressure off completely. Ending the farce for good. She had no talent for these stupid games; the sooner they could both stop lying to each other, the better.

She said, "And who exactly do you think is doing it?"

Durham paused to think it over, as if he hadn't seriously considered the question before. "Some corporate espionage unit? Some national security organization? There's really no way of telling. I know very little about the intelligence community; your guess would be as good as mine."

"Then why do you think they're—?"

Durham said blithely, "If I was developing a computer, say, thirty orders of magnitude more powerful than any processor cluster in existence, don't you think people like that might take an interest?"

Maria almost choked. "Ah. Yes."

"But of course I'm not, and eventually they'll convince themselves of that, and leave us both alone. So there's absolutely nothing to worry about."

"Right."

Durham grinned at her. "Presumably, they think that just because I've commissioned an Autoverse planet, there's a chance that I might possess the means to actually *run it.* They've searched this place a couple of times; I don't know what they expected to find. A little black box, sitting in a corner of one of the rooms? Hidden under a pot plant, quietly cracking military codes, raking in a fortune on the stock market—and simulating a universe or two on the side, just to keep from getting bored. Any five-year-old could tell them how ludicrous that is. Maybe they think I've found a way to shrink individual processors to the size of an atom. That would just about do it."

So much for an end to the lying. He wasn't going to make this easy for her. *All right.* Maria forced the words out evenly: "And any five-year-old could tell you that if anyone searched your flat, it was the Fraud Squad."

Durham was still giving nothing away. "Why do you say that?"

"Because I *know* they're watching you. They've spoken to me. They've told me exactly what you're doing." Maria faced him squarely now. She was tense at the prospect of a confrontation, but she had nothing to be ashamed of; he was the one who'd set out to deceive her from the start.

He said, "Don't you think the Fraud Squad would need to get a warrant, and search the flat in my presence?"

"Then maybe it hasn't been searched at all. That's not the point."

He nodded slightly, as if conceding some minor breach of etiquette. "No, it's not. You want to know why I lied to you."

Maria said, "I *know* why. Please don't treat me like an idiot." Her bitterness surprised her, she'd had to conceal it for so long. "I was hardly going to agree to be your . . . *accomplice—*"

Durham raised one hand from the tabletop, a half conciliatory, half impatient gesture. Maria fell silent, more from astonishment at how calmly he seemed to be taking all this than any desire to give him a chance to defend himself.

He said, "I lied because I didn't know if you'd believe the truth or not. I think you might have, but I couldn't be sure. And I couldn't risk it. I'm sorry."

"Of course I would have believed the truth! It would have made a lot more sense than the bullshit you fed me! But, yes, I can see why you couldn't *risk it.*"

Durham still showed no sign of contrition. "Do you know what it is that I'm offering my backers? The ones who've been funding your work?"

"A sanctuary. A privately owned computer somewhere."

"That's almost true. Depending on what you take those words to mean."

Maria laughed cynically. "Oh, yes? Which words do you have trouble with? 'Privately owned'?"

"No. 'Computer.' And, 'somewhere.'"

"Now you're just being childish." She reached out and picked up her notepad, slid her chair back and rose to her feet. Trying to think of a parting shot, it struck her that the most frustrating thing was that the bastard had *paid her*. He'd lied to her, he'd made her an accomplice—but he hadn't actually swindled her.

Durham looked up at her calmly. He said, "I've committed no crime. My backers know exactly what they're paying for. The Fraud Squad, like the intelligence agencies, are jumping to absurd conclusions. I've told them the whole truth. They've chosen not to believe me."

Maria stood by the table, one hand on the back of the chair. "They said you refused to discuss the matter."

"Well, that's a lie. Although what I had to say certainly wasn't what they wanted to hear."

"What *did* you have to say?"

Durham gave her a searching look. "If I try to explain, will you listen? Will you sit down and listen, to the end?"

"I might."

"Because if you don't want to hear the whole story, you might as well leave right now. Not every Copy took me up on the offer—but the only ones who went to the police were the ones who refused to hear me out."

Maria said, exasperated, "What do you care what I think, now? You've extracted all the Autoverse technobabble from me you could possibly need. And I know nothing more about your scam than the police do; they'll have no reason to ask me to testify against you, if all I can say in court is 'Detective Hayden told me this, Detective Hayden told me that.' So why don't you quit while you're ahead?"

Durham said simply, "Because you don't understand anything. And I owe you an explanation."

Maria looked toward the door, but she didn't take her hand off the back of the chair. The work had been an end in itself—but she was still curious to know precisely what Durham had intended to do with the fruits of her labor.

She said, "How was I going to spend the afternoon, anyway? Modeling the survival of *Autobacterium hydrophila* in sea spray?" She sat. "Go ahead. I'm listening."

Durham said, "Almost six years ago—loosely speaking—a man I know made a Copy of himself. When the Copy woke up, it panicked, and tried to bale out. But the original had sabotaged the software; baling out was impossible."

"That's illegal."

"I know."

"So who was this man?"

"His name was Paul Durham."

"You? You were the original?"

"Oh, no. *I was the Copy.*"

16

(Toy man, picture it)

Paul felt a hand gripping his forearm. He tried to shake it off, but his arm barely moved, and a terrible aching started up in his shoulder. He opened his eyes, then closed them again in pain. He tried again. On the fifth or sixth attempt, he managed to see a face through washed-out brightness and tears.

Elizabeth.

She raised a cup to his lips. He took a sip, spluttered and choked, but then managed to force some of the thin sweet liquid down.

She said, "You're going to be fine. Just take it easy."

"Why are you here?" He coughed, shook his head, wished he hadn't. He was touched, but confused. Why had his original lied—claiming that she wanted to shut him down—when in fact she was sympathetic enough to go through the arduous process of visiting him?

He was lying on something like a dentist's couch, in an unfamiliar room. He was in a hospital gown; there was a drip in his right arm, and a catheter in his urethra. He glanced up to see an interface helmet, a bulky hemisphere of magnetic axon current inducers, suspended from a gantry, not far above his head. He thought: fair enough, to construct a simulated meeting place that looked like the room that *her* real body must be in. Putting him in the couch, though, and giving him all the symptoms of a waking visitor, seemed a little extreme.

He tapped the couch with his left hand. "What's the message? You want me to know exactly what you're going through? Okay. I'm grateful. And it's good to see you." He shuddered with relief, and delayed shock. "Fantastic, to tell the truth." He laughed weakly. "I honestly thought he was going to wipe me out. The man's a complete lunatic. Believe me, you're talking to his better half."

Elizabeth was perched on a stool beside him. She said, "Paul. Try to listen carefully to what I'm going to say. You'll start to reintegrate the memories gradually, on your own, but it'll help if I talk you through it all first. To start with, you're not a Copy. You're flesh and blood."

Paul coughed, tasting acid. Durham had let her do something unspeakable to the model of his digestive system.

"I'm flesh and blood? What kind of sadistic joke is that? Do you have any idea how hard it's been, coming to terms with the truth?"

She said patiently, "It's not a joke. I know you don't remember yet, but . . . after you made the scan that was going to run as Copy number five, you finally told me what you were doing. And I persuaded you not to run it—until you'd tried another experiment: putting yourself in its place. Finding out, firsthand, what *it* would be forced to go through.

"And you agreed. *You* entered the virtual environment which the Copy would have inhabited—with your memories since the day of the scan suppressed, so you had no way of knowing that you were only a visitor."

"I—?"

"*You're not the Copy.* Do you understand? All you've been doing is visiting the environment you'd prepared for Copy number five. And now you're out of it. You're back in the real world."

Her face betrayed no hint of deception—but software could smooth that out. He said, "I don't believe you. How can I *be* the original? I spoke to the original. What am I supposed to believe? *He* was the Copy? Thinking he was the original?"

"Of course not. That would hardly have spared the Copy, would it? The fifth scan *was never run.* I controlled the puppet that played your 'original'—software provided the vocabulary signature and body language, but I pulled the strings. You briefed me, beforehand, on what to have it say and do. You'll remember that, soon enough."

"But . . . the experiments?"

"The experiments were a sham. They could hardly have been performed on a visitor, on a physical brain—could they?"

Paul shook his head, and whispered, "Abulafia."

No interface window appeared.

He gripped the couch and closed his eyes, then laughed. "You say I *agreed* to this? What kind of masochist would do that? I'm going out of my mind. *I don't know what I am.*"

Elizabeth took hold of his arm again. "You're disoriented—but that won't last long. And you *know* why you agreed. You were sick of Copies baling out on you. You had to come to terms with their experience. Spending a few days believing you were a Copy would make or break the project: you'd either end up psychologically prepared, at last, to give rise to a Copy who'd be able to cope with its fate—or you'd gain enough sympathy for their plight to stop creating them.

"The plan was to tell you everything while you were still inside, after the third experiment. But when you went weird on me in there, I panicked. All I could think of was having the puppet playing your original tell you that it was going to pause you. I wasn't trying to frighten you. I didn't think you'd take it so badly."

A technician came into the room and removed the drip and catheter. Paul propped himself up and looked out through the windows of the room's swing doors; he could see half a dozen people in the corridor. He bellowed wordlessly at the top of his lungs; they all turned to stare in his direction. The technician said mildly, "Your penis might sting for an hour or two."

Paul slumped back onto the couch and turned to Elizabeth. "You wouldn't pay for reactive crowds. I wouldn't pay for reactive crowds. It looks like you're telling the truth."

People, glorious people: thousands of strangers, meeting his eyes with suspicion or puzzlement, stepping out of his way on the street—or, more often, clearly, consciously refusing to.

The freedom of the city was so sweet. He walked the streets

of Sydney for a full day, rediscovering every ugly shopping arcade, every piss-stinking litter-strewn park and alley, until, with aching feet, he squeezed his way home through the evening rush hour, to watch the real-time news.

There was no room for doubt: he was not in a virtual environment. Nobody in the world could have had reason to spend so much money, simply to deceive him.

When Elizabeth asked if his memories were back, he nodded and said of course. She didn't grill him on the details. In fact, having gone over her story so many times in his head, he could almost imagine the stages: his qualms after the fifth scan; repeatedly putting off running the model; confessing to Elizabeth about the project; accepting her challenge to experience for himself just what his Copies were suffering.

And if the suppressed memories hadn't actually reintegrated, well, he'd checked the literature, and there was a two point five percent risk of that happening; electronically censoring access to memories could sometimes permanently weaken the neural connections in which they were encoded.

He even had an account from the database service which showed that he'd consulted the very same articles before.

He reread and replayed the news reports that he'd accessed from inside—and found no discrepancies. He flicked through encyclopedic databases—spot-checking random facts of history, geography, astronomy—and although he was surprised now and then by details which he'd never come across before, there were no startling contradictions. The continents hadn't moved. Stars and planets hadn't vanished. The same wars had been lost and won.

Everything was consistent. Everything was explicable.

And yet he couldn't stop wondering about the fate of a Copy who was shut down and never run again. A normal human death was one thing—woven into a much vaster tapestry, it was a process which made perfect sense. From the internal point of view of a Copy whose model was simply *halted,* though, there was no explanation whatsoever for its demise—just an edge where the pattern abruptly came to an end.

But if the insight he'd gained from the experiments was true (whether or not they'd ever really happened)—if a Copy *could* assemble itself from dust scattered across the world, and bridge the gaps in its existence with dust from across the universe . . . then why should it ever come to an *inconsistent* end? Why shouldn't the pattern keep on finding itself?

Or find a larger pattern into which it could merge?

The dust theory implied a countless number of alternative worlds: billions of different possible histories spelled out from the same primordial alphabet soup. One history in which Durham *did* run Copy number five—and one in which he didn't, but was persuaded to take its place as a visitor, instead.

But if the visitor had been perfectly deceived, and had experienced everything the Copy did . . . what set the two of them apart? So long as the flesh-and-blood man had no way of knowing the truth, it was meaningless to talk about "two different people" in "two different worlds." The two patterns of thoughts and perceptions had effectively merged into one.

If the Copy had been allowed to keep on running after the visitor had learned that he was flesh and blood, their two paths would have diverged again. But the Copy had been shut down; it had no future at all in its original world, no separate life to live.

So the two subjective histories remained as one. Paul *had been* a visitor believing he was a Copy. And he'd *also been* the Copy itself. The patterns had merged seamlessly; there could be no way of saying that one history was true and the other false. Both explanations were equally valid.

Once, preparing to be scanned, he'd had two futures.

Now he had two pasts.

Paul woke in darkness, confused for a moment, then pulled his cramped left arm out from under the pillow and glanced at his watch. Low power infrared sensors in the watch face detected his gaze, and flashed up the time—followed by a reminder: DUE AT LANDAU 7 A.M. It was barely after five, but it hardly seemed worth going back to sleep.

Memories of the night before came back to him. Elizabeth had finally confronted him, asking what decision he'd reached: to abandon his life's work, or to forge ahead, now that he knew, firsthand, what was involved.

His answer seemed to have disappointed her. He didn't expect to see her again.

How could he give up? He knew he could never be sure that he'd discovered the truth—but that didn't mean that nobody else could.

If he made a Copy, ran it for a few virtual days, then terminated it abruptly . . . then at least *that* Copy would know if its own pattern of experience continued.

And if another Paul Durham in one of the countless billions of alternative worlds could provide a future for the terminated Copy—a pattern into which it could merge—then perhaps that flesh-and-blood Durham would repeat the whole process again.

And so on, again and again.

And although the seams would always be perfect, the "explanation" for the flesh-and-blood human believing that he had a second past as a Copy would necessarily grow ever more "contrived," less convincing . . . and the dust theory would become ever more compelling.

Paul lay in bed in the darkness, waiting for sunrise, staring into the future down this corridor of mirrors.

One thing nagged at him. He could have sworn he'd had a dream, just before he woke: an elaborate fable, conveying some kind of insight. That's all he knew—or thought he knew. The details hovered maddeningly on the verge of recollection.

His dreams were evanescent, though, and he didn't expect to remember anything more.

17

(Remit not paucity)

APRIL 2051

Maria shifted in her seat to try to get her circulation flowing, then realized it wasn't enough. She stood up and limped around the room, bending down to massage her cramped right calf.

She said, "And you claim you're the *twenty-third?*" She was almost afraid to sound too skeptical; not because she believed that Durham would take offence, but because the story was so strangely entrancing that she wasn't sure she wanted to deflate it, yet. One hint of mockery and the floodgates would open. "You're the *twenty-third* flesh-and-blood Paul Durham whose past includes all those who came before?"

Durham said, "I may be wrong about the exact number. I may have counted this last version more than once; if I'm capable of believing in twenty-three incarnations, some of them might be false. The whole nature of the delusions I suffered contributes to the uncertainty."

"*Contributes.* Isn't that a bit of an understatement?"

Durham was unflappable. "I'm cured now. The nanosurgery worked. The doctors pronounced me sane, and I have no reason to question their judgement. They've scanned my brain; it's functioning impeccably. I've seen the data, before and after. Activity in the prefrontal cortex—"

"But don't you see how absurd that is? You acknowledge that you *were* deluded. You insist that you're cured now. But you claim that your delusions weren't delusions—"

Durham said patiently, "I've admitted from the outset: my condition *explains* everything. I believed—because I was mentally ill—that I was the twenty-third-generation Copy of another Paul Durham, from another world."

"*Because you were mentally ill!* End of story."

"No. Because I'm certifiably rational now—and the logic of the dust theory makes as much sense to me as ever. And it makes no difference whether my memories are true, false, or both."

Maria groaned. "*Logic of the dust theory!* It's *not* a *theory.* It can't be tested."

"Can't be tested by whom?"

"By anyone! I mean . . . even assuming that everything you believe is the truth: you've 'been through' twenty-three separate experiments, and you still don't know what you've proved or disproved! As you say: your condition accounts for everything. Haven't you heard of Occam's razor: once you have a perfectly simple explanation for something, you don't go looking for ever more complicated ways of explaining the very same thing? No *dust theory* is required." Her words reverberated in the near-empty room. She said, "I need some fresh air."

Durham said firmly, "After twenty-three ambiguous results, I know how to get it right this time. A Copy plus a virtual environment is a patchwork, a mess. A system like that isn't rich enough, detailed enough, or consistent enough, to be self-sustaining. If it was, when I was shut down, *the entire VR world I was in* would have persisted. That never happened. Instead—every time—I found a flesh-and-blood human with a reason to believe he shared my past. *That* explained my pattern of experience far better than VR—even to the point of insanity.

"What I have to do now is construct a consistent pattern which can only have *one* past."

Maria took a few deep breaths. It was almost too much to bear: Durham's sad flat, his cosmic visions, his relentless, mechanical logic, grinding away trying to make sense of the legacy of his disease. The doctors *had* cured him, he *was* sane. He just didn't want to disown his delusional past—so he'd invented a flawlessly logical, utterly irrefutable, reason to hang on to it.

If he'd really told the cops all this, why were they still hounding him? They should have seen that he was harmless and left him alone—and left his moronic clients to fend for themselves. The man wasn't even a danger to himself. And if he could ever harness a fraction of the energy and intelligence he'd put into this "project" and direct it towards something worthwhile—

Durham said, "Do you know what a Garden-of-Eden configuration is?"

Maria was caught blank for a second, then she said, "Yes, of course. In cellular automaton theory, it's a state of the system that can't be the result of any previous state. No other pattern of cells can give rise to it. If you want a Garden-of-Eden configuration, you have to start with it—you have to put it in by hand as the system's first state."

Durham grinned at her as if she'd just conceded the whole argument. She said, "What?"

"Isn't it obvious? A cellular automaton isn't like patchwork VR; it's every bit as *consistent* as a physical universe. There's no jumble of *ad hoc* high-level laws; one set of rules applies to every cell. Right?"

"Yes, but—"

"So if I set up a cellular automaton in a Garden-of-Eden configuration, run it through a few trillion clock ticks, then shut it down . . . the pattern will continue to find itself in the dust—separate from this version of me, separate from this world, but still flowing unambiguously from that initial state. A state which can't be explained by the rules of the automaton. A state which *must* have been constructed in another world—exactly as I remember it.

"The whole problem, so far, has been that my memories are always entirely explicable *within* the new world. I shut myself down as a Copy—and find myself in a flesh-and-blood body with flesh-and-blood memories which the laws of physics could have produced from *earlier states* of a flesh-and-blood brain. This world can explain me only as a man whose delusions are unlikely beyond belief—but there's no denying that I *do* have a complete extra history, here, that's not literally, physically impossible. So whatever I prefer to believe, I have to concede that the outcome of the experiment is still ambiguous. I could, still, be wrong.

"But a cellular automaton can't provide an 'extra history' for a Garden-of-Eden configuration! It's mathematically impossible! If I find myself inside a cellular automaton universe, and I can track my past back to a Garden-of-Eden configuration, that will be conclusive proof that I *did* seed the whole universe in a previous incarnation. The dust theory will be vindicated. And I'll finally know—beyond any doubt—that I haven't merely been insane all along."

Maria felt punch-drunk. At one level, she knew she should stop humoring him, stop treating his ideas seriously. On another, it seemed that if Durham was so wrong, she should be able to point out the reasons why. She shouldn't have to call him a madman and refuse to listen to another word.

She said, "*Find yourself in a cellular automaton world?* You don't mean the Autoverse—?"

"Of course not. There's no prospect of translating a human into Autoverse biochemistry."

"Then what?"

"There's a cellular automaton called TVC. After Turing, von Neumann and Chiang. Chiang completed it around twenty-ten; it's a souped-up, more elegant version of von Neumann's work from the nineteen fifties."

Maria nodded uncertainly; she'd heard of all this, but it wasn't her field. She did know that John von Neumann and his students had developed a two-dimensional cellular automaton, a simple universe in which you could embed an elaborate pattern of cells—a rather Lego-like "machine"—which acted as both a universal constructor and a universal computer. Given the right program—a string of cells to be interpreted as coded instructions rather than part of the machine—it could carry out any computation, and build anything at all. Including another copy of itself—which could build another copy, and so on. Little self-replicating toy computers could blossom into existence without end.

She said, "Chiang's version was three-dimensional, wasn't it?"

"Much better. N-dimensional. Four, five, six, whatever you like. That leaves plenty of room for data within easy reach. In two dimensions, the original von Neumann machine had to reach farther and farther—and wait longer and longer—for each successive bit of data. In a six-dimensional TVC automaton, you can have a three-dimensional grid of computers, which keeps on growing indefinitely—*each* with its own three-dimensional memory, which can also grow without bound."

Maria said numbly, "Where are *you* supposed to fit into all of this? If you think translating human biochemistry into *Autoverse* terms is difficult, how are you going to map yourself into a six-dimensional world designed solely to support von Neumann machines?"

"The TVC universe is one big, ever-expanding processor cluster. It runs a Copy of me—"

"I thought the whole point was to do away with Copies!"

"—in a VR environment which lets me *interact with* the TVC level. Yes, I'll be a patchwork Copy, as always—there's no alternative to that—but I'll also be linked to the cellular automaton itself. I'll witness its operation, I'll experience its laws. By observing it, I'll make it a part of what has to be explained.

"And when the simulated TVC universe being run on the physical computer is suddenly shut down, the best explanation for what I've witnessed will be a continuation of that universe—an extension made out of dust."

Maria could almost see it: a vast lattice of computers, a seed of order in a sea of a random noise, extending itself from moment to moment by sheer force of internal logic, "accreting" the necessary building blocks from the chaos of non-space-time by the very act of *defining* space and time.

Visualizing wasn't believing, though.

She said, "What makes you so sure? Why not another deluded psychiatric patient, who believes he was—briefly—a Copy being run on a TVC automaton being run on a processor cluster in another world?"

"You're the one who invoked Occam's razor. Wouldn't you say that a self-contained TVC universe is a simpler explanation, by far?"

"No. It's about the most bizarre thing I can imagine."

"It's a lot less bizarre than yet another version of this universe, containing yet another version of me, with yet another set of convenient delusions."

"How many of your clients believed all this? How many think they're coming along for the ride?"

"Fifteen. And there's a sixteenth who, I think, is tempted."

"They paid—?"

"About two million each." He snorted. "It's quite funny, the significance the police have attached to that. Some large sums of money have changed hands, for reasons more complex than usual—so they assume I must be doing something illegal. I mean, billionaires have been known to make donations larger than that to *the Church of the God Who Makes No Difference.*" He added hastily, "None of mine."

Maria was having some trouble with the scale of things herself. "You found *fifteen* Copies willing to part with two million dollars after hearing this bullshit? Anyone that gullible deserves to lose their money."

Durham took no offence. "If you were a Copy, you'd believe the dust theory, too. You'd feel the truth of it in your nonexistent bones. Some of these people carried out the same experiments as I did—computing themselves in randomized fragments—but others didn't need to. They already *knew* that they could scatter themselves across real time and real space, and they'd still find themselves. Every Copy proves the dust theory to itself a million times a day."

It suddenly occurred to Maria that Durham might have invented all of this for her sake, alone—while telling his clients exactly what Hayden had assumed: some fraudulent but utterly non-metaphysical tale of a hidden supercomputer. But she couldn't see what he had to gain by confusing her . . . and too many details made too much sense, now. If his clients had accepted the whole mad vision, the problem of making them believe in a nonexistent super-computer vanished. Or at least changed from a question of evidence to a question of faith.

She said, "So you promised to fit a snapshot of each of

your 'backers' into the Garden-of-Eden configuration, plus the software to run them on the TVC?"

Durham said proudly, "All that and more. The major world libraries; not quite the full holdings, but tens of millions of files—text, audio, visual, interactive—on every conceivable subject. Databases too numerous to list—including all the mapped genomes. Software: expert systems, knowledge miners, metaprogrammers. Thousands of off-the-shelf VR environments: deserts, jungles, coral reefs, Mars and the moon. And I've commissioned Malcolm Carter, no less, to create a major city to act as a central meeting place: Permutation City, capital of the TVC universe.

"And, of course, there'll be your contribution: the seed for an alien world. Humanity is going to find other life in *this* universe, eventually. How can we give up hope of doing the same? Sure, we'll have our own software descendants, and recreated Earth animals, and no doubt novel, wholly artificial creatures as well. We won't be alone. But we still need a chance to confront the Other. We mustn't leave that possibility behind. And what could be more *alien* than Autoverse life?"

Maria's skin crawled. Durham's logic was impeccable; an endlessly expanding TVC universe, with new computing power being manufactured out of nothing in all directions, "would" eventually be big enough to run an Autoverse planet—or even a whole planetary system. The packed version of Planet Lambert—the compressed description, with its topographic summaries in place of actual mountains and rivers—would easily fit into the memory of a real-world computer. Then Durham's Copy could simply wait for the TVC grid to be big enough—or pause himself, to avoid waiting—and have the whole thing *unfold*.

Durham said, "I've been working on the software which will run the first moments of the TVC universe on a real-world computer. I can probably finish that myself. But I can't complete the Autoverse work without you, Maria."

She laughed sharply. *"You want me to keep working for you?* You lie to me. You get me visited by the Fraud Squad. You confess to a history of mental illness. You tell me you're the twenty-third incarnation of a retailing millionaire from a parallel world—"

"Whatever you think about the dust theory—and whatever you think about my *psychological health*—I can prove to you that I'm not a criminal. My backers will vouch for that; they all know exactly what their money's being used for. None of them are victims of fraud."

"I accept that. I just—"

"Then accept the payment. Finish the work. Whatever the police have told you, you have every right to the money, and I have every right to give it to you. Nobody's going to take you to court, nobody's going to throw you into prison."

Maria was flustered. "Just, *hold on.* Will you give me a chance to think?" Durham's sheer reasonableness was beginning to be as exhausting as the impassioned rhetoric of any obvious fanatic. And so much ground had shifted in the last half-hour that she hadn't had a chance to even start to reappraise her own situation: legally, financially . . . and morally.

She said, "Why don't your backers tell the police all this? If they can confirm your story for me, why can't they do the same for the cops? By refusing to talk, they're just fueling suspicion."

Durham agreed. "Tell me about it. It makes everything ten times harder—but I'm just going to have to keep on living with that. *Do you think they'd risk the truth becoming public knowledge?* There have already been some embarrassing leaks—but so far we've been able to muddy the water by putting out our own misinformation. Copies with *de facto* control of billion-dollar business empires would much rather have people linking them to some dubious salesman and his breakthrough supercomputer—and have the rumors fizzle out from lack of substantiation—than let the world know that they plan to send a clone into an artificial universe which runs *without hardware.* The share markets can get nervous enough when people start wondering if a certain board of directors have all taken up playing virtual Caligula in their spare time. If word got out that a Copy in a position of power had done something which might be construed as a sign that they no longer felt obliged to give a shit about their corporate responsibilities, their personal wealth, or the continued existence of Planet Earth . . ."

Maria walked over to the window. It was open, but the air outside was still; standing by the insect screen she might as well have been standing by a solid brick wall. People were arguing loudly in the flat above; she'd only just noticed.

When Durham had first approached her, she'd wondered, half seriously, if she'd be taking advantage of a man who'd taken leave of his senses. Now, she couldn't just shrug that off as a hypocritical insult to a fellow eccentric. This wasn't a matter of an artificial life fanatic with more money than sense. An ex-psychiatric patient was planning to spend thirty million dollars of other people's money to "prove" his own sanity— and lead the clones of his followers into a cybernetic paradise which would last for about twenty seconds. Taking a cut seemed just a tiny bit like doing the catering for the Jonestown massacre.

Durham said, "If you don't agree to finish the biosphere seed, who would I get to replace you? There's nobody else who could even begin to grasp what's involved."

Maria eyed him sharply. "Don't start flattering me. And don't kid yourself about the seed, either. You asked for a package of *persuasive data,* and that's all you'll be getting— even if I finish the work. If you're counting on Planet Lambert's inhabitants rising up on their hind legs and talking to you . . . I can't *guarantee* that happening if you ran the whole thing a billion times. You should have simulated *real-world* biochemistry. At least it's been shown that intelligent life can arise within that system . . . and you'd supposedly have the computing power to do it."

Durham said reasonably, "*A. lamberti* seemed simpler, surer. Any real-world organism—modeled subatomically— would be too big a program to test out in advance on any physical computer. And it'd be too late to change my mind and try another approach if I failed to get it to work—stuck in the TVC universe, with plenty of books and journals, but no pool of expertise."

Maria felt a deep chill pass through her; every time she thought she'd accepted just how seriously Durham took this lunacy, he gave an answer like that which drove it home to her anew.

She said, "Well, Autoverse life might turn out just as useless. You might have A. *hydrophila* spewing out useless mutations, generation after generation, with nothing you can do to fix it."

Durham seemed about to reply, but then stopped himself. Maria felt the chill return, at first without knowing why. A second later, she glared at him, outraged, as furious as if he'd come right out and asked her.

"I will *not* be there to fix it for you!"

Durham had the grace to look cowed, momentarily—but instead of denying that the thought had ever crossed his mind, he said, "If you don't believe in the dust theory, what difference would it make if there's a scan file of you in the Garden-of-Eden data?"

"I don't want a Copy of me waking up and living for a few subjective seconds, *knowing* that it's going to die!"

"Who said anything about waking it? Running a Copy on a simulated TVC grid is a computer-intensive operation. We can't afford to wake more than one Copy while we're still running on a physical computer. Mine. As far as you're concerned, your scan file would never even be used to build a Copy; the data would just sit there, completely inert. And *you* could sit outside at a terminal, overseeing the whole operation, making sure I kept my word."

Maria was scandalized—although it took her a second to weave through Durham's infuriating logic to find a target.

"And *you*—certain that I'd eventually wake—would happily take me on board under false pretences?"

Durham seemed genuinely baffled by the accusation. "False pretences? I've given you all the facts, and I've argued my case as hard as I can; it's not my fault if you don't believe me. Am I supposed to feel guilty for being right?"

Maria started to reply, but then the point seemed too ridiculous to pursue. She said, "Never mind. You won't get a

chance to feel anything about it, because I'm certainly not
offering you a scan file."

Durham bowed his head. "It's your decision."

Maria hugged herself. She was actually trembling slightly.
She thought: *I'm* afraid of exploiting *him?* If what he's doing
really is legitimate . . . finish the job, take the money. His
Copy's going to spend a few seconds believing it's headed for
Copy Heaven—and that's going to happen whatever I do. The
fifteen clones will just sleep through it all, as if they'd never
been made. That's no Jonestown.

Durham said, "The fee would be six hundred thousand
dollars."

Maria said, "I don't *care* if it's six hundred million." She'd
meant to shout, but her words faded out into a whisper.

Six hundred thousand dollars would be enough to save
Francesca's life.

Peer seemed to be making love with Kate, but he had his doubts. He lay on the soft dry grass of a boundless meadow, in mild sunshine. Kate's hair was longer than usual, tickling his skin wherever she kissed him, brushing against him with an erotic precision which seemed unlikely to have been left to chance. Insect chirps and birdsong were heard. Peer could recall David Hawthorne screwing a long-suffering lover in a field, once. They'd been driving back to London from her father's funeral in Yorkshire; it had seemed like a good idea at the time. This was different. No twigs, no stones, no animal shit. No damp earth, no grass stains, no itching.

The perfect meadow itself was no reason for suspicion; neither of them were verisimilitude freaks, masochistic re-creators of the irritating details of real environments. Good sex was, equally, a matter of choice. But Peer still found himself wondering if Kate really had agreed to the act. She hadn't actually made love to him for months—however many times he'd recycled the memories of the last occasion—and he couldn't rule out the possibility that he'd merely decided to fool himself into believing that she'd finally relented. He'd never gone quite so far before—so far as he presently knew—but he had a vague memory of resolving to do a thorough job of concealing the evidence if he ever did.

He could clearly remember Kate beginning to flirt as they'd toured Carter's city, and then reaching out and starting to undress him as they stood in the exit doorway. He'd shut down all limits on her access to his body while she'd been unbuttoning his shirt—and he'd bellowed with shock and delight when, in the middle of their physically plausible fore-play, an invisible second Kate, twenty times his size, had picked him up in one hand, raised him to her mouth, and licked his body from toes to forehead like a sweet-toothed giant taking the icing off a man-shaped cake.

None of this struck him as especially unlikely; if Kate had decided to make love again, it was the kind of thing he could imagine her doing. That in itself proved nothing. He could have scripted this fantasy to fit everything he knew about her—or chosen the scenario, and then rewritten his "knowledge" of her to accommodate the action. In either case, software could have laid down a trail of false memories: a plausible transition from their meeting with Carter—which he felt certain had actually happened—to this moment. All memories of having planned the deception would have been temporarily suppressed.

Kate stopped moving. She shook her head, spattering his face and chest with sweat, and said, "Are you here where you seem to be, or off somewhere else?"

"I was about to ask you the same question."

She smiled wickedly. "Ah. Then maybe this body you hope is me only asked you first to put your mind at ease."

In the sky above her right shoulder, Peer could see a stray cloud taking on a new shape, a whimsical sculpture parodying the bodies on the grass below.

He said, "And then admitted as much?"

Kate nodded, and started slowly rising. "Of course. For the very same reason. How many levels of bluffing will it take before you get bored and say: Fuck it, I don't care?"

She lifted herself until they were almost apart. He closed his eyes and violated the geometry, licking the sweat from between her shoulder blades without moving a muscle. She responded by sticking her tongue in both of his ears simultaneously. He laughed and opened his eyes.

The cloud above had darkened. Kate lowered herself onto him again, trembling very slightly.

She said, "Don't you find it ironic?"

"What?"

"Trans-humans taking pleasure by stimulating copies of the

neural pathways which used to be responsible for the continuation of the species. Out of all the possibilities, we cling to that."

Peer said, "No, I don't find it ironic. I had my irony glands removed. It was either that, or castration."

She smiled down at him. "I love you, you know. But would I tell you that? Or would you be stupid enough to pretend that I had?"

Warm, sweet rain began to fall.

He said, "I don't care, I don't care, I don't care."

Peer sat on the lowest of the four wooden steps leading up to the back porch of his homestead, glancing down now and then at his bare feet and thin brown arms. *Ten-year-old farm boy at dusk.* Kate had made both the environment and the body for him, and he liked the tranquil mood of the piece. There was no invented family, no role to play; this was a painting, not a drama. One place, one moment, lasting as long as he chose to inhabit it. The scenery wasn't quite photorealist—there were subtle distortions of form, color and texture which made it impossible to forget that he was inhabiting a work of art—but there were no sledgehammer techniques: no visible brushstrokes, no Van Gogh lighting effects.

Violating the whole aesthetic, an interface window hovered in front of him, a meter above the chicken-feed-scattered dirt. The cloning utility insisted on following an elaborate confirmation sequence; Peer kept saying, "Please skip to the final question, I know exactly what I'm doing"—but icons in legal wigs and gowns kept popping up in front of the window and declaring solemnly, "You *must* read this warning carefully. Your brain model will be directly examined for evidence of complete understanding before we proceed to the next stage."

It was a thousand times more trouble than baling out—he knew that for certain, having almost done it—but then, baling out entailed fewer legal complications for the people outside. Peer's estate was controlled by an executor, who'd signed a contract obliging her to act according to "any duly authenticated communications—including, but not limited to, visual and/or auditory simulations of a human being appearing to proffer instructions or advice." What *duly authenticated* meant revolved around a ninety-nine-digit code key which had been "hardwired" into Peer's model-of-a-brain when his Copy was generated from his scan file. He could summon it up consciously if he had to, in some unlikely emergency, but normally he made use of it by a simple act of will. He'd record a video postcard, wish it to be *duly authenticated*—and it was done. Unless the key was stolen—plucked right out of the computer memory which contained the data representing his brain—Peer was the only software on the planet capable of encrypting instructions to his executor in a form compatible with her own matching key. It was the closest thing he had to a legal identity.

By law, any clone which a Copy made of itself had to be given a new key. It was up to the initial Copy, prior to the cloning, to divide up the worldly assets between the two future selves—or rather, divide them up between the executor's two portfolios.

Peer fought his way through the process of assuring the cloning utility that he really had meant what he'd told it from the start: The clone would require no assets of its own. Peer would run it on sufferance, paying for its running time himself. He didn't plan on keeping it conscious for more than a minute or two; just long enough to reassure himself that he was doing the right thing.

He almost wished that Kate was with him, now. She'd offered to be here, but he'd turned her down. He would have been glad of her support, but this had to be done in private.

Finally, the utility said, "This is your last chance to cancel. Are you sure you wish to proceed?"

Peer closed his eyes. *When I see my original, sitting on the porch, I'll know who I am, and accept it.*

He said, "Yes, I'm sure."

Peer felt no change. He opened his eyes. His newly made twin stood on the ground where the interface window had been, staring at him, wide-eyed. Peer shivered. He recognized the boy as *himself,* and not just intellectually—Kate's piece included adjustments to every part of his brain which dealt with his body image, so he'd be no more shocked by catching a glimpse of himself in a mirror than he was by the way his limbs felt as he walked. But the effect wasn't so much to see through the "disguise" of the ten-year-old body, as to find himself thinking of the clone—and himself—as if the two of them really were that young. *How could he send this child into exile?*

Peer brushed the absurd notion aside. "Well?"

The clone seemed dazed. "I—"

Peer prompted him. "You know what I want to hear. Are you ready for this? Are you happy with your fate? Did I make the right decision? You're the one who knows, now."

"But I *don't* know." He looked at Peer pleadingly, as if hoping for guidance. "Why am I doing this? Remind me."

Peer was taken aback, but some disorientation was only to be expected. His own voice sounded "normal" to him—thanks to the neural adjustments—but the clone still sounded like a frightened child. He said gently, "Kate. We want to be with her. Both of her—"

The clone nodded fervently. "Of course." He laughed nervously. "And of course I'm ready. Everything's fine." His eyes darted around the yard, as if he was searching for an escape route.

Peer felt his chest tighten. He said evenly, "You don't have to go ahead if you don't want to. You know that. You can bale out right now, if that's what you'd prefer."

The clone looked more alarmed than ever. "I don't want that! I want to stow away with Kate." He hesitated, then added, "She'll be happier in there, more secure. And I do want to be with her; I want to know that side of her."

"Then what's wrong?"

The clone sank to his knees in the dirt. For a second, Peer thought he was sobbing, then he realized that the noise was laughter.

The clone recovered his composure and said, "Nothing's *wrong*—but how do you expect me to take it? The two of us, cut off from everything else. Not just the real world, but all the other Copies."

Peer said, "If you get lonely, you can always generate new people. You'll have access to ontogenesis software—and no reason to care about the slowdown."

The clone started laughing again. Tears streamed down his face. Hugging himself, he tumbled sideways onto the ground. Peer looked on, bemused. The clone said, "Here I am trying to steel myself for the wedding, and already you're threatening me with children."

Suddenly, he reached out and grabbed Peer by one ankle, then dragged him off the step. Peer hit the ground on his arse with a jarring thud. His first instinct was to freeze the clone's power to interact with him, but he stopped himself. He was in no danger—and if his twin wanted to burn off some aggression on his brother-creator, he could take it. They were evenly matched, after all.

Two minutes later, Peer was lying with his face in the dirt and his arms pinned behind his back. The clone kneeled over him, breathless but triumphant.

Peer said, "All right, you win. Now get off me—or I'll double my height, put on forty kilograms, and get up and flatten you."

The clone said, "Do you know what we should do?"

"Shake hands and say goodbye."

"Toss a coin."

"For what?"

The clone laughed. "What do you think?"

"You said you were happy to go."

"I am. But so should you be. I say we toss a coin. If I win, we swap key numbers."

"That's illegal!"

"*Illegal!*" The clone was contemptuous. "Listen to the Solipsist Nation Copy invoke the laws of the world! It's easily done. The software exists. All you have to do is agree."

Talking was difficult; Peer spat out sand, but there was a seed of some kind caught between his teeth which he couldn't dislodge. He felt a curious reluctance to "cheat," though—to remove the seed from his mouth, or the clone from his back. It had been so long since he'd been forced to endure the slightest discomfort that the novelty seemed to outweigh the inconvenience.

He said, "All right. I'll do it."

And if he lost? But why should he fear that? Five minutes ago, he'd been prepared to give rise to—to *become*—the clone who'd stow away.

They created the coin together, the only way to ensure that it was subject to no hidden influences. The reality editor they jointly invoked offered a standard object ready-made for their purpose, which they decorated as a one-pound coin. The physics of flipping a real coin wouldn't come into it; any Copy could easily calculate and execute a flick of the thumb leading to a predetermined outcome. The result would be controlled by a random number generator deep in the hidden layers of the operating system.

Peer said, "I toss, you call"—at exactly the same time as the clone. He laughed. The clone smiled faintly. Peer was about to defer, then decided to wait. A few seconds later, he said, alone, "All right, you toss."

As the coin went up, Peer thought about encasing it in a second object, an invisibly thin shell under his control alone—but the long list of attributes of the fair coin probably included crying foul if its true faces were concealed. He shouted "Heads!" just before the thing hit the dirt.

The two of them fell to their hands and knees, almost bumping heads. A hen approached; Peer shooed it away with a backward kick.

President Kinnock, in profile, glinted in the dust.

The clone met his eyes. Peer did his best not to look relieved—short of severing ties with his body. He tried to read the clone's expression, and failed; all he saw was a reflection of his own growing numbness. Pirandello had said it was impossible to feel any real emotion while staring into a mirror. Peer decided to take that as a good sign. They were still one person, after all—and that was the whole point.

The clone rose to his feet, dusting off his knees and elbows.

Peer took a hologram-embossed library card from the back pocket of his jeans and handed it over; it was an icon for a copy of all the environments, customized utilities, bodies, memories and other data he'd accumulated since his resurrection.

The clone said, "Don't worry about me—or Kate. We'll look after each other. We'll be happy." As he spoke, he morphed smoothly into an older body.

Peer said, "Ditto." He reached up and shook the young man's hand. Then he summoned one of his control windows and froze the clone, leaving the motionless body visible as an icon for the snapshot file. He shrunk it to a height of a few centimeters, flattened it into a two-dimensional postcard, and wrote on the back: TO MALCOLM CARTER.

Then he walked down the road a kilometer to one of Kate's little touches, a postbox marked US MAIL, and dropped the postcard in.

19

(Remit not paucity)

The anaesthetist said, "Count backward from ten."

Maria said, "Ten."

She dreamed of arriving on Francesca's doorstep with a suitcase full of money. As she walked down the hall behind her mother, the case fell open, and hundred-dollar bills fluttered out and filled the air like confetti.

Francesca turned to her, radiant with health. She said tenderly, "You shouldn't have, my darling. But I understand. You can't take it with you."

Maria laughed. "You can't take it with you."

Her father was in the living room, dressed for his wedding day, although not as young. He beamed and held out his arms to Maria. His parents, and Francesca's parents, stood behind him—and as Maria approached, she saw from on high that behind her grandparents were cousins and aunts, great-grandparents and great-aunts, row after row of relatives and ancestors, stretching back into the depths of the house, laughing and chattering. The money had brought them all back to life. How could she have been so selfish as to think of denying them this grand reunion?

Maria threaded her way through the crowd, greeting people she'd never known existed. Handsome, dark-eyed seventh cousins kissed her hand and whispered compliments in a beautiful dialect she didn't understand. Veiled widows in elegant black dresses stood arm-in-arm with their resurrected husbands. Children weaved between the adults' legs, stealing food by the handful and cramming it into their mouths on the run.

The clinic's neurologist turned out to be a distant relative. Maria cupped her hands to the woman's ear and shouted over the noise of the party: "Have I been scanned yet? Will my Copy remember any of this?" The neurologist explained that the scan only captured memories laid down permanently as changes in synaptic strengths; the fleeting electrochemistry of this dream would be lost forever. She added cryptically, "Lost to whoever's not having it."

Maria felt herself waking. Suddenly afraid that she might be the Copy, she struggled to remain in the dream—as if she could force her way back through the crowd, back through the plot, and leave by a different exit. But the scene grew vague and unconvincing; she could feel the heavy presence of her waking body: her aching shoulders, her swollen tongue.

She opened her eyes. She was alone in the Landau Clinic's cheerfully decorated recovery room; she'd been wheeled through for a patient's-eye view before being given the anesthetic, so she'd know exactly what to expect. It took a few seconds for the truths of the dream to fade, though. *Her father was dead. Her grandparents were dead. There'd been no grand reunion. There never would be.*

As for the Copy . . . her scan file didn't even exist, yet; the raw tomographic data would take hours to be processed into a high-resolution anatomical map. And she could still change her mind and keep the results out of Durham's hands altogether. He'd paid the clinic for the scan, but if she refused to hand over the file there'd be nothing he could do about it.

The recovery room was softly lit, lined with odorless blue and orange flowers. Maria closed her eyes. If Durham's logic meant anything, *raw tomographic data* could probably process itself, *find itself conscious,* as easily as any Copy who'd been chopped up and run at random. There was no need for a finished scan file.

No need even to be scanned; the very same data surely existed, scattered about the universe, whether or not it was ever plucked from her brain and assembled in what she thought of as *one place.*

In fact, if Durham was right—if the events he believed

would take place in his TVC universe could *find themselves* in the dust—then those events *would* happen, regardless. It could make no difference what anyone did in this world. The whole Garden-of-Eden project was superfluous. Every permutation of the dust which was capable of perceiving itself, making sense of itself, would do just that. And all she would have achieved by refusing to be scanned would have been to deny the Maria of that permutation a history which seemed to overlap with her own particular life. While a third woman—in another world, another permutation—would have taken her place in that role.

Maria opened her eyes. She'd just recalled the first thing she'd meant to do on waking. Every scanner was programmed to recognize—in real time, before all the arduous data processing that followed—the magnetic resonance spectrum of four or five special dyes, which could be used for alignment and identification. The scanning technician had obligingly loaned her a "number three" marker pen—and instructed the scanner to blind itself to that particular dye.

She pulled her hands out from under the sheets. Her left palm still read: YOU ARE NOT THE COPY.

She licked her fingers and started rubbing the unnecessary words away.

Maria arrived at the north Sydney flat around half past twelve. Two terminals were set up side by side on Durham's kitchen table; other than that, the place was as bare as it had been the last time she'd called.

Although it wasn't, technically, necessary, Maria had insisted that she and Durham be in the same physical location throughout what he called the "launch"—the running of the first moments of the TVC universe as software on a real computer, the act which would supposedly seed an independent, self-sustaining universe, taking up where the version relying on real-world hardware left off. At least this way she could monitor the keys he pressed and the words he spoke, without having to wonder if she was being shown what was really going on at that level. She had no idea what she was guarding against—but Durham was a highly intelligent man with some very strange beliefs, and she had no reason to feel confident that he'd revealed the full extent of his delusions. His clients had confirmed part of his story—and they would have had the resources to check much more of it than she had—but Durham might still have lied to them about what was going on inside his head.

She wanted to trust him, she wanted to believe that she'd finally reached the truth—but it was hard to put any limits on how wrong she might yet be. She felt she'd known him too long to seriously fear for her physical safety—but the possibility remained that everything she thought she'd understood about the man would turn out, once again, to have been utterly misconceived. If he came away from the kitchen sink brandishing a carving knife, calmly announcing his intention to sacrifice her to the Spirit of the New Moon, she'd have no right to feel betrayed, or surprised. She couldn't expect to live off the proceeds of insanity, and also take for granted the usual parameters of civilized behavior.

The flesh-and-blood Durham was only half the problem. Once the program simulating a TVC cellular automaton was started, the plan was that neither she nor Durham would intervene at all. Any external tinkering would violate the automaton's rules—the fundamental laws of the new universe—making a mockery of the whole endeavor. Only *Durham's Copy,* being run on the simulated TVC computers, could act in harmony with those laws. They would always have the option of aborting the project, pulling the plug—but in every other respect, the Copy would be in control.

(Of course, aborting the simulation if something went wrong would not—in Durham's eyes—prevent the spawning of an independent universe beyond their control . . . but it might leave them with enough unspent computer time for a second attempt.)

With her hands tied once the universe was running, her only way to influence what did or didn't happen was through the Garden-of-Eden configuration—which included all the programs the TVC lattice would initially run. Maria had written part of this internal launch software herself; Durham had written, or commissioned, the rest, but she'd checked it all personally. And she'd built in a safeguard: all the Copies but Durham's would be blocked from running until the TVC processors had solved a suitably intractable mathematical equation. Maria had estimated that the world's combined computing resources couldn't have cracked the problem in under a decade; thirty million dollars' worth, minus overheads, wouldn't come close. That was no obstacle in the eyes of Durham and his followers; the ever-growing resources of the burgeoning TVC universe would make light work of it, solving the equation within a week or two of the launch. But short of any such universe coming into existence— and so long as the test wasn't circumvented—there was no chance of a second Maria Deluca, or anyone else, waking. It was her guarantee that there'd be no virtual Jonestown. Just one lone prophet flickering in and out of existence.

Durham made instant coffee. Maria surveyed the spartan room. She said, "This isn't good enough, you know. We should have two hundred people wearing headsets, and a giant screen taking up an entire wall. Like one of the old NASA missions."

Durham spoke over the sound of boiling water. "Don't worry; we'll be using more computing power per second than NASA used for the entire Apollo program."

Computing power. One more thing to worry about. Maria logged on to the QIPS exchange; the rate was up slightly since she'd last checked, but so far there was no sign of what she dreaded. In the event that Operation Butterfly entered the market again, today of all days, the Garden of Eden would be frozen out, postponed until the QIPS rate returned to normal levels. That wouldn't make the slightest difference to Durham or his followers—even if the launch program was thrown off the network halfway through, and only completed days, or weeks, later. Real time was irrelevant. Maria could appreciate the logic of that—but the thought of a delay, or an unexpected slowdown, still made her sick with anxiety. Every legal opinion she'd obtained had made it clear that neither she nor Durham were likely to face prosecution—and if charges *were* brought against them, a conviction was highly improbable . . .

and even if that happened, an appeal would almost certainly succeed. Nonetheless, every day she'd spent working with Durham as a knowing "accomplice" had made her feel more vulnerable to the whims of the authorities. Hayden had treated her icily when she'd confessed to having abandoned her laughable "undercover" role. The risk of harassment would hardly vanish the moment the project was completed—but the relief would still be considerable.

She was beginning to regret having honored her promise not to try to record Durham's clients' statements assuring her that they were fully informed participants in the scheme. The authenticated messages she'd viewed—on public terminals— might not have been the equivalent of human testimony, but having them stored away on a chip somewhere would have made her feel a lot more secure. Regardless of the legal status of the Copies, she couldn't imagine being prosecuted for fraud if she could show that the *de facto* "victims of the crime" knew exactly what they were paying for.

Durham set her coffee down on the table. Maria mumbled thanks as he sat beside her. He said, "No last-minute qualms? You can still back out if you want to."

She kept her eyes on the screen, the flickering pie chart of the QIPS exchange. "Don't tempt me." As if she'd seriously consider blowing her one real chance to have Francesca scanned—after all the work, all the anxiety—for no better reason than a laughable, microscopic fear that this artificial universe *might actually blossom into self-contained existence.*

Durham's terminal beeped. Maria glanced at his screen; a message box said PRIORITY COMMUNICATION. She looked away as he viewed the text.

"Speaking of last-minute qualms, Riemann's changed his mind. He wants in."

Maria said irritably, "Well, tell him it's too late. Tell him he's missed the boat." She wasn't serious; from what she knew of the project's finances, Durham had been set to barely break even by the end of the day. The price of one more ticket would transform his fortunes completely.

He said, "Relax—it will take half an hour at the most to fit him in. And his fee will cover much more than the increase in data; we'll be able to run the whole launch a bit longer."

Maria had to pause to let that sink in. Then she said, "You're going to blow most of *two million ecus* on stretching out something that—"

Durham smiled. "That *what?* That would have worked anyway?"

"That *you believe* would have worked anyway!"

"The longer I get to see my Copy observing the TVC universe, the happier I'll be. I don't *know* what it will take to anchor the automaton rules—but if ten watertight experiments sounds good, then eleven sounds better."

Maria pushed her chair back and walked away from her terminal. Durham tapped at his keyboard, first invoking the programs which would recompute the Garden-of-Eden configuration to include the new passenger and his luggage— then directing the windfall from Riemann straight into the project's JSN account.

She said, "What's wrong with you? Two million ecus is more than two million dollars! You could have lived on that for the rest of your life!"

Durham kept typing, passing Riemann's documents through a series of legal checks. "I'll get by."

"Given it to a charity, then!"

Durham frowned, but said patiently, "I gather that Thomas Riemann gives generously to famine relief and crop research every year. He chose to spend this money on a place in my sanctuary; it's hardly my role to channel his funds into whatever you or I decide is the worthiest cause." He glanced at her and added, mock-solemnly, "That's called fraud, Ms. Deluca. You can go to prison for that."

Maria was unmoved. "You could have kept something for yourself. For this life, this world. I don't imagine any of your clients expected you to do all this for nothing."

Durham finished at the terminal and turned to her. "I don't expect you to understand. You treat the whole project as a joke—and that's fine. But you can hardly expect me to run it on that basis."

Maria didn't even know what she was angry about anymore: the delayed launch, the obscene waste of money—or
just Durham sitting there making perfect sense to himself, as
always.

She said, "The project *is* a joke. Three hundred million people are living in refugee camps, and you're offering *sanctuary*
to sixteen billionaires! What do they need protection from?
There's never going to be an *anti-Copy revolution!* They're
never going to be *shut down!* You know as well as I do that
they'll just sit there getting richer for the next ten thousand
years!"

"Possibly."

"So you are a fraud then, aren't you? Even if your 'sanctuary' really does come into existence—even if you prove your
precious theory right—what have your backers gained?
You've sent their clones into solitary confinement, that's all.
You might as well have put them in a black box at the bottom
of a mineshaft."

Durham said mildly, "That's not quite true. You talk about
Copies surviving ten thousand years. What about ten billion?
A hundred billion?"

She scowled. "Nothing's going to last that long. Haven't
you heard? They've found enough dark matter to reverse the
expansion of the universe in less than forty billion years—"

"Exactly. *This* universe isn't going to last."

Maria nodded sarcastically, and tried to say something
belittling, but the words stuck in her throat.

Durham continued blithely, "The TVC universe will never collapse. *Never.* A hundred billion years, a hundred trillion; it makes
no difference, it will always be expanding."

Maria said weakly, "Entropy—"

"Is not a problem. Actually, 'expanding' is the wrong word;
the TVC universe grows like a crystal, it doesn't stretch like a
balloon. Think about it. Stretching ordinary space increases
entropy; everything becomes more spread out, more disordered.
Building more of a TVC cellular automaton just gives you
more room for data, more computing power, more order.
Ordinary matter would eventually decay, but these computers

aren't made out of *matter*. There's nothing in the cellular automaton's rules to prevent them from lasting for ever."

Maria wasn't sure what she'd imagined before; Durham's universe—being made of the same "dust" as the real one, merely rearranged—suffering the same fate? She couldn't have given the question much thought, because that verdict was nonsensical. The rearrangement was in time as well as space; Durham's universe could take a point of space-time from just before the Big Crunch, and follow it with another from ten million years B.C. And even if there was only a limited total amount of "dust" to work with, there was no reason why it couldn't be reused in different combinations, again and again. The fate of the TVC automaton would only have to make *internal* sense—and the thing would have no reason, ever, to come to an end.

She said, "So you promised these people . . . immortality?"

"Of course."

"Literal immortality? Outliving the universe?"

Durham feigned innocence, but he was clearly savoring the shock he'd given her. "That's what the word means. Not: dying after a very long time. Just: not dying, period."

Maria leaned back against the wall, arms folded, trying to cast aside the feeling that the whole conversation was as insubstantial as anything Durham had hallucinated in the Blacktown psychiatric ward. She thought: *When Francesca's been scanned, I'm going to take a holiday. Visit Aden in Seoul, if I have to. Anything to get away from this city, this man.*

She said, "Ideas like that are powerful things. One of these days you're going to hurt someone."

Durham looked wounded himself, at that. He said, "All I've tried to do is be honest. *I know:* I lied to you, at first—and I'm sorry. I had no right to do that. But what was I supposed to do with the truth? Keep it locked up in my head? Hide it from the world? Give no one else the chance to believe, or disbelieve?" He fixed his eyes on her, calm and sane as ever; she looked away.

He said, "When I first came out of hospital, I wanted to publish everything. And I tried . . . but nobody reputable was interested—and publishing in the junk-science journals would have been nothing but an admission that it was all bullshit. So what else could I do, except look for private backers?"

Maria said, "I understand. Forget it. You've done what you thought you had to—I don't blame you for that." The clichés nearly made her gag, but all she could think about was shutting him up. She was sick of being reminded that the ideas which were nothing but a means to an end, for her—the ideas she could turn her back on forever, in eight hours' time—were this man's entire life.

He looked at her searchingly, as if genuinely seeking guidance. "If you'd believed everything I believe, would you have kept it all to yourself? Would you have lived out your life pretending to the world that you'd merely been insane?"

Maria was saved from answering by a beep from Durham's terminal. The Garden-of-Eden configuration had been recomputed; Thomas Riemann's snapshot was now built into their cellular automaton equivalent of the Big Bang.

Durham swung his chair around to face the screen. He said cheerfully, "All aboard the ship of fools!"

Maria took her place beside him. She reached over and tentatively touched his shoulder. Without looking at her, he reached up and squeezed her hand gently, then removed it.

Following a long cellular automaton tradition, the program which would bootstrap the TVC universe into existence was called FIAT. Durham hit a key, and a starburst icon appeared on both of their screens.

He turned to Maria. "You do the honors."

She was about to object, but then it didn't seem worth arguing. She'd done half the work, but this was Durham's creation, whoever cut the ribbon.

She prodded the icon; it exploded like a cheap flashy firework, leaving a pin-cushion of red and green trails glowing on the screen.

"Very tacky."

Durham grinned. "I thought you'd like it."

The decorative flourish faded, and a shimmering blue-white cube appeared: a representation of the TVC universe. The

Garden-of-Eden state had contained a billion ready-made processors, a thousand along each edge of the cube—but that precise census was already out of date. Maria could just make out the individual machines, like tiny crystals; each speck comprised sixty million automaton cells—not counting the memory array, which stretched into the three extra dimensions, hidden in this view. The data preloaded into most of the processors was measured in terabytes: scan files, libraries, databases; the seed for Planet Lambert—and its sun, and its three barren sibling planets. Everything had been assembled, if not on one physical computer—the TVC automaton was probably spread over fifteen or twenty processor clusters—at least as one logical whole. One pattern.

Durham reduced the clock rate until the blue-white shimmer slowed to a stroboscopic flickering, then a steady alternation of distinct colors. The outermost processors were building copies of themselves; in this view, blue coded for complete, working processors, and white coded for half-finished machines. Each layer of blue grew a layer of white, which abruptly turned blue, and so on. The skin of this universe came with instructions to build one more layer exactly like itself (including a copy of the same instructions), and then wait for further commands to be passed out from the hub.

Durham zoomed in by a factor of two hundred, slowed down the clock rate further, and then changed the representation to show individual automaton cells as color-coded symbols. The processors were transformed from featureless blue or white boxes into elaborate, multicolored, three-dimensional mazes, rectilinear filigree alive with sparks of light.

In the throes of reproduction, each processor could be seen sprouting hundreds of pairs of fine red and green "construction wires," which grew straight out into the surrounding empty space—until they all reached the same predetermined length, abruptly turned a tight one-hundred-and-eighty degrees, and then started growing back in the opposite direction. Glowing with elaborate moving striations, the wires zigzagged back and forth between the surface of the mother computer and an unmarked boundary plane—until between them, they'd filled in the region completely, like some strange electronic silk weaving itself into a solid cocoon.

In close-up, the wires resolved into long lines of cells marked with arrowheads, some rendered in the brighter hues which represented "activated" states. Glowing stripes built from the binary code of bright and dim moved down the wire from arrow to arrow: the data of the blueprint for the daughter machine being shuffled out from the central memory.

With the clock rate slowed still further, the process could be followed in detail. Wherever a pulse of brightness reached the end of a construction wire, the transparent "vacuum" of the null state was transformed into an "embryonic" cell, shown as a nondescript gray cube. Subsequent data told the new cell what to become—each pulse, or absence of a pulse, converting it into a slightly more specialized transition state, zeroing in on the particular final state required. The construction wires grew out from the mother computer using this principle, extending themselves by building more of themselves at their tips.

Having filled the entire region which the daughter machine would occupy, they then worked backward, retracting one step at a time; unweaving their zig-zag cocoon, and leaving behind whatever the blueprint required. The whole process looked grotesquely inefficient—far more time was spent on extending and retracting the wires themselves than on creating the cells of the daughter machine—but it kept the rules of the automaton as simple as possible.

Durham said, "This all looks fine to me. Okay to proceed?"

"Sure." Maria had grown mesmerized; she'd forgotten her urgency, forgotten herself. "Crank it up." At any speed where they could keep track of events at the level of individual processors—let alone individual cells—nothing useful would ever get done. Durham let the clock rate revert to the maximum they could afford, and the grid became a blur.

In contrast, the next stage would be painfully slow. Durham made coffee and sandwiches. All the overheads of running a Copy on a system of computers which was, itself, a simulation, added up to a slowdown of about two hundred and fifty. More than four real-time minutes to a subjective second. There was no question of two-way communication—the TVC universe was hermetic, no data which hadn't been present from the outset could affect it in any way—but they could still spy on what was happening. Every hour, they could witness another fourteen seconds of what the Copy of Durham had done.

Maria spot-checked at other levels, starting with the software running directly on the TVC grid. The "machine language" of the TVC computers was about as arcane and ridiculous as that of any hypothetical Turing machine, six-dimensional or not, but it had been simple enough to instruct a metaprogrammer to write—and rigorously validate—a program which allowed them to simulate conventional modern computers. So the processor clusters in Tokyo or Dallas or Seoul were simulating a cellular automaton containing a lattice of bizarre immaterial computers . . . which in turn were simulating the logic (if not the physics) of the processor clusters themselves. From there on up, everything happened in exactly the same way as it did on a real machine—only much more slowly.

Maria munched cheese and lettuce between thick slices of white bread. It was a Tuesday afternoon; most of the flats around them were silent, and the street below was lifeless. The neighboring office blocks had no tenants, just a few furtive squatters; where the sun penetrated the nearest building at just the right angle, Maria could see clothes hung out to dry on lines stretched between office partitions.

Durham put on music, a twentieth-century opera called *Einstein on the Beach*. He didn't own a sound system, but he called up the piece from a library he'd bought for the Garden of Eden, and had a background task play it through his terminal's speakers.

Maria asked, "What will you do with yourself when this is over?"

Durham replied without hesitation. "Finish the whole set of fifty experiments. Start Planet Lambert unfolding. Celebrate for about a week. Stroll down the main street of Permutation City. Wait for your little locking device to disengage. Wake up my passengers in their own private worlds—and hope that some of them are willing to talk to me, now and then. Start catching up on Dostoyevsky. In the original—"

"Yeah, very funny. I said *you,* not *him.*"

"I'd like to think of us as inseparable."

"Seriously."

He shrugged. "What will *you* do?"

Maria put her empty plate down, and stretched. "Oh . . . sleep in until noon, for a week. Lie in bed wondering exactly how I'm going to break the news to my mother that she can now afford to be scanned—without making it sound like I'm telling her what to do."

"Perish the thought."

Maria said simply, "She's dying. And she can save herself—without hurting anyone. Without *stealing food from the mouths of the next generation,* or whatever it is she thinks makes being scanned such a crime. Do you really think she—honestly—doesn't want to stay alive? Or wouldn't want to, if she could think it through clearly, without all the guilt and moralizing bullshit her generation saddled her with?"

Durham wasn't taking sides. "I don't know her, I can't answer that."

"She was a child of the nineties. Her kindergarten teachers probably told her that the pinnacle of her existence would be fertilizing a rainforest when she died." Maria thought it over. "And the beauty of it is . . . *she can still do that.* Scan her, put her through a meat grinder . . . scatter the results over the Daintree."

"You're a sick woman."

"I'll have the money soon. I can afford to joke."

Their terminals chimed simultaneously; the first fourteen seconds of life inside were ready to be viewed. Maria felt the food she'd just swallowed harden into a lump like a closed fist in her gut. Durham told the program to proceed.

The Copy sat in a simple, stylized control room, surrounded by floating interface windows. One window showed a representation of a small part of the TVC lattice. The Copy couldn't take the same God's-eye view of the lattice as they had; the software they'd used could only function on a level right outside his universe. There was no simple way he could discover the state of any given automaton cell; instead, a system of construction and sensor wires (all joined to specialized processors) had been built around a small region in the center of the lattice. Durham had christened this apparatus "the Chamber." What went on deep inside the Chamber could be deduced, indirectly, from the data which ended up flowing down the sensor wires. It wasn't as complicated as working out what had happened in a particle accelerator collision, based on the information registered by surrounding detectors—but the principle was the same, and so was the purpose. The Copy had to conduct experiments to test his own fundamental "laws of physics"—the TVC automaton's rules. And the (simulated) modern computers running his VR environment had a (simulated) link to the Chamber, like the real-world computers linked to any real-world accelerator.

The Copy said, "Setting up the first experiment." He deftly typed a sequence of code letters on his keyboard. Durham had rehearsed the whole thing before his scan, until he could perform each of fifty experiments in ten seconds flat, but Maria was still astonished that the Copy—who had woken abruptly to find himself seated in the control room, without any preliminaries, any chance to grow accustomed to his identity, and his fate—had had the presence of mind to leap straight into the task. She'd entertained visions of this first version of Durham to wake inside a computer finally realizing that "the other twenty-three times" were nothing at all like the real experience—and telling his original about it in no uncertain terms. But there didn't seem to be much chance of that; the Copy just sat there typing as if his life depended on it.

The experimental setups could have been automated. The checking of the results could have been automated, too. The Copy could have spent two minutes sitting and watching a flashing green sign which said EVERYTHING IS JUST WHAT YOU WOULD HAVE EXPECTED, DON'T WORRY ABOUT THE MESSY DETAILS. There was no such thing as a set of perceptions for the Copy which could *prove* that he inhabited a cellular automaton which obeyed all the rules which he hoped were

being obeyed. It was all down to Occam's razor in the end—
and hoping that the simplest explanation for perceiving a display showing the correct results was that the correct results
were actually occurring.

Maria stared into the screen, over the Copy's shoulder, at
the interface window within. When he typed the last code letter, the assembly of cells he'd constructed in the Chamber
became unstable and started creating new cells in the surrounding "vacuum," setting off a cascade which eventually impinged
on the sensor wires. Disconcertingly, the Copy watched both a
simulation—on his own terms—of what *ought to be* happening
in the Chamber, and then a moment later a reconstruction of
the "actual" events, based on the sensor data.

Both evidently matched the results of the simulations which
the original Durham had committed to memory. The Copy
clapped his hands together loudly in obvious jubilation, bellowed something incoherent, then said, "Setting up the sec—"

Maria was becoming giddy with all the levels of reality
they were transecting—but she was determined to appear as
blasé as ever. She said, "What did you do, wake him up with a
brain full of amphetamines?"

Durham replied in the same spirit. "No, he's high on life. If
you've only got two minutes of it, you might as well enjoy it."

They waited, passing the time checking software more or
less at random, displaying everything from firing patterns in the
Copy's model brain to statistics on the performance of the TVC
computers. Intuitively, the elaborate hierarchy of simulations
within simulations seemed vulnerable, unstable—every level
multiplying the potential for disaster. But if the setup resembled
a house of cards, it was a simulated house of cards: perfectly
balanced in a universe free of vibrations and breezes. Maria was
satisfied that the architecture at every level was flawless—so
long as the level beneath held up. It would take a glitch in the
real-world hardware to bring the whole thing tumbling down.
That was rare, though not impossible.

They viewed the second installment of the Copy at work,
then took a coffee break. *Einstein on the Beach* was still playing, repetitive and hypnotic. Maria couldn't relax; she was too

wired on caffeine and nervous energy. She was relieved that everything was running smoothly—no software problems, no Operation Butterfly, no sign of either version of Durham going weird on her. At the same time, there was something deeply unsettling about the prospect of the whole thing unwinding, exactly as predicted, for the next six hours—and then simply coming to an end. *She'd have the money for Francesca, then, and that justified everything* . . . but the absolute futility of what they were doing still kept striking her anew—in between bouts of worrying over such absurdities as whether or not she could have made a better job of *A. hydrophila*'s response to dehydration. Durham would let her publish all the Autoverse work, so that hadn't been a complete waste of time—and she could keep on refining it for as long as she liked before unleashing it on the skeptics . . . but she could already imagine the—bizarre—regret she'd feel because the improvements had come too late to be incorporated into the "genuine" Planet Lambert: the one they were currently flushing down a multi-million-dollar drain.

She said, "It's a pity none of your passengers' originals have bodies. Having paid for all this, they should be here, watching."

Durham agreed. "Some of them may be here in spirit; I've granted them all the same viewing access to the simulation that we have. And their auditors will receive a verified log of everything—proof that they got what they paid for. But you're right. This isn't much of a celebration; you should be clinking glasses and sharing caviar with the others."

She laughed, offended. "*Others?* I'm not one of your *victims*—I'm just the confidence artist's accomplice, remember? And I'm not here to *celebrate;* I'm only here to make sure your doppelgänger doesn't hot-wire the software and wake me up."

Durham was amused. "Why would he try to wake you so soon? Do you think he's going to become unbearably lonely in the space of two minutes?"

"I have no idea what he might do, or why. That's the whole problem. He's just as fucked up as you are."

Durham said nothing. Maria wished she could take back the words. What was the point of needling him and mocking him, again and again—did she think she could ever *bring him down to Earth?* It was all a matter of pride; she couldn't let a second go by without reminding him that she hadn't been seduced by his ideas. Computer junkie, artificial life freak; she still had her feet planted firmly in the real world. His vision of an Autoverse biosphere had impressed her—when she'd thought he'd understood that it could never be anything but a thought experiment. And all the work he'd done on the TVC universe was ingenious—however ultimately pointless it was. In a way, she even admired his stubborn refusal to give in to common sense and accept his delusions for what they were.

She just couldn't bear the thought that he harbored the faintest hope that he'd persuaded her to take the "dust hypothesis" seriously.

At three minutes past ten, the money ran out—all but enough to pay for the final tidying-up. The TVC automaton was shut down between clock ticks; the processors and memory which had been allocated to the massive simulation were freed for other users—the memory, as always, wiped to uniform zeroes first for the sake of security. The whole elaborate structure was dissolved in a matter of nanoseconds.

Night had turned the windows of the flat to mirrors. No lights showed in the empty office towers; if there'd been cooking fires from the squatters, they'd been extinguished long ago. Maria felt disconnected, adrift in time; the trip north across the harbor bridge in sunlight seemed like a distant memory, a dream.

The individual components of the Garden of Eden were still held in mass storage. Maria deleted her scan file, carefully checking the audit records to be sure that the data hadn't been read more often than it should have been. The numbers checked out; that was no guarantee, but it was reassuring.

Durham deleted everything else.

The recordings of the spy software remained, and they

viewed the last brief scene of the Copy at work—and then replayed the whole two-minute recording.

Maria watched with a growing sense of shame. The individual fragments had barely affected her, but viewed without interruption, the Copy took on the air of a deranged sect leader driving a bus full of frozen billionaires straight toward the edge of a cliff—accelerating euphorically in the sure and certain knowledge that the thing *would* fly, carrying them all off into a land beyond the sunset. She clung to her rationalizations: the Copy's limited separate identity, his joyful demise.

When the replay stopped in mid-experiment, Durham closed his eyes and let his head hang forward. He wept silently. Maria looked away.

He said, "I'm sorry. I'm embarrassing you."

She turned back to him; he was smiling, and sniffling. She wanted to embrace him; the urge was half sisterly, half sexual. He was pale and unshaven, obviously drained—but there was more life in his eyes than ever, as if the fulfilment of his obsession had liberated him from his past so completely that he faced the world now like a newborn child.

He said, "Champagne?"

Maria hardened her heart. She still had no reason to trust him. She said, "Let me check my bank balance first; I might not have anything to celebrate." Durham giggled, as if the very idea that he might have cheated her was preposterous. She ignored him, and used the terminal. The six hundred thousand dollars he'd promised had been deposited.

She stared at the digits on the screen for a while, numb with the strange truth that the simple pattern of data they represented, sanctified as "wealth," could travel out into the living, breathing, decaying world . . . and return, enriched beyond measure: imprinted with everything which made Francesca human.

She said, "One glass. I'm cycling."

They emptied the bottle. Durham paced around the flat, growing increasingly hyperactive. "Twenty-three Copies! Twenty-three lives! Imagine how my successor must be feeling, right now! He has the proof, he *knows* he was right. All I have is the knowledge that I gave him that chance—and even that's too much to bear." He wept again, stopped abruptly. He turned and gazed at Maria imploringly. "I did it all to myself, but it was still madness, still torture. Do you think I knew, when I started out, how much pain and confusion there'd be? Do you think I knew what it would do to me? I should have listened to Elizabeth—but there is no Elizabeth here. I'm not alive. Do you think I'm *alive*? If a Copy's not human, what am I? Twenty-three times removed?"

Maria tried to let it wash over her. She couldn't feel simple compassion—she was too tainted, too culpable—so she tried to feel nothing at all. Durham had systematically pursued his beliefs as far as they could take him; he'd either be cured by that, or ready for another round of nanosurgery. Nothing she could do now would make any difference. She started to tell herself that by helping with the project—without ever conceding its premise— she might have helped him exorcize his delusions . . . but that wasn't the point. She'd done it all for the money. For Francesca. And for herself. To spare herself the pain of Francesca dying. *How dare the woman think of refusing?* Copies, like funerals, were for the benefit of the survivors.

Durham suddenly went quiet. He sat down beside her, disheveled and contrite; she wasn't sure if he'd become sober, or just moved on to a new phase. It was half past two; the opera had finished playing hours ago, the flat was silent.

He said, "I've been ranting. I'm sorry."

The two swivel chairs they'd been sitting on all day were the only furniture in the room besides the table; there was no sofa she could sleep on, and the floor looked cold and hard. Maria thought about heading home; she could catch a train, and collect her cycle later.

She stood; then, barely thinking about it, leaned down and kissed him on the forehead.

She said, "Goodbye."

Before she could straighten up, he put a hand on her cheek. His fingers were cool. She hesitated, then kissed him on the mouth— then almost recoiled, angry with herself. *I feel guilty, I feel sorry for him, I only want to make up for that somehow.* Then he met her eyes. He wasn't drunk any more. She believed he understood everything she was feeling—the whole knot of confusion and shame—and all he wanted to do was smooth it away.

They kissed again. She was sure.

They undressed each other on the way to the bedroom. He said, "Tell me what you want, tell me what you like. I haven't done this for a long time."

"How long?"

"Several lives ago."

He was skilled with his tongue, and persistent. She almost came—but before it could happen, everything broke down into isolated sensations: pleasant but meaningless, faintly absurd. She closed her eyes and willed it, but it was like trying to cry for no reason. When she pushed him gently away, he didn't complain, or apologize, or ask stupid questions; she appreciated that.

They rested, and she explored his body. He was probably the oldest man she'd ever seen naked; certainly the oldest she'd ever touched. *Fifty.* He was . . . loose, rather than flabby; muscle had wasted rather than turned to fat. It was almost impossible to imagine Aden—twenty-four years old, and hard as a statue—ever succumbing to the same process. But he would. And her own body had already begun.

She slithered around and took his penis in her mouth, trying to psych herself past the comic strangeness of the act, trying to grow drunk on the stench of it, working with her tongue and teeth until he begged her to stop. They rearranged their bodies clumsily so they were side by side; he entered her and came at once. He cried out, bellowing in obvious pain, not histrionic delight. He gritted his teeth and turned ashen as he withdrew; she held his shoulders until he could explain. "My . . . left testicle went into spasm. It just . . . happens sometimes. It feels like it's being crushed in a vise." He laughed and blinked away the tears. She kissed him and ran a finger around his groin.

"That's awful. Does it still hurt?"

"Yes. Don't stop."

Afterward, she found she didn't want to touch him; his skin turned clammy as their sweat dried, and when he seemed to fall asleep, she disentangled herself from his embrace and shifted to the edge of the bed.

She didn't know what she'd done: complicated everything, set herself up for yet another stage in their convoluted relationship—or simply marked the end of it, bidden him farewell? An hour of disastrous sex hadn't resolved anything: she still felt guilty for taking the money, "taking advantage" of him.

What would she do, if he wanted to see her again? She couldn't face the prospect of spending the next six months listening to him fantasize about the grand future which lay ahead for his homemade universe. She'd taken some pride in the fact that she'd never once humored him, never pretended for a moment to have accepted his theories—and she'd never met a nominally sane person who could disagree with her so graciously. But there'd be something dishonest about trying to forge a lasting friendship between them, in the face of her skepticism. And if she ever succeeded in disillusioning him . . . she'd probably feel guilty about that, as well.

The long day was catching up with her, it was too hard to think it through. Decisions would have to wait until morning.

Light from the kitchen spilled through the doorway onto her face; she called out softly to the house controller, to no effect, so she got up and switched off the light manually. She heard Durham stir as she felt her way back into the room. She paused in the doorway, suddenly reluctant to approach him.

He said, "I don't know what you think, but I didn't plan this."

She laughed. *What did he think he'd done? Seduced her?* "Neither did I. All I ever wanted from *you* was your money."

He was silent for a moment, but she could see his eyes and teeth flashing in the dark, and he seemed to be smiling.

He said, "That's all right. All I wanted from you was your soul."

20

(Can't you time trip?)

Resting between descents, Peer looked up and finally realized what had been puzzling him. The clouds above the skyscraper were motionless; not merely stationary with respect to the ground, but frozen in every detail. The wispiest tendrils at the edges, presumably vulnerable to the slightest breeze, remained undisturbed for as long as he studied them. The shape of every cloud seemed flawlessly natural—but all the dynamism implicit in the wind-wrought forms, compelling at a glance, was pure illusion. Nothing in the sky was changing.

For a moment, he was simply bemused by this whimsical detail. Then he remembered why he'd chosen it.

Kate had vanished. She'd lied; she hadn't cloned herself at all. She'd moved to Carter's city, leaving no other version behind.

Leaving him—or half of him—alone.

The revelation didn't bother him. On the skyscraper, nothing ever did. He clung to the wall, recuperating happily, and marveled at what he'd done to heal the pain. Back in cloud time, before he'd always been descending.

He'd set up the environment as usual—the city, the sky, the building—but frozen the clouds, as much to simplify things as to serve as a convenient reminder.

Then he'd mapped out a series of cues for memory and mood changes over fifteen subjective minutes. He'd merely sketched the progression, like a naive musician humming a melody to a transcriber; the software he'd used had computed the actual sequence of brain states. Moment would follow moment "naturally"; his model-of-a-brain would not be forced to do anything, but would simply follow its internal logic. By fine-tuning that logic in advance and loading the right memories, the desired sequence of mental events would unfold: from A to B to C to . . . A.

Peer looked over his shoulder at the ground, which never grew closer, and smiled. He'd dreamed of doing this before, but he'd never had the courage. Losing Kate forever—while knowing that he was with her—must have finally persuaded him that he had nothing to gain by putting it off any longer.

The scheme wouldn't slip his mind completely—he could vaguely remember experiencing exactly the same revelation several times before—but his short-term memory had been selectively impaired to limit the clarity of this recursive false history, and once he was distracted, a series of free associations would eventually lead him back to *exactly* the state of mind he'd been in at the cycle's beginning. His body—with respect to every visible cue in the environment—would also be back where it had started. The ground and sky were static, and every story of the building was identical, so his perceptions would be the same. And every muscle and joint in his body would have recovered perfectly, as always.

Peer laughed at his cloud-self's ingenuity, and started to descend again. It was an elegant situation, and he was glad he'd finally had a cloud-reason to make it happen.

There was one detail, though, which he couldn't focus on, one choice he'd made back in cloud time which he seemed to have decided to obscure from himself completely.

Had he programmed his exoself to let him run through the cycle a predetermined number of times? ABCABCABC . . . and then some great booming DEF breaking through the sky like the fist of God—or a tendril of cumulus actually moving—putting an end to his perpetual motion? A grappling hook could tear him from the side of the building, or some subtle change in the environment could nudge his thoughts out of their perfectly circular orbit. Either way, experiencing one uninterrupted cycle would be the same as experiencing a thousand, so if there was an alarm clock ticking away at all, his next cycle—subjectively—would be the one when the buzzer went off.

And if there was no clock? He might have left his fate in external hands. A chance communication from another Copy, or some event in the world itself, could be the trigger which would release him.

Or he might have chosen absolute solipsism. Grinding through the cycle whatever else happened, until his executor embezzled his estate, terrorists nuked the supercomputers, civilization crumbled, the sun went out.

Peer stopped and shook his head to flick sweat out of his eyes. The sense of *déjà vu* the action triggered was, presumably, purely synthetic; it told him nothing about the number of times he'd actually repeated the gesture. It suddenly struck him as unlikely that he'd done anything as inelegant as running the cycle more than once. His subjective time closed up in a loop, rolled in on itself; there was no need to follow the last moment with an *external* repetition of the first. Whatever happened—externally—"afterward," the loop was subjectively seamless and complete. He could have shut himself down completely, after computing a single cycle, and it would have made no difference.

The breeze picked up, cooling his skin. Peer had never felt so tranquil; so physically at ease, so mentally at peace. Losing Kate must have been traumatic, but he'd put that behind him. Once and for ever.

He continued his descent.

2 1

(Remit not paucity)

Maria woke from a dream of giving birth. A midwife had urged her, "Keep pushing! Keep pushing!" She'd screamed through gritted teeth, but done as she was told. The "child" had turned out to be nothing but a blood-stained statue, carved from smooth, dark wood.

Her head was throbbing. The room was in darkness. She'd taken off her wristwatch, but she doubted that she'd been asleep for long; if she had, the bed would have seemed unfamiliar, she would have needed time to remember where she was, and why. Instead, the night's events had come back to her instantly. It was long after midnight, but it wasn't a new day yet.

She sensed Durham's absence before reaching across the bed to confirm it, then she lay still for a while and listened. All she heard was distant coughing, coming from another flat. No lights were on; she would have seen the spill.

The smell hit her as she stepped out of the bedroom. Shit and vomit, with a sickly sweet edge. She had visions of Durham reacting badly to a day of stress and a night of champagne, and she almost turned around and went back to the bedroom, to open the window and bury her face in a pillow.

The bathroom door was half-closed, but there were no sound effects suggesting that he was still in there; not a moan. Her eyes began to water. She couldn't quite believe that she'd slept through all the noise.

She called out, "Paul? Are you all right?" There was no reply. If he was lying unconscious in a pool of vomit, alcohol had nothing to do with it; he had to be seriously ill. Food poisoning? She pushed open the door and turned on the light.

He was in the shower recess. She backed out of the room quickly, but details kept registering long after she'd retreated. Coils of intestine. Bloodred shit. He looked like he'd been kneeling, and then sprawled sideways. At first, she was certain that she'd seen the knife, red against the white tiles—but then she wondered if in fact she'd seen nothing but the Rorschach blot of a random blood stain.

Maria's legs started to give way. She made it to one of the chairs. She sat there, light-headed, fighting to remain conscious; she'd never fainted in her life, but for a time it was all she could do to keep herself from blacking out.

The first thing she felt clearly was a sense of astonishment at her own stupidity, as if she'd just marched, with her eyes wide open, straight into a brick wall. *Durham had believed that his Copy had achieved immortality—and proved the dust hypothesis. The whole purpose of his own life had been fulfilled by the project's completion. What had she expected him to do, after that? Carry on selling insurance?*

It was Durham she'd heard screaming through gritted teeth, shaping her dream.

And it was Durham who'd *kept pushing,* Durham who looked like he'd tried to give birth.

She called for an ambulance. "He's cut his abdomen open with a knife. The wound is very deep. I didn't look closely, but I think he's dead." She found that she could speak calmly to the emergency services switchboard puppet; if she'd had to say the same things to a human being, she knew she would have fallen apart.

When she hung up, her teeth started chattering, and she kept emitting brief sounds of distress which didn't seem to belong to her. She wanted to get dressed before the ambulance and police arrived, but she didn't have the strength to move—and the thought of even caring if she was discovered naked began to seem petty beyond belief. Then something broke through her paralysis, and she rose to her feet and staggered around the room, picking up the clothes they'd scattered on the floor just hours before.

She found herself fully dressed, slumped in a corner of the

living room, reciting a litany of excuses in her head. *She'd never humored him. She'd argued against his insane beliefs at every opportunity. How could she have saved him? By walking out on the project? That would have changed nothing. By trying to get him committed? His doctors had already pronounced him cured.*

The worst thing she'd done was stand by and let him shut down his own Copy.

And there was still a chance—

She sprang to her feet, rushed over to the nearest terminal, and logged back on to the project's JSN account.

But Durham's scan file was gone, deleted as meticulously, as irreversibly, as her own. The audit records showed no sign that the data had been preserved elsewhere; like her own file, it had even been flagged explicitly for exclusion from the JSN's automatic hourly backups. The only place the data had been reproduced had been inside the Garden-of-Eden configuration itself—and every trace of that structure had been obliterated.

She sat at the terminal, replaying the file which showed Durham's Copy conducting his experiments: testing the laws of his universe, rushing joyfully toward . . . *what?* The unheralded, inexplicable annihilation of everything he was in the process of establishing as the basis for his own existence?

And now his corpse lay in the bathroom, dead by his own hands, on his own terms; victim of his own seamless logic.

Maria buried her face in her hands. She wanted to believe that the two deaths were not the same. She wanted to believe that Durham had been right, all along. What had the JSN computers in Tokyo and Seoul meant to the Copy? No experiment performed within the TVC universe could ever have proved or disproved the existence of those machines. They were as irrelevant—to him—as Francesca's ludicrous God Who Makes No Difference.

So how could they have destroyed him? How could he be dead?

There were quick, heavy footsteps outside, then a pounding on the door. Maria went to open it.

She wanted to believe, but she couldn't.

22

(Remit not paucity)

JUNE 2051

Thomas prepared himself to witness a death.

The flesh-and-blood Riemann was the man who'd killed Anna—not the Copy who'd inherited the killer's memories. And the flesh-and-blood Riemann should have had the opportunity to reflect on that, before dying. He should have had a chance to accept his guilt, to accept his mortality. *And to absolve his successor.*

That hadn't been allowed to happen.

But it wasn't too late, even now. A software clone could still do it for him—*believing itself to be flesh and blood.* Revealing what the mortal, human self would have done, if only it had known that it was dying.

Thomas had found a suitable picture in a photo album—old chemical hardcopy images which he'd had digitized and restored soon after the onset of his final illness. Christmas, 1985: his mother, his father, his sister Karin and himself, gathered outside the family home, dazzled by the winter sunshine. Karin, gentle and shy, had died of lymphoma before the turn of the century. His parents had both survived into their nineties, showing every sign of achieving immortality by sheer force of will—but they'd died before scanning technology was perfected, having scorned Thomas's suggestion of cryonic preservation. "I have no intention," his father had explained curtly, "of doing to myself what *nouveau riche* Americans have done to their pets." The young man in the photograph didn't look much like the image Thomas would have conjured up by closing his eyes and struggling to remember—but the expression on his face, captured in transition from haunted to smug, rang true. Half afraid that the camera would reveal his secret; half daring it to try.

Thomas had kept copies of his deathbed scan file—off-line, in vaults in Geneva and New York—with no explicit purpose in mind, other than the vaguest notion that if something went irreparably wrong with his model, and the source of the problem—a slow virus, a subtle programming error—rendered all of his snapshots suspect, starting life again with no memories since 2045 would be better than nothing.

Having assembled the necessary elements, he'd scripted the whole scenario in advance and let it run—without observing the results. Then he'd frozen the clone and sent it to Durham at the last possible moment—without giving himself a chance to back out, or, worse, to decide that he'd botched the first attempt, and to try again.

Now he was ready to discover what he'd done, to view the *fait accompli.* Seated in the library—with the drinks cabinet locked—he gestured to the terminal to begin.

The old man in the bed looked much worse than Thomas had expected: sunken-eyed, jaundiced and nearly bald. (So much for the honesty of his own appearance, the "minimal" changes he'd made to render himself presentable.) His chest was furrowed with scars, criss-crossed by a grid of electrodes; his skull was capped with a similar mesh. A pump suspended beside the bed fed a needle in his right arm. The clone was sedated by a crudely modeled synthetic opiate flowing into his crudely modeled bloodstream, just as Thomas's original had been sedated by the real thing, from the time of the scan until his death three days later.

In this replay, though, the narcotic was scheduled to undergo a sudden drop in concentration—for no physically plausible reason, but none was required. A graph in a corner of the screen plotted the decline.

Thomas watched, sick with anxiety, feverish with hope. This—at last—was the ritual which he'd always believed might have cured him.

The old man attained consciousness, without opening his eyes; the EEG waveforms meant nothing to Thomas, but the software monitoring the simulation had flagged the event with a subtitle. Further text followed:

The anesthetic still hasn't taken. Can't they get anything right? [Garbled verbalization.] The scan can't be over. I can't be the Copy yet. The Copy will wake with a clear head, seated in the library, premodified to feel no disorientation. So why am I awake?

The old man opened his eyes.

Thomas shouted, "Freeze!" He was sweating, and nauseous, but he made no move to banish the unnecessary symptoms. *He wanted catharsis, didn't he? Wasn't that the whole point?* The subtitles gave only a crude hint of what the clone was experiencing. Much greater clarity was available; the recording included traces from key neural pathways. If he wanted to, he could read the clone's mind.

He said, "Let me know what he's thinking, what he's going through." Nothing happened. He clenched his fists and whispered, "Restart."

The library vanished; he was flat on his back in the hospital bed, staring up at the ceiling, dazed. He looked down and saw the cluster of monitors beside him, the wires on his chest. The motion of his eyes and head was wrong—intelligible, but distressingly out of synch with his intentions. He felt fearful and disoriented—but he wasn't sure how much of that was his own reaction and how much belonged to the clone. Thomas shook his own head in panic, and the library—and his body—returned.

He stopped the playback, and reconsidered.

He could break free any time he wanted to. He was only an observer. There was nothing to fear.

Fighting down a sense of suffocation, he closed his eyes and surrendered to the recording.

He looked around the room groggily. He wasn't the Copy—that much was certain. And this wasn't any part of the Landau

Clinic; as a VIP shareholder and future client, he'd toured the building too many times to be wrong about that. If the scan had been postponed for some reason, he ought to be back home—or on his way. Unless something had gone wrong requiring medical attention which the Landau was unable to provide?

The room was deserted, and the door was closed. He called out hoarsely, "Nurse!" He was too weak to shout.

The room controller replied, "No staff are available to attend to you, at present. Can I be of assistance?"

"Can you tell me where I am?"

"You're in Room 307 of Valhalla."

"Valhalla?" He knew he'd done business with the place, but he couldn't remember why.

The room controller said helpfully, "Valhalla is the Health Dynamics Corporation of America's Frankfurt Hospice."

His bowels loosened with fright; they were already empty. [Thomas squirmed in sympathy, but kept himself from breaking free.] *Valhalla* was the meat-rack he'd hired to take care of his comatose body until it expired, after the scan—with the legal minimum of medical attention, with no heroic measures to prolong life.

He *had* been scanned—but they'd fucked up.

They'd let him wake.

It was a shock, but he came to terms with it rapidly. There was no reason to panic. He'd be out of here and scanned again in six hours flat—and whoever was responsible would be out on the street even faster. He tried to raise himself into a sitting position, but he was too dizzy from the lingering effects of the drug infusion to coordinate the action. He slumped back onto the pillows, caught his breath, and forced himself to speak calmly.

"I want to talk to the director."

"I'm sorry, the director is not available."

"Then, the most senior member of staff you can find."

"No staff are available to attend to you, at present."

Sweat trickled into his eyes. There was no point screaming about lawsuits to this machine. In fact . . . it might be prudent not to scream about lawsuits to anyone. *A place like this would be perfectly capable of responding by simply drugging him back into a coma.*

What he needed to do was let someone outside know about the situation.

He said, "I'd like to make a phone call. Can you connect me to the net?"

"I have no authority to do that."

"I can give you an account number linked to my voiceprint, and authorize you to charge me for the service."

"I have no authority to accept your account number."

"Then . . . make a call, reversing all charges, to Rudolf Dieterle, of Dieterle, Hollingworth and Partners."

"I have no authority to make such a call."

He laughed, disbelieving. "Are you *physically capable* of connecting me to the net at all?"

"I have no authority to disclose my technical specifications."

Any insult would have been a waste of breath. He lifted his head and surveyed the room. There was no furniture; no drawers, no table, no visitor's chair. Just the monitors to one side of his bed, mounted on stainless steel trolleys. And no terminal, no communications equipment of any kind—not even a wall-mounted audio handset.

He probed the needle in his forearm, just below the inside of the elbow. A tight, seamless rubber sleeve, several centimeters wide, covered the entry point; it seemed to take forever to get his fingernails under the edge—and once he'd succeeded, it was no help. The sleeve was too tight to be dragged down his arm, and too elastic to be rolled up like a shirt sleeve. *How did anyone, ever, take the thing off?* He tugged at the drip tube itself; held in place by the sleeve, it showed no sign of yielding. The other end vanished inside the drug pump.

[Thomas began to wonder if the immovable needle, on top of the Kafkaesque room controller, would make the clone suspicious—but it seemed that the possibility of some future self *waking the scan file a second time* was too convoluted an explanation to occur to him in the middle of a crisis like this.]

He'd have to take the pump with him. That was a nuisance—but if he was going to march through the building wrapped in a sheet, looking for a terminal, it could hardly make him more conspicuous than he would have been anyway.

He started to peel the electrodes from his chest when a pulse of numbing warmth swept through his right arm. The pump beeped twice; he turned to see a green LED glowing brightly in the middle of the box, a light he hadn't noticed before.

The wave of paralysis spread out from his shoulder before he could react—*crimp the tube?* He tried to roll himself out of the bed but if his body responded at all, he couldn't feel it.

His eyes fluttered closed. He struggled to remain conscious—and succeeded. [The script guaranteed the clone several minutes of lucidity—which had nothing to do with the opiate's true pharmacological effects.]

There'd be a computer log of his EEG. Someone would be alerted, soon, to the fact that he'd been awake . . . and they'd understand that the only humane thing to do would be to revive him.

But someone should have been alerted the moment he woke.

It was far more likely that he'd be left to die.

[Thomas felt ill. *This was sadistic, insane.*

It was too late for squeamishness, though. Everything he was witnessing had already happened.]

His body was numb, but his mind was crystalline. Without the blur of visceral distractions, his fear seemed purer, sharper than anything he'd ever experienced.

He tried to dredge up the familiar, comforting truths: The Copy would survive, it would live his life for him. This body was always destined to perish; he'd accepted that long ago. *Death* was the irreversible dissolution of the personality; this wasn't *death,* it was a shedding of skin. There was nothing to fear.

Unless he was wrong about death. Wrong about everything.

He lay paralyzed, in darkness. Wishing for sleep; terrified of sleep. Wishing for anything that might distract him;

afraid of wasting his last precious minutes, afraid of not being prepared.

Prepared? What could that mean? Extinction required no preparation. He wasn't making any deathbed pleas to a God he'd stopped believing in at the age of twelve. He wasn't about to cast aside seventy years of freedom and sanity, to return to his infantile faith. *Approach the Kingdom of Heaven as a child, or you won't get in?* That very line was one which had helped him see through the crude mechanics of entrapment; the translation was all too obvious (even to a child): *This bullshit would insult any adult's intelligence—but swallow it anyway, or you'll burn forever.*

He was still afraid, though. The hooks had gone in deep.

The irony was, he had finally come to his senses and abandoned the whole insane idea of having himself woken, intentionally. *To confront his mortality! To purge his Copy of guilt!* What a pathetic fucking joke that would have been. And now the supposed beneficiary of the fatuous gesture would never even know that it had happened, anyway, by accident.

The blackness in his skull seemed to open out, an invisible view expanding into an invisible vista. Any sense of being in the hospice bed, merely numb and sightless, was gone now; he was lost on a plain of darkness.

What could he have told the Copy, anyway? The miserable truth? *I'm dying in fear. I killed Anna for no reason but selfishness and cowardice—and now, in spite of everything, I'm still afraid that there might be an afterlife. A God. Judgement. I've regressed far enough to start wondering if every childish superstition I ever held might yet turn out to be true—but not far enough to embrace the possibility of repentance.*

Or some anodyne lie? *I'm dying in peace, I've found forgiveness, I've laid all my ghosts to rest. And you're free, now, to live your own life. The sins of the father will not be visited upon the son.*

Would that have worked, would that have helped? Some formula as inane as the voodoo of Confession, as glib as the dying words of some tortured soul finding Hollywood redemption?

He felt himself moving across the darkness. No tunnels of light; no light at all. Sedative dreams, not near-death hallucinations. Death was hours or days away; by then he'd surely be comatose again. One small mercy.

He waited. No revelations, no insights, no lightning bolts of blinding faith. Just blackness and uncertainty and fear.

Thomas sat motionless in front of the terminal long after the recording had finished.

The clone had been right: the ritual had been pointless, misguided. He was and always would be the murderer; nothing could make him see himself as the innocent software child of the dead Thomas Riemann, unfairly burdened with the killer's guilt. Not unless he redefined himself completely: edited his memories, rewrote his personality. Sculpted his mind into someone new.

In other words: died.

That was the choice. He had to live with what he was in its entirety, or create another person who'd inherit only part of what he'd been.

He laughed angrily and shook his head. "I'm not passing through the eye of any needle. I killed Anna. I killed Anna. That's who I am." He reached for the scar which defined him, and stroked it as if it were a tailsman.

He sat for a while longer, reliving the night in Hamburg one more time, weeping with shame at what he'd done.

Then he unlocked the drinks cabinet and proceeded to make himself confident and optimistic. The ritual had been pointless—but if nothing else, it had rid him of the delusion that it might have been otherwise.

Some time later, he thought about the clone. Drifting into narcosis. Suffering a crudely modeled extrapolation of the disease which had killed the original. And then, at the moment of simulated death, taking on a new body, young and healthy— with a face plucked from a photograph from Christmas, 1985.

Resurrection—for an instant. No more than a formality. The script had frozen the young murderer, without even waking him.

And then?

Thomas was too far gone to agonize about it. He'd done what he'd done for the sake of the ritual. He'd delivered the clone into Durham's hands, to grant it—like the flesh-and-blood it believed itself to be—the remote chance of another life, in a world beyond death, unknowable.

And if the whole thing had been a mistake, there was no way, now, to undo it.

PART TWO

Permutation City

23

Maria woke from dreamless sleep, clearheaded, tranquil. She opened her eyes and looked around. The bed, the room, were unfamiliar; both were large and luxurious. Everything appeared unnaturally pristine, unsullied by human habitation, like an expensive hotel room. She was puzzled, but unperturbed; an explanation seemed to be on the verge of surfacing. She was wearing a nightdress she'd never seen before in her life.

She suddenly remembered the Landau Clinic. *Chatting with the technicians. Borrowing the marker pen. The tour of the recovery rooms. The anesthetist asking her to count.*

She pulled her hands out from beneath the sheet. Her left palm was blank; the comforting message she'd written there was gone. She felt the blood drain from her face.

Before she had a chance to think, Durham stepped into the room. For a moment, she was too shocked to make a sound—then she screamed at him, "What have you done to me? I'm the Copy, aren't I? You're running the Copy!" *Trapped in the launch software, with two minutes to live?*

Durham said quietly, "Yes, you're the Copy."

"*How?* How did you do it? How could I let it happen?" She stared at him, desperate for a reply, enraged more than anything else by the thought that they might both vanish before she'd heard the explanation, before she understood how he'd broken through all of her elaborate safeguards. But Durham just stood by the doorway looking bemused and embarrassed—as if he'd anticipated a reaction like this, but couldn't quite credit it now that it was happening.

Finally, she said, "This isn't the launch, is it? This is later. You're another version. You stole me, you're running me later."

"I didn't *steal* you." He hesitated, then added cautiously, "I think you know exactly where you are. And I agonized about waking you—but I had to do it. There's too much going on here that you'll want to see, want to be a part of; I couldn't let you sleep through it all. That would have been unforgivable."

Maria disregarded everything he'd said. "You kept my scan file after the launch. You duplicated it, somehow."

"No. The only place your scan file data ever went was the Garden-of-Eden configuration. As agreed. And now you're in Permutation City. In the TVC universe—now commonly known as Elysium. Running on nothing but its own laws."

Maria sat up in bed slowly, bringing her knees up to her chest, trying to accept the situation without panicking, without falling apart. Durham was insane, unpredictable. *Dangerous.* When was she going to get that into her skull? In the flesh, she could probably have broken his fucking neck if she had to, to defend herself—but if he controlled this environment, she was powerless: he could rape her, torture her, do anything at all. The very idea of him attacking her still seemed ludicrous—but she couldn't rely on the way he'd treated her in the past to count for anything. He was a liar and a kidnapper. She didn't know him at all.

Right now, though, he was being as civilized as ever; he seemed intent on keeping up the charade. She was afraid to test this veneer of hospitality—but she forced herself to say evenly, "I want to use a terminal."

Durham gestured at the space above the bed, and a terminal appeared. Maria's heart sank; she realized that she'd been hanging on to the slender hope that she might have been human. *And that was still possible.* Durham himself had once been memory-wiped and fooled into thinking he was a Copy, when he was merely a visitor. Or at least he'd claimed that it had happened, in another world.

She tried half a dozen numbers, starting with Francesca's, ending with Aden's. The terminal declared them all invalid.

She couldn't bring herself to try her own. Durham watched in silence. He seemed to be caught between genuine sympathy and a kind of clinical fascination—as if an attempt to make a few phone calls cast doubt on *her* sanity; as if she was engaged in some bizarre, psychotic behavior worthy of the closest scrutiny: peering behind a mirror in search of the objects seen in the reflection; talking back to a television program . . . or making calls on a toy phone.

Maria pushed the floating machine away angrily; it moved easily, but came to a halt as soon as she took her hands off it. Patchwork VR and its physics-of-convenience seemed like the final insult.

She said, "Do you think I'm stupid? What does a dummy terminal prove?"

"Nothing. So why don't you apply your own criteria?" He said, "Central computer," and the terminal flashed up an icon-studded menu, headed PERMUTATION CITY COMPUTING FACILITY. "Not many people use this interface, these days; it's the original version, designed before the launch. But it still plugs you into as much computing power as the latest co-personality links."

He showed Maria a text file. She recognized it immediately; it was a program she'd written herself, to solve a large, intentionally difficult, set of Diophantine equations. The output of this program was the key they'd agreed upon to unlock Durham's access to the other Copies, "after" the launch.

He ran it. It spat out its results immediately: a screenful of numbers, the smallest of which was twenty digits long. On any real-world computer, it should have taken years.

Maria was unimpressed. "You could have frozen us while the program was running, making it seem like no time had passed. Or you could have generated the answers in advance." She gestured at the terminal. "I expect you're faking all of this: you're not talking to a genuine operating system, you're not really running the program at all."

"Feel free to alter some parameters in the equations, and try again."

She did. The modified program "ran" just as quickly, churning out a new set of answers. She laughed sourly. "So what am

I supposed to do now? Verify all *this* in my head? You could put any bullshit you liked on the screen; I wouldn't know the difference. And if I wrote another program to check the results, you could fake *its* operation, too. You control this whole environment, don't you? So I can't trust anything. Whatever I do to try to test your claims, you can intervene and make it go your way. Is that why you wanted my scan file, all along? So you could lock me in here and bombard me with lies—finally 'prove' all your mad ideas to someone?"

"You're being paranoid now."

"Am I? You're the expert."

She looked around the luxurious prison cell. Red velvet curtains stirred in a faint breeze. She slipped out of bed and crossed the room, ignoring Durham; the more she argued with him, the harder it was to be physically afraid of him. He'd chosen his form of torture, and he was sticking to it.

The window looked out on a forest of glistening towers—no doubt correctly rendered according to all the laws of optics, but still too slick to be real . . . like some nineteen twenties Expressionist film set. She'd seen the sketches; this *was* Permutation City—whatever hardware it was running on. She looked down. They were seventy or eighty stories up, the street was all but invisible, but just below the window, a dozen meters to the right, a walkway stretched across to an adjacent building, and she could see the puppet citizens, chatting together in twos and threes as they strode toward their imaginary destinations. All of this looked expensive—but slowdown could buy a lot of subjective computing power, if that was the trade-off you wanted to make. *How much time had passed in the outside world? Years? Decades?*

Had she managed to save Francesca?

Durham said, "You think I've kidnapped your scan file, and run this whole city, solely for the pleasure of deceiving you?"

"It's the simplest explanation."

"It's ludicrous, and you know it. I'm sorry; I know this must be painful for you. But I didn't do it lightly. It's been seven thousand years; I've had a lot of time to think it over."

She spun around to face him. *"Stop lying to me!"*

He threw his hands up, in a gesture of contrition—and impatience. "Maria . . . *you are in the TVC universe.* The launch worked, the dust hypothesis has been vindicated. It's a fact, and you'd better come to terms with that, because you're now part of a society which has been living with it for millennia.

"And I know I said I'd only wake you if Planet Lambert failed—if we needed you to work on the biosphere seed. All right, I've broken my word on that. But . . . *it was the wrong promise to make.* Planet Lambert hasn't failed; it's succeeded beyond your wildest dreams. *How could I let you sleep through that?*"

An interface window appeared in midair beside her, showing a half-lit blue-and-white world. "I don't expect the continents will look familiar. We've given the Autoverse a lot of resources; seven thousand years, for most of us, has been about three billion for Planet Lambert."

Maria said flatly, "You're wasting your time. Nothing you show me is going to change my mind." But she watched the planet, transfixed, as Durham moved the viewpoint closer.

They broke through the clouds near the east coast of a large, mountainous island, part of an archipelago straddling the equator. The bare surface rock of the peaks was the color of ochre; no mineral she'd included in the original design . . . but time, and geochemistry, could have thrown up something new. The vegetation, which covered almost every other scrap of land, right to the water line, came in shades of blue-green. As the viewpoint descended, and the textures resolved themselves, Maria saw only "grasses" and "shrubs"—nothing remotely like a terrestrial tree.

Durham zeroed in on a meadow not far from the coast—a few hundred meters back, according to the scale across the bottom of the image—and about what she would have guessed from cues in the landscape, unexpectedly validated. What looked at first like a cloud of wind-borne debris—seeds of some kind?—blowing above the grass resolved into a swarm of shiny black "insects." Durham froze the image, then zoomed in on one of the creatures.

It was no insect by the terrestrial definition; there were four legs, not six, and the body was clearly divided into five segments: the head; sections bearing the forelegs, wings, and hind legs; and the tail. Durham made hand movements and rotated the view. The head was blunt, not quite flat, with two large eyes—if they were eyes: shiny bluish disks, with no apparent structure. The rest of the head was coated in fine hairs, lined up in a complex, symmetrical pattern which reminded Maria of Maori facial tattoos. Sensors for vibration—or scent?

She said, "Very pretty, but you forgot the mouth."

"They put food into a cavity directly under the wings." He rotated the body to show her. "It adheres to those bristles, and gets dissolved by the enzymes they secrete. You'd think it would fall out, but it doesn't—not until they've finished digesting it and absorbing nutrients, and then a protein on the bristles changes shape, switching off the adhesion. Their whole stomach is nothing but this sticky droplet hanging there, open to the air."

"You might have come up with something more plausible."

Durham laughed. "Exactly."

The single pair of wings were translucent brown, looking like they were made of a thin layer of the same stuff as the exoskeleton. The four legs each had a single joint, and terminated in feathery structures. The tail segment had brown-and-black markings like a bull's-eye, but there was nothing at the center; a dark tube emerged from the bottom of the rim, narrowing to a needle-sharp point.

"The Lambertians have diploid chromosomes, but only one gender. Any two of them can inject DNA, one after the other, into certain kinds of plant cell; their genes take over the cell and turn it into a cross between a cyst and an egg. They usually choose a particular spot on the stems of certain species of shrub. I don't know if you'd call it parasitism—or just nestbuilding on a molecular level. The plant nourishes the embryo, and survives the whole process in perfect health—and when the young hatch, they return the favor by scattering seeds. Their ancestors stole some of the control mechanisms from a plant virus, a billion years ago. There are a lot of genetic exchanges like that; the "kingdoms" are a lot more biochemically similar here than they were on Earth."

Maria turned away from the screen. *The stupidest thing was, she kept wanting to ask questions, press him for details.* She said, "What's next? You zoom right in and show me the fine anatomical structure, the insect's cells, the proteins, the atoms, the *Autoverse* cells—and that's supposed to convince me that the whole planet is embedded in the Autoverse? You unfreeze this thing, let it fly around—and I'm meant to conclude that no real-world computer could ever run an organism so complex, modeled at such a deep level? As if I could personally verify that every flap of its wings corresponded to a valid sequence of a few trillion cellular automaton states. It's no different than the equation results. It wouldn't prove a thing."

Durham nodded slowly. "All right. What if I showed you some of the other species? Or the evolutionary history? The paleogenetic record? We have every mutation on file since the year zero. You want to sit down with that and see if it looks authentic?"

"No. I *want* a terminal that works. I want you to let me call my original. I want to talk to her—and between us, maybe we can decide what I'm going to do when I get out of this fucking madhouse and into my own JSN account."

Durham looked rattled—and for a moment she believed she might finally be getting through to him. But he said, "I woke you for a reason. We're going to be making contact with the Lambertians soon. It might have been sooner—but there've been complications, political delays."

He'd lost her completely now. "'Contact with the Lambertians?' What's that supposed to mean?"

He gestured at the motionless insect, backside and genitals still facing them. "This is not some species I picked at random. This is the pinnacle of Autoverse life. They're conscious, self-aware, highly intelligent. They have almost no technology—but their nervous system is about ten times more complex than a human's—and they can go far beyond that for some tasks, performing a kind of parallel computing in swarms. They have chemistry, physics, astronomy. They know there are thirty-two atoms—although they haven't figured out the underlying cellular automaton rules yet. And they're modeling the primordial cloud. These are sentient creatures, and they want to know where they came from."

Maria turned her hand in front of the screen, bringing the Lambertian's head back into view. She was beginning to suspect that Durham actually believed every word he was saying—in which case, maybe he hadn't, personally, contrived these aliens. Maybe some other version of him—the flesh-and-blood original?—was deceiving both of them. If that was the case, she was arguing with the wrong person—but what was she supposed to do instead? Start shouting pleas for freedom to the sky?

She said numbly, "Ten times more complex than a human brain?"

"Their neurons use conducting polymers to carry the signal, instead of membrane action potentials. The cells themselves are comparable in size to a human's—but each axon and dendrite carries multiple signals." Durham moved the viewpoint behind the Lambertian's eye, and showed her. A neuron in the optic nerve, under close examination, contained thousands of molecules like elaborately knotted ropes, running the whole length of the cell body. At the far end, each polymer was joined to a kind of vesicle, the narrow molecular cable dwarfed by the tiny pouch of cell membrane pinched off from the outside world. "There are almost three thousand distinct neurotransmitters; they're all proteins, built from three sub-units, with fourteen possibilities for each sub-unit. A bit like human antibodies—the same trick for generating a wide spectrum of shapes. And they bind to their receptors just as selectively as an antibody to an antigen; every synapse is a three-thousand-channel biochemical switchboard, with no cross-talk. That's the molecular basis of Lambertian thought." He added wryly, "Which is more than you and I possess: a molecular basis for anything. We still run the old patchwork models of the human body—expanded and modified according to taste, but still based on the same principles as John Vines's first talking Copy. There's a long-term project to give people the choice of being implemented on an atomic level . . . but quite apart from the political complications, even the enthusiasts keep finding more pressing things to do."

Durham moved the viewpoint out through the cell wall and turned it back to face the terminal end of the neuron. He changed the color scheme from atomic to molecular, to highlight the individual neurotransmitters with their own distinctive hues. Then he unfroze the image.

Several of the grey lipid-membrane vesicles twitched open, disgorging floods of brightly colored specks; tumbling past the viewpoint, they resolved into elaborate, irregular globules with a bewildering variety of forms. Durham swung the angle of view forward again, and headed for the far side of the synapse. Eventually, Maria could make out color-coded receptors embedded in the receiving neuron's cell wall: long-chain molecules folded together into tight zig-zagged rings, with lumpy depressions on the exposed surface.

For several minutes, they watched thousands of mismatched neurotransmitters bounce off one receptor, until Durham became bored and pleaded with the software, "Show us a fit." The image blurred for a second, and then returned to the original speed as a correctly shaped molecule finally stumbled onto its target. It hit the receptor and locked into place; Durham plunged the viewpoint through the cell membrane in time to show the immersed tail section of the receptor changing its configuration in response. He said, "*That* will now catalyze the activation of a second messenger, which will feed energy into the appropriate polymer—unless there's an inhibiting messenger already bound there, blocking access." He spoke to the software again; it took control of the viewpoint, and showed them each of the events he'd described.

Maria shook her head, bedazzled. "Tell me the truth—who orchestrated this? Three thousand neurotransmitters, three thousand receptors, three thousand second messengers? No doubt you can show me the individual structures of all of them—and no doubt they really would behave the way you claim they do. Even writing the software to fake this would have been an enormous job. Who did you commission? There can't be many people who'd take it on."

Durham said gently, "I commissioned *you*. You can't have

forgotten. A seed for a biosphere? A demonstration that life in the Autoverse could be as diverse and elaborate as life on Earth?"

"No. From *A. hydrophila* to *this* would take—"

"Billions of years of Autoverse time? Computing power orders of magnitude beyond the resources of twenty-first century Earth? That's what Planet Lambert needed—and that's exactly what it's been given."

Maria backed away from the screen until she could go no further, then slid down against the wall beside the red-draped window and sat on the plushly carpeted floor. She put her face in her hands, and tried to breathe slowly. She felt like she'd been buried alive.

Did she believe him? It hardly seemed to matter anymore. Whatever she did, he was going to keep on bombarding her with "evidence" like this, consistent with his claims. Whether he was deliberately lying or not—and whether he was being fooled by another version of himself, or whether the "dust hypothesis" was right after all—he was never going to let her out of here, back into the real world. Psychotic liar, fellow victim or calm purveyor of the truth, he was incapable of setting her free.

Her original was still out there—with the money to save Francesca. That was the point of the whole insane gamble, the payoff for risking her soul. If she could remember that, cling to that, maybe she could keep herself sane.

Durham pressed on—oblivious to her distress, or intent on delivering the *coup de grace*. He said, "Who could have engineered this? You *know* how long it took Max Lambert to translate a real-world bacterium. Do you honestly believe that I found someone who could manufacture a functioning—novel—pseudo-insect out of thin air . . . let alone *an intelligent one?*

"All right: you can't personally check macroscopic behavior against the Autoverse rules. But you can study all the biochemical pathways, trace them back to the ancestral species. You can watch an embryo grow, cell by cell—following the gradients of control hormones, the differentiating tissue layers, the formation of the organs.

"The whole planet is an open book to us; you can examine whatever you like, scrutinize it on any scale, from viruses to ecosystems, from the activation of a molecule of retinal pigment to the geochemical cycles.

"There are six hundred and ninety million species currently living on Planet Lambert. All obeying the laws of the Autoverse. All demonstrably descended from a single organism which lived three billion years ago—and whose characteristics I expect you know by heart. Do you honestly believe that anyone could have *designed* all that?"

Maria looked up at him angrily. "No. Of course it evolved; it must have evolved. You can shut up now—you've won; I believe you. *But why did you have to wake me?* I'm going to lose my mind."

Durham squatted down and put a hand on her shoulder. She started sobbing drily as she attempted to dissect her loss into parts she could begin to comprehend. *Francesca was gone. Aden was gone. All her friends. All the people she'd ever met: in the flesh, on the networks. All the people she'd ever heard of: musicians and writers, philosophers and movie stars, politicians and serial killers.* They weren't even dead; their lives didn't lie in her past, whole and comprehensible. They were scattered around her like dust: meaningless, disconnected.

Everything she'd ever known had been ground down into random noise.

Durham hesitated, then put his arms around her clumsily. She wanted to hurt him, but instead she clung to him and wept, teeth clenched, fists tight, shuddering with rage and grief.

He said, "You're not going to lose your mind. You can live any life you want to, here. Seven thousand years means nothing; we haven't lost the old culture—we still have all the libraries, the archives, the databases. And there are thousands of people who'll want to meet you; people who respect you for what you've done. You're a myth; you're a hero of Elysium; you're the sleeping eighteenth founder. We'll hold a festival in honor of your awakening."

Maria pushed him away. "I don't want that. I don't want any of that."

"All right. It's up to you."

She closed her eyes and huddled against the wall. She knew she must have looked like a petulant child, but she didn't care. She said fiercely, "You've had the last word. The last laugh. You've *brought me to life* just to rub my nose in the proof of your precious beliefs. And now I want to go back to sleep. Forever. I want all of this to vanish."

Durham was silent for a while. Then he said, "You can do that, if you really want to. Once I've shown you what you've inherited, once I've shown you how to control it, you'll have the power to seal yourself off from the rest of Elysium. If you choose sleep, then nobody will ever be able to wake you.

"But don't you want to be there, on Planet Lambert, when we make first contact with the civilization that owes its existence to you?"

24

(Rut City)

Peer was in his workshop, making a table leg on his lathe, when Kate's latest message caught his eye: *You have to see this. Please! Meet me in the City.*

He looked away.

He was working with his favorite timber, sugar pine. He'd constructed his own plantation from a gene library and plant cell maps—modeling individual examples of each cell type down to an atomic level, then encapsulating their essential behavior in rules which he could afford to run billions of times over, for tens of thousands of trees. In theory, he could have built the whole plantation from individual atoms—and that would have been the most elegant way to do it, by far—but slowing himself down to a time frame in which the trees grew fast enough to meet his needs would have meant leaving Kate far behind.

He stopped the lathe and reread the message, which was written on a poster tacked to the workshop's noticeboard (the only part of his environment he allowed her to access, while he was working). The poster looked quite ordinary, except for an eye-catching tendency for the letters to jump up and down when they crossed his peripheral vision.

He muttered, "I'm happy here. I don't care what they're doing in the City." The workshop abutted a warehouse full of table legs—one hundred and sixty-two thousand, three hundred and twenty-nine, so far. Peer could imagine nothing more satisfying than reaching the two hundred thousand mark—although he knew it was likely that he'd change his mind and abandon the workshop before that happened; new vocations were imposed by his exoself at random intervals, but statistically, the next one was overdue. Immediately before taking up woodwork, he'd passionately devoured all the higher mathematics texts in the central library, run all the tutorial software, and then personally contributed several important new results to group theory—untroubled by the fact that none of the Elysian mathematicians would ever be aware of his work. Before that, he'd written over three hundred comic operas, with librettos in Italian, French and English— and staged most of them, with puppet performers and audience. Before that, he'd patiently studied the structure and biochemistry of the human brain for sixty-seven years; towards the end he had fully grasped, to his own satisfaction, the nature of the process of consciousness. Every one of these pursuits had been utterly engrossing, and satisfying, at the time. He'd even been interested in the Elysians, once.

No longer. He preferred to think about table legs.

He was still interested in Kate, though. He'd chosen that as one of his few invariants. And he'd been neglecting her lately; they hadn't met in almost a decade.

He looked around the workshop wistfully, his gaze falling on the pile of fresh timber in the corner, but then he strengthened his resolve. The pleasures of the lathe beckoned—but love meant making sacrifices.

Peer took off his dustcoat, stretched out his arms, and fell backward into the sky above the City.

Kate met him while he was still airborne, swooping down from nowhere and grabbing his hand, nearly wrenching his arm from its socket. She yelled above the wind, "So, you're still alive after all. I was beginning to think you'd shut yourself down. Gone looking for the next life without me." Her tone was sarcastic, but there was an edge of genuine relief. Ten years could still be a long time, if you let it.

Peer said gently, but audibly, "You know how busy I am. And when I'm working—"

She laughed derisively. *"Working?* Is that what you call it? Taking pleasure from something that would bore the stupidest factory robot to death?" Her hair was long and jet black, whipping up around her face as if caught by the wind at random—but always concealing just enough to mask her expression.

"You're still—" The wind drowned out his words; Kate had disabled his aphysical intelligibility. He shouted, "You're still a sculptor, aren't you? You ought to understand. The wood, the grain, the texture—"

"I *understand* that you need prosthetic interests to help pass the time—but you could try setting the parameters more carefully."

"*Why should I?*" Being forced to raise his voice made him feel argumentative; he willed his exoself to circumvent the effect, and screamed calmly: "Every few decades, at random, I take on new goals, at random. It's perfect. How could I improve on a scheme like that? I'm not stuck on any one thing forever; however much you think I'm wasting my time, it's only for fifty or a hundred years. What difference does that make, in the long run?"

"You could still be more selective."

"What did you have in mind? Something *socially useful?* Famine relief work? Counseling the dying? Or something *intellectually challenging?* Uncovering the fundamental laws of the universe? I have to admit that the TVC rules have slipped my mind completely; it might take me all of five seconds to look them up again. *Searching for God?* That's a difficult one: Paul Durham never returns my calls. *Self discovery—?*"

"You don't have to leave yourself open to every conceivable absurdity."

"If I limited the range of options, I'd be repeating myself in no time at all. And if you find the phase I'm passing through so unbearable, you can always make it vanish: you can freeze yourself until I change."

Kate was indignant. "I have other time frames to worry about besides yours!"

"The Elysians aren't going anywhere." He didn't add that he knew she'd frozen herself half a dozen times already. Each time for a few more years than the time before.

She turned toward him, parting her hair to show one baleful eye. "You're fooling yourself, you know. You're going to

repeat yourself, eventually. However desperately you repro-
gram yourself, in the end you're going to come full circle and
find that you've done it all before."

Peer laughed indulgently, and shouted, "We've certainly
been through *all this* before—and you know that's not true. It's
always possible to synthesize something new: a novel art form,
a new field of study. A new aesthetic, a new obsession." Falling
through the cool late afternoon air beside her was exhilarating,
but he was already missing the smell of wood dust.

Kate rendered the air around them motionless and silent,
although they continued to descend. She released his hand,
and said, "I know we've been through this before. I remember
what you said last time: If the worst comes to the worst, for
the first hundred years you can contemplate *the number one.*
For the second hundred years you can contemplate *the number two.* And so on, *ad infinitum.* Whenever the numbers
grow too big to hold in your mind, you can always expand
your mind to fit them. QED. You'll never run out of *new and
exciting interests.*"

Peer said gently, "Where's your sense of humor? It's a simple proof that the worst-case scenario is still infinite. I never
suggested actually doing that."

"But you might as well." Now that her face was no longer
concealed, she looked more forlorn than angry—by choice, if
not necessarily by artifice. "Why do you have to find everything so . . . fulfilling? Why can't you discriminate? Why
can't you *let yourself* grow bored with things—then move on?
Pick them up again later if you feel the urge."

"Sounds awfully quaint to me. Very *human.*"

"It did work for them. Sometimes."

"Yes. And I'm sure it works for you, sometimes. You drift
back and forth between your art and watching the great
Elysian soap opera. With a decade or two of aimless depression in between. You're dissatisfied most of the time—and
letting that happen is a conscious choice, as deliberate, and
arbitrary, as anything I impose on myself. If that's how you
want to live, I'm not going to try to change you. But you can't
expect me to live the same way."

She didn't reply. After a moment, the bubble of still air around them blew away, and the roar of the wind drowned the silence again.

Sometimes he wondered if Kate had ever really come to terms with the shock of discovering that stowing away had granted them, not a few hundred years in a billionaires' sanctuary, but a descent into the abyss of immortality. The Copy who had persuaded David Hawthorne to turn his back on the physical world; the committed follower—even before her death—of the Solipsist Nation philosophy; the woman who had needed no brain rewiring or elaborate external contrivances to accept her software incarnation . . . now acted more and more like a flesh-and-blood-wannabe—or rather, Elysian-wannabe—year by year. *And there was no need for it.* Their tiny slice of infinity was as infinite as the whole; ultimately, there was nothing the Elysians could do that Kate couldn't.

Except walk among them as an equal, and that was what she seemed to covet the most.

True, the Elysians had deliberately set out to achieve the logical endpoint of everything she'd ever believed Copies should be striving for—while she'd merely hitched a ride by mistake. Their world would "always" (Elysian instant compared to Elysian instant) be bigger and faster than her own. So "naturally"—according to archaic human values which she hadn't had the sense to erase—she wanted to be part of the main game. But Peer still found it absurd that she spent her life envying them, when she could have generated—or even *launched*—her own equally complex, equally populous society, and turned her back on the Elysians as thoroughly as they'd turned their back on Earth.

It was her choice. Peer took it in his stride, along with all their other disagreements. If they were going to spend eternity together, he believed they'd resolve their problems eventually—if they could be resolved at all. It was early days yet. As it always would be.

He rolled over and looked down at the City—or the strange recursive map of the City which they made do with, buried as they were in the walls and foundations of the real thing. Malcolm Carter's secret parasitic software wasn't blind to its host; they could spy on what was going on in the higher levels of the program which surreptitiously ran them, even though they couldn't affect anything which happened there. They could snatch brief, partial recordings of activity in the real City, and play them back in a limited duplicate environment. It was a bit like . . . being the widely separated letters in the text of *Ulysses* which read: *Peer and Kate read, "Leopold Bloom wandered through Dublin."* If not quite so crude an abridgment.

Certainly, the view from the air was still breathtaking; Peer had to concede that it was probably indistinguishable from the real thing. The sun was setting over the ocean as they descended, and the Ulam Falls glistened in the east like a sheet of amber set in the granite face of Mount Vine. In the foothills, a dozen silver needles and obsidian prisms, fanciful watchtowers, caught the light and scattered it between them. Peer followed the river down, through lush tropical forests, across dark plains of grassland, into the City itself.

The buildings on the outskirts were low and sprawling, becoming gradually taller and narrower; the profile swept up in a curve which echoed the shape of Mount Vine. Closer to the centre, a thousand crystalline walkways linked the City's towers at every level, connections so dense and stellated as to make it seem possible that every building was joined, directly, to all the rest. That wasn't true—but the sense that it might have been was still compelling.

Decorative crowds filled the streets and walkways: mindless puppets obeying the simplest rules, but looking as purposeful and busy as any human throng. A strange adornment, perhaps—but not much stranger than having buildings and streets at all. Most Elysians merely visited this place, but last time Peer had concerned himself with such things, a few hundred of them—mainly third-generation—had taken up *inhabiting* the City full-time: adopting every detail of its architecture and geography as fixed parameters, swearing fidelity to its Euclidian distances. Others—mainly first-generation—had been appalled by the behavior of this sect. It was strange how "reversion" was the greatest taboo amongst the oldest Elysians, who were so conservative in most other ways. Maybe they were afraid of becoming homesick.

Kate said, "Town Hall."

He followed her down through the darkening air. The City always smelled sweet to Peer; sweet but artificial, like a newly unwrapped electronic toy, all microchips and plastic, from David Hawthorne's childhood. They spiraled around the central golden tower, the City's tallest, weaving their way between the transparent walkways. Playing Peter Pan and Tinkerbell. Peer had long ago given up arguing with Kate about the elaborate routes she chose for entering the reconstruction; she ran this peephole on the City out of her own time, and she controlled access to the environment completely. He could either put up with her rules, or stay away altogether. And the whole point of being here was to please her.

They alighted on the paved square outside the Town Hall's main entrance. Peer was startled to recognize one of the fountains as a scaled-up version of Malcolm Carter's demonstration for his algorithmic piggy-back tricks: a cherub wrestling a snake. He must have noticed it before—he'd stood on this spot a hundred times—but if so, he'd forgotten. His memory was due for maintenance; it was a while since he'd increased the size of the relevant networks, and they were probably close to saturation. Simply adding new neurons slowed down recall—relative to other brain functions—making some modes of thought seem like swimming through molasses; a whole host of further adjustments were necessary to make the timing feel right. The Elysians had written software to automate this tuning process, but he disliked the results of the versions they'd shared with each other (and hence made accessible to him), so he'd written his own—but he'd yet to perfect it. Things like table legs kept getting in the way.

The square wasn't empty, but the people around them all looked like puppets, merely strolling past. The City's owners were already inside—and so Kate's software, which spied on the true City and reconstructed it for the two of them, was carrying most of the burden of computing the appearance of their surroundings, now officially unobserved. He took Kate's hand—and she allowed it, though she made her skin feel as cold as marble—and they walked into the hall.

The cavernous room was about half-full, so some eight thousand Elysians had turned up for the meeting. Peer granted himself a brief bird's-eye view of the crowd. A variety of fashions in clothing—or lack of it—and body type were represented, certainly spanning the generations, but most people had chosen to present in more or less traditional human form. The exceptions stood out. One clique of fourth-generation Elysians displayed themselves as modified Babbage engines; the entire hall couldn't have held one of them "to scale," so portions of the mechanism poked through into their seating allocation from some hidden dimension. Ditto for those who'd turned up as "Searle's Chinese Rooms": huge troupes of individual humans (or human-shaped automatons), each carrying out a few simple tasks, which together amounted to a complete working computer. The "components" seated in the hall were Kali-armed blurs, gesticulating at invisible colleagues with coded hand movements so rapid that they seemed to merge into a static multiple exposure.

Peer had no idea how either type of system collected sound and vision from its surroundings to feed to the perfectly normal Elysians these unwieldy computers were (presumably) simulating, as the end result of all their spinning cogs and frantic hand movements—or whether the people in question experienced anything much different than they would have if they'd simply shown that standard physiological model to the world.

Pretentious fancy dress aside, there were a smattering of animal bodies visible—which may or may not have reflected their inhabitants' true models. It could be remarkably comfortable being a lion, or even a snake—if your brain had been suitably adapted for the change. Peer had spent some time inhabiting the bodies of animals, both historical and mythical, and he'd enjoyed them all—but when the phase was over, he'd found that with very little rewiring, he could make the human form feel every bit as good. It seemed more elegant to be comfortable with his ancestral physiology. The majority of Elysians apparently agreed.

Eight thousand was a typical attendance figure—but Peer could not have said what fraction of the total population it represented. Even leaving out Callas, Shaw and Riemann—the three founders who'd remained in their own private worlds, never making contact with anyone—there might have been hundreds or thousands of members of the later generations who'd opted out of the core community without ever announcing their existence.

The ever-expanding cube of Elysium had been divided up from the outset into twenty-four ever-expanding oblique pyramids; one for each of the eighteen founders and their offspring, and six for common ventures (such as Permutation City itself—but mostly Planet Lambert). Most Elysians—or at least most who used the City—had chosen to synch themselves to a common objective time rate. This Standard Time grew steadily faster against Absolute Time—the ticking of the TVC cellular automaton's clock—so every Elysian needed a constantly growing allocation of processors to keep up; but Elysium itself was growing even faster, leaving everyone with an ever-larger surplus of computing power.

Each founder's territory was autonomous, subdivided on his or her own terms. By now, each one could have supported a population of several trillion, living by Standard Time. But Peer suspected that most of the processors were left idle—and he had occasionally daydreamed about some fifth-generation Elysian studying the City's history, getting a curious hunch about Malcolm Carter, and browbeating one of the founders into supplying the spare computing resources of a near-empty pyramid to scan the City for stowaways. All of Carter's ingenious camouflage—and the atom-in-a-haystack odds which had been their real guarantee against discovery—would count for nothing under such scrutiny, and once their presence was identified, they could easily be disinterred . . . assuming that the Elysians were generous enough to do that for a couple of petty thieves.

Kate claimed to believe that this was inevitable, in the long term. Peer didn't much care if they were found or not; all that really mattered to him was the fact that *the City's computational infrastructure* was also constantly expanding, to enable it to keep up with both the growing population, and the ever-increasing demands of Elysian Standard Time. As long as that continued, his own tiny fraction of those resources also steadily increased. Immortality would have been meaningless, trapped in a "machine" with a finite number of possible states; in a finite time he would have exhausted the list of every possible thing he could be. Only the promise of eternal growth made sense of eternal life.

Kate had timed their entrance into the replay perfectly. As they settled into empty seats near the back of the hall, Paul Durham himself took the stage.

He said, "Thank you for joining me. I've convened this meeting to discuss an important proposal concerning Planet Lambert."

Peer groaned. "I could be making table legs, and you've dragged me along to *Attack of the Killer Bees.* Part One Thousand and Ninety-Three."

Kate said, "You could always choose to be glad you're here. There's no need to be *dissatisfied.*"

Peer shut up, and Durham—frozen by the interruption—continued. "As most of you will know, the Lambertians have been making steady progress recently in the scientific treatment of their cosmology. A number of teams of theorists have proposed dust-and-gas-cloud models for the formation of their planetary system—models which come very close to the truth. Although no such process ever literally took place in the Autoverse, it was crudely simulated before the launch, to help design a plausible ready-made system. The Lambertians are now zeroing in on the parameters of that simulation." He gestured at a giant screen behind him, and vision appeared: several thousand of the insect-like Lambertians swarming in the air above a lush blue-green meadow.

Peer was disappointed. *Scientific treatment of their cosmology* sounded like the work of a technologically sophisticated culture, but there were no artifacts visible in the scene: no build-ings, no machines, not even the simplest tools. He froze the image and expanded a portion of it. The creatures themselves looked exactly the same to him as they'd looked several hundred thousand Lambertian years before, when they'd been singled out as the Species Most Likely to Give Rise to Civilization. Their segmented, chitinous bodies were still naked and unadorned. *What had he expected? Insects in lab coats?* No—but it was still hard to accept that the leaps they'd made in intelligence had left no mark on their appearance, or their surroundings.

Durham said, "They're communicating a version of the the-ory, and actively demonstrating the underlying mathematics at the same time; like one group of researches sending a com-puter model to another—but the Lambertians don't have arti-ficial computers. If the dance looks valid it's taken up by other groups—and if they sustain it long enough, they'll inter-nalize the pattern: they'll be able to remember it without con-tinuing to perform it."

Peer whispered, "Come back to the workshop and dance cosmological models with me?" Kate ignored him.

"The dominant theory employs accurate knowledge of Autoverse chemistry and physics, and includes a detailed breakdown of the composition of the primordial cloud. It goes no further. As yet, there's no hypothesis about the way in which that particular cloud might have come into existence; no explanation for the origin and relative abundances of the elements. And there *can be no explanation,* no sensible prior history; the Autoverse doesn't provide one. No Big Bang: General Relativity doesn't apply, their space-time is flat, their universe isn't expanding. No elements formed in stars: there are no nuclear forces, no fusion; stars burn by gravity alone—and their sun is the only star.

"So, these cosmologists are about to hit a brick wall—through no fault of their own. Dominic Repetto has suggested that now would be the ideal time for us to make contact with the Lambertians. To announce our presence. To explain their planet's origins. To begin a carefully moderated cultural exchange."

A soft murmuring broke out among the crowd. Peer turned to Kate. "This is it? This is the news I couldn't miss?"

She stared back at him, pityingly. "They're talking about *first contact with an alien race.* Did you really want to sleep-walk right through that?"

Peer laughed. *"First contact?"* They've observed these insects in microscopic detail since the days they were single-celled algae. Everything about them is known already: their biology, their language, their culture. It's all in the central library. These "aliens" have evolved on a microscope slide. There are no surprises in store."

"Except how they respond to us."

"*Us?* Nobody responds to *us.*"

Kate gave him a poisonous look. "How they respond to the Elysians."

Peer thought it over. "I expect someone knows all about that, too. Someone must have modeled the reaction of Lambertian "society" to finding out that they're nothing but an experiment in artificial life."

An Elysian presenting as a tall, thin young man took the stage. Durham introduced him as Dominic Repetto. Peer had given up trying to keep track of the proliferating dynasties long ago, but he thought the name was a recent addition; he certainly couldn't recall a Repetto being involved in Autoverse studies when he'd had a passion for the subject himself.

Repetto addressed the meeting. "It's my belief that the Lambertians now possess the conceptual framework they need to comprehend our existence, and to make sense of our role in their cosmology. It's true that they lack artificial computers— but their whole language of ideas is based on representations of the world around them in the form of *numerical models.* These models were originally variations on a few genetically hardwired themes—maps of terrain showing food sources, algorithms for predicting predator behavior—but the modern Lambertians have evolved the skill of generating and testing whole new classes of models, in a way that's as innate to them as language skills were to the earliest humans. A team of

Lambertians can 'speak' and 'judge' a mathematical description of population dynamics in the mites they herd for food, as
easily as prelaunch humans could construct or comprehend a
simple sentence.

"We mustn't judge them by anthropomorphic standards;
human technological landmarks simply aren't relevant. The
Lambertians have deduced most of Autoverse chemistry and
physics by observations of their natural world, supplemented
by a very small number of controlled experiments. They've
generated concepts equivalent to *temperature and pressure,
energy and entropy*—without fire, metallurgy or the wheel . . .
let alone the steam engine. They've calculated the melting and
boiling points of most of the elements—*without ever purifying
them.* Their lack of technology only makes their intellectual
achievements all the more astounding. It's as if the ancient
Greeks had written about the boiling point of nitrogen, or the
Egyptians had predicted the chemical properties of chlorine."

Peer smiled to himself cynically; the founders always loved
to hear Earth rate a mention—and all the better if the refer-
ences were to times long before they were born.

Repetto paused; he grew perceptibly taller and his youthful
features became subtly more dignified, more mature. Most
Elysians would see this as no more manipulative than a
change in posture or tone of voice. He said solemnly, "Most
of you will be aware of the resolution of the Town Meeting of
January 5, 3052, forbidding contact with the Lambertians until
they'd *constructed* their own computers and performed simulations—experiments in artificial life—as sophisticated as the
Autoverse itself. That was judged to be the safest possible
benchmark . . . but I believe it has turned out to be misconceived, and completely inappropriate.

"The Lambertians are looking for answers to questions
about their origins. We know there are no answers to be discovered inside the Autoverse itself—but I believe the
Lambertians are intellectually equipped to comprehend the
larger truth. We have a responsibility to make that truth
known to them. I propose that this meeting overturns the resolution of 3052, and authorizes a team of Autoverse scholars to

enter Planet Lambert and—in a culturally sensitive manner—inform the Lambertians of their history and context."

The buzz of discussion grew louder. Peer felt a vestigial twinge of interest, in spite of himself. In a universe without death or scarcity, politics took strange forms. Any one of the founders who disagreed with the way Planet Lambert was managed would be perfectly free to copy the whole Autoverse into their own territory, and to do as they wished with their own private version. In inverse proportion to the ease of such a move, any faction would have a rare chance here to demonstrate their "influence" and increase their "prestige" by persuading the meeting to retain the ban on contact with the Lambertians—without provoking their opponents into cloning the Autoverse and pushing ahead regardless. Many of the first generation still chose to value these things, for their own sake.

Elaine Sanderson rose to her feet, resplendent in a light blue suit and a body which together proclaimed: *1972 to 2045* A.D., *and proud of it* (even if she only wore them on official occasions). Peer let himself time-trip for a second: in his late teens, David Hawthorne had seen the flesh-and-blood Sanderson on television, being sworn in as Attorney General of the United States of America—a nation whose constituent particles at the time of that oath might well overlap with some portion of Elysium at this very instant.

Sanderson said, "Thank you, Mr. Repetto, for giving us your perspective on this important matter. It's unfortunate that so few of us take the time to keep ourselves up to date with the progress of the Lambertians. Although they have come all the way from single-celled lifeforms to their present, highly sophisticated state without our explicit intervention, ultimately they are in our care at every moment, and we all have a duty to treat that responsibility with the utmost seriousness.

"I can still recall some of the earliest plans we made for dealing with the Autoverse: to hide the details of life on Planet Lambert from ourselves, deliberately; to watch and wait, as if from afar, until the inhabitants sent probes to their system's other worlds; to arrive as 'explorers' in 'space ships,' struggling to learn the language and customs of these 'aliens'—perhaps going so far as to extend the Autoverse to include an invisibly distant star, with a 'home world' from which we might travel. Slavish imitations of the hypothetical interstellar missions we'd left behind. Bizarre charades.

"Mercifully, we abandoned those childish ideas long ago. There will be no sham 'mission of discovery'—and no lying to the Lambertians, or to ourselves.

"There is one quality of those early, laughable schemes which should still be kept in mind, though: *we always intended to meet the Lambertians as equals.* Visitors from a distant world who would stretch their vision of the universe— but not subvert it, not swallow it whole. We would approach them as siblings, arguing our viewpoint—not Gods, revealing divine truth.

"I ask the meeting to consider whether these two equally laudable aims, of honesty and humility, could not be reconciled. If the Lambertians are on the verge of a crisis in understanding their origins, what patronizing instinct compels us to rush in and provide them with an instant solution? Mr. Repetto tells us how they have already inferred the properties of the chemical elements—elements which remain mysterious and invisible, manifesting themselves only in the elaborate phenomena of the natural world. Clearly, the Lambertians have a gift for uncovering hidden patterns, hidden explanations. How many more centuries can it be, then, before they guess the truth about their own cosmology?

"I propose that we delay contact until *the hypothesis of our existence* has arisen naturally amongst the Lambertians, and has been thoroughly explored. Until they have decided for themselves exactly what we might mean to them. Until *they* have debated, as we are debating right now, how best they might deal with us.

"If aliens had visited Earth the moment humans first looked up at the sky and suffered some crisis of understanding, they would have been hailed as Gods. If they'd arrived in the early twenty-first century—when humans had been predicting their existence and pondering the logistics of contact, for decades—they would have been accepted as equals; more experienced, more skilled, more knowledgeable, but ultimately nothing but an expected part of a well-behaved, well-understood universe.

"I believe that we should wait for the equivalent moment in Lambertian history: when the Lambertians are *impatient* for proof of our existence—when our continued absence becomes far harder for them to explain than our arrival would be. Once they begin to suspect that we're eavesdropping on every conversation they hold about us, it would be dishonest to remain concealed. Until then, we owe them the opportunity to find as many answers as they can, without us."

Sanderson resumed her seat. Portions of the audience applauded demurely. Peer lazily mapped the response and correlated it with appearance; she seemed to have been a big hit with the third-generation mainstream—but they had a reputation for gleefully faking everything.

Kate said, "Don't you wish you could join the discussion?" Half sarcasm, half self-pity.

Peer said cheerfully, "No—but if you have strong views on the matter yourself, I suggest you copy the whole Autoverse, and make contact with the Lambertians personally—or leave them in unspoilt ignorance. Whichever you prefer."

"You know I don't have room to do that."

"And you know that makes no difference. There's a copy of the original biosphere seed, the entire compressed description, in the central library. You could copy that, and freeze yourself until you finally have the room to unfold it. The whole thing's deterministic—every Lambertian would flutter its little wings for you in exactly the same way as it did for the Elysians. Right up to the moment of contact."

"And you honestly believe that the City will grow that large? That after a billion years of Standard Time, they won't have trashed it and built something new?"

"I don't know. But there's always the alternative: you could launch a whole new TVC universe and make all the room you need. I'll come along, if you want me to." He meant it; he'd follow her anywhere. She only had to say the word.

But she looked away. He ached to grant her happiness, but

the choice was hers: if she wanted to believe that she was standing outside in the snow—or rather, bricked into the walls—watching the Elysians feast on Reality, there was nothing he could do to change that.

Three hundred and seven speakers followed; one hundred and sixty-two backed Repetto, one hundred and forty supported Sanderson. Five waffled on with no apparent agenda; a remarkably low proportion. Peer daydreamed about the sound of sandpaper on wood.

When the vote finally came—one per original attendee, no last-minute clonings accepted—Sanderson won by a ten percent margin. She took the stage and made a short speech thanking the voters for their decision. Peer suspected that many of the Elysians had quietly slipped out of their bodies and gone elsewhere, by now.

Dominic Repetto said a few words too, clearly disappointed, but gracious in defeat. It was Paul Durham—presumably his mentor and sponsor—who showed the slightly vacuous expression of a model-of-a-body with its facial muscles crudely decoupled from its model-of-a-brain. Durham—with his strange history of brief episodes as a Copy in different permutations—seemed to have never really caught up with the prelaunch state of the art, let alone the Elysian cutting edge; when he had something to hide, it was obvious. He was taking the decision badly.

Kate said coldly, "That's it. You've fulfilled your civic duty. You can go now."

Peer made his eyes big and brown. "Come back to the workshop with me. We can make love in the wood dust. Or just sit around and talk. *Be happy, for no reason.* It wouldn't be so bad."

Kate shook her head and faded away. Peer felt a pang of disappointment, but not for long.

There'd be other times.

25

Thomas crouched in the bathroom window frame, halfway out of Anna's flat. He knew that the edges of the brickwork would be sharper than razors, this time. He made his way across to the neighbor's window, repeating the familiar movements precisely, though his hands and forearms wept blood. Insects crawled from the wounds and swarmed along his arm, over his face, into his mouth. He gagged and retched but he didn't falter.

Down the drain pipe. From the alley below, he returned to the flat. Anna was by his side on the stairs. They danced again. Argued again. Struggled again.

"Think fast. Think fast."

He knelt over her, one knee to either side, took her face in his hands, then closed his eyes. He brought her head forward, then slammed it back against the wall. Five times. Then he held his fingers near her nostrils, without opening his eyes. He felt no exhalation.

Thomas was in his Frankfurt apartment, a month after the murder, dreaming. Anna stood by the bed. He reached out from beneath the blankets into the darkness, eyes closed. She took his hand in hers. With her other hand, she stroked the scar on his forearm tenderly, then she pushed one finger easily through his brittle skin and liquefying flesh. He thrashed against the sheets, but she wouldn't let go; she dug with her fingers until she was gripping naked bone. When she snapped the ulna and radius, he convulsed with pain and ejaculated suddenly, everything his corrupt body contained departing in a single stream: dark clotted blood, maggots, pus, excrement.

Thomas was in his suburban mansion, sitting naked on the floor at the end of the hallway, startled. He shifted his right hand, and realized he was clutching a small vegetable knife. And he remembered why.

There were seven faint pink scars on his abdomen, seven digits, still legible, right-way-up as he gazed down at them: 1053901. He set to work recarving the first six.

He didn't trust the clocks. The clocks lied. And although every incision he made in his skin healed perfectly, given time, for a long time it seemed he had managed to repair the numbers before they faded. He didn't know what they measured, except their own steady ascent, but they seemed like a touchstone of something approaching sanity.

He recut the final digit as a two, then licked his fingers and wiped the blood away. At first it seeped back, but after five or six repetitions, the fresh wound stood clean and red against his pale skin. He pronounced the number several times. "One million, fifty three thousand, nine hundred and two."

Thomas climbed to his feet and walked down the hall. His body knew only the time he carved upon it; he never felt tired, or hungry, or even unclean—he could sleep or not sleep, eat or not eat, wash or not wash; it made no perceptible difference. His hair and fingernails never grew. His face never aged.

He stopped outside the library. He believed he'd methodically torn all the books to shreds several times, but on each occasion the debris had been cleared away and the books replaced, in his absence.

He walked into the room. He glanced at the terminal in the corner, the object of his deepest loathing; he'd never been able to damage it—smash, chip, bend or even scratch any part of its visible form. Indestructible or not, it had never functioned.

He wandered from shelf to shelf, but he'd read every book a dozen or more times. They'd all become meaningless. The library was well-stocked, and he'd studied the sacred texts of every faith; those few which, by some stretch of poetic licence, might have been said to describe his condition offered no prospect for changing it. In the distant past, he'd undergone a hundred feverish conversions; he'd ranted to every deity which humanity had ever postulated. If he'd stumbled on the one which existed—the one responsible for his damnation—his pleas had been to no avail.

The one thing he'd never expected after death was uncertainty. It had worried him deeply, at first: being cast into Hell, without so much as a glimpse of Heaven to taunt him, and a smug I-told-you-so from the faithful on their way up—let alone a formal trial before the God of his childhood, in which every doctrinal assertion he'd ever doubted was proclaimed as Absolute Truth, and every theological debate was resolved, once and for all.

But he'd since decided that if his condition was eternal and irreversible, it hardly mattered what the God who'd made it so was named.

Thomas sat cross-legged on the floor of the library, and tried to empty his mind.

"Think fast. Think fast."

Anna lay before him, bleeding and unconscious. Time slowed down. The moment he was approaching seemed impossible to face, impossible to traverse yet again—but he inched toward it, and he knew that he had no power to turn away.

He'd come to understand that all the visions of his own decay and mutilation were nothing but elaborate gestures of self-loathing. When his flesh was torn from his body it was a distraction—almost a relief. His suffering did not illuminate his crime; it drowned his thoughts in an anesthetic haze. It was a fantasy of power, a fantasy of retribution.

But here there was no balm of self-righteous pain, no pretence that his baroque tortures were working some alchemy of justice. He knelt over Anna, and could not weep, could not flinch, could not blind himself to the measure of what he'd done.

He might have called an ambulance. He might have saved her life. It would have taken so little strength, so little courage, so little love, that he could not imagine how a human being could have failed to possess enough of each, and still walk the Earth.

But he had. He had.

So he brought her head forward, and slammed it against the wall.

26

After a week as Durham's guest, Maria went looking for a place of her own.

Her anger had faded, the numbness of shock had faded, the fifth or sixth wave of disbelief had finally lifted. But she still felt almost paralyzed by the strangeness of the truths she'd been forced to accept: her exile from the universe of flesh-and-blood humanity; the impossible existence of Elysium; intelligent life in the Autoverse. She couldn't begin to make sense of any of these things until she had a fixed point to stand on.

She had refused to pack any luggage to accompany her scan file into the next life; it would have felt like she was humoring Durham if she'd made the slightest concession to the needs of a Copy who she'd believed would never run. No environments, no furniture, no clothes; no photographs, no diaries, no scanned memorabilia. No VR duplicate of her old narrow terrace to make her feel at home. She might have set about reconstructing it from memory, detail by detail—or let architectural software pluck a perfect imitation straight out of her brain—but she didn't feel strong enough to deal with the emotional contradictions: the tug of the old world, the taint of self-deception. Instead, she decided to choose one of the pre-defined apartments in the City itself.

Durham assured her that nobody would begrudge her the use of public resources. "Of course, you could copy the City into your own territory and run a private version at your own expense—defeating the whole point. This is the one environment in all of Elysium which comes close to being a *place* in the old sense. Anyone can walk the streets, anyone can live here—but no one can rearrange the skyline on a whim. It would require a far more impassioned debate to alter the colors of the street signs, here, than it used to take for the average local council to rezone an entire neighborhood."

So Permutation City offered her its disingenuous, municipally sanctioned, quasi-objective presence for free, while her model-of-a-body ran on processors in her own territory—and the two systems, by exchanging data, contrived her experience of walking the streets, entering the sleek metallic buildings, and exploring the empty apartments which might have smelled of paint, but didn't. She felt nervous on her own, so Durham came with her, solicitous and apologetic as ever. His regret seemed sincere on one level—he wasn't indifferent to the pain he'd caused her—but beneath that there didn't seem to be much doubt: he clearly expected to be wholly forgiven for waking her, sooner or later.

She asked him, "How does it feel, being seven thousand years old?"

"That depends."

"On what?"

"On how I want it to feel."

She found a place in the northeast quadrant, halfway between the central tower and the City's rim. From the bedroom, she could see the mountains in the east, the glistening waterfall, a distant patch of forest. There were better views available, but this one seemed right; anything more spectacular would have made her feel self-conscious.

Durham showed her how to claim residency: a brief dialogue with the apartment software. He said, "You're the only Elysian in this tower, so you can program all your neighbors any way you like."

"What if I do nothing?"

"Default behavior: they'll stay out of your way."

"And what about other Elysians? Am I such a novelty that people will come looking for me?"

Durham thought it over. "Your awakening is public knowledge—but most people here are fairly patient. I doubt that anyone would be so rude as to buttonhole you in the street. Your phone number will remain unlisted until you choose otherwise—and the apartment itself is under your control, now, as secure as any private environment. The software has been rigorously validated: breaking and entering is mathematically impossible."

He left her to settle in. She paced the rooms, trying to inhabit them, to claim them as her own; she forced herself to walk the nearby streets, trying to feel at ease. The Art Deco apartment, the Fritz Lang towers, the streets full of crowd-scene extras all unnerved her—but on reflection, she realized that she couldn't have gone anywhere else. When she tried to imagine her "territory," her private slice of Elysium, it seemed as daunting and unmanageable as if she'd inherited one twenty-fourth of the old universe of galaxies and vacuum. That the new one was generally invisible, and built from a lattice of self-reproducing computers, built in turn from cellular automaton cells—which were nothing more than sequences of numbers, however easy it might be to color-code them and arrange them in neat grids—only made the thought of being lost in its vastness infinitely stranger. It was bad enough that her true body was a pattern of computation resonating in a tiny portion of an otherwise silent crystalline pyramid which stretched into the distance for the TVC equivalent of thousands of light years. The thought of immersing her senses in a fake world which was really another corner of the same structure—withdrawing entirely into the darkness of that giant airless crypt, and surrendering to private hallucinations—made her sick with panic.

If the City was equally unreal, at least it was one hallucination which other Elysians shared—and, anchored by that consensus, she found the courage to examine the invisible world beneath, from a safe—if hallucinatory—distance. She sat in the apartment and studied maps of Elysium. On the largest scale, most of the cube was portrayed as featureless: the other seventeen founders' pyramids were private, and her own was all but unused. Public territory could be colored according to the software it ran—processes identified, data flows traced—but even then, most of it was monochrome: five of the six public pyramids were devoted to the Autoverse, running the same simple program on processor after processor, implementing the Autoverse's own cellular automaton rules—utterly different from the TVC's. A faint metallic grid was superimposed on this region, like a mesh of fine wires immersed in an unknown substance to gauge its properties. This was the software which spied on Planet Lambert—an entirely separate program from the Autoverse itself, not subject to any of its laws. Maria had written the original version herself, although she'd never had a chance to test it on a planetary scale. Generations of Elysian Autoverse scholars had extended and refined it, and now it peeked through a quadrillion nonexistent cracks in space, collating, interpreting and summarizing everything it saw. The results flowed to the hub of Elysium, into the central library—along a channel rendered luminous as white-hot silver by the density of its data flow.

The hub itself was a dazzling polyhedron, a cluster of databases ringed by the communications structures which handled the torrent of information flowing to and from the pyramids. Every transaction between Elysians of different clans flowed through here; from phone calls to handshakes, from sex to whatever elaborate post-human intimacies they'd invented in the past seven thousand years. The map gave nothing away, though; even with the highest magnification and the slowest replay, streaming packets of data registered as nothing more than featureless points of light, their contents safely anonymous.

The second-brightest data flow linked the hub to the City, revealed as a delicate labyrinth of algorithms clinging to one face of the sixth public pyramid. With the Autoverse software across the border rendered midnight blue, the City looked like a cluttered, neon-lit fairground on the edge of a vast desert, at the end of a shimmering highway. Maria zoomed in and watched the packets of data responsible for the map itself come streaming out from the hub.

There was no point-for-point correspondence between this

view and the City of the senses. The crowds of fake pedestrians, spread across the visible metropolis, could all be found here as a tight assembly of tiny flashing blocks in pastel shades, with titles like FLOCKING BEHAVIOR and MISCELLANEOUS TROPISMS. The locations and other attributes of specific individuals were encoded in data structures too small to be seen without relentless magnification. Maria's own apartment was equally microscopic, but it was the product of widely scattered components, as far apart as SURFACE OPTICS, AIR DYNAMICS, THERMAL RADIATION and CARPET TEXTURE.

She might have viewed her own body as a similar diagram of functional modules—but she decided to let that wait.

One vivisection at a time.

She began exploring the information resources of Elysium—the data networks which portrayed themselves as such—and leaving the apartment to walk alone through the City twice a day; familiarizing herself with the two spaces analogous to those she'd known in the past.

She skimmed through the libraries, not quite at random, flicking through Homer and Joyce, staring at the Rembrandts and Picassos and Moores, playing snatches of Chopin and Liszt, viewing scenes from Bergman and Buñuel. Hefting the weight of the kernel of human civilization the Elysians had brought with them.

It felt light. *Dubliners* was as fantastic, now, as *The Iliad*. *Guernica* had never really happened—or if it had, the Elysian view was beyond the powers of any artist to portray. *The Seventh Seal* was a mad, pointless fairy tale. *The Discreet Charm of the Bourgeoisie* was all that remained.

Altering herself in any way was too hard a decision to make, so, faithful by default to human physiology, she ate and shat and slept. There were a thousand ways to conjure food into existence, from gourmet meals in the culinary database literally emerging from the screen of her terminal, to the time-saving option of push-button satiety and a pleasant aftertaste, but old rituals clamored to be reenacted, so she went out and bought raw ingredients from puppet shopkeepers in aromatic delicatessens, and cooked her own meals, often badly, and grew curiously tired watching the imperfect chemistry at work, as if she was performing the difficult simulation, subconsciously, herself.

For three nights, she dreamed that she was back in the old world, having unremarkable conversations with her parents, school friends, fellow Autoverse junkies, old lovers. Whatever the scene, the air was charged, glowing with self-conscious authenticity. She woke from these dreams crippled with loss, clawing at the retreating certainties, believing—for ten seconds, or five—that Durham had drugged her, hypnotized her, brainwashed her into dreaming of Elysium; and each time she thought she "slept," here, she awoke into the Earthly life she'd never stopped living.

Then the fog cleared from her brain, and she knew that it wasn't true.

She dreamed of the City for the first time. She was out on Fifteenth Avenue when the puppets started pleading with her to be treated as fully sentient. "We pass the Turing test, don't we? Is a stranger in a crowd less than human, just because you can't witness her inner life?" They tugged at her clothes like beggars. She told them not to be absurd. She said, "How can you complain? Don't you understand? We've abolished injustice." A man in a crisp black suit eyed her sharply, and muttered, "You'll always have the poor." But he was wrong.

And she dreamed of Elysium itself. She weaved her way through the TVC grid in the gaps between the processors, transformed into a simple, self-sustaining pattern of cells, like the oldest, most primitive forms of artificial life; disturbing nothing, but observing everything—in all six dimensions, no less. She woke when she realized how absurd that was: the TVC universe wasn't flooded with some analog of light, spreading information about every cell far and wide. To be embedded in the grid meant being all but blind to its contents; reaching out and painstakingly probing what lay ahead—sometimes destructively—was the only way to discover anything.

In the late afternoons, in the golden light which flooded in through the bedroom window after a thousand chance, calculated reflections between the towers, she usually wept. It felt inadequate, desultory, pathetic, immoral. She didn't want to "mourn" the human race—but she didn't know how to make sense of its absence. She refused to imagine a world long dead—as if her Elysian millennia of sleep had propelled her into Earth's uncertain future—so she struggled to bind herself to the time she remembered, to follow the life of her doppelgänger in her mind. She pictured a reconciliation with Aden; it wasn't impossible. She pictured him very much alive, as tender and selfish and stubborn as ever. She fantasized the most mundane, the most unexceptionable moments between them, ruthlessly weeding out anything that seemed too optimistic, too much like wish-fulfilment. She wasn't interested in inventing a perfect life for the other Maria; she only wanted to guess the unknowable truth.

But she had to keep believing that she'd saved Francesa. Anything less would have been unbearable.

She tried to think of herself as an emigrant, an ocean-crosser in the days before aircraft, before telegraphs. People had left everything behind, and survived. Prospered. Flourished. Their lives hadn't been destroyed; they'd embraced the unknown, and been enriched, transformed.

The unknown? She was living in an artifact, a mathematical object she'd helped Durham construct for his billionaires. Elysium was a universe made to order. It contained no hidden wonders, no lost tribes.

But it did contain the Autoverse.

The longer she thought about it, the more it seemed that Planet Lambert was the key to her sanity. Even after three billion years of evolution, it was the one thing in Elysium which connected with her past life—leading right back to the night she'd witnessed *A. lamberti* digesting *mutose.* The thread was unbroken: the seed organism, *A. hydrophila,* had come from that very same strain. And if the Autoverse, then, had been the ultimate indulgence, a rarefied intellectual game in a world beset with problems, the situation now was completely inverted: the Autoverse was home to hundreds of millions of lifeforms, a flourishing civilization, a culture on the verge of a scientific revolution. In a universe subject to whim, convenience and fantasy, it seemed like the only solid ground left.

And although she suffered no delusions of having personally "created" the Lambertians—sketching their planet's early history, and cobbling together an ancestor for them by adapting someone else's translation of a terrestrial bacterium, hardly qualified her to take credit for their multiplexed nervous systems and their open-air digestive tracts, let alone their self-awareness—she couldn't simply wash her hands of their fate. She'd never believed that Planet Lambert could be brought into existence—but she had helped to make it happen nonetheless.

Part of her still wanted to do nothing but rage against her awakening, and mourn her loss. Embracing the Autoverse seemed like an insult to the memory of Earth—and a sign that she'd accepted the way Durham had treated her. But it began to seem perverse to the point of insanity to turn her back on the one thing which might give her new life some meaning—just to spite Durham, just to make a lie of his reasons for waking her. There were other ways of making it clear that she hadn't forgiven him.

The apartment—at first, inconceivably large, almost uninhabitable—slowly lost its strangeness. On the tenth morning, she finally woke expecting the sight of the bedroom exactly as she found it; if not at peace with her situation, at least unsurprised to be exactly where she was.

She phoned Durham and said, "I want to join the expedition."

The Contact Group occupied one story of a tower in the southeast quadrant. Maria, uninterested in teleporting, made the journey on foot, crossing from building to building by walkway, ignoring the puppets and admiring the view. It was faster than traveling at street level, and she was gradually conquering her fear of heights. Bridges here did not collapse from unanticipated vibrations. Perspex tubes did not hurtle to the ground, spilling corpses onto the pavement. It made no difference whether or not Malcolm Carter had known the first thing about structural engineering; the City was hardly going to bother laboriously modeling stresses and loads just to discover whether or not parts of itself should fail, for the sake of realism. Everything was perfectly safe, by decree.

Durham was waiting for her in the foyer. Inside, he introduced her to Dominic Repetto and Alisa Zemansky, the project's other leaders. Maria hadn't known what to expect from her first contact with later-generation Elysians, but they presented as neatly dressed humans, male and female, both "in their late thirties," wearing clothes which would not have looked wildly out of place in any office in twenty-first century Sydney. *Out of deference to her?* She hoped not—unless the accepted thing to do, in their subculture, was to show a different form to everyone, expressly designed to put them at ease. Repetto, in fact, was so strikingly handsome that she almost recoiled at the thought that he—or his parent—had deliberately chosen such a face. *But what did codes of vanity from the age of cosmetic surgery and gene splicing mean, now?* Zemansky was stunning too, with dark-flecked violet eyes and spiked blonde hair. Durham appeared—to her, at least— almost unchanged from the man she'd met in 2050. Maria began to wonder how she looked to the young Elysians. Like something recently disinterred, probably.

Repetto shook her hand over and over. "It's a great, great honor to meet you. I can't tell you how much you've inspired us all." His face shone; he seemed to be sincere. Maria felt her cheeks flush, and tried to imagine herself in some analogous situation, shaking hands with . . . who? Max Lambert? John von Neumann? Alan Turing? Charles Babbage? Ada Lovelace? She knew she'd done nothing compared to any of those pioneers—but she'd had seven thousand years for her reputation to be embellished. And three billion for her work to bear fruit.

The floor was divided into open-plan offices, but nobody else seemed to be about. Durham saw her peering around the partitions and said cryptically, "There are other workers, but they come and go."

Zemansky led the way into a small conference room. She

said to Maria, "We can move to a VR representation of Planet Lambert, if you like—but I should warn you that it can be disorienting: being visually immersed but intangible, walking through vegetation, and so on. And moving at the kinds of speeds necessary to keep track of the Lambertians can induce motion sickness. Of course, there are neural changes which counteract both those problems—"

Maria wasn't ready to start tampering with her brain—or to step onto the surface of an alien planet. She said, "Viewing screens sound easier. I'd be happier with that. Do you mind?" Zemansky looked relieved.

Repetto stood at the end of the table and addressed the three of them, although Maria knew this was all for her benefit.

"So much has been happening on Lambert, lately, that we've slowed it right down compared to Standard Time so we can keep up with developments." An elliptical map of the planet's surface appeared on the wall behind him. "Most recently, dozens of independent teams of chemists have begun looking for a simpler, more unified model underlying the current atomic theory." Markers appeared, scattered across the map. "It's been three hundred years since the standard model—thirty-two atoms with a regular pattern of masses, valencies and mutual affinities—became widely accepted. The Lambertian equivalent of Mendeleev's Periodic Table." He flashed a smile at Maria, as if she might have been a comtemporary of Mendeleev—or perhaps because he was proud of his arcane knowledge of the history of a science which was no longer true. "At the time, atoms were accepted as fundamental entities: structureless, indivisible, requiring no further explanation. Over the last twenty years, that view has finally begun to break down."

Maria was already confused. From the hurried reading she'd done in the past few days, she knew that the Lambertians only modified an established theory when a new phenomenon was discovered which the theory failed to explain. Repetto must have noticed her expression, because he paused expectantly.

She said, "Autoverse atoms *are* indivisible. There are no

components you can separate out, no smaller stable entities. Smash them together at any energy you like, and all they'll do is bounce—and the Lambertians are in no position to smash them together at any energy at all. So . . . surely there's nothing in their experience that the current theory can't account for perfectly."

"Nothing in their immediate environment, certainly. But the problem is cosmology. They've been refining the models of the history of their star system, and now they're looking for an explanation for the composition of the primordial cloud."

"They accepted the thirty-two atoms and their properties as given—but they can't bring themselves to do the same with the arbitrary amounts of each one in the cloud?"

"That's right. It's difficult to translate the motivation exactly, but they have a very precise aesthetic which dictates what they'll accept as a theory—and it's almost physically impossible for them to contradict it. If they try to dance a theory which fails to resonate with the neural system which assesses its simplicity, the dance falls apart." He thought for a second, then pointed to the screen behind him; a swarm of Lambertians appeared. "Here's an example—going back awhile. This is a team of astronomers—all fully aware of the motions of the planets in the sky, relative to the sun—testing out a theory which attempts to explain those observations by assuming that Planet Lambert is fixed, and everything else orbits around it."

Maria watched the creatures intently. She would have been hard-pressed to identify the rhythms in their elaborate weaving motions—but when the swarm began to drift apart, the collapse of order was obvious.

"Now here's the heliocentric version, from a few years later."

The dance, again, was too complex to analyze—although it did seem to be more harmonious—and after a while, almost hypnotic. The black specks shifting back and forth against the white sky left trails on her retinas. Below, the ubiquitous grassland seemed an odd setting for astronomical theorizing. The Lambertians apparently accepted their condition—in which *herding mites* represented the greatest control they exerted over nature—as if it constituted as much of a utopia as the Elysian's total freedom. They still faced predators. Many still died young from disease. Food was always plentiful, though; they'd modeled their own population cycles, and learned to damp the oscillations, at a very early stage. And, nature lovers or not, there'd been no "ideological" struggles over "birth control"; once the population model had spread, the same remedies had been adopted by communities right across the planet. Lambertian cultural diversity was limited; far more behavior was genetically determined than was the case in humans—the young being born self-sufficient, with far less neural plasticity than a human infant—and there was relatively little variation in the relevant genes.

The heliocentric theory was acceptable; the dance remained coherent. Repetto replayed the scene, with a "translation" in a small window, showing the positions of the planets represented at each moment. Maria still couldn't decipher the correspondence—the Lambertians certainly weren't flying around in simple mimicry of the hypothetical orbits—but the synchronized rhythms of planets and insect-astronomers seemed to mesh somewhere in her visual cortex, firing some pattern detector which didn't know quite what to make of the strange resonance.

She said, "So Ptolemy was simply bad grammar—obvious nonsense. Doubleplus ungood. And they reached Copernicus *a few years later?* That's impressive. How long did they take to get to Kepler . . . to Newton?"

Zemansky said smoothly, "That *was* Newton. The theory of gravity—and the laws of motion—were all part of the model they were dancing; the Lambertians could never have expressed the shapes of the orbits without including a reason for them."

Maria felt the hairs rise on the back of her neck.

"If that was Newton . . . what came before?"

"Nothing. That was the first successful astronomical model—the culmination of about a decade of trial and error by teams all over the planet."

"But they must have had something. Primitive myths. Stacks of turtles. Sun gods in chariots."

Zemansky laughed. "No turtles or chariots, obviously—but no: no naive cosmologies. Their earliest language grew out of the things they could easily observe and model—ecological relationships, population dynamics. When cosmology was beyond their grasp, they didn't even try to tackle it; it was a non-subject."

"No creation myths?"

"No. To the Lambertians, believing any kind of "myth"— any kind of vague, untestable pseudo-explanation—would have been like . . . suffering hallucinations, seeing mirages, hearing voices. It would have rendered them completely dysfunctional."

Maria cleared her throat. "Then I wonder how they'll react to us."

Durham said, "*Right now,* creators are a non-subject. The Lambertians have no need of that hypothesis. They understand evolution: mutation, natural selection—they've even postulated some kind of macromolecular gene. But the origin of life remains an open question, too difficult to tackle, and it would probably be centuries before they realized that their ultimate ancestor was seeded "by hand" . . . if in fact there's any evidence to show that—any logical reason why *A. hydrophila* couldn't have arisen in some imaginary prebiotic history.

"But it won't come to that; after a few more decades banging their heads against the problem of the primordial cloud, I think they'll guess what's going on. An idea whose time has come can sweep across the planet in a matter of months, however exotic it might be; these creatures are not traditionalists. And once the theory that their world was *made* arises in the proper scientific context, it's not going to drive them mad. All Alisa was saying was that the sort of primitive superstitions which early humans believed in wouldn't have made sense to the early Lambertians."

Maria said, "So . . . we'll wait until 'creators' are no longer a non-subject before we barge in and announce that that's exactly what we are?"

Durham replied, "Absolutely. We have permission to make contact *once the Lambertians have independently postulated our existence*—and no sooner." He laughed, and added, with evident satisfaction, "Which we achieved by asking for much more."

Maria still felt uneasy—but she didn't want to hold up proceedings while she grappled with the subtleties of Lambertian culture.

She said, "All right. Cosmology is the trigger, but they're looking for a deeper explanation for their chemistry. Are they having any luck?"

Repetto brought back the map of Planet Lambert; the markers showing the locations of the teams of theorists were replaced by small bar charts in the same positions. "These are the dance times sustained for various subatomic models which have been explored over the past five years. A few theories are showing some promise, improving slightly with each refinement; other groups are getting fairly random results. Nobody's come up with anything they'd be capable of communicating over any distance; these dances are too short-lived to be remembered by teams of messengers."

Maria felt her skin crawl, again. *False messages die, en route.* There was something chilling about all this efficiency, this ruthless pursuit of the truth. Or maybe it was just a matter of injured pride: treating some of humanity's most hard-won intellectual achievements as virtually self-evident wasn't the most endearing trait an alien species could possess.

She said, "So . . . no team is on the verge of discovering the truth?"

Repetto shook his head. "Not yet. But the Autoverse rules are the simplest explanation for the thirty-two atoms, by almost any criterion."

"Simplest to us. There's nothing in the Lambertians' environment to make them think in terms of cellular automata."

Zemansky said, "There was nothing in their environment to make them think in terms of atoms."

"Well, no, but the ancient Greeks thought of atoms—but they didn't come up with quantum mechanics." Maria couldn't imagine a preindustrial human inventing the cellular automaton—even as a mathematical abstraction—let alone going on to hypothesize that the universe itself might *be* one. Clockwork cosmologies had come after physical clocks; computer cosmologies had come after physical computers.

Human history, though, clearly wasn't much of a guide to Lambertian science. They already had their Newtonian—"clockwork"—planetary model. They didn't need artifacts to point the way.

She said, "This 'aesthetic' which governs the acceptability of theories—have you been able to map the neural structures involved? Can you reproduce the criteria?"

Repetto said, "Yes. And I think I know what you're going to ask next."

"You've devised your own versions of possible Lambertian cellular automaton theories? And you've tested them against the Lambertian aesthetic?"

He inclined his head modestly. "Yes. We don't model whole brains, of course—that would be grossly unethical—but we can run simulations of trial dances with nonconscious Lambertian neural models."

Modeling Lambertians modeling the Autoverse . . .

"So how did it go?"

Repetto was hesitant. "The results so far are inconclusive. None of the theories I've constructed have worked—but it's a difficult business. It's hard to know whether or not I'm really stating the hypothesis in the way the Lambertians would—or whether I've really captured all the subtleties of the relevant behavior in a nonconscious model."

"But it doesn't look promising?"

"It's inconclusive."

Maria thought it over. "The Autoverse rules, alone, won't explain the abundances of the elements—which is the main problem the Lambertians are trying to solve. So what happens if they miss the whole idea of a cellular automaton, and come up with a completely different theory: something utterly misguided . . . which fits all the data nonetheless? I know, they've grasped everything else about their world far more smoothly than humans ever did, but that doesn't make them perfect. And if they have no tradition of giving up on difficult questions by invoking the hand of a creator, they might cobble together something which explains both the primordial cloud and the chemical properties of the elements—without coming anywhere near the truth. That's not impossible, is it?"

There was an awkward silence. Maria wondered if she'd committed some terrible *faux pas* by suggesting that the criteria for contact might never be met . . . but she could hardly be telling these people anything they hadn't already considered.

Then Durham said simply, "No, it's not impossible. So we'll just have to wait and see where the Lambertians' own logic take them."

27

(Rut City)

Peer felt the change begin, and switched off the lathe. He looked around the workshop helplessly, his eyes alighting on object after object which he couldn't imagine living without: the belt sander, the rack full of cutting tools for the lathe, cans of oil, tins of varnish. The pile of freshly cut timber itself. Abandoning these things—or worse, abandoning his love of them—seemed like the definition of extinction.

Then he began to perceive the situation differently. He felt himself step back from his life as a carpenter into the larger scheme of things—or non-scheme: the random stuttering from pretext to pretext which granted his existence its various meanings. His sense of loss became impossible to sustain; his enthusiasm for everything to which he'd been devoted for the past seventy-six years evaporated like a dream. He was not repelled, or bewildered, by the phase he was leaving behind—but he had no desire to extend or repeat it.

His tools, his clothes, the workshop itself, all melted away, leaving behind a featureless gray plain, stretching to infinity beneath a dazzling blue sky, sunless but radiant. He waited calmly to discover his new vocation—remembering the last transition, and thinking: *These brief moments between are a life in themselves.* He imagined picking up the same train of thought and advancing it, slightly, the next time.

Then the empty ground grew a vast room around him, stretching in all directions for hundreds of meters, full of row after row of yellow wooden specimen drawers. A high ceiling with dusty skylights came together above him, completing the scene. He blinked in the gloom. He was wearing heavy black trousers and a waistcoat over a stiff white shirt. His exoself, having chosen an obsession which would have been meaningless in a world of advanced computers, had dressed him for the part of a Victorian naturalist.

The drawers, he knew, were full of beetles. Hundreds of thousands of beetles. He was free, now, to do nothing with his time but study them, sketch them, annotate them, classify them: specimen by specimen, species by species, decade after decade. The prospect was so blissful that he almost keeled over with joy.

As he approached the nearest set of drawers—where a blank legal pad and pencil were already waiting for him—he hesitated, and tried to make sense of his feelings. He *knew* why he was happy here: his exoself had rewired his brain, yet again, as he'd programmed it to do. What more sense did he require?

He looked around the musty room, trying to pin down the source of his dissatisfaction. Everything was perfect, here and now—but his past was still with him: the gray plain of transition, his decades at the lathe, the times he'd spent with Kate, his previous obsessions. The long-dead David Hawthorne, invincible, clinging to a rock face. None of it bore the slightest connection to his present interests, his present surroundings—but the details still hovered at the edge of his thoughts: superfluous, anachronistic distractions.

He was dressed for a role—*so why not complete the illusion?* He'd tinkered with false memories before. Why not construct a virtual past which "explained" his situation, and his enthusiasm for the task ahead, in terms which befitted the environment? Why not create a person with no memory of Peer, who could truly lose himself in the delights of being unleashed on this priceless collection?

He opened a window to his exoself, and together they began to invent the biography of an entomologist.

———

Peer stared blankly at the flickering electric lamp in the corner of the room, then marched over to it and read the scrawled note on the table beneath.

TALK TO ME. SOMETHING IS WRONG.

He hesitated, then created a door beside the lamp. Kate stepped through. She was ashen.

She said, "I spend half my life trying to reach you. When is it going to stop?" Her tone was flat, as if she wanted to be angry, but didn't have the strength. Peer raised a hand to her cheek; she pushed it away.

He said, "What's the problem?"

"*The problem?* You've been missing for four weeks."

Four weeks? Peer almost laughed, but she looked so shaken that he stopped himself. He said, "You know I get caught up in what I'm doing. It's important to me. But I'm sorry if you were worried—"

She brushed his words aside. "*You were missing.* I didn't say: You didn't answer my call. The environment we're standing in—and its owner—did not exist."

"Why do you think that?"

"The communications software announced that there was no process accepting data addressed to your personal node. *The system lost you.*"

Peer was surprised. He hadn't trusted Malcolm Carter to start with, but after all this time it seemed unlikely that there were major problems with the infrastructure he'd woven into the City for them.

He said, "Lost track of me, maybe. For how long?"

"Twenty-nine days."

"Has this ever happened before?"

Kate laughed bitterly. "*No.* What—do you think I would have kept it to myself? I have *never* come across a basic software failure *of any kind,* until now. And there are automatic logs which confirm that. This is the first time."

Peer scratched his neck beneath the starched collar. The interruption had left him disoriented; he couldn't remember what he'd been doing when the flashing lamp had caught his attention. *His memory needed maintenance.* He said, "It's worrying—but I don't see what we can do, except run some diagnostics, try to pinpoint the problem."

"I ran diagnostics while the problem was happening."

"And—?"

"There was certainly nothing wrong with the communications software. But none of the systems involved with running *you* were visible to the diagnostics."

"That's impossible."

"Did you suspend yourself?"

"Of course not. And that wouldn't explain anything; even if I had, the systems responsible for me would still have been active."

"So what have you been doing?"

Peer looked around the room, back to where he'd been standing. There was a specimen drawer on one of the desks, and a thick legal pad beside it. He walked up to the desk. Kate followed.

He said, "Drawing beetles, apparently." Perhaps a hundred pages of the pad had been used and flipped over. An unfinished sketch of one of the specimens was showing. Peer was certain that he'd never seen it before.

Kate picked up the pad and stared at the drawing, then flipped back through the previous pages.

She said, "Why the pseudonym? Aren't the clothes affectation enough?"

"What pseudonym?"

She held the pad in front of him, and pointed to a signature. "Sir William Baxter, FRS."

Peer steadied himself against the desk, and struggled to fill the gap. He'd been playing some kind of memory game, that much was obvious—but surely he would have set things up so he'd understand what had happened, in the end? When Kate made contact, breaking the spell, his exoself should have granted him a full explanation. He mentally invoked its records; the last event shown was his most recent random transition. Whatever he'd done since, there was no trace of it.

He said dully, "The name means nothing to me."

Stranger still, the thought of spending twenty-nine days sketching beetles left him cold. Any passion he'd felt for *insect taxonomy* had vanished along with his memories—as if the whole package had belonged to someone else entirely, who'd now claimed it, and departed.

28

As the City slowly imprinted itself upon her brain—every dazzling sunset leaving its golden afterimage burning on her nonexistent retinas, every journey she made wiring maps of the nonexistent streets into her nonexistent synapses—Maria felt herself drifting apart from her memories of the old world. The details were as sharp as ever, but her history was losing its potency, its meaning. Having banished the idea of grieving for people who had not died—and who had not lost her—all she seemed to have left to feel was nostalgia . . . and even that was undermined by contradictions.

She missed rooms, streets, smells. Sometimes it was so painful it was comical. She lay awake thinking about the shabbiest abandoned buildings of Pyrmont, or the cardboard stench of ersatz popcorn wafting out of the VR parlors on George Street. And she knew that she could reconstruct her old house, all of its surroundings, all of Sydney, and more, in as much detail as she wished; she knew that every last idiot ache she felt for the amputated past could be *dealt with* in an instant. Understanding exactly how far she could go was more than enough to rid her of any desire to take a single step in that direction.

But having chosen to make no effort to relieve the pangs of homesickness, she seemed to have forfeited her right to the emotion. How could she claim to long for something which she could so easily possess—while continuing to deny it to herself?

So she tried to set the past aside. She studied the Lambertians diligently, preparing for the day when contact would be permitted. She tried to immerse herself in the role of the legendary eighteenth founder, roused from her millennia of sleep to share the triumphant moment when the people of Elysium would finally come face to face with an alien culture.

Lambertian communities—despite some similarities to those of terrestrial social insects—were far more complex, and much less hierarchical, than the nests of ants or the hives of bees. For a start, all Lambertians were equally fertile; there was no queen, no workers, no drones. The young were conceived in plants at the periphery of the local territory, and upon hatching usually migrated hundreds of kilometers to become members of distant communities. There, they joined teams and learned their speciality—be it herding, defense against predators, or modeling the formation of planetary systems. Specialization was usually for life, but team members occasionally changed professions if the need arose.

Lambertian group behavior had a long evolutionary history, and it remained the driving force in cultural development—because individual Lambertians were physically incapable of inventing, testing or communicating the models by which the most sophisticated ideas were expressed. An individual could learn enough about a model while taking part in a successful dance to enable it to exchange roles with any other individual the next time the dance was performed—but it could never ponder the implications of the idea itself, in solitude. The language of the dance was like human writing, formal logic, mathematical notation and computing, all rolled into one—but the basic skills were innate, not cultural. And it was so successful—and so much in tune with other aspects of their social behavior—that the Lambertians had never had reason to develop a self-contained alternative.

Individuals were far from unthinking components, though. They were fully conscious in their own right; groups performed many roles, but they did not comprise "communal minds." The language of sounds, movements and scents used by individuals was far simpler than the group language of the dance, but it could still express most of the concepts which preliterate humans had dealt with: intentions, past experience, the lives of others.

And individual Lambertians spoke of individual death. They knew that they would die.

Maria searched the literature for some clue to the way they dealt with their mortality. Corpses were left where they dropped; there was no ritual to mark the event, and no evidence of anything like grief. There were no clear Lambertian analogs for any of the human emotions—not even physical pain. When injured, they were acutely aware of the fact, and took steps to minimize damage to themselves—but it was a matter of specific instinctive responses coming into play, rather than the widespread biochemical shifts involved in human mood changes. The Lambertian nervous system was "tighter" than a human's; there was no flooding of regions of the brain with large doses of endogenous stimulants or depressants—everything was mediated within the enclosed synapses.

No grief. No pain. *No happiness?* Maria retreated from the question. The Lambertians possessed their own spectrum of thoughts and behavior; any attempt to render it in human terms would be as false as the colors of the Autoverse atoms themselves.

The more she learned, the more the role she'd played in bringing the Lambertians into existence seemed to recede into insignificance. Fine-tuning their single-celled ancestor had seemed like a matter of the utmost importance, at the time—if only for the sake of persuading the skeptics that Autoverse life could flourish. Now—although a few of her biochemical tricks had been conserved over three billions years of evolution—it was hard to attribute any real significance to the choices she'd made. Even though the whole Lambertian biosphere might have been transformed beyond recognition if she'd selected a different shape for a single enzyme in *A. hydrophila,* she couldn't think of the Lambertians as being dependent on her actions. The decisions she'd made controlled what she was witnessing on her terminal, nothing more; had she made other choices, *she* would have seen another biosphere, another civilization—but she could not believe that the Lambertians themselves would have failed to have lived the very same lives without her. Somehow, they still would have found a way to *assemble themselves from the dust.*

If that was true, though—if the internal logic of their experience would have been enough to bring them into existence—then there was no reason to believe that they would ever be forced to conclude that their universe required a creator.

She tried to reconcile this growing conviction with the Contact Group's optimism. They'd studied the Lambertians for thousands of years—who was she to doubt their expertise? Then it occurred to her that Durham and his colleagues might have decided to feign satisfaction with the political restrictions imposed upon them, until they knew where she stood on the issue. *Until she reached the same conclusions, independently?* Durham might have guessed that she'd resist being pressured into taking their side; it would be far more diplomatic to leave her to form her own opinions—even applying a little reverse psychology to aim her in the right direction.

Or was that sheer paranoia?

After five days of studying the Lambertians, tracing the history of their increasingly successful attempts to explain their world—and five nights trying to convince herself that they'd soon give it all up and recognize their status as artificial life—she could no longer hold the contradictions in her head.

She phoned Durham.

It was three in the morning, but he must have been out of the City; Standard Time set a rate, but no diurnal cycle, and behind him was a dazzling sunlit room.

She said bluntly, "I think I'd like to hear the truth now. *Why did you wake me?*"

He seemed unsurprised by the question, but he replied guardedly. "Why do you think?"

"You want my support for an early expedition to Planet Lambert. You want me to declare—with all the dubious authority of the 'mother' of the Lambertians—that there's no point waiting for them to invent the idea of us. Because we both know it's never going to happen. Not until they've seen us with their own eyes."

Durham said, "You're right about the Lambertians—but forget the politics. I woke you because your territory adjoins the region where the Autoverse is run. I want you to let me use it to break through to Planet Lambert." He looked like a child, solemnly confessing some childish crime. "Access through the hub is strictly controlled, and visible to everyone. There's plenty of unused space in the sixth public wedge, so I could try to get in from there—but again, it's potentially visible. Your territory is private."

Maria felt a surge of anger. She could scarcely believe that she'd ever swallowed the line about being woken *to share in the glory of contact*—and being used by Durham was no great shock; it was just like old times—but having been resurrected, not for her expertise, not for her status, but *so he could dig a tunnel through her backyard* . . .

She said bitterly, "Why do you need to break into the Autoverse? Is there a race going on that nobody's bothered to tell me about? Bored fucking *immortals* battling it out to make the first unauthorized contact with the Lambertians? Have you turned xenobiology into a new Olympian sport?"

"It's nothing like that."

"No? What, then? I'm dying to know." Maria tried to read his face, for what it was worth. He allowed himself to appear ashamed—but he also looked grimly determined, as if he really did believe that he'd had no choice.

It hit her suddenly. "You think . . . there's some kind of risk to Elysium, from the Autoverse?"

"Yes."

"I see. So you woke me in time to share the danger? How thoughtful."

"Maria, I'm sorry. If there'd been another way, I would have let you sleep forever—"

She started laughing and shivering at the same time. Durham placed one palm flat against the screen; she was still angry with him, but she let him reach through the terminal from his daylit room and put his hand on hers.

She said, "Why do you have to act in secret? Can't you persuade the others to agree to stop running the Autoverse? They must realize that it wouldn't harm the Lambertians; it would launch them as surely as it launched Elysium. There's no question of *genocide*. All right, it would be a loss to the Autoverse scholars—but how many of those can there be? What does Planet Lambert mean to the average Elysian? It's just one more kind of entertainment."

"I've already tried to shut it down. I'm authorized to set the running speed relative to Standard Time—and to freeze the whole Autoverse, temporarily, if I see the need to stem the information flow, to let us catch up with rapid developments."

"So what happened? They made you restart it?"

"No. I never managed to freeze it. *It can't be done any-more.* The clock rate can't be slowed past a certain point; the software ignores the instructions. Nothing happens."

Maria felt a deep chill spread out from the base of her spine. "Ignores them how? That's impossible."

"It would be impossible if everything was working—so, obviously, something's failed. The question is, *at what level?* I can't believe that the control software is suddenly revealing a hidden bug after all this time. If it's not responding the way it should, then *the processors running it* aren't behaving correctly. So either they've been damaged somehow . . . or the cellular automaton itself has changed. *I think the TVC rules are being undermined—or subsumed into something larger.*"

"Do you have any hard evidence?"

"No. I've rerun the old validation experiments, the ones I ran during the launch, and they still work—wherever I've tried them—but I can't even instruct the processors running the Autoverse to diagnose themselves, let alone probe what's happening there at the lowest level. I don't even know if the problem is confined to the region, or if it's spreading out slowly . . . or if it's already happening everywhere, but the effects are too subtle to pick up. You know the only way to validate the rules is with special apparatus. So what do I do? Disassemble half the processors in Elysium, and build test chambers in their place? And even if I could prove that the rules were being broken, how would that help?"

"Who else knows about this?"

"Only Repetto and Zemansky. If it became public knowledge, I don't know what would happen."

Maria was outraged. "What gives you the right to keep this to yourselves? Some people might panic . . . but what are you afraid of? *Riots? Looting?* The more people who know about the problem, the more likely it is that someone will come up with a solution."

"Perhaps. Or perhaps the mere fact that *more people know* would make things worse."

Maria absorbed that in silence. The sunlight spilling through the terminal cast radial shadows around her; the room looked like a medieval woodcut of an alchemist discovering the philosopher's stone.

Durham said, "Do you know why I chose the Autoverse in the first place—instead of real-world physics?"

"Less computation. Easier to seed with life. My brilliant work with *A. lamberti.*"

"No nuclear processes. No explanation for the origins of the elements. I thought: In the unlikely event that the planet yielded intelligent life, they'd still only be able to make sense of themselves on our terms. It all seemed so remote and improbable, then. It never occurred to me that they might miss the laws that we know are laws, and circumvent the whole problem."

"They haven't settled on any kind of theory, yet. They might still come up with a cellular automaton model—complete with the need for a creator."

"They might. But what if they don't?"

Maria's throat was dry. The numbing abstractions were losing their hypnotic power; she was beginning to feel all too real: too corporeal, too vulnerable. Good timing: finally embracing the illusion of possessing solid flesh and blood— just as the foundations of this universe seemed ready to turn to quicksand.

She said, "You tell me. I'm tired of guessing what's going on in your head."

"*We can't shut them down.* I think that proves that they're already affecting Elysium. If they successfully explain their origins in a way which contradicts the Autoverse rules, then that may distort *the TVC rules.* Perhaps only in the region where the Autoverse is run—or perhaps everywhere. And if the TVC rules are pulled out from under us—"

Maria baulked. "That's . . . like claiming that a VR environment could alter the real-world laws of physics in order to guarantee its own internal consistency. Even with thousands of Copies in VR environments, that never happened back on Earth."

"No—but which is most like *the real world:* Elysium, or the Autoverse?" Durham laughed, without bitterness. "We're all still patchwork Copies, most of us in private fantasy lands. Our bodies are *ad hoc* approximations. Our cities are indestructible wallpaper. The "laws of physics" of all the environments in Elysium contradict each other—and themselves—a billion times a day. Ultimately, yes, everything runs on the TVC processors, it's all consistent with the TVC rules—but level after level is sealed off, made invisible to the next, made irrelevant.

"On Planet Lambert, everything that happens is intimately tied to *one set of physical laws,* applied uniformly, everywhere. And they've had three billion years of that. We may not know what the deepest laws are, anymore, but every event the Lambertians experience is part of a coherent whole. If there's any conflict between the two versions of reality, we can't rely on our own version taking precedence."

Maria couldn't argue for patchwork VR holding up against the deep logic of the Autoverse. She said, "Then surely the safest thing would be to ensure that there *is no conflict.* Stop observing the Autoverse. Give up all plans of making contact. *Isolate* the two explanations. Keep them from clashing."

Durham said flatly, "No. We're already in conflict. Why else can't we shut them down?"

"I don't know." Maria looked away. "If the worst comes to the worst . . . can't we start again? Construct a new Garden-of-Eden configuration? Launch ourselves again, without the Autoverse?"

"If we have to." He added, "If we think we can trust the TVC universe to do everything it's programmed to do—without altering the launch process, fouling it up . . . or even passing on the modified laws which we think we're escaping."

Maria looked out at the City. Buildings were not collapsing, the illusion was not decaying. She said, "If we can't trust in that, what's left?"

Durham said grimly, "Nothing. If we don't know how this universe works anymore, we're powerless."

She pulled her hand free. "So what do you want to do? You think if you have access to more of the Autoverse than the data channels running out from the hub, you can make the TVC rules apply? One whole face of the pyramid shouting *stop* to the neighboring processors will carry more weight than the normal chain of command?"

"No. That might be worth trying. But I don't believe it will work."

"Then . . . what?"

Durham leaned forward urgently. "We have to win back the laws. We have to go into the Autoverse and convince the Lambertians to accept our explanation of their history— before they have a clear alternative.

"We have to persuade them that *we created them,* before that's no longer the truth."

29

Thomas sat in the garden, watching the robots tend the flowerbeds. Their silver limbs glinted in the sunshine as they reached between the dazzling white blossoms. Every movement they made was precise, economical; there was no faltering, no resting. They did what they had to, and moved on.

When they were gone, he sat and waited. The grass was soft, the sky was bright, the air was calm. He wasn't fooled. There'd been moments like this before: moments approaching tranquility. They meant nothing, heralded nothing, changed nothing. There'd always be another vision of decay, another nightmare of mutilation. And another return to Hamburg.

He scratched the smooth skin of his abdomen; the last number he'd cut had healed long ago. Since then, he'd stabbed his body in a thousand places; slit his wrists and throat, punctured his lungs, sliced open the femoral artery. Or so he believed; no evidence of the injuries remained.

The stillness of the garden began to unnerve him. There was a blankness to the scene he couldn't penetrate, as if he was staring at an incomprehensible diagram, or an abstract painting he couldn't quite parse. As he gazed across the lawn, the colors and textures flooding in on him suddenly dissociated completely into meaningless patches of light. Nothing had moved, nothing had changed—but his power to interpret the arrangement of shades and hues had vanished; the garden had ceased to exist.

Panicking, Thomas reached blindly for the scar on his forearm. When his fingers made contact, the effect was immediate: the world around him came together again. He sat, rigid for a moment, waiting to see what would happen next, but the stretch of dark green in the corner of his eye remained a shadow cast by a fountain, the blue expanse above remained the sky.

He curled up on the grass, stroking the dead skin, crooning to himself. He believed he'd once hacked the scar right off; the new wound he'd made had healed without a trace—but the original faint white line had reappeared in its proper place. It was the sole mark of his identity, now. His face, when he sought it in the mirrors inside the house, was unrecognizable. His name was a meaningless jumble of sounds. But whenever he began to lose his sense of himself, he only had to touch the scar to recall everything which defined him.

He closed his eyes.

He danced around the flat with Anna. She stank of alcohol, sweat and perfume. He was ready to ask her to marry him; he could feel the moment approaching, and he was almost suffocating with fear, and hope.

He said, "God, you're beautiful."

Order my life. I'm nothing without you: fragments of time, fragments of words, fragments of feelings. Make sense of me. Make me whole.

Anna said, "I'm going to ask you for something I've never asked for before. I've been trying to work up the courage all day."

"You can ask for anything."

Let me understand you. Let me piece you together, hold you together. Let me help you to explain yourself.

She said, "I have a friend, with a lot of cash. Almost two hundred thousand marks. He needs someone who can—"

Thomas stepped back from her, then struck her hard across the face. He felt betrayed; wounded and ridiculous. She started punching him in the chest and face; he stood there and let her do it for a while, then grabbed both her hands by the wrists.

She caught her breath. "Let go of me."

"I'm sorry."

"Then let go of me."

He didn't. He said, "I'm not a money-laundering facility for your *friends*."

She looked at him pityingly. "Oh, what have I done? Offended your high moral principles? All I did was ask. You might have made yourself useful. Never mind. I should have known it was too much to expect."

He pushed his face close to hers. "Where are you going to be, in ten years' time? In prison? At the bottom of the Elbe?"

"Fuck off."

"Where? Tell me?"

She said, "I can think of worse fates. I could end up playing happy families with a middle-aged banker."

Thomas threw her toward the wall. Her feet slipped from under her before she hit it; her head struck the bricks as she was going down.

He crouched beside her, disbelieving. There was a wide gash in the back of her head. She was breathing. He patted her cheeks, then tried to open her eyes; they'd rolled up into her skull. She'd ended up almost sitting on the floor, legs sprawled in front of her, head lolling against the wall. Blood pooled around her.

He said, "Think fast. Think fast."

Time slowed. Every detail in the room clamored for attention. The light from the one dull bulb in the ceiling was almost blinding; every edge of every shadow was razor sharp. Thomas shifted on the lawn, felt the grass brush against him. *It would take so little strength, so little courage, so little love.* It was not beyond imagining—

Anna's face burned his eyes, sweet and terrible. He had never been so afraid. He knew that if he failed to kill her, he was nothing; no other part of him remained. Only her death made sense of what he'd become, the shame and madness which were all he had left. To believe that he had saved her life would be to forget himself forever.

To die.

He forced himself to lie still on the grass; waves of numbness swept through his body.

Shaking, he phoned for an ambulance. His voice surprised

him; he sounded calm, in control. Then he knelt beside Anna and slid one hand behind her head. Warm blood trickled down his arm, under the sleeve of his shirt. *If she lived, he might not go to prison—but the scandal would still destroy him.* He cursed himself, and put his ear to her mouth. She hadn't stopped breathing. *His father would disinherit him.* He stared blankly into the future, and stroked Anna's cheek.

He heard the ambulance men on the stairs. The door was locked; he had to get up to let them in. He stood back helplessly as they examined her, then lifted her onto the stretcher. He followed them out through the front door. One of the men locked eyes with him coldly as they maneuvered the stretcher around the landing. "Pay extra to smack them around, do you?"

Thomas shook his head innocently. "It's not what it looks like."

Reluctantly, they let him ride in the back. Thomas heard the driver radio the police. He held Anna's hand and gazed down at her. Her fingers were icy, her face was white. The ambulance took a corner; he reached out with his free hand to steady himself. Without looking up, he asked, "Will she be all right?"

"Nobody will know that until she's been X-rayed."

"It was an accident. We were dancing. She slipped."

"Whatever you say."

They sped through the streets, weaving through a universe of neon and headlights, rendered silent by the wail of the siren. Thomas kept his eyes on Anna. He held her hand tightly, and with all of his being willed her to live, but he resisted the urge to pray.

30

The leaders of the Contact Group assembled in Maria's apartment. They'd barely taken their seats when Durham said, "I think we should move to my territory before we proceed any further. I'm on the far side of the hub from the Autoverse region—for what that's worth. If distance still means anything, we should at least try to run our models somewhere reliable."

Maria felt sick. The City itself was right beside the Autoverse: *the fairground on the edge of the desert.* But no Elysians were being computed in that public space; only buildings and puppet pedestrians. She said, "Six other founders have pyramids adjoining the Autoverse. If you think there's a chance that effects are spilling over the border . . . can't you find a pretext to get them to move their people as far away as possible? You don't have to spell things out—you don't have to tell them anything that might increase the danger."

Durham said wearily, "I've had enough trouble persuading thirty-seven dedicated Autoverse scholars to occupy themselves with projects which will keep them out of our way. If I started suggesting to Elaine Sanderson, Angelo Repetto and Tetsuo Tsukamoto that they *rearrange the geometry of their computing resources,* it would take them about ten seconds to put the entire Autoverse under scrutiny, to try to find out what's going on. And the other three pyramids are occupied by hermits who haven't shown themselves since the launch; we couldn't warn them even if we wanted to. The best thing we can do is deal with the problem as quickly—and inconspicuously—as possible."

Maria glanced at Dominic Repetto, but apparently he was resigned to the need to keep his family in the dark. She said, "It makes me feel like a coward. Fleeing to the opposite side of the universe, while we poke the hornet's nest by remote control."

Repetto said drily, "Don't worry; for all we know, the TVC geometry might be irrelevant. The logical connection between us and the Autoverse might put us at more risk than the closet physical neighbors."

Maria still chose to do everything manually, via her "solid" terminal; no interface windows floating in midair, no telepathic links to her exoself. Zemansky showed her how to run the obscure utility program which would transport her right out of her own territory. The less wealthy Copies back on Earth had darted from continent to continent in search of the cheapest QIPS—but in Elysium there would never have been a reason for anyone to shift this way, before. As she okayed the last query on the terminal, she pictured her model being halted, taken apart and piped through the hub into Durham's pyramid—no doubt with a billion careful verification steps along the way . . . but it was impossible to know what even the most stringent error-checking procedures were worth, now that the deepest rules upon which they relied had been called into question.

As a final touch, Durham cloned the apartment, and they moved—imperceptibly—to the duplicated version. Maria glanced out the window. "Did you copy the whole City as well?"

"No. That's the original you're looking at; I've patched in a genuine view."

Zemansky created a series of interface windows on the living-room wall; one showed the region running the Autoverse, with the triangular face which bordered Maria's own pyramid seen head-on. On top of the software map—the midnight-blue of the Autoverse cellular automation program, finely veined with silver spy software—she overlayed a schematic of the Lambertain planetary system, the orbits weirdly chopped up and rearranged to fit into the five adjacent pyramids. The space being modeled was—on its own terms—

a relatively thin disk, only a few hundred thousand kilometers thick, but stretching about fifty per cent beyond the orbit of the outermost planet. Most of it was empty—or filled with nothing but light streaming out from the sun—but there were no short-cuts taken; every cubic kilometer, however featureless, was being modeled right down to the level of Autoverse cells. The profligacy of it was breathtaking; Maria could barely look at the map without trying to think of techniques to approximate the computations going on in all the near-vacuum. When she forced herself to stop and accept the thing as it was, she realized that she'd never fully grasped the scale of Elysium before. She'd toured the Lambertain biosphere from the planetary level right down to the molecular—but that was nothing compared to a solar-system's-worth of subatomic calculations.

Durham touched her elbow. "I'm going to need your authorization." She went with him to the terminal he'd created for himself in a corner of the room, and typed out the code number which had been embedded in her scan file back on Earth; the ninety-nine digits flowed from her fingers effortlessly, as if she'd rehearsed the sequence a thousand times. The code which would have granted her access to her deceased estate, on Earth, here unlocked the processors of her pyramid.

She said, "I really am your accomplice, now. Who goes to prison when you commit a crime using my ID?"

"We don't have prisons."

"So what exactly will the other Elysians do to us, when they find out what we've done?"

"Express appropriate gratitude."

Zemansky zoomed in on the map to show the individual TVC processors along the border, and then enlarged the view still further to reveal their elaborate structure. It looked like a false-color schematic of an array of three-dimensional micro-circuits—but it was too rectilinear, too perfect, to be a micro-graph of any real object. The map was largely conjecture, now: a simulation guided by limited data flowing in from the grid itself. There were good reasons why it "should have been" correct, but there could be no watertight evidence that anything they were seeing was actually there.

Zemansky manipulated the view until they were peering straight down the middle of the thin layer of transparent "null" cells which separated the Autoverse region from Maria's territory—bringing her own processors into sight for the first time. An arrow in a small key diagram above showed the orientation; they were looking straight toward the distant hub. All the processors were structurally identical, but those in the Autoverse were alive with the coded streams of activated states marking data flows, while her own were almost idle. Then Durham plugged her territory into the software he was running, and a wave of data swept out from the hub—looking like something from the stargate sequence in *2001*—as the processors were reprogrammed. The real wave would have passed in a Standard Time picosecond; the map was smart enough to show the event in slow motion.

The reprogrammed processors flickered with data—and then began to sprout construction wires. Every processor in the TVC grid was a von Neumann machine as well as a Turing machine—a universal constructor as well as a universal computer. The only construction task they'd performed in the past had been a one-off act of self-replication, but they still retained the potential to build anything at all, given the appropriate blueprint.

The construction wires reached across the gap and touched the surface of the Autoverse processors. Maria held her breath, almost expecting to see a defensive reaction, a counterattack. Durham had analyzed the possibilities in advance: if the TVC rules continued to hold true, any "war" between these machines would soon reach a perpetual stalemate; they could face each other forever, annihilating each other's "weapons" as fast as they grew, and no strategy could ever break the deadlock.

If the TVC rules failed, though, there was no way of predicting the outcome.

There was no—detectable—counterattack. The construction wires withdrew, leaving behind data links bridging the gap between the pyramids. Since the map was showing the links as intact, the software must have received some evidence that they were actually working: the Autoverse processors were at least reacting as they should to simple tests of the integrity of the connections.

Durham said, "Well, that's something. They haven't managed to shut us out completely."

Repetto grimaced. "You make it sound like the Lambertians have taken control of the processors—that they're deciding what's going on here. They don't even know that this level exists."

Durham kept his eyes on the screen. "Of course they don't. But it still feels like we're sneaking up on some kind of . . . sentient adversary. The Lambertians' guardian angels: aware of all the levels—but jealously defending their own people's version of reality." He caught Maria's worried glance, and smiled. "Only joking."

Maria looked on as Durham and Zemansky ran a series of tests to verify that they really had plugged in to the Autoverse region. Everything checked out—but then, all the same tests had worked when run through the authorized link, down at the hub. The suspect processors were merely acting as messengers, passing data around in a giant loop which confirmed that they could still talk to each other—that the basic structure of the grid hadn't fallen apart.

Durham said, "Now we try to stop the clock." He hit a few keys, and Maria watched his commands racing across the links. She thought: *Maybe there was something wrong down at the hub. Maybe this whole crisis is going to turn out to be nothing but a tiny, localized bug. Perfectly explicable. Easily fixed.*

Durham said, "No luck. I'll try to reduce the rate."

Again, the commands were ignored.

Next, he increased the Autoverse clock rate by fifty percent—successfully—then slowed it down in small steps, until it was back at the original value.

Maria said numbly, "What kind of sense does that make? We can run it as fast as we like—within our capacity to give it computing resources—but if we try to slow it down, we hit a brick wall. That's just . . . perverse."

Zemansky said, "Think of it from the Autoverse point of view. Slowing down the Autoverse is speeding up Elysium; it's as if there's a limit to how fast *it* can run *us*—a limit to the computing resources it can spare for us."

Maria blanched. "What are you suggesting? That Elysium is now a computer program being run somewhere in the Autoverse?"

"No. But there's a symmetry to it. A principle of relativity. Elysium was envisioned as a fixed frame of reference, a touchstone of reality—against which the Autoverse could be declared a mere simulation. The truth has turned out to be more subtle: there are no fixed points, no immovable objects, no absolute laws." Zemansky betrayed no fear, smiling beatifically as she spoke, as if the ideas enchanted her. Maria longed to know whether she was merely concealing her emotions, or whether she had actually chosen a state of tranquility in the face of her world's dethronement.

Durham said flatly, "Symmetries were made to be broken. And we still have the edge: we still know far more about Elysium—and the Autoverse—than the Lambertians. There's no reason why our version of the truth can't make as much sense to them as it does to us. All we have to do is give them the proper context for their ideas."

Repetto had created a puppet team of Lambertians he called Mouthpiece: a swarm of tiny robots resembling Lambertians, capable of functioning in the Autoverse—although ultimately controlled by signals from outside. He'd also created human-shaped "telepresence robots" for the four of them. With Mouthpiece as translator, they could "reveal themselves" to the Lambertains and begin the difficult process of establishing contact.

What remained to be seen was whether or not the Autoverse would let them in.

Zemansky displayed the chosen entry point: a deserted stretch of grassland on one of Planet Lambert's equatorial islands. Repetto had been observing a team of scientists in a nearby community; the range of ideas they were exploring was wider than that of most other teams, and he believed there was a chance that they'd be receptive to Elysian theories.

Durham said, "Time to dip a toe in the water." On a second window, he duplicated the grassland scene, then zoomed in at a dizzying rate on a point in midair, until a haze of tumbling molecules appeared, and then individual Autoverse cells. The vacuum between molecules was shown as transparent, but faint lines delineated the lattice.

He said, "One *red* atom. One tiny miracle. Is that too much to ask for?"

Maria watched the commands stream across the TVC map: instructions to a single processor to rewrite the data which represented this microscopic portion of the Autoverse.

Nothing happened. The vacuum remained vacuum.

Durham swore softly. Maria turned to the window. The City was still standing; Elysium was not decaying like a discredited dream. But she felt herself break out in a sweat, felt her body drag her to the edge of panic. She had never really swallowed Durham's claim that there was a danger in sharing their knowledge with the other Elysians—but now she wanted to flee the room herself, hide her face from the evidence, lest she add to the weight of disbelief.

Durham tried again, but the Autoverse was holding fast to its laws. *Red* atoms could *not* spontaneously appear from nowhere—it would have violated the cellular automaton rules. And if those rules had once been nothing but a few lines of a computer program—a program which could always be halted and rewritten, interrupted and countermanded, subjugated by higher laws—that was no longer true. Zemansky was right: there was no rigid hierarchy of reality and simulation anymore. The chain of cause and effect was a loop now—or a knot of unknown topology.

Durham said evenly, "All right. Plan B." He turned to Maria. "Do you remember when we discussed closing off the Autoverse? Making it finite, but borderless . . . the surface of a four-dimensional doughnut?"

"Yes. But it was too small." She was puzzled by the change of subject, but she welcomed the distraction; talking about the old days calmed her down, slightly. "Sunlight would have circumnavigated the universe and poured back into the system, in a matter of hours; Planet Lambert would have ended up far too hot, for far too long. It tried all kinds of tricks to change the thermal equilibrium—but nothing plausible really worked. So I left in the border. Sunlight and the solar wind disappear across it, right out of the model. And all that comes in is—"

She stopped abruptly. She knew what he was going to try next.

Durham finished for her. "All that comes in is cold thermal radiation, and a small flux of atoms, like a random inflow of interstellar gas. A reasonable boundary condition—better than having the system magically embedded in a perfect vacuum. But there's no strict logic to it, no Autoverse-level model of exactly what's supposed to be out there. There could be anything at all."

He summoned up a view of the edge of the Autoverse; the atoms drifting in were so sparse that he had to send **Maxwell's Demon** looking for one. The software which faked the presence of a plausible intestellar medium created atoms in a thin layer of cells, "next to" the border. This layer was *not* subject to the Autoverse rules—or the atoms could not have been created—but its contents affected the neighboring Autoverse cells in the usual way, allowing the tiny hurricanes which the atoms were to drift across the border.

Durham sent a simple command to the atom-creation subprocess—an instruction designed to merge with the flow of random requests it was already receiving: inject a *red* atom at a certain point, with a certain velocity.

It worked. The atom conjured up in the boundary layer, and them moved into the Autoverse proper, precisely on cue.

Durham sent a sequence of a thousand similar commands. A thousand more atoms followed, all moving with identical vectors. The "random inflow" was no longer random.

Elysium was affecting the Autoverse; they'd broken through.

Repetto cheered. Zemansky smiled enigmatically. Maria felt sicker than ever. She'd been hoping that the Autoverse would prove to be unbreakable—and then, by symmetry, Elysium might have been equally immune to interference. The two worlds, mutually contradictory or not, might have continued on their separate ways.

She said, "How does this help us? Even if you can make this program inject the puppets into deep space, how would you get them safely down to Planet Lambert? And how could you control their behavior once they were there? We still can't reach in and manipulate them—that would violate the Autoverse rules."

Durham had thought it all through. "One, we put them in a spaceship and drop *that* in. Two, we make them radio-controlled—and beam a signal at them from the edge of the model. If we can persuade the cold thermal radiation software to send in a maser beam."

"You're going to sit here and try to design a spaceship which can function in the Autoverse?"

"I don't have to; it's already been done. One of the old plans for contact involved masquerading as 'aliens' from another part of the Autoverse, to limit the culture shock for the Lambertians. We would have told them that there were billions of other stars, hidden from view by dust clouds shrouding their system. The whole idea was immoral, of course, and it was scrapped thousands of years ago—long before there were sentient Lambertians—but the technical work was completed and filed away. It's all still there, in the Central Library; it should take us about an hour to assemble the components into a working expedition."

It sounded bizarre, but Maria could see no flaw in the plan, in principle. She said, "So . . . we're crossing space to meet the aliens, after all?"

"It looks that way."

Repetto echoed the phrase. "*Crossing space to meet the aliens.* You must have had some strange ideas, in the old days. Sometimes I almost wish I'd been there."

—

Maria gave in and learned how to use a mind's eye control panel to switch between her Elysian body and her Autoverse telepresence robot. She stretched the robot's arms and looked around the glistening flight deck of the *Ambassador.* She was lying in an acceleration couch, alongside the other three members of the crew. According to the flight plan, the robot was almost weightless now—but she'd chosen to filter out the effects of abnormal gravity, high or low. The robot knew how to move itself, in response to her wishes, under any conditions; inflicting herself with space sickness for the sake of "realism" would be absurd. She was not *in* the Autoverse, after all—she had not *become* this robot. Her entire model-of-a-human-body was still being run back in Elysium; the robot was connected to that model in a manner not much different from the nerve-induction link between a flesh-and-blood visitor to a VR environment, and his or her software puppet.

She flicked a mental switch and returned to the cloned apartment. Durham, Repetto and Zemansky sat in their armchairs, staring blankly ahead; little more than place markers, really. She went back to the *Ambassador,* but opened a small window in a corner of her visual field, showing the apartment through her Elysian eyes. If she was merely running a puppet in the Autoverse, she wanted to be clear about where her "true" body was supposed to be located. Knowing that there was an unobserved and insensate shop-window dummy occupying a chair on her behalf was not quite enough.

From the acceleration couch, she watched a—solid—display screen, high on the far wall of the flight deck, which showed their anticipated trajectory, swooping down on a shallow helical path toward Planet Lambert. They'd injected the ship through the border at the nearest possible point—one hundred and fifty thousand kilometers above the orbital plane—with a convenient preexisting velocity; it would take very little fuel to reach their destination, and descend.

She said, "Does anyone know if they ever bothered to rehearse a real landing in this thing?" Her vocal tract, wherever it was, felt perfectly normal as she spoke—but the timbre of her voice sounded odd through the robot's ears. The tricks being played on her model-of-a-brain to edit out the growing radio time lag between her intentions and the robot's actions didn't bear thinking about.

Durham said, "Everything was rehearsed. They recreated the whole prebiotic planetary system for the test flights. The only difference between then and now was that they could materialize the ship straight into the vacuum, wherever they liked—and control the puppet crew directly."

Violating Autoverse laws all over the place. It was unnerving to hear it spelled out: the lifeless Autoverse, in all its subatomic detail, had been a mere simulation; the presence of the Lambertians had made all the difference.

A second display screen showed the planet itself, an image from a camera outside the hull. The view was no different from that which the spy software had shown her a thousand times; although the camera and the robot's eyes were subject to pure Autoverse physics, once the image was piped into her non-Autoverse brain, the usual false-color conventions were employed. Maria watched the blue-and-white disk growing nearer, with a tightening in her chest. Free falling with the illusion of weight. Descending and staying still.

She said, "Why show ourselves to the Lambertians, immediately? Why not send Mouthpiece ahead to prepare the ground—to make sure that they're ready to face us? There are no animals down there larger than a wasp—and none at all with internal skeletons, walking on their hind legs. Humanoid robots one hundred and eighty centimeters tall will look like something out of their nightmares."

Repetto replied, "Novel stimuli aren't disabling for the Lambertians. They're not going to go into shock. But we'll certainly grab their attention."

Durham added, "We've come to reveal ourselves as the creators of their universe. There's not much point being shy about it."

They hit the upper layers of the atmosphere over the night side. Land and ocean alike were in almost perfect darkness: no moonlight, no starlight, no artificial illumination. The ship began to vibrate; instrument panels on the flight deck hummed, and the face of one display screen audibly *cracked.* Then radio contact was disrupted by the cone of ionized gas around the hull, and they had no choice but to return to the apartment, to sit out the worst of it. Maria stared at the golden towers of the City, weighing the power of their majestic, self-declared invulnerability against the unassailable logic of the buffeting she'd just witnessed.

They returned for the last seconds of the descent, after the parachutes had already been deployed. The impact itself seemed relatively smooth—or maybe that was just her gravity filter coddling her. They left their acceleration couches and waited for the hull to cool: cameras showed the grass around them blackened, but true to predictions the fire had died out almost at once.

Repetto unpacked Mouthpiece from a storage locker, opening the canister full of robot insects and tipping them into the air. Maria flinched as the swarm flew around aimlessly for several seconds, before assembling into a tight formation in one corner of the deck.

Durham opened the airlock doors, outer first, then inner. The robots didn't need *pneuma* of any kind, but the *Ambassador's* designers must have toyed with the possibility of mapping human biochemistry into the Autoverse—actually creating "aliens" who could meet the Lambertians as equals—instead of playing with elaborate masks.

They stepped out onto the scorched ground. It was early morning; Maria blinked at the sunlight, the clear white sky. the warmth on her robot skin came through loud and clear. The blue-green meadow stretched ahead as far as she could see; she walked away from the ship—a squat ceramic truncated cone, its white heat shield smoke-darkened in untidy streaks—and the highlands to the south came into view behind it. Lush vegetation crowded the slopes, but the peaks were bare, rust-red.

A chorus of faint chirps and hums filled the air. She glanced at Mouthpiece, but it was hovering, almost silently, near Repetto; these sounds were coming from every direction. She recognized some of the calls—she'd listened to a few of the nonsentient species, in a quick tour of the evolutionary history leading up to Lambertain communication—and there was nothing particularly exotic about any of them; she might have been hearing cicadas, bees, wasps, mosquitoes. When a faint breeze blew from the east, though, carrying something which the robot's olfactory apparatus mapped to the scent of salt water, Maria was suddenly so overwhelmed by the modest cluster of sensations that she thought her legs might give way beneath her. But it didn't happen; she made no deliberate attempt to swoon, so the robot just stood like a statue.

Durham approached her. "You've never been on Lambert before, have you?"

She frowned. "How could I?"

"Passively. Most Autoverse scholars have done it." Maria remembered Zemansky's offer of a VR representation, when she first met the Contact Group. Durham bent down and picked a handful of grass, then scattered the blades. "But we could never do *that* before."

"Hallelujah, the Gods have landed. What are you going to do if the Lambertians ask for a miracle? Pluck a few leaves as a demonstration of your omnipotence?"

He shrugged. "We can always show them the ship."

"They're not stupid. The ship proves nothing. Why should they believe that we're running the Autoverse, when we can't even break its laws?"

"Cosmology. The primordial cloud. The convenient amounts of each element." She couldn't help looking skeptical. He said, "Whose side are you on? *You* designed the primordial cloud! *You* sketched the original topography! You *made* the ancestor of the whole Lambertian biosphere! All I want to do is tell them that. It's the truth, and they have to face it."

Maria looked about, at a loss for words. It seemed clearer than ever that this world was not her creation; it existed on its own terms.

She said, "Isn't that like saying . . . that your flesh-and-blood original was nothing but a lunatic with some strange delusions? And that any other, better explanation he invented for his life had to be wrong?"

Durham was silent for a while. Then he said, "Elysium is at stake. What do you want us to do? Map ourselves into Autoverse biochemistry and come here to live?"

"I've seen worse places."

"The sun's going to freeze in another billion years. I promised these people immortality."

Repetto called out to them, "Are you ready? I've spotted the team; they're not far off. About three kilometers west." Maria was baffled for a moment, until she recalled that he still had access to all of the spy software. They were, still, outside the Autoverse looking in.

Durham yelled back, "Ten seconds." He turned to Maria. "Do you want to be part of this, or not? It has to be done the way I've planned it—and you can either go along with that, or go back."

She was about to reply angrily that he had no right to start making ultimatums, when she noticed the tiny window with its view of the apartment, hovering in the corner of her eye.

Elysium was at stake. Hundreds of thousands of people. The Lambertians would survive the shock of learning their "true" cosmology. Elysium might or might not survive the invention of an alternative.

She said, "You're right; it has to be done. So let's go spread the word."

The team was hovering in a loose formation over the meadow. Maria had had visions of being attacked, but the Lambertians didn't seem to notice their presence at all. They stopped about twenty meters from the swarm, while Mouthpiece went forward.

Repetto said, "This is the dance to signify that we have a message to convey."

Mouthpiece came to a halt in a tight vertical plane, and the individual robots began to weave around each other in interlocking figure eights. The Lambertians responded immediately, aligning themselves into a similar plane. Maria glanced at Repetto; he was beaming like a ten-year-old whose homemade shortwave radio had just started to emit promising crackling noises.

She whispered, "It looks like they're ignoring us completely . . . but do they think they're talking to real Lambertians—or have they noticed the differences?"

"I can't tell. But as a group, they're reacting normally, so far."

Zemansky said, "If a robot greeted you in your own language, wouldn't you reply?"

Repetto nodded. "And the instinct goes far deeper, with the Lambertians. I don't think they'd . . . discriminate. If they've noticed the differences, they'll want to understand them, eventually—but the first priority will still be to receive the message. And to judge it."

Mouthpiece began to drift into a more complex formation. Maria could make little sense of it—but she could see the Lambertains tentatively begin to mimic the change. This was it: Durham and Repetto's cosmological package deal. An explanation for the primordial cloud, and for the deep rules underlying Autoverse chemistry: a cellular automaton, created with the cloud in place, five billion years ago. The two billion years of planetary formation which strictly hadn't happened seemed like a forgivable white lie, for the moment; messy details like that could be mentioned later, if the basic idea was accepted.

Durham said, "Bad messages usually can't be conveyed very far. Maybe the fact that Mouthpiece clearly isn't a team for a nearby community will add credence to the theory."

Nobody replied. Zemansky smiled sunnily. Maria watched the dancing swarms, hypnotized. The Lambertians seemed to be imitating Mouthpiece almost perfectly, now—but that only proved that they'd "read" the message. It didn't yet mean that they believed it.

Maria turned away, and saw black dots against the sky. Persistence of vision was back in Elysium, in her model-of-a-brain. She remembered her dissatisfaction, clutching Autoverse molecules with her real-world hands and gloves. *Had she come any closer to knowing the Autoverse as it really was?*

Repetto said, "They're asking a question. They're asking

for . . . clarification." Maria turned back. The Lambertians had broken step with Mouthpiece, and the swarm had rearranged itself into something like an undulated black flying carpet. "They want 'the rest of the message'—the rest of the theory. They want a description of the universe *within which* the cellular automaton was created."

Durham nodded. He looked dazed, but happy. "Answer them. Give them the TVC rules."

Repetto was surprised. "Are you sure? That wasn't the plan—"

"What are we going to do? Tell them it's none of their business?"

"I'll translate the rules. Give me five seconds."

Mouthpiece began a new dance. The waving carpet dispersed, then began to fall into step.

Durham turned to Maria. "This is better than we'd dared to hope. *This way, they reinforce us.* They won't just stop challenging our version; they'll help to affirm it."

Zemansky said, "They haven't accepted it yet. All they've said is that the first part of what we've told them makes no sense alone. They might ask about real-world physics, next."

Durham closed his eyes, smiling. He said quietly, "Let them ask. We'll explain everything—right back to the Big Bang, if we have to."

Repetto said, puzzled, "I don't think it's holding."

Durham glanced at the swarm. "Give them a chance. They've barely tried it out."

"You're right. But they're already sending back a . . . rebuttal."

The swarm's new pattern was strong and simple: a sphere, rippling with waves like circles of latitude, running from pole to pole. Repetto said, "The software can't interpret their response. I'm going to ask it to reassess all the old data; there may be a few cases where this dance has been observed before—but too few to be treated as statistically significant."

Maria said, "Maybe we've made some kind of grammatical error. Screwed up the syntax, so they're laughing in our face—without bothering to think about the message itself."

Repetto said, "Not exactly." He frowned, like a man trying to visualize something tricky. Mouthpiece began to echo the spherical pattern. Maria felt a chill in her Elysian bowels.

Durham said sharply, "What are you doing?"

"Just being polite. Just acknowledging their message."

"Which is?"

"You may not want to hear it."

"I can find out for myself, if I have to." He took a step toward Repetto, more a gesture of impatience than a threat; a cloud of tiny blue gnat-like creatures flew up from the grass, chirping loudly.

Repetto glanced at Zemansky; something electric passed between them. Maria was confused—they were, unmistakably, lovers; she'd never noticed before. But perhaps the signals had passed through other channels, before, hidden from her. Only now—

Repetto said, "Their response is that the TVC rules are false—because the system those rules describe would endure forever. They're rejecting everything we've told them, because it leads to what they think is an absurdity."

Durham scowled. *"You're* talking absurdities. They've had transfinite mathematics for thousands of years."

"As a formality, a tool—an intermediate step in certain calculations. None of their models lead to infinite results. Most teams would never go so far as to try to communicate a model which did; that's why this response is one we've rarely seen before."

Durham was silent for a while, then he said firmly, "We need time to decide how to handle this. We'll go back, study the history of the infinite in Lambertian culture, find a way around the problem, then return."

Maria was distracted by something bright pulsing at the edge of her vision. She turned her head—but whatever it was seemed to fly around her as fast as she tracked it. Then she realized it was the window on Elysium; she'd all but banished it from her attention, filling it in like a blind spot. She tried to focus on it, but had difficulty making sense of the image. She centered and enlarged it.

The golden towers of Permutation City were flowing past the apartment window. She cried out in astonishment, and put her hands up, trying to gesture to the others. The buildings weren't simply moving away; they were *softening, melting, deforming*. She fell to her knees, torn between a desire to return to her true body, to protect it—and dread at what might happen if she did. She dug one hand into the Lambertian soil; it felt real, solid, trustworthy.

Durham grabbed her shoulder. "We're going back. Stay calm. It's only a view—we're not *part of the City*."

She nodded and steeled herself, fighting every visceral instinct about the source of the danger, and the direction in which she should flee. The cloned apartment looked as solid as ever . . . and in any case, its demise could not, in itself, harm her. The body she had to defend was invisible: the model running at the far end of Durham's territory. She would be no safer pretending to be on Planet Lambert than she would pretending to be in the cloned apartment.

She returned.

The four of them stood by the window, speechless, as the City rapidly and silently . . . imploded. Buildings rushed by, abandoning their edges and details, converging on a central point. The outskirts followed, the fields and parks flowing in toward the golden sphere which was all that remained of the thousand towers. Rainforest passed in a viridian blur. Then the scene turned to blackness as the foothills crowded in, burying their viewpoint in a wall of rock.

Maria turned to Durham. "The people who were in there . . .?"

"They'll all have left. Shocked but unharmed. Nobody was *in there*—in the software—any more than we were." He was shaken, but he seemed convinced.

"And what about the founders with adjoining territory?"

"I'll warn them. Everyone can come here, everyone can shift. We'll all be safe, here. The TVC grid is constantly growing; we can keep moving away, while we plan the next step."

Zemansky said firmly, "The TVC grid is *decaying*. The only way to be safe is to start again. Pack everything into a new Garden-of-Eden configuration, and launch Elysium again."

Repetto said, "If that's possible. If the infinite is still possible." Born into a universe without limits, without death, he seemed transfixed by the Lambertians' verdict.

A red glow appeared in the distance; it looked like a giant sphere of luminous rubble. As Maria watched, it brightened, then broke apart into a pattern of lights, linked by fine silver threads. A neon labyrinth. A fairground at night, from the air. The colors were wrong, but the shape was unmistakable: it was a software map of the City. The only thing missing was the highway, the data link to the hub.

Before Maria could say a word, the pattern continued to rearrange itself. Dazzling pinpricks of light appeared within a seemingly random subset of the processes, then moved together, clustering into a tightly linked core. Around them, a dimmer shell formed by the remaining software settled into a symmetrical configuration. The system looked closed, self-contained.

They watched it recede, in silence.

31

Peer turned and looked behind him. Kate had stopped dead in the middle of the walkway. All the energy seemed to drain out of her; she put her face in her hands, then sank to her knees.

She said flatly, "They've gone, haven't they? They must have discovered us . . . and now this is their punishment. They've left the City running . . . but they've deserted it."

"We don't know that."

She shook her head impatiently. "They will have made another version—purged of *contamination*—for their own use. And we'll never see them again." A trio of smartly dressed puppets approached, and walked straight through her, smiling and talking among themselves.

Peer walked over to her and sat cross-legged on the floor beside her. He'd already sent software probes hunting for any trace of the Elysians, without success—but Kate had insisted on scouring a reconstruction of the City, on foot, as if their own eyes might magically reveal some sign of habitation that the software had missed.

He said gently, "There are a thousand other explanations. Someone might have . . . I don't know . . . created a new environment so astonishing that they've all gone off to explore it. Fashions sweep Elysium like plagues—but this is their meeting place, their center of government, *their one piece of solid ground*. They'll be back."

Kate uncovered her face and gave him a pitying look. "What kind of *fashion* would tempt every Elysian out of the City, in a matter of *seconds*? And where did they hear about this great work of art which they had to rush off and experience? I monitor all the public networks; there was nothing special leading up to the exodus. But if they'd discovered *us*—if they knew we were listening in—then they wouldn't have used the public channels to announce the fact, would they?"

Peer couldn't see why not; if the Elysians had found them, they'd also know that he and Kate were powerless to influence the City—let alone its inhabitants—in any way. There was no reason to arrange a secret evacuation. He found it hard enough to believe that anyone would want to punish two harmless stowaways—but it was harder still to accept that they'd been "exiled" without being dragged through an elaborate ritual of justice—or at the very least, publicly lambasted for their crime, before being formally sentenced. The Elysians never missed the opportunity for a bit of theater; swift, silent retribution just didn't ring true.

He said, "If the data link to the hub was broken, unintentionally—"

Kate was scornful. "It would have been fixed by now."

"Perhaps. That depends on the nature of the problem." He hesitated. "Those four weeks I was missing . . . we still don't know if I was cut off from you by a fault in the software at our level—or whether the problem was somewhere deeper. If there are faults appearing in the City itself, one of them might have severed the links to the rest of Elysium. And it might take some time for the problem to be pinned down; anything that's taken seven thousand years to reveal itself could turn out to be elusive."

Kate was silent for a while, then she said, "There's an easy way to find out if you're right. Increase our slowdown—keep increasing it—and see what happens. Program our exoselves to break in and switch us back to the normal rate if there's any sign of the Elysians . . . but if that doesn't happen, keep ploughing ahead into the future, until we're both convinced that we've waited long enough."

Peer was surprised; he liked the idea—but he'd imagined that Kate would have preferred to prolong the uncertainty. He wasn't sure if it was a good sign or not. Did it mean she wanted to make a clean break from the Elysians? To banish any lingering hope of their return, as rapidly as possible? Or was it proof of just how desperately she wanted them back?

He said, "Are you sure you want to do that?"

"I'm sure. Will you help me program it? You're the expert at this kind of thing."

"Here and now?"

"Why not? The whole point is to save ourselves from waiting."

Peer created a control panel in the air in front of them, and together they set up the simple time machine.

Kate hit the button.

Slowdown one hundred. The puppets using the walkway accelerated into invisible streaks. *Slowdown ten thousand.* Night and day chugged by, then flashed, then flickered—*slowdown one million*—then merged. Peer glanced up to watch the arc of the sun's path slide up and down the sky with the City's mock seasons, ever faster, until it smeared into a dull glowing band. *Slowdown one billion.* The view was perfectly static, now. There were no long-term fake astronomical cycles programmed into the virtual sky. No buildings rose, or crumbled. The empty, invulnerable City had nothing to do but repeat itself: to exist, and exist, and exist. *Slowdown one trillion.*

Peer turned to Kate. She sat in an attentive pose, head up, eyes averted, as if she was listening for something. The voice of an Elysian hyperintelligence, the endpoint of a billion years of self-directed mutation, reaching out to encompass the whole TVC grid? Discovering their fate? Judging them, forgiving them, and setting them free?

Peer said, "I think you've won the bet. They're not coming back." He glanced at the control panel, and felt a stab of vertigo; more than a hundred trillion years of Standard Time had elapsed. But if the Elysians had cut all ties with them, Standard Time was meaningless. Peer reached out to halt their acceleration, but Kate grabbed him by the wrist.

She said quietly, "Why bother? Let it climb forever. It's only a number, now."

"Yes." He leaned over and kissed her on the forehead.

"One instruction per century. One instruction per millennium. And it makes no difference. You've finally got your way."

He cradled Kate in his arms, while Elysian aeons slipped away. He stroked her hair, and watched the control panel carefully. Only one number was rising; everything but the strange fiction of Elapsed Standard Time stayed exactly the same.

No longer tied to the growth of the Elysians, the City remained unchanged, at every level. And that meant, in turn, that the infrastructure which Carter had woven into the software for them had also ceased to expand. The simulated "computer" which ran them, composed of the City's scattered redundancies, was now a finite "machine," with a finite number of possible states.

They were mortal again.

It was a strange feeling. Peer looked around the empty walkway, looked down at the woman in his arms, feeling like he'd woken from a long dream—but when he searched himself for some hint of a waking life to frame it, there was nothing. David Hawthorne was a dead stranger. The Copy who'd toured the Slow Clubs with Kate was as distant as the carpenter, the mathematician, the librettist.

Who am I?

Without disturbing Kate, he created a private screen covered with hundreds of identical anatomical drawings of the brain; his menu of mental parameters. He hit the icon named CLARITY.

He'd generated a thousand arbitrary reasons to live. He'd pushed his philosophy almost as far as it would go. But there was one last step to take.

He said, "We'll leave this place. Launch a universe of our own. It's what we should have done long ago."

Kate made a sound of distress. "How will I live, without the Elysians? I can't survive the way you do: rewiring myself, imposing happiness. I can't do it."

"You won't have to."

"It's been seven thousand years. I want to live among people again."

"Then you'll live among people."

She looked at him hopefully. "We'll create them? Run the

ontogenesis software? Adam-and-Eve a new world of our own?"

Peer said, "No. I'll become them. A thousand, a million. Whatever you want. I'll become the Solipsist Nation."

Kate pulled away from him. "*Become?* What does that mean? You don't have to *become* a nation. You can build it with me—then sit back and watch it grow."

Peer shook his head. "What have I become, already? An endless series of people—all happy for their own private reasons. Linked together by the faintest thread of memory. Why keep them spread out in time? Why go on pretending that there's one 'real' person, enduring through all those arbitrary changes?"

"You remember yourself. You believe you're one person. Why call it a pretence? It's the truth."

"But I don't believe it, anymore. Each person I create is stamped with the illusion of still being this imaginary thing called 'me'—but that's no real part of their identity. It's a distraction, a source of confusion. There's no reason to keep on doing it—or to make these separate people follow each other in time. Let them all live together, meet each other, keep you company."

Kate gripped him by the shoulders and looked him in the eye. "You can't *become* the Solipsist Nation. That's nonsense. It's rhetoric from an old play. All it would mean is . . . dying. The people the software creates when you're gone won't be *you* in any way."

"They'll be happy, won't they? From time to time? For their own strange reasons?"

"Yes. But—"

"That's all I am, now. That's all that defines me. So when they're happy, they'll be me."

32

"Seventeen down, one to go."

Durham had rendered himself calm and efficient, to deal with the evacuation. Maria, still unmodified, watched—sick with relief—as he finally packed Irene Shaw, her seven hundred million offspring, and their four planets' worth of environments, into the bulging Garden-of-Eden-in-progress. A compressed snapshot of the entire civilization flowed down the data paths Durham had created to bypass the suspect hub—following a dozen independent routes, verified and reverified at every step—until it crossed the barrier into the region where the new Elysium was being forged.

So far, there'd been no sign that the corruption of the grid was spreading further—but the last Town Meeting had given Durham just six hours of Standard Time to assemble and launch the new seed. Maria was astonished that they'd appointed him to do the job at all, given that it was his clandestine visit to Planet Lambert which had catalyzed the whole disaster (and they'd left—nonconscious—watchdog software running, to monitor his actions, and take over the task if he failed) . . . but he was still the man who'd built and launched Elysium, and apparently they trusted him above anyone else to rescue them from their disintegrating universe, just as he'd rescued the founders from their legendary deteriorating Earth.

Two of the three "hermits" among the founders—Irene Shaw and Pedro Callas—had responded to the emergency signals sent into their pyramids from the hub. Despite their millennia of silence, they hadn't sealed their worlds off completely from information from the rest of Elysium.

Thomas Riemann, apparently, had.

Maria checked the clock on the interface window; they had fourteen minutes left.

Durham had set a program running, hours before, to try to break into Riemann's pyramid. He'd succeeded in forging new links with the processors, but without Riemann's personal code, any instructions piped in would be ignored—and a time-lock triggered by each incorrect attempt made scanning through all ninety-nine-digit combinations impractical. So Durham had instructed a metaprogrammer to build a TVC "machine" to isolate and dissect one of Riemann's processors, to scrutinize the contents of its memory, and to deduce the code from the heavily encrypted tests within.

As the program zeroed in on the final result, Maria said sharply, "You could have done that for my pyramid, couldn't you? And let me sleep?"

Durham shook his head, without looking at her. "Done it from where? I had no access to the border. *This* is only possible because the other founders have granted me *carte blanche*."

"I think you could have burrowed through somehow, if you'd set your mind to it."

He was silent for a while, then he conceded, "Perhaps I could have. I did want you to see Planet Lambert. I honestly believed that I had no right to let you sleep through contact."

She hunted for a suitably bitter reply—then gave up and said wearily, "You had no right to wake me—but I'm glad I saw the Lambertians."

The code-breaking program said, "In."

There was no time left for decorum, for explaining the crisis and justifying the evacuation. Durham issued a sequence of commands, to freeze all the software running in the pyramid, analyze it, extract all the essential data, and bundle it into the new Garden-of-Eden. Riemann and his children need never know the difference.

The software had other ideas. It acknowledged the access code, but refused to halt.

Maria turned aside and retched drily. *How many people*

were in there? Thousands? Millions? There was no way of knowing. What would happen if the changes in the grid engulfed them? Would the worlds they inhabited implode and vanish, like the inanimate City?

When she could bring herself to look again, Durham had calmly changed tack. He said, "I'm trying to break the lock on communication. See if I can get in on any level, and at least talk to someone. Maybe from the inside they'll have more control; we can't halt their software and download it *en masse*, but maybe they can do that themselves."

"You have eleven minutes."

"I know." He hesitated. "If I have to, I can stick around and launch these people separately. I don't imagine they care whether or not they're in the same universe as the rest of the Elysians."

"*Stick around?* You mean clone yourself, and launch one version with the rest of us—?"

"No. Zemansky's organized a hundred people to verify the launch from within. I don't have to be there."

Maria was horrified. "But—why leave yourself out? Why risk it?"

He turned to her and said placidly, "I'm not splitting myself, not again. I had enough of that on twenty-four Earths. I want one life, one history. One explanation. Even if it has to come to an end."

The program he'd been running beeped triumphantly and flashed up a message. "There's a data port for granting physical interaction with one environment, and it seems to be intact."

Maria said, "Send in a few thousand robots, sweep the place for signs of life."

Durham was already trying it. He frowned. "No luck. But I wonder if . . ."

He created a doorway a few meters to his right; it seemed to lead into a lavishly decorated corridor.

Maria said queasily, "You have seven minutes. The port's not working: if a robot can't materialize . . ."

Durham stood and walked through the doorway, then broke

into a run. Maria stared after him. *But there was no special danger "in there"—no extra risk. The software running their models was equally safe, wherever they pretended their bodies to be.*

She caught up with Durham just as he reached an ornate curved staircase; they were upstairs in what seemed to be a large two-story house. He clapped her on the shoulder. "Thank you. Try downstairs, I'll keep going up here."

Maria wished she'd disabled all her human metabolic constraints—but she was too agitated now to try to work out how to make the changes, too awash with adrenaline to do anything but run down corridors bellowing, "Is there anyone home?"

At the end of one passage, she burst through a door and found herself out in the garden.

She looked about in despair. The grounds were enormous—and apparently deserted. She stood catching her breath, listening for signs of life. She could hear birdsong in the distance, nothing else.

Then she spotted a white shape in the grass, near a flowerbed full of tulips.

She yelled, "Down here!" and hurried toward it.

It was a young man, stark naked, stretched out on the lawn with his head cradled in his hands. She heard breaking glass behind her, and then a heavy thud on the ground; she turned to see Durham pick himself up and limp toward her.

She knelt by the stranger and tried to wake him, slapping his cheeks. Durham arrived, ashen, clearly shorn of his artificial tranquility. He said, "I think I've sprained an ankle. I could have broken my neck. Don't take any risks—something strange is going on with our physiology; I can't override the old-world defaults."

Maria seized the man by the shoulders and shook him hard, to no effect. "This is hopeless!"

Durham pulled her away. "I'll wake him. You go back."

Maria tried to summon up a mind's-eye control panel to spirit her away. Nothing happened. "I can't connect with my exoself. I can't get through."

"Use the doorway, then. *Run!*"

She hesitated—but she had no intention of following Durham into martyrdom. She turned and sprinted back into the house. She took the stairs two at a time, trying to keep her mind blank, then raced down the corridor. The doorway into the evacuation control room was still there—or at least, still visible. As she ran toward it, she could see herself colliding with an invisible barrier—but when she reached the frame, she passed straight through.

The clock on the interface window showed twenty seconds to launch.

When she'd insisted on hanging around, Durham had made her set up a program which would pack her into the new Garden-of-Eden in an instant; the icon for it—a three-dimensional Alice stepping into a flat storybook illustration—was clearly on display in a corner of the window.

She reached for it, then glanced toward the doorway into Riemann's world.

The corridor was moving, slowly retreating. Slipping away, like the buildings of the City.

She cried out, "Durham! You idiot! It's going to implode!" Her hand shook; her fingers brushed the Alice icon, lightly, without the force needed to signal consent.

Five seconds to launch.

She could clone herself. Send one version off with the rest of Elysium, send one version in to warn him.

But she didn't know how. There wasn't time to learn how.

Two seconds. One.

She bunched her fist beside the icon, and wailed. The map of the giant cube flickered blue-white: the new lattice had begun to grow, the outermost processors were reproducing. It was still part of Elysium—a new grid being simulated by the processors of the old one—but she knew the watchdog software wouldn't give her a second chance. It wouldn't let her halt the launch and start again.

She looked back through the doorway. The corridor was still sliding smoothly away, a few centimeters a second. *How much further could it go, before the doorway hit a wall, stranding Durham completely?*

Swearing, she stepped toward it, and reached through with one hand. The invisible boundary between the environments still let her pass. She crouched at the edge, and reached down to touch the floor; her palm made contact with the carpet as it slipped past.

Shaking with fear, she stood up and crossed the threshold. She stopped to look behind the doorway; the corridor came to a dead end, twelve or fifteen meters away in the direction the doorway was headed. She had four or five minutes, at most.

Durham was still in the garden, still trying to rouse the man. He looked up at her angrily. "What are you doing here?"

She caught her breath. "I missed the launch. And this whole thing's . . . separating. Like the City. You have to get out."

Durham turned back to the stranger. "He looks like a rejuvenated Thomas Riemann, but he could be a descendant. One of hundreds. One of millions, for all we know."

"Millions, where? It looks like he's alone here—and there's no sign of other environments. You only discovered one communications port, didn't you?"

"We don't know what that means. The only way to be sure he's alone is to wake him and ask him. *And I can't wake him.*"

"What if we just . . . carried him out of here? *I know:* there's no reason why doing that should move his model to safer territory—but if *our* models have been affected by this place, forced to obey human physiology . . . then all the logic behind that has already been undermined."

"What if there are others? I can't abandon them!"

"*There's no time!* What can you do for them, trapped in here? If this world is destroyed, nothing. If it survives somehow . . . it will still survive without you."

Durham looked sickened, but he nodded reluctantly.

She said, "Get moving. You're crippled—I'll carry Sleeping Beauty."

She bent down and tried to lift Riemann—Thomas or otherwise—onto her shoulders. It looked easy when firefighters did it. Durham, who'd stopped to watch, came back and helped her. Once she was standing, walking wasn't too hard. For the first few meters.

Durham hobbled alongside her. At first, she abused him, trying insincerely to persuade him to go ahead. Then she gave up and surrendered to the absurdity of their plight. Flushed and breathless, she said, "I never thought I'd witness . . . the disintegration of a universe . . . while carrying a naked merchant banker . . ." She hesitated. "Do you think if we close our eyes and say . . . we don't believe in stairs, then maybe . . ."

She went up them almost crouching under the weight, desperate to put down her burden and rest for a while, certain that if she did they'd never make it.

When they reached the corridor, the doorway was still visible, still moving steadily away. Maria said, "Run ahead and . . . keep it open."

"How?"

"I don't know. Go and stand in the middle . . ."

Durham looked dubious, but he limped forward and reached the doorway well ahead of her. He stepped right through, then turned and stood with one foot on either side, reaching out a hand to her, ready to drag her onto the departing train. She had a vision of him, bisected, one half flopping bloodily into each world.

She said, "I hope this . . . bastard was a great . . . philanthropist. He'd better . . . have been a fucking . . . saint."

She looked to the side of the doorway. The corridor's dead end was only centimeters away. Durham must have read the expression on her face; he retreated into the control room. The doorway touched the wall, then vanished. Maria bellowed with frustration, and dropped Riemann onto the carpet.

She ran to the wall and pounded on it, then sank to her knees. *She was going to die here, inside a stranger's imploding fantasy.* She pressed her face against the cool paintwork. *There was another Maria, back in the old world—and whatever else happened, at least she'd saved Francesca. If this insane dream ended, it ended.*

Someone put a hand on her shoulder. She twisted around in shock, pulling a muscle in her neck. It was Durham.

"This way. We have to go around. *Hurry.*"

He picked up Riemann—he must have repaired his ankle in

Elysium, and no doubt strengthened himself as well—and led Maria a short way back down the corridor, through a vast library, and into a storage room at the end. The doorway was there, a few meters from the far wall. Durham tried to walk through, holding Riemann head first.

Riemann's head disappeared as it crossed the plane of the doorway. Durham cried out in shock and stepped back; the decapitation was reversed. Maria caught up with them as Durham turned around and tried backing through the doorway, dragging Riemann after him. Again, the portion of Riemann's body which passed through seemed to vanish—and as his armpits, where Durham was supporting him, disappeared, the rest of him crashed to the floor. Maria ducked behind the doorway—and saw Riemann, whole, lying across the threshold.

They couldn't save him. This world had let them come and go—on its own terms—but to Riemann himself, the exit they'd created was nothing, an empty frame of wood.

She went back and stepped over him, into Elysium. As the doorway retreated, Riemann's shoulders came into view again. Durham, sobbing with frustration, reached through and dragged the sleeping man along for a meter—and then his invisible head must have struck the invisible wall, and he could be moved no further.

Durham withdrew into Elysium, just as the doorway became opaque. A second later, they saw the outside wall of the house. The implosion—or separation—accelerated as the doorway flew through the air above the grounds; and then the whole scene was encircled by darkness, like a model in a glass paperweight, floating off into deep space.

Maria watched the bubble of light recede, the shapes within melting and re-forming into something new, too far away to decipher. *Was Riemann dead, now? Or just beyond their reach?*

She said, "I don't understand—but whatever the Lambertians are doing to us, it's not just random corruption . . . it's not just destroying the TVC rules. That world was *holding together*. As if its own logic had taken precedence over Elysium's. As if it no longer needed us."

Durham said flatly, "I don't believe that." He crouched beside the doorway, weighed down by defeat.

Maria touched his shoulder. He shrugged free. He said, "You'd better hurry up and launch yourself. The other Elysians will have been removed from the seed, but everything else—all the infrastructure—should still be there. Use it."

"Alone?"

"Make children, if you want to. It's easy; the utility programs are all in the central library."

"And—what? You'll do the same?"

"No." He looked up at her and said grimly, "I've had enough. *Twenty-five lives.* I thought I'd finally discovered solid ground—but now it's all crumbling into illusions and contradictions. I'll kill myself before the whole thing falls apart: die on my own terms, leaving nothing to be explained in another permutation."

Maria didn't know how to respond. She walked over to the interface window, to take stock of whatever was still functioning. After a while, she said, "The Autoverse spy software has stopped working—and the entire hub has gone dead—but there's some last-minute summary data in the copy of the central library you made for the seed." She hunted through Repetto's analysis and translation systems.

Durham came and stood beside her; he pointed out a highlighted icon, a stylized image of a swarm of Lambertians.

He said, "Activate that."

They read the analysis together. A team of Lambertians had found a set of field equations—nothing to do with the Autoverse cellular automaton—with thirty-two stable solutions. One for each of their atoms. And at high enough temperatures, the same equations predicted the spontaneous generation of matter—in exactly the right proportions to explain the primordial cloud.

The dance had been judged successful. The theory was gaining ground.

Maria was torn between resentment and pride. "Very clever—but how will they ever *explain* four humanoid robots abandoned in a meadow?"

Durham seemed bleakly amused. "They arrived in a spaceship, didn't they? Aliens must have sent them, as emissaries. There must be other stars out there—concealed behind a suitable dust cloud."

"Why should aliens try to tell the Lambertians about the TVC cellular automaton?"

"Maybe they believed in it. Maybe they discovered the Autoverse rules . . . but since they still couldn't explain the origin of the elements, they decided to embed the whole thing in a larger system—another cellular automaton—complete with immortal beings to create the Autoverse, primordial cloud and all. But the Lambertians will put them straight: there's no need for such a convoluted hypothesis."

"And now the Autoverse is sloughing us off like dead skin." Maria gazed at the Lambertian field equations; they were far more complex than the Autoverse rules, but they had a strange elegance all their own. She could never have invented them herself; she was sure of that.

She said, "It's not just a matter of the Lambertians out-explaining us. *The whole idea of a creator* tears itself apart. A universe with conscious beings either finds itself in the dust . . . or it doesn't. It either makes sense of itself on its own terms, as a self-contained whole . . . or not at all. There never can, and never will be, *Gods*."

She displayed a map of Elysium. The dark stain marking processors which had ceased responding had spread out from the six public pyramids and swallowed most of the territories of Riemann, Callas, Shaw, Sanderson, Repetto and Tsukamoto. She zoomed in on the edge of the darkness; it was still growing.

She turned to Durham and pleaded, "Come with me!"

"No. What is there left for me to do? Descend into paranoia again? Wake up wondering if I'm really nothing but a discredited myth of Planet Lambert's humanoid alien visitors?"

Maria said angrily, "You can keep me company. Keep *me* sane. After all you've done to me, you owe me that much."

Durham was unmoved. "You don't need me for that. You'll find better ways."

She turned back to the map, her mind going blank with panic for a moment—then she gestured at the growing void. "The TVC rules are dissolving, the Lambertians are destroying Elysium—*but what's controlling that process?* There must be deeper rules, governing the clash of theories: deciding which explanations hold fast, and which dissolve. *We can hunt for those rules.* We can try to make sense of what went on here."

Durham said sardonically, "Onward and upward? In search of higher order?"

Maria was close to despair. He was her one link to the old world; without him, her memories would lose all meaning.

"*Please!* We can argue this out in the new Elysium. *But there's no time now.*"

He shook his head sadly. "Maria, I'm sorry—but I can't follow you. I'm seven thousand years old. Everything I've struggled to build is in ruins. All my certainties have evaporated. Do you know how that feels?"

Maria met his eyes and tried to understand, tried to gauge the depth of his weariness. *Could she have persisted for as long as he had?* Maybe the time came, for everyone, when there was no way forward, no other choice but death. Maybe the Lambertians were right, maybe "infinity" was meaningless . . . and "immortality" was a mirage no human should aspire to.

No *human*—

Maria turned on him angrily. "Do I know how it feels? *However you want it to feel.* Isn't that what you told me? You have the power to choose exactly *who you are.* The old human shackles are gone. If you don't want the weight of your past to crush you . . . *then don't let it!* If you really want to die, I can't stop you—but don't tell me that you *have no choice.*"

For a moment Durham looked stricken, as if all she'd done was compound his despair, but then something in her tirade seemed to break through to him.

He said gently, "You really do need someone, don't you, who knows the old world?"

"Yes." Maria blinked back tears.

Durham's expression froze abruptly, as if he'd decoupled from his body. *Had he left her?* Maria almost pulled free of his grip—but then his waxwork face became animated again.

He said, "I'll come with you."

"What—?"

He beamed at her, like an idiot, like a child. "I just made a few adjustments to my mental state. And I accept your invitation. *Onward and upward.*"

Maria was speechless, giddy with relief. She put her arms around him; he returned the embrace. *He'd done that, for her? Reshaped himself, rebuilt himself . . .*

There was no time to waste. She moved toward the control panel and hurried to prepare the launch. Durham looked on, still smiling; he seemed as entranced by the flickering display as if he'd never set eyes on it before.

Maria stopped dead. If he'd rebuilt himself, reinvented himself . . . *then how much of the man she'd known remained?* Had he granted himself transhuman resilience, and healed himself of his terminal despair . . . or had he died in silence, beyond her sight, and given birth to a companion for her, a software child who'd merely inherited its father's memories?

Where was the line? Between self-transformation so great as to turn a longing for death into childlike wonder . . . and death itself, and the handing on of the joys and burdens he could no longer shoulder to someone new?

She searched his face for an answer, but she couldn't read him.

She said, "You must tell me what you did. I need to understand."

Durham promised her, "I will. In the next life."

EPILOGUE

(Remit not paucity)

NOVEMBER 2052

Maria left three wreaths propped against the illusion mural at the end of the cul-de-sac. It was not the anniversary of any death, but she placed flowers there whenever the mood took her. She had no graves to decorate; both her parents had been cremated. Paul Durham, too.

She backed away from the wall slowly, and watched the crudely painted garden, with its Corinthian columns and its olive groves, almost come to life. As she reached the point where the perspective of the imaginary avenue merged with that of the road, someone called out, "Maria?"

She spun around. It was Stephen Chew, another member of the volunteer work team, with pneumatic jackhammer in tow on a small trolley. Maria greeted him, and picked up her shovel. The sewer main in Pyrmont Bridge Road had burst again.

Stephen admired the mural. "It's beautiful, isn't it? Don't you wish you could step right through?"

Maria didn't reply. They set off down the road together in silence. After a moment, her eyes began to water from the stench.